W9-AXT-818

GREEN

GREEN

FRANCES

SHERWOOD

Farrar, Straus and Giroux

NEW YORK

Library of Congress Cataloging-in-Publication Data
Sherwood, Frances
Green / Frances Sherwood. — 1st ed.
    p.   cm.
      I. Title.
PS3569.H454G74   1995   813'.54—dc20   94-24436   CIP

The author gratefully acknowledges permission to reprint material from the
following previously published sources: "You," by D. H. Lawrence, from The
Complete Works of D. H. Lawrence edited by V. de Sola Pinto and F. W.
Roberts. Copyright © 1964, 1971 by Angelo Ravagli and C. M. Weekly,
Executors of the Estate of Frieda Lawrence Ravagli. Used by permission of Viking
Penguin, a division of Penguin Books USA Inc. Two lines from "Howl," from
Howl and Other Poems, by Allen Ginsberg. Copyright © 1956 by Allen
Ginsberg. Copyright renewed. Reprinted by permission of HarperCollins, Inc. One
line from "How Does A Poem Mean," by Lawrence Ferlinghetti. Copyright ©
1958 by Lawrence Ferlinghetti. Reprinted by permission of New Directions, Inc.
Three lines from Collected Poems, by Federico García Lorca, edited by
Christopher Maurer. Copyright © 1989, 1990, 1991 by Herederos de Federico
García Lorca and Will Kirkland. Used by permission of Farrar, Straus and Giroux.
Four lines from "Kaddish," from Collected Poems 1947–1980, by Allen
Ginsberg. Copyright © 1959 by Allen Ginsberg. Copyright renewed. Reprinted by
permission of HarperCollins Publishers, Inc. Six lines from Red Emma Speaks:
An Emma Goldman Reader, edited by Alix Kates Shulman. Copyright ©
1972. Reprinted by permission of Random House.

As always,

to my children:

Lark, Leander, and Ceres Madoo

•

And also to

Frederick Slaski

and Michael Kouroubetes

SECTIONS

I was born white girl. Bird of ill omen flew over hospital.
His plumage was bloodred, bright orange, and dirty snow.
He said: Girl, watch yourself.
And that is exactly what I have done ever since.

[**IN THE 1950s,** when the cars had fins like fishes and the Cold War-orama was heating up, the name for me was teenager.

Of course, my parents didn't let me wear lipstick. My mother, however, smeared red waxy color on her mouth, thick as butter and bright enough to match her name, Ruby, every single day of the week. Sitting at her dressing table, she'd hold her lips a little open like a movie star.

"What do you think, Zoe?"

She was gorgeous, and often slightly drunk, what could I say.

"Like there's no tomorrow, huh, Zoe?"

"Yeah."

My mother wore those dresses they had on television and in ads —the new look with the flared skirts, cinched waist—and always she was in little piggy-hoof high heels. And when she was stone-cold sober, she acted as if vacuuming the living room created order in the universe.

The vacuum was a Eureka automatic, which beat, swept, and suction-cleaned. We paid twenty dollars a month at Monkey Ward's, installments. Our whole decor was a muted sandpiper beige, including pictures of the early pioneers on the Mormon Trail, the wagons of 1849, 1850, and 1851, bad cholera years. The bathroom, however, was upbeat, a bright turquoise, which made me feel whenever I had to use the toilet that I was jumping into an aquarium.

As Mormons, we were followers of Joseph Smith, who in the early part of the nineteenth century found, with the guidance of the angel Moroni, *The Book of Mormon*, the Sacred Tablets documenting Christ's second coming on the American continent. Every week my father taped a scripture calendar to our refrigerator. That meant each night a member of our family would read something from the Bible or *Doctrine and Covenants* or *The Book of Mormon* for our mutual edification.

Every morning before my father left for work, we'd have prayers, and, of course, at eight years old, I had been taken into the basement of our church by our Bishop and, in a white dress, I had been dunked in a pool, duly baptized.

Furthermore, my parents had been married in the Temple, thus sealed for time and all eternity, and they were given special underwear which, protecting them from evil, had to be worn constantly. My father had become a deacon after *his* baptism, a teacher when he was fourteen, then a priest. My mother was Sister Ruby. She belonged to the church's Relief Society.

So we *tried* to be a righteous family. When my mother was attending to her household duties, she cut recipes from slick-covered women's magazines: casseroles, meat loaf, cottage cheese with canned cling peaches arranged in the pattern of a sailboat, Swift premium bacon laced around macaroni and cheese. All the mothers in our ward had little file boxes for that very purpose, alphabetically arranged recipes from apple pie à la mode to yellow Jell-O with baby marshmallows.

We were also a modern family. The couches in our home, sectional sofas arranged in the shape of an L, were a shade darker than our carpeting, and the Danish teak coffee table, glass-topped (which I fell through once), took pride of place in front of the couches. But the rumpus room, our old, comfortable stuff, was pine and plaid. That's where my dad kept his fly-fishing equipment in little metal toolboxes —hooks disguised as brilliantly colored insects, fantasy creatures with wispy tails and dangerous emerald eyes—and my mother did her sewing, if she was in the rare sewing mood. That's where we ate popcorn on Family Home Night. When my father was a kid, they pulled taffy on Family Home Night. Those were the days, he said, back in old Salt Lake City, the Mormon capital.

Even Brigham Young, who led our people to Zion in Utah, had Family Home Nights, he and his fifty-seven kids and twenty-six wives. All accounts report happiness and harmony in the beehive house. That's what they called it then, and the beehive still is the motif on the Utah state flag, signifying industry.

Our house was hardly a beehive. Or an anthill. Snake pit? Bear's lair? Like all the one-level houses in our neighborhood in Pacific Grove, California, we had wall-to-wall carpets and tiny, cell-like bedrooms, and the linoleum in our kitchen was full of white swirls speckled with sparkles. It was the latest style. When my mother got drunk and tread diligently across the kitchen floor, I thought of her as tripping the light fantastic along the Milky Way: swirls white and delightsome. *White and delightsome* was a Mormon term in those days that meant us, the white, chosen Mormon people.

"Zoe," my mother would say at those times in her mock Southern accent, signaling a change in tone, mood, a ruffle in the smooth functioning of our Free World family life, "Froggy, fetch your mother a wedge of lime." She could throw her head back like Blanche Dubois in *Streetcar*, or Scarlett O'Hara of *Gone with the Wind*.

"A girl needs a drink now and then, so don't look at me over your glasses."

My mother was a proud, fierce woman who would have us know she was caught in a time-and-place warp. She was made for long swishy skirts, the stage, adulation. Instead she converted to Mormonism, married my dad.

"Z-o-eeee, fetch your motttheer a wedge of lime."

After a few gin and tonics she would sing her favorites from American musicals like *Annie Get Your Gun*, *Oklahoma!* and *The Pajama Game*. Her singing was inevitably accompanied by a little soft-shoe, sometimes a slight slip, often a little fall.

"Whoops, give your mother a helping hand, Froggy, would you please."

"Gads," I'd groan. If anybody in my school could have seen me, I knew I would have had to die instantly.

"Be a good girl."

If I *was* a good girl, I'd brace myself, give her the old heave-ho, accompany her to bed, and, sitting in the lounge chair by her bed, relate the entire plot of a movie—"and then the creature from the black lagoon in real-life 3-D hauled himself out of the mud and slime"— until she fell into a deep and troubled sleep.

But when I was bad, I was very bad, and I would just leave her there kerplop all over the floor, a loose bundle of flesh, the new look askew on her waist, her heels abandoned, and her acid wit slurred to a stupid silly.

"You are going to get it," I would hear her call at me as I fled down the hallway.

"You are going to get it," getting fainter and fainter.

She would then crawl around the kitchen like something caught in a pen.

"You are going to get it."

"Get what?" I would return to the kitchen for a final, victorious look. She would rear her large head, shake her heavy mane. If I had not been a child, I would have felt sorry for her.

"Don't get smart, young lady." Except it came out like the roar of a wounded animal: Doontgeetsmat.

"How could you just leave her there?" my father would ask when he came home from work and called me. I would be in the locked bathroom, trying to concentrate on a sneaked comic book, *True Love Confidences*, the scalloped bubble of our heroine's thoughts whispering: "When I looked into Melvin's eyes, I knew I would be tempted to go all the way, but my mother had taught me that if a girl does not respect herself, who can she respect. Yet, I dreamed of his lips and his hands and his arms and eyes."

"How could you just leave her?" my father would ask, standing outside the bathroom door.

Easy, I thought, didn't say, emerging from my turquoise refuge.

"Your own mother." My father was only a little taller than I, and rather thin, too, but his words carried weight.

"I know." He was right. I was wrong. She was my own mother. I began blinking like mad.

By then, my mother would be curled up asleep like one of those curlicue insects that can make themselves into tight little balls.

"Can you tell me why, Zoe," my father persisted, "you would treat your mother this way?"

"I don't know, Daddy." Of course, I did know. She made me sick.

At that point, my mother would be snoring, quite indifferent to the little drama being played about her. I realized I could have at least put a blanket around her.

"You will be put on restriction for this."

I would dutifully hang my head, although my whole life was restriction as far as I was concerned.

My father fancied himself stern but fair. In the Mormon church, he was, of course, a priest, let us never forget.

My mother fancied herself Ginger Rogers, Betty Grable, Vivien Leigh, and Gloria Swanson, and her hair *was* blond and long, a dyed blond, pulled into a ponytail so tight it gave her what the kids at high school would call chinky eyes, and when it started to grow out to the natural black, it looked like a row of ants were marching across her scalp underneath the amber waves of grain.

Naturally, I fancied myself adopted, or at least misplaced. They had made a mistake at the hospital. I knew I didn't belong with those people. But, like my unreal mother, I had an imagination, and, like my not-real father, I was harsh. I wanted to be a Christian, yes, but more along the lines of Mary Magdalene than of the Prophet, Bishops, Apostles, and Priests of the Mormon Church. I didn't think they swooned. Temperamentally I was more in tune with the sinner Mary than the mother Mary.

"Your mother," my father repeated, "loves you."

"Yes," but I knew that was not true.

"You love your mother."

My love for my mother was one of the flashy fly-fishing hooks my father tied caught in my heart like an earring in a pierced Catholic ear, something I could not dislodge. My love for my father fashioned itself after the sinker on the fish line, a little metal weight. Yet, I'd been taught in Sunday School to love my parents and that the meaning of life was happiness.

[**UNFORTUNATELY**, I looked like my dad. Not just glasses—black plastic cat-woman glasses for me, old-time wire frames for him—but springy orange hair, bunched curls parted in the middle like all the McLarens. At school they called me Better Dead Than Red. My dad's great-grandfather McLaren, also a redhead, was in the 1856 Mormon migration, coming over from Scotland by ship, and then walking, pushing a handcart from Iowa, going over the Platte, passing the Mormon landmarks of Devil's Gate, Chimney Rock, Scottsbluff, burying the dead at night, suffering exhaustion, near starvation, traveling more than fourteen hundred miles to Zion, Salt Lake City, Utah to practice his religion freely. The Mormons had been driven out of every state they lived in.

But Great-grandfather Harold survived, and old photographs show the McLaren patriarch in sepia, his Adam's apple and turkey-wattle neck as obscene as some freak sex organ. His six wives, all crinkly old hens in bonnets, staunchly proper, are ranged about their husband. Accounts verify they each had a separate room in the Utah ranch house on the sheep ranch and each night Great-grandfather McLaren did his husbandly duty.

On the seventh day he rested.

The first Harold's hair also had that strict line with waves of kink bulging up on either side, reminding me of the Red Sea parting, Charlton Heston in the lead of the Israelites, those other desert people, holding that staff that could turn into a snake when necessary.

On the other hand, my mother's hair couldn't take a part in it if it wanted to, it was so silky-wild, and I could imagine how it must have been when I was born in 1939, at the Monterey County Hospital in Salinas, the smell of fertilizer on the lettuce fields undeniable, some old gangster car parked low in the dust, the distance between mother and child already visible, our fate sealed. I, with my bad eyes in my red kinky hair; she, in her arrow-straight black hair like her twin, like Pearl. They were sleek seals. I was Raggedy Ann coming apart at the seams.

My mother told me that when she was a little girl and woke up from a nightmare, seeing Pearl's face would reassure her. Of course, then, before her blond change, it would have been like looking in a mirror.

The two sisters inherited the Gatehouse, a historic landmark overlooking Monterey Bay in Pacific Grove, from their father, the owner of a sardine boat, a purse seiner. Originally a Methodist camp, Pacific Grove was still dry, and Lovers' Point was not a make-out spot but where the Lovers of Christ had Easter Service at sunrise, huddled and freezing with the prairie dogs or whatever the rodent was that popped up between the rocks. When it was first populated by white people, Pacific Grove had a big fence all around to keep the devil and other riffraff out. The Gatehouse, which is where my mother and aunt grew up, was where the sentry lived with a telescope and a periscope and hot-fire tongs. Then one night, an irate Montereyan, a Catholic it is rumored, chopped down the fence to Pacific Grove in order to get inside.

My aunt said her father bought the Gatehouse for a song. I wondered what song. "Hernando's Hideaway?"

In order to keep up the old mansion after their father died, Aunt Pearl and my mother worked canning sardines in the Portola Cannery. When the whistle blew, signaling that the catch was in, they put on their special shower caps, making them look like Christopher Columbus. They flocked down the hill along with all the other women in their caps, an army of discoverers of America, on the way to Cannery Row. The air over the boats in the bay would be thick with reeling sea gulls and skinny black cormorants. The wharf would be bustling, the canneries chugging. Double time, triple time, heads tails, heads tails. On the assembly line, my aunt secretly dreamed of being a ballerina, my mother of being a costume designer. I think they might have prayed to Saint Bartholomew, patron saint of Armenia and nervous tics, to save them.

Instead, one day my father came by the Gatehouse, Harold McLaren, on his bicycle, a part in his hair and *The Book of Mormon* under his arm. He was wearing a white shirt and a tie. He told them about Christ reappearing in A.D. 34 in the Americas and about the golden tablets found by one Joseph Smith in New York State in the 1800s. He warned them about poisoning their bodies with caffeine, alcohol, and nicotine. He advised chastity, promised heaven.

"How fascinating," my mother must have said.

In the Gatehouse, each room had a nationality, and, ironically, the two Armenian sisters even had a Turkish room with gold tassels, an elephant holding up a brass tray with little demitasses. My father had developed a taste for the exotic after his missionary stint in Honduras.

"Yes, we have no bananas," my mother must have said, throwing her heavy mane of hair back from her face, giving him her toothy smile. She was olive-skinned, rather magnificent, and she offered him Turkish coffee (which as a Mormon he couldn't drink) and macaroons. Several months later they were married in the Temple for time and all eternity, and donned magic Mormon underwear, making them, as far as I was concerned, as invulnerable as Superman. My aunt opened The World Is Your Oyster Ballet School, and I was born.

The summer I was twelve, we were at the Great Salt Lake on a vacation with my great-aunts and grandmother when I realized that my mother, in her black bathing suit with a sharp, jutting bow across one breast, was the most beautiful woman on the beach and that she was in the wrong lake.

That day I got salt in my eyes, and my father held me up so I could rub my face in his hair. In the distance I saw, bobbing along, Noah's ark headed for Armenia, for Mount Ararat. Only a mirage. Only the salt. Only the heat. But even as a kid, though I was not Armenian or always kind to my poor mother, I began to understand what it meant to be part of a vanquished and destroyed people. Leaving out the part about the canneries, she confided in me her dream to become a famous costume designer. She was saving her money to go to New York. Instead she had to content herself with making my costume for the Butterfly Parade the Pine Avenue Elementary had each year to welcome the Monarch butterflies back for their mating season on the Monterey peninsula.

[**MY MOTHER'S BENDERS,** as my Dad called them, happened about once every two weeks, and were Our Big Secret, our family cross, because in the Mormon Church: "Tea and coffee and tobacco we despise. Drink no liquor and we eat but very little meat. Hark, hark, the children sing."

"Your mother is a very sick woman," my father would say, no doubt very advanced in his thinking in that one area.

Sometimes, my mother was so drunk she would pull me into the closet with her. There we'd be. "Cozy as two bugs in a rug," my mother would slur, her nails talons in my side.

It would be dark, stuffy. I would be blinking in the dark, nobody to witness my distress but God. I would wonder about the oxygen level, the hems of her silk dresses brushing against my face like ghosts, and the lumpy pile of high heels digging into my bottom. Sometimes I'd beg to be let up, have to pee in my pants. Then a suspicious puddle would seep out from under the closed door. My fault. I was a baby. Peeyou. The smell of wet leather. At school, they joked about a book called *The Yellow Stream* by I. P. Freely. Little did they know how the joke made me want to shrivel up and blow away.

"Oklahoma," my mother would sing, her voice getting faster and faster. "Oklahoma, Oklahoma."

"Ruby, Ruby, where are you?"

My father would finally come home from work.

My mother, ever vigilant, would put her hand over my mouth. Mum's the word.

"Ruby, Zoe?" We could hear his shoes, his hand jingling the change in his pants pocket.

"Ruby?"

All quiet.

Then he would quickly pick up the phone.

"Pearl, get over here."

Pearl, my mom's twin sister, the one who stayed Armenian, the one who didn't convert, the one who didn't marry, and the one who drove a Pontiac Chieftain that was red and white and very sharp-looking, knew what to do. Aunt Pearl, who had the World Is Your Oyster Ballet School and was going to help me go to college, was fifteen minutes older than my mother, and if Pearl said, Jump, my mother said, What bridge?

This would be Pearl entering our house: the fast pad-pad-pad of her ballet slippers and tangling of her longish peasant skirt. Her long earrings, which looked like my father's fishing flies, tinkled like bells. But all this delicacy would be countered by her breathing. When angry, Pearl snorted like a horse before the race.

"Again?" she would ask my father. "Ruby is at it again?"

"Yes, Pearl, she's at it again."

"The closet, Harold?"

"The closet, Pearl."

The closet door would be yanked open.

Two long lines above Pearl's very straight nose would deepen to crevices.

"Do you know what you are doing? Are you crazy? What is the matter with you? Let the child go, Ruby."

I would be instantly released, and feel at once both ashamed and shameless. My dress would be wet. I would have to run straight to the bathroom, hearing my mother's sobs, Pearl's scolding.

"What is wrong with you?"

"Oh God, Pearl."

"You are ruining your life and terrorizing the child. What do you expect your husband to do with you?"

"I didn't mean to."

"You're a grown woman, for God's sake, with a family. You have a beautiful house. Tell me what the hell is going on."

Our house wasn't all that nice, not picture-perfect *House Beautiful.* In Del Monte Forest they had split-levels and ranch houses with huge flagstone fireplaces. Our house was basically a box, a little box. But still.

"I know, Pearl. I mean, I don't know."

The voices got softer, but in our house, of pasteboard dividing walls, you could hear everything from any room.

"Are you mad?"

"Maybe I am."

"No, you're not. Don't say that."

"I am not crazy, but Pearl . . ."

"Pearl what? Tell me."

Then they would whisper in Armenian.

Toon arants hooysi es.

You are without hope.

Yes hoovs oonem.

I have hope.

Inchi hamar sireli kuyr.

For what, dear sister?

Kez hamar, ashkari hamar, mer boloris hamar, payts mievneoyn e yes dkhoor em, yev im gyankn animast e tvoom.

For you, for the world, for all of us, but still I am sad, and my life seems pointless.

Oh, Ruby, Ruby.

Aynkan teivar e, Pearl.

It's so hard, Pearl.

Kidem, kidem.

I know, I know.

Chem kider ardyock grnam aysbes sharoungel.

I don't know if I can go on.

Payts bedk e sharounages.

But you must.

Inchou?

Why?

Haroldin hamar.

For Harold.

Harold was my father.

Zoein hamar.

For Zoe.

That was me. I was running a bath for myself.

Inkzinkit hamar.

For yourself.

For herself.

And my mother would come out of the closet and cry a little on my father's shoulder, and I, bathed and in my flannel pj's with a bluebell pattern and blue piping along the breast pocket, would return, would let her now hug me to her. My mother would ask me to forgive her, which, of course, I did, at least for that moment.

"You must not forget the child," Pearl would announce as if she were in a play.

Even when she was not dealing with my mother, Pearl's style was emphatic and dramatic. Of course I idolized her. As a ballet teacher, she barked out commands (plié, first, second, fifth position, tendu, arms port de bras). She had a long stick shaped like a staff to keep beat.

"First arabesque, second arabesque, hold that head up, third arabesque, arabesque penchée, arabesque. Bend it, girls, bend it."

Pearl and my mother were born in Armenia, but I thought of Aunt Pearl as European. She wore her bright black hair in a tight ballerina bun, carried herself with the posture of a diva, and her eyes snapped fire. She had practically raised my mother when their father died.

"Zoe is the future, Ruby. She is our blood," she would continue during those evenings she retrieved us from the closet.

My father, in the face of these twin sisters, seemed negligible, as if my birth were virginal or the result of spontaneous combustion or twin conspiracy, something utterly mysterious cooked up by the two women.

"Come, Ruby," he would say gently, trying to get control back, to remind us who was who and what was what and whose house, after all, we were in. "Let's go to bed."

Pearl would drop her head. She was standing in the face of a marriage, no doubt a bad one, but marriage nonetheless, something she respected.

"Yes, Ruby, go on, go with your husband."

And my mother and father would limp off together to the master cell, and I would kiss my Aunt Pearl good night and turn out the lights after she backed down the driveway, and go back to my comic book:

"I knew I should be a good girl, yet I couldn't stop myself. But luckily, the face of my mother appeared before me. Sheila, she said, remember what is true and what is false. I pushed him away and ran."

The next afternoon, my mother would get up out of her sour, rumpled bed, and by the time I came home from school, she would be sitting on the toilet seat in her pink chenille bathrobe, with an Old Gold hanging from her mouth. Brandishing a frizzled toothbrush, she would ask me to dye her black hair roots strand by strand. Meanwhile, she would be reading an article in her *Ladies' Home Journal* as she plucked at her bathrobe, leaving little pink tufts all over the floor, along with the ashes.

And on Sunday, we would go to church as if nothing had ever happened. If it was the first Sunday of the month, Fast Sunday, Sacrament Service, we would have the Bearing of Testimonies, in which people would come forward to the pulpit and bear testimony, proclaiming their faith individually, often telling us all their problems and how God and the Gospel had helped them get through a particularly trying time, ending always with the phrase "I say this in the name of Jesus Christ, Our Lord, Amen." And I would know better than to say anything about our life because it was going to be fine anyway.

In Sunday school, when the lesson of the week was the Lord's Law of Health, from *Doctrine and Covenants*, where it is written that the body is a tabernacle and that we must eschew all stimulants, narcotics, and deleterious substances, I would feel hopeful that the danger was over.

And when I met in the third hour of Sunday service with the young women, the Laurels, and there was further testimony about our "little problems growing up," I kept quiet, chanting with the others the thirteenth article of faith:

We believe in being honest, true, chaste, benevolent, virtuous, and in doing good to all men; indeed, we may say that we follow the admonition of Paul—we believe in all things, we hope of all things, we have endured many things, we hope to be able to endure all things.

[**OF MY HIGH SCHOOL** life, I can say these four words: I was not popular.

Imagine us, September 1957, Monterey Union High School, Monterey, California, we, the senior girls, clumped together in the auditorium, Midnight in Paris heavy in the air, no boys allowed.

The sperm is traveling from the left side of the screen up to the right corner where the egg sits smug and saucy.

The sperm clips right along.

What a frisky fellow.

The egg gloats.

The sperm's little tail twizzles and twists, but his head is aiming straight ahead, no wavering, a torpedo in action.

Soon, any second now . . .

Suddenly there is a rumble and a fumble.

The lights pop on.

"There's a boy in the auditorium," comes a frightened female cry.

The Encyclopaedia Britannica voice slows to a dull roar. The celluloid film in the projector gets off track, slaps over and over again on the table. Whop, whop.

"A boy is in the auditorium." This time it is our Dean of Women's voice. Mrs. Manitee is gruff, rough, and favors tweeds, and, it was rumored, girls.

Although, of course, I didn't know what that meant then.

She had hair on her hands and always wore her raincoat. That, everybody said, was because she had hair on her chest.

I liked hair and was ashamed that my pubic patch was a mere tuft of orange. During a school excursion, I had seen wreaths in the Sonoma County frontier museum made out of dead people's hair. My, my, my, I had thought, what a memento. A dream of mine was to have a man as hairy as a bear lie on me, the kind that had hair growing up out of his collar and down his back and a V on his stomach and down his butt, and his equipment, whatever that might be, would be placed like a small rose on a large, hairy doily.

For you, my darling.

"Please file back to your classroom, girls."

"Drats," we all said, like Felix in the comic strip *Felix the Cat.*

Margo, the Negro girl, who had been sitting in front of me with her big hairy hair half obstructing my view, turned around and said: "Well, I guess I'll just have to depend on the Kinsey reports and Henry Miller and Dorothy Parker and 'The Man in the Brooks Brothers Shirt.' "

I didn't know what she was talking about. I didn't even know what the movie was about. The tadpole image confused me. I thought It was like free-floating pollen that emanated from boys' bodies and wafted over your way. The important thing was to keep your back to the wall so nothing could approach your bottom. Nobody told me about water and frogs. Did that mean you couldn't go swimming? Did their stuff just swim at you from their bathing suit to yours? Across the Rio Grande, so to speak? Didn't my stiff Esther Williams bathing suit made by Jantzen protect me? The world was indeed a perilous place, with babies lurking not only behind every cabbage head but just about everywhere you could think.

"We saw a movie," I began that night at home after grace.

"We thank you, Father, for the food we eat."

We were having mashed potatoes and gravy over sliced turkey, left over from Sunday. My bread had gotten really soggy, and I didn't know if I could finish it all. In all honesty, I was sick to my stomach. We were in the kitchen, the table poised on the milky way, because my mom, in a fit of repentance, was cutting out a dress on the dining room table. The soft beige thin-sheeted Butterick pattern was pinned over white fabric dotted with little bunches of buttercups. It was to have a sash in the back. I dreaded the day of its completion.

"Sit up straight, Zoe. Do you want to grow up with a hunchback?"

"Saw a movie, dear?" My mother had been sober a good two weeks. My dad and I were crossing our fingers.

"It was a little confusing."

Actually, seeing movies in school was nothing new.

We had seen *Dating Dos and Don'ts, Are You Popular?, Are Manners Important?, Shy Guy, When You Don't Know What to Do to Fit In, The Gossip, How to Get in the Pep Club*, and all about being a "swell kid," in addition to the usual boring science films about flowers growing out of the ground at a very fast pace.

"Rather, we started to see a movie . . . Only the girls got to see it," I said. "It was about swimming when you are grown up, I think."

"Slouching gives a very negative impression," my father said, pressing my back with one hand and pulling up my neck with the other. Obviously, he wanted a giraffe for a daughter.

"I wonder why the boys couldn't come," I ventured.

My mother glanced nervously over at my father.

"What you don't know won't hurt you, but bad posture signals moral turpitude," my father answered.

I thought just the opposite. I liked *The Hunchback of Notre Dame* and cried through the whole last part. And there was a case in our school of a girl who had a baby, which she put in a shoe box and hid in the sand dunes in Seaside. She was expelled and not allowed to graduate because of something like moral turpitude. I didn't tell my parents that I wondered if she had failed to keep her back to the wall. With a hunchback, I would think you would tend to slip in and out of rooms with your best face forward, so to speak. Did my mother actually think I was going to wear a dress with a sash to school? Wittingly or unwittingly, she was keeping me pinned to the wall, the wallflower agenda. What I didn't know *was* hurting me.

"Curiosity killed the cat," my father continued, giving my mother a knowing look.

"How?"

"Zoe, finish your dinner, and stop acting smart."

"The movie," my mother concluded, "was, no doubt, about growing up, becoming a woman."

"Oh."

When my period started, two years earlier, I'd thought I was hemorrhaging. I had awakened in a pool of blood.

"Call the ambulance," I had screamed, not daring to budge, and wondering where the tourniquet should be applied—my waist?—but my mother said it was only part of being a woman, the curse, and I'd better get used to Kotex, which we hid in the cabinet under the sink. One time, and one time only, I forgot and left a dirty Kotex out. Spare the rod, spoil the child, was one of my father's sayings.

"Women get the curse," my mother had gone on the day my period began. "It's our lot in life, we are cursed."

This little conversation, a rare burst of opinion from my mother, was held in the bathroom with the door locked. We were in the aquarium, under water, bubbling. We could have been goldfish, for all I knew. My mother sat on the edge of the bathtub and I on the toilet seat, which was covered with a furry turquoise thing with our family initials on it. H.M. My mother was really R.M. and I was Z.M., and sometimes at school, they called me B.M.

"Every month," my mother continued, "until we're old and dried up."

"Is it like the mark of Cain, Mother?" I began to blink.

"You could say so. The mark of Eve, Zoe. Here, you hook it on this belt," she said. She said this tenderly, as if rather than welcoming me into the ranks of women she bemoaned the loss of my childhood. You, too, she seemed to be saying, are now trapped by your anatomy. The belt was pink elastic and harmless enough, but it had two metal clips hanging down, fore and aft, with rather sharp teeth. You pulled the paper of the Kotex over the teeth and wore it under your underpants. One had to marvel at modern technology, but it was not infallible. For what if the Kotex fell off and out of your pants and down your leg and the metal teeth snagged your hairy patch in a deadly and painful grip? Or what if the blood saturated your Kotex and bled on through the pants and everybody saw. Or what if . . .

I *was* cursed.

"You are not cursed," Margo said to me when we discussed the matter later on in our school cafeteria.

"But . . ."

"My butt, Zoe."

"Margo?"

"Because that, like much of what is told about being a woman and everything else, is a bunch of cockamamy nonsense. Your body is just doing its job during your period, and you can thank your lucky stars you're not pregnant. So it is a blessing, if you want to use archaic religious language. Get it?"

"I think so."

"I know so. So, if you just put your mind to yourself, as much as you put it to those stupid romances you read, you will find that there is a conspiracy going on trying to keep you, me, the rest of us dumb, down, and dirty."

"Dumb, down, and dirty?"

"You got it, Einstein."

[**NEEDLESS TO SAY**, I could not invite Margo over, because my father thought Negroes were cursed by God; and actually, I never brought anybody home from school, because I couldn't count on what I would find. The only time I could bank on peace and quiet was when we practiced getting bombed.

If the City Hall whistle honked three times, honk, honk, honk, instructions were to *walk*, do not run, to your nearest bomb shelter, just like at the swimming pool. My father, the insurance agent, thought ahead. In our backyard bomb shelter, we had supplies stocked up, including fifty Sugar Daddy lollipops, for Armageddon. On Family Home Night we pretended that we heard the three blasts of the City Hall whistle. My father used a bicycle horn.

Honk, honk, honk.

"Hurry up, hurry up."

"Put your fingers in your ears," my father would command as we sat there on our bomb cots. "And your head between your legs. Pray."

My mother and I would obey—I quickly, she reluctantly.

"Sh," my father would say, trying to make it all as authentic as possible.

"Nobody is there," my mother would comment in her bored way. She would want a cigarette, like bad, and a drink even worse. The bomb shelter was like our house, but smaller.

"You never can tell," my father would say. "Pray, Ruby, pray, Zoe."

What were they worried about, I wondered. They were married in the Temple, sealed for all eternity, and had magic underwear which made them bullet-proof. Plus they were Latter-day Saints, my father a priest destined for heaven, and since my father knew my mother's secret name, she could go to heaven, too. Actually, before I went to high school, I could hardly wait to get my secret name, my entrance to heaven when I got married in the Temple, if I got married in the Temple, if I got married. I wanted to be Joanna, just like a pioneer woman of old who had traveled the Mormon Trail.

"Joanna? Time to come to heaven."

"Coming Zeke." Zeke short for Ezekiel.

Yet truthfully, I had doubts about my faith as well as my looks. Hunkered down in our bunker—To the Bunker, men—I did not think about My Heavenly Father. Instead, I dreamed of the ballet dancer Nijinsky. My Aunt Pearl had a photograph of him in his *Afternoon of a Faun* costume in her Russian room. The ballet I fancied him in, though, was *Petrouchka*, where he is a puppet come alive. I had read the story of Petrouchka, the clown, many times. Once, when I was older, however, I saw a portrait of Nijinsky as Petrouchka painted by Franz Kline, which made him look sinister. And Margo told me that the presence of the villainous Moor in the Petrouchka story made it a prejudiced ballet. Her father, she said, was an expert on another Moor, Othello. And Nijinsky, himself, she explained, was probably a fairy, which she also had to spell out to me. What did I know, I told her, I was a kid. Innocence is no excuse, she said.

Until Margo, my code name to heaven if I were Petrouchka's wife would have been Ballerina. In my girlish dreams Nijinsky would be waiting for me in a little house in a forest of tall trees with two thousand flowering daffodils in between. He would be in his tight tights, and the rounded bulge between his legs would look as firm as a robin redbreast, but, when touched, would be soft as butter in my hands.

My knowledge of that particular aspect of anatomy was hazy before I knew Margo. The few times I had stared at Catholic crucifixes, peeking in at Saint Anthony's on Central Avenue, I pretended that Christ descended, dropped his loin cloth, showing what indeed made him man —something never mentioned in Sunday school or at the Relief Society.

"Come, little Zoenochka, da, da, da."

Nijinsky's *Afternoon of a Faun* picture in my aunt's Gatehouse was housed with the silver samovar and the embroidered tablecloth and painted Easter eggs—Nijinsky, his head thrown back, elegantly fey, waiting to have his throat cut. My aunt, in her Russian room, served hot tea from her silver samovar in glasses with silver holders. Then the record player would be dragged in from the Italian room and Aunt Pearl would put on Stravinsky's *Rite of Spring*.

My mother would be smoking, of course, black Russian cigarettes from God knows where, and sneaking vodka with her tea. The sisters, my aunt and mother, I knew, had never given up the game of dress-up.

Meanwhile, my dad worried that the FBI had tapes going and bugs planted and informants crouched in the bushes. Jack Webb, from the television show *Dragnet*, would step in, "the names changed to protect the innocent," arrest my aunt, and disgrace would fall on the whole family because of her Russian room. Are you now or have you ever been a member of the Communist Party, Roy Cohn and Senator McCarthy presiding.

"Pearl," my dad would beg, "think of somebody besides yourself for a change. Do you want to implicate my whole family, become part of the files, get on some list?"

"I do, Harold, I do think of everybody. It is a White Russian room, not Red Russia."

"You never can tell how you will be interpreted, Pearl. You never can tell. Appearances are deceiving."

My dad's insurance business logo was an umbrella. Underneath were the words Protect Your Family.

I sometimes thought of Great-grandfather McLaren and his six wives and thirty children under the umbrella.

Honk, honk, honk. That was the signal we could come out of our basement bomb shelter.

"We can ascend, praise God," my father would announce theatrically, as if we had journeyed to the center of the earth.

"Proceed cautiously," I imagined I-Like-Ike telling us through the gold-flecked cloth of our Telefunken radio.

"Ali, ali, oxen free." The Civil Defense Team at City Hall could blast through Pacific Grove.

[MARGO.

On the first day of school in my senior year, Mr. Watkins asked us all what we wanted to be, including the girls. Margo said she wanted to be a writer because she believed in lovers.

"Love," Mr. Watkins corrected.

"No, lovers," Margo insisted.

"I don't quite get the connection," Mr. Watkins said, rubbing his crew cut. Mr. Watkins wouldn't. His favorite poet was Emily Dickinson.

"Casa Mañana," Margo said, her eyes narrowed.

"Next." Mr. Watkins pointed at me.

I said I wanted to be an anthropologist like Margaret Mead, because she was the only famous woman I knew about other than dead ones like Charlotte Brontë, Jane Austen, Emily Brontë and Emily Dickinson, George Eliot and George Sand. I would have said ornithologist if I'd known some women bird-watchers.

When Mr. Watkins asked what we had read over the summer, Margo said she'd read Camus's *The Stranger*.

"An existentialist book," Margo added.

Mr. Watkins asked her to define existentialism.

"Existentialism," Margo began, "is a philosophical movement which asserts that since there is no God or external, absolute meaning to our existence, our existence itself is the only meaning."

"No God?" tittered the class.

I was intrigued. Humpty Dumpty falling off the wall? All the king's horses and all the king's men?

"For example," Margo continued, "the stranger is initially without values, but in the end, near his own death, he comes to venerate his own life. Life."

I was fascinated. The boys snickered.

Margo.

Margo sat in the school cafeteria by herself. The other Negro kids sat together, but because of her adoptive family she really didn't qualify as a real Negro, and, of course, she was not white at all. Her hair was stiff and bristly. She looked like an electrified porcupine.

"You are a Mormon. You are Mormon and you are prejudiced," she said when she saw me standing beside her.

I had never heard Mormon and prejudice used as accusations, although I knew my father called Brazil nuts niggertoes, and Negroes were definitely not the "white and delightsome."

"You're in the band," I accused back. I had seen her practicing formations in the morning for halftime at football games. Our school song and standard came from Bizet's *Carmen*. We sang:

> *Toreadors, who wear the green and gold,*
> *Fight for your name, fight for your fame.*
> *Fight, fight, fight, win the game.*

"You probably think I'm a Baptist, right?" Margo was a Negro, but also by birth half white. She had café-au-lait skin and big green eyes.

"I thought you said you were an existentialist. Remember in class when Mr. Watkins asked what you read this summer and you said *The Stranger?*

"That's right. I'm an atheist. When I was in grammar school, I never bowed my head when we got our free milk."

I didn't quite know what she meant, although in civics class I had heard Mr. Mitchell use the term "Commie Jewish atheists." It was hard to be lower than that, he said. It meant scum of the earth, he said, ungrateful wretches, ungrateful un-Americans.

"They come over here and gripe," he said. "Who invited them? Love it or leave it."

"Yeah," all the boys said, crossing their arms. "Who do they think they are?"

I could think of worse: Commie, nigger, Jewish, atheist, fat woman. Or how about Commie, nigger, Jew atheist, fat-woman spinster.

My dad said my Aunt Pearl was on her way to spinsterhood and that *nothing* could be worse, for nobody would know her name in heaven. I hated to think of Aunt Pearl in hell, although there was something about her that made you believe that, wherever, whatever, she would fare well.

"I'm kind of live and let live," I told Margo.

"You mean you don't care what religion I am or not?"

"Not really."

If we, the Toreadors, didn't win the game, our school stoned and broke the windows of the visiting bus. To me, that was prejudice in action.

"I don't believe in religious wars," I said. "Any war. Take the Crusades for example."

"Would you defend your mother against foreign invaders?"

I thought of my mother prostrate on the kitchen floor while her ingrate-daughter didn't even give her a helping hand.

"I'm adopted," Margo said. I noticed her nails were down to nubs. But on her it was *très chic,* as was her bad posture. She read too much, worried a lot. She wore long scarves and big earrings.

"That's nice." I knew she was adopted. Everybody knew.

"You think it's nice to be adopted?"

"Better than like Dickens, you know, having to eat gruel in an orphanage, and sometimes I think I don't belong to my parents or that it would be nice to be in a boarding school or, you know, like away."

"Solid," she said. "Solid."

"Actually, I'm beat." That was a spur-of-the-moment ploy. The only beat thing I knew was *Howl*, Ginsberg's famous poem, and Kerouac's *On the Road*, which had come out in sections in the *Paris Review* and *New World Writing*.

"Beat? You must be out of your mind. Do you know any beatnik girls?"

"Not yet."

"Well, the girls are sex slaves and the guys are fairies."

I sort of knew what fairies were, but I wasn't sure exactly what they did, other than flutter their fingers and hop around. I knew they didn't get married or have girlfriends. We had one in our school.

"Kerouac is not a fairy," I insisted. "He played football in college, and if the beats are fairies, how can the girls be sex slaves?"

Margo stood up. She was much shorter than I.

"I remember you from homemaking," she said, "but you've grown. How old are you?"

"Two inches over the summer. Seventeen."

"Is that so? How tall are you now?"

"Five feet, ten inches." I could have been on the basketball team, the only one we had, the boys' team.

"Doesn't it bother you to be so tall?"

"You mean for a girl?"

"Well."

"What's wrong with tall?" I said this as if I didn't agonize over it, as I did over the color of my hair, my freckles, and everything else about my face and body. But around Margo, I knew I should keep a stiff upper lip.

"I have to go to trig," she said slowly. "You want to go to the music store after school?"

"Okay."

"You like to read?"

"Yes," I said. Although I didn't like what we read in school. In American lit, we were reading about a happy Armenian family who lived in Fresno. They were not at all like my mother and aunt. The Fresno Armenians were salt of the earth. My mother and aunt were bats out of hell.

"Read this."

It was Howard Fast's *Citizen Tom Paine*.

"What's it about?"

"It's about a professional revolutionary atheist."

"Hey," I answered, "no sweat."

"Why do you talk jive?"

"I'm not talking jive."

"Yes, you are."

"I can talk any way I want."

"Oh my, a little rebel without a cause."

"I have a cause."

"And what is that?"

"Freedom." I flinched as I said it.

"And you're Mormon?" She narrowed her eyes.

"If I want to be." I folded my arms like the boys did.

She folded *her* arms. "My dad was in Spain during a war. You know that picture by Picasso, *Guernica*?

"Yes." No, I didn't. I was lying.

"That's the war."

"No lie?"

"Cross my heart, hope to die."

"Wow."

"You were in the Girl Scouts, right?"

"For a little while."

"Well, it shows. You probably think I look cool," she said.

"Oh yes," I answered. "You do look fine."

The music store was on Alvarado Street in Monterey. We could try out records—78s, 45s, and LPs—in the soundproof practice rooms with soundproof glass all around. It was there that Margo introduced me to Elvis Presley, Chubby Checker, Little Richard, Miles Davis, and Antonio Vivaldi.

"Listen," Margo said that first day. "No offense about the beatniks. I mean, the important thing is, they reject middle-class values, right?"

It was going on five o'clock. I wondered if my mother was okay, if she had had a good day. Usually I came home right after school. Now my father was due home any moment. If he found her alone . . .

"The important thing," I repeated after her, "is to reject middle-class values?"

Middle class was my father and my town and everything I knew from experience. Middle class was all my Mormon relatives gathered for a funeral—the dull, ill-fitting clothes and listless conversation. The men returned from work with large tin lunch boxes swinging in their hands. Days came and went, open the door, close the curtain, make the bed, turn down the bed. Wash day, bread-making day, birthday, weddings in the spring. Yet they seemed too poor to be middle-class.

Furthermore, Kerouac ate baloney sandwiches. Was that middle-class? Burroughs had gone to Harvard. That was high-class. But Ginsberg had gotten kicked out of Columbia for writing dirty words on his window. That was cool.

"What class are you, Margo?" I knew her family had more money than mine.

"The intellectual class. We are the ones who foment revolutions. In France, in Russia, it is always the intellectuals."

"I see."

After the music store, we went to the soda fountain, where people looked at us funny, but it was not Mississippi. Margo *could* sit at the counter. I was still punchy from our session in the listening room, the enclosed box of sound, and then walking down the aisle bordered by bins of records without our having the least intention of buying anything.

And, quite frankly, I had not been to the soda fountain that much either. "Shrimp Boats" was playing on the jukebox. The soda jerk was all in white. White pants, white shirt, little white pillbox hat. He leaned over the counter as if he owned it, put his hand on his chin, smirked at us. But his face was red with pimples, little pustules ready to pop. Obviously, he didn't know about the remedies advertised on the radio, like Noxzema.

"I'm not real hungry," Margo said.

"Come on."

"Okay. I'll have a hot fudge sundae with chocolate ice cream, whipped cream, nuts, and a cherry."

"Crazy," I said. "Me, too."

"I, too," she corrected.

I froze. My home was a house of correction.

"Just kidding," she said. "You can't take a joke?"

"It depends."

"I dig you. I don't want to hurt your feelings."

"Neat." Did she mean it?

All the soda-fountain equipment gleamed: the silvery nozzles and swishers, the long tube holding firm the large malted milk containers, the ice-cream-sundae cups, tall and fluted like tulips. Everything was spit-and-polish clean, about face, in order, and the soda jerks in their white could have been working in a military hospital instead of scooping out balls of maple nut and rocky road, vanilla, chocolate, chunky strawberry.

Was Margo going to be my friend?

Our swivel stools were covered in tight red vinyl and banded in silver. The other girls there sported June Allyson pageboy hairdos, each strand curled under, plaid skirts, white blouses with Peter Pan collars, white bucks.

"The thing I like about you, Zoe, is you're not afraid," Margo said.

"Sure I am." I started to blink.

"Of what? Tell me."

I tried to think of something that had to do with my parents.

"Like what scares you?"

I tried to think of something that really scared me. All I could think of was a dream I had once in which a dark man on a motorcycle approached me. The bike had no handlebars, no brakes.

"Want to go for a ride?" he asked me.

I said yes because he was cute.

"I'm not keen on snakes," I said.

"Oh, everybody is scared of them."

"Really?"

"Do you want to go to San Francisco on Saturday on the Del Monte Express, come back at the end of the day? We can go to City Lights Books, get a date with some poets."

"How much does it cost?"

"I'll pay the train fare. The poets come free."

"Sure," I said, feeling very queasy and needing a drink of water after all the ice cream.

"You know what Woody Guthrie said?" Margo asked as we left the soda fountain.

"No." I didn't know who Woody Guthrie was, so how could I know what he said.

"He said, 'Take it easy . . . but take it.'"

[**SAN FRANCISCO** was only three hours away on the train, but I had never been there by myself.

"Going to the library to study," I announced on Saturday, "all day."

"The library?" my mother said, examining her nails.

We were in the living room. On our glass coffee table was a photograph of the Mormon Tabernacle Choir, my least favorite singing group.

"The library."

"Well, okay."

She was in her pink chenille bathrobe and her hair was down. She looked smashing, and I knew that after a virtuous walk to Monterey to the liquor store she would be smashed.

"I'll be gone all day," I said, trying not to let a hint of excitement creep into my voice.

I could tell that my mother thought something was up, but she looked at me forlornly and said, "Have fun."

Luckily my father was sleeping in.

"What did you tell them?" Margo whispered at the train station. I pointed to my books.

"Ah."

"What did you say?"

"That I was going to San Francisco."

"You didn't have to lie?"

"Nope."

How amazing.

We were both in black, of course. Black turtlenecks, one that she lent me, and a black skirt, and hastily in the bathroom we put black eyeliner on. We looked like raccoons in mourning.

"You look great," Margo oozed.

"Ditto."

We each hoped to meet a poet at the City Lights bookstore. He would be in a black turtleneck, too, and a black beret, thin-fingered, moist-mouthed, and not prejudiced.

"Would you go with a Negro guy?" Margo asked.

"If the shoe fits," I said. It was one of my father's expressions, and I liked, more than anything, to use his words against him.

"What is that supposed to mean, something nasty?"

"If he's handsome."

"You think he could be handsome, a Negro?"

"Is this only a test or something, Margo? You know, we probably won't meet anybody, white, Negro, prejudiced, bereted . . ."

But of course we did. After getting lost for a couple of hours, we finally got on the right cable car and made it over to North Beach. Margo was in the W fiction section for Richard Wright, *Native Son*, and I was in C for Willa Cather, *My Antonia*, and he was in M for Norman Mailer, *The Naked and the Dead*. How perfect can you get?

And he was indeed in a black beret. His turtleneck was dark green, but I let that pass because at least it was dirty.

When I asked him if he wrote poetry, he replied, "Of course."

Margo looked over.

I made my eyebrows go up.

She nodded a yes.

It occurred to me that I really wasn't prepared for this. My sex education began and ended at that school movie, which was so rudely interrupted.

"Scat," she hissed.

"But what about you? I don't want to leave you alone."

"What makes you think I'll be alone?"

"I mean . . ."

He took me to his room over the New Pisa restaurant in North

Beach in the middle of the afternoon. I could hear the cars on the street, and the smell of soy sauce drifted over from Chinatown.

"Take off your glasses."

I did. I began to blink.

"Very nice," he said. "Take off your pants."

Somehow I hadn't planned on that. I thought we just might swoon away on cloud nine. I had never even kissed a boy. I had the proper makeup, the proper black sweater and skirt, but unfortunately I was also wearing my saddle shoes, and my underwear was little-girl cotton, the waistband held together with a small gold safety pin. I didn't want to show my pants. They weren't that good.

"Take off your pants," he repeated hoarsely. He swayed a bit. I knew he was a little drunk. And I could see now that his fingernails were dirty. Somehow that didn't rate as well as the dirty turtleneck.

I thought of Margo, who had given me a knowing look in the bookstore. Our virginity hung heavily on our hands. It was getting to be a bother, and yet, on the one hand, who cared other than ourselves, and on the other hand, should our virginity therefore be thrown away to the winds or on unworthy souls? And what about babies? Margo said losing our virginity was a big thing in our womanhood, the beginning of it. I didn't know. I thought of my mother back at home, probably pouring herself a nice stiff drink. I hated the sound of the gin splashing in the tall jelly glass. But once, she and my father had been innocents together. I saw them as very white, whiter than the sheets, excruciatingly white, that naked.

"Well."

My father would just die if he could see me. Little did he know that Margo existed and that she was, of all things, a Negro, and little did Margo know that she would not be allowed in my house by my father, who thought Negroes descended from Ham, Noah's bad-boy son, or was it the tribe of Ishmael? Anyway, would *she* get anybody on this day of days? Who would she meet? A Negro man? How many of them went into bookstores? And white men? God, I felt sick, sick and tired. The poet's room, I realized, was tawdry, cheap. His bed, with a sag in the middle, signaled Death Valley, and he may have had, for all I knew, babies in his pocket. He could kill me for sport, nobody the wiser. Alcatraz hung at the window, right there in the middle of the bay. And if he was a poet, where were his books?

"Do you want me to take you back to the bookstore?" the man asked.

"Oh no. No." Perish the thought. I didn't want to hurt his feelings.

"What is your name?" he asked. We stood facing each other. In the bookstore, he had looked in his twenties. Now, with his beret off, I saw lots of gray in his hair. We stood facing each other, the bed a coffin behind us.

"Zoe, my name is Zoe." Then I thought I should have given him a fake name. You never could tell.

"I'm Gary."

"Is that your real name?"

"Of course. Are you waiting for Santa Claus, Zoe?" he asked.

"No."

"Well then."

So I hastily stepped out of my pants, kicked them under the bed. He took out his teeth, setting them on the bed stand.

Then, going under the umbrella of my skirt, he began to gum me.

I stood straight and tall like a good girl, staring at his teeth on the bed stand. I thought of them in a glass, on the sink, tap-dancing, clacking down the hall. I hadn't thought of the man as that old. The man wasn't old. Was he old? I wondered what had happened and vowed to brush my teeth more regularly. My father had warned me regularly about gingivitis.

When he was finished, I fished for my pants under the bed, wondering if I was still a virgin. We went downstairs for dinner at the New Pisa restaurant. I had veal scallopine, with an antipasto, garden salad, soup du jour, minestrone, and ravioli, for $2.25. My love had half of a roasted spring chicken and everything else I had except for the veal, for $1.95.

I paid. It was a month of my allowance.

He escorted me gallantly back to City Lights, where Margo was waiting and reading a book called *Nadja* by André Breton.

"Listen to this," she said, reading from the book. " 'Who am I?' "

I swallowed hard.

"Well?"

"I don't have the slightest idea, Margo, who I am."

"Finished?"

"Finished," I said.

"Oh, by the way, I'm not a virgin anymore." This I announced on the train, as we pulled out of San Francisco.

"Wow."

"Yeah," I said. "It was easy."

"Aren't you bleeding?"

"Like a pig."

I wondered if, with teeth, you did bleed.

"So what did it feel like?"

I searched for the right word, something that might apply. I looked out the window. It had started to rain. I saw a group of cows huddled together under an oak. An old bathtub was their chalice.

"A bit on the gummy side. Wetish. It was like taking a sponge bath."

"Oh. Is that all?"

I would have to look it up in her parents' Kinsey reports.

"A very nice bath."

I thought of Solomon and Bathsheba, of how he spied on her when she took a bath on her roof. Burt Lancaster, I think, and Susan Hayward. How did she, also a redhead, turn out so different?

"So are you in love?" Margo asked on the train.

"Oh yes. Can you get pregnant from saliva?"

"Of course not. What are you talking about?"

"This is only a test, Margo."

"Yeah, like everything else."

We were passing Gilroy, garlic capital of the world. I was holding a fashion magazine, looking at an ad for a girdle. It said that the little *x* girdle was considered the most important advance in girdle design in years. Two criss-crossing stretch panels slimmed the waist, sleeked the hips, smoothed the tummy, and yet it let you move freely. It was made of nylon power net, dainty trim, and came in lovebird pink, bluebird blue, white, and black.

Margo seemed sad, left out. I wanted to tell her that it was awful, that it was nothing, that she had been better off in the bookstore, or the coffeehouse, anywhere else. But I had to save face. I looked out the window again, saw a huge set of teeth hovering in the sky. They weren't even in a face.

"What did you guys talk about?" Margo asked.

"Oh, he recited *Howl* to me."

"He *recited* the whole of *Howl* to you? The whole thing?"

"The first line." I stood up in the empty train, began: "I have seen the best minds of my generation destroyed by madness, starving hysterical naked, dragging themselves through the . . ." Then I stopped.

"You can say it; we're in California, Zoe. It's 1957."

I wasn't thinking of that. I was thinking I might hurt her feelings.

"Negro streets, Margo," I said, taking her hand. "Negro streets," I repeated softly. "Negro streets at dawn looking for an angry fix, angelheaded hipsters burning for the ancient heavenly connection to the starry dynamo in the machinery of night, / who poverty and tatters and hollow-eyed and high sat up smoking in the supernatural darkness of cold-water flats floating across the tops of cities . . .

"Margo."

"Contemplating jazz," she answered.

"Contemplating jazz."

[**CONTEMPLATING JAZZ?** The real beats were a good ten years older than I was, and I had never written a word except for school. If my first kiss was that sloshy conjugation of tongue and clitoris, if that was a preview of coming attractions, I was in for some trouble. I could not imagine, or rather I *could* imagine, how it might have been had he aimed for my mouth. Gary, his name was Gary. I think I would have known immediately what was teeth and what was gums. Was sex supposed to be that lurid? Was I supposed to feel that indifferent? I had my fantasies, which were anything but cold, but my father had called me cold, and perhaps I was. Certainly I was cold when I was swimming serenely in my family's bathroom, the door securely locked while wars were waged home, home on the range.

Furthermore, at school, we were preparing for our eventual death, just like in my father's bomb shelter. One blast for earthquake, get under your desk; two blasts for fire, get out on the playground; and three blasts for the bomb, get under your desk, protect your lower parts. My main worry about potential disaster was not the loss of procreation but getting trampled to death.

No white picket fences. No vacuum cleaners, no Westinghouse appliances. No Dick and Jane. Ozzie and Harriet start yelling at each other. John Wayne melts, puddles. Marilyn Monroe baby-talks herself into sudden haghood. I am pressed flat to the ground by a hundred pairs of panicked feet.

And then the whistle blows again. Except by then I am a paper cutout. They must scrape me up, a Zoescrape. My mother frames me, puts me in the hallway. This is our daughter, Zoe, had a bad accident way back when.

In the movie *Invasion of the Body Snatchers*, which I saw at the Grove theater, outer-space aliens arriving in mysterious pods supposedly take over our bodies and make us into zombies. But the point of the movie was that the lay of the land was the day of the dead, and we already were pod people, the silent generation. That is what I secretly believed: annihilation was in the air and contagious polio in the water. Paranoia was a household idol and we were all twins with our Toni home perms. But if I let my bravado drop a moment, I would have to admit that I, too, lived in a tract house.

"Margo, I'm going to graduate from high school and not be engaged." I hadn't even started my cedar hope chest, where I could accumulate all the accoutrements of a happy marriage—pillowcases, curtains, tablecloths, and such.

"Big deal." Margo was doing a book report, eating a cucumber sandwich with mustard on it, and polishing her toenails perfect pink. Margo always did three things at once and she always used green ink for book reports. She wrote not sitting at her desk but thrown across her bed, something on the radio all the time. If she couldn't think of what to write next, she bit her fingernails, and it would come to her.

"I'm serious, Margo." I wrote in pencil because I always had to erase, and sometimes I erased holes straight through my papers, and I had a habit of wetting the tip of my pencil with my tongue. I was good at school, but basically grubby and disorganized.

"It *is* too bad you're not engaged, Zoe. Why don't you just ask somebody and buy yourself a ring."

Easy for her, I thought. Her parents wanted to send her to college. Mine didn't. And what was I supposed to do? Get a job I hated?

My only hope was my aunt. However, her ballet school The World Is Your Oyster was actually not doing too well.

The studio was housed in downtown Monterey in an old adobe-brick building next to the first jail and first theater in California, where they ringed the stage with candles encased in holders cut out of tin. When I was about to graduate from high school, the walls of picturesque adobe sagged, and the wood floor my aunt had installed in her studio was warped, and the mirrors were rusted at the edges. Only four little girls in ill-fitting leotards lined up at the bar for each lesson. The record player had replaced the piano accompanist, and my aunt beat out the rhythm with a bamboo cane, not her former wooden staff.

41

Glissés, ronds de jambe par terre, ronds de jambe en l'air.

I had been through it myself, up to toe shoes. They were pink satin with pink bows, but my toes scrunched up in the little box of wood could not endure the torture. Thus, my career as a dancer ended when I was twelve, as if another door had closed.

"College?" My father was incredulous every time I brought up the subject.

"I have the grades."

My books were kept under my bed, or rather the library's books. I could read the whole length of my bed in a month during the summer.

"Why should a girl go to college, answer me that?"

"To earn more money," I offered.

This was our usual discussion during my senior year, when we all sat down to dinner and my mother, chastened and repentant from a recent fall from grace, cooked and dutifully cleared the table. I did the dishes. She dried. I put them away. My father read the paper. I polished his shoes. God was in heaven. Our set of dishes was an aqua Melmac, miraculously unbreakable.

"College costs money, four years of earnings lost to begin with, and then what, then who would marry you once you graduated?"

"I could work."

"At what?"

"Being a lawyer," I threw out.

My mother flitted back and forth, the door between the kitchen and dining room swinging open, shut, open, shut. In *Happy Marriage*, issue number 20, ten cents, the cover had a picture of a poor husband asleep. His wife, fully dressed, is thinking in her scalloped bubble: "Oh no, he is asleep again. This job is killing my marriage. Maybe Mother had the right idea . . . If I'm not home, who knows what may happen?"

Below are the warning words: "Divided between marriage and career . . . Working wife, her own WORST ENEMY."

"A lady lawyer?" my father exclaimed. "Who ever heard of that?"

"They have them in New York." Actually, Margo told me that the legal counsel of the NAACP had a woman lawyer.

"New York? A Mormon girl in New York?"

"I'm sure I could find other Mormons." New York was not exactly Sodom and Gomorrah, but to my father anything east of Salt Lake smacked of sedition. Actually finding Mormons was not one of my priorities, except, of course, in order to get married. But I didn't believe in secret names, did I? Or heaven? Although I wanted to cover all bases, I don't know what I believed in, except loneliness. That I was familiar with, and perhaps in New York I would meet people like me, people who liked me, people who . . .

"Where will you live in New York?" my father threw out.

"In an apartment."

I would have one of those beds you could pull from the wall. I would have my own telephone, and the elevator in the building would be small and cozy, closed by folding links. I would eat dinner in the Automat and see a Broadway play every week.

"Stop that blinking, will you, Zoe. How do you expect to get married if you can't hold your eyes open?"

"Married?"

"You can be a secretary in my office until you get married."

"I don't want to be a secretary." I could type only twenty-five words a minute.

"Dear, don't argue with your father. Your father is right."

My mother, sober, was grateful for small mercies. After all, some husbands would not put up with what my father did. I could see the cover of the pulp magazine: "I drowned my marriage in a bottle, and the next day I was out on the street, washed up."

"Your mother is right, Zoe."

"Your father is right."

It's *Invasion of the Body Snatchers* all over again, that telltale vacant look. Yourfatherisrightyourmotherisright.

"Your mother is right."

My father, always right, had plans. I would start with filing, he had explained, work up to answering the telephone. It would give me poise, be a kind of finishing-school experience. Furthermore, what was good enough for him was good enough for me, and that was that.

I didn't know, of course, that we were barely middle-class, and that between my mother's drinking and my father's lack of salesmanship we really didn't have any money for college. All I knew was that we owned our house and were making regular payments on everything in it. Surely if that was possible . . .

Waste not, want not, my father said at the end of every meal, as he made that terrible scraping sound with his knife to get up every last bit.

But it was at three, the hour of the wolf, when my father couldn't sleep, that he confided his worldly philosophy.

First, I would see his lean shadow bending over my bed, and his hushed voice—"Zoe, Zoe, get up"—as if he were an eerie guardian angel, a moth summoning me outside on the grass to see the moon before he died. I would put on my bathrobe quickly, and there in the quiet of that hour a kind of awful intimacy would grow up between us.

"Your mother is a very sick woman," my father would begin quietly, as if she were some kind of romantic figure and her disease was consumption or faintness of heart, "and she needs you."

Meanwhile, my mother snored away. I would be on my knees scrubbing the woodwork in the kitchen while my father watched.

"As I was saying, your mother is a very sick woman. She does not realize that the body is a tabernacle."

This was our mystery, our own private taboo, and nobody but us knew, he would whisper, so as not to wake up the world. He seemed thrilled by my mother's problem. Suffering and sacrifice were our lot in life, he informed me. He liked the hour of the wolf. He liked our secret, my mother's "disease."

"Mum's the word," he said, putting a narrow finger up to his narrow lips. "Sh."

I am rubbing the area along the doorway near our refrigerator with a rag made out of an old sock of mine, wondering how I will perform on an algebra test at eight o'clock in the morning.

"Are you listening to me?"

"Mum's the word."

My father is in his shorts and bathrobe, one leg crossed. I have never seen him naked and never want to, not even his chest. But during these sessions, I get a glimpse of pink. Sometimes, while I am scrubbing, he works on his fishhooks, although he rarely goes fishing, just as he spends every Saturday afternoon in the hardware store but rarely fixes anything around the house.

Sometimes, while I am scrubbing, he reads *The Monterey Herald*, turning the pages back with a vengeance; he does not know what the world is coming to, what with juvenile delinquency on the rise and all the fuss over that kid in Mississippi. Emmett? Emmett Till? Was that his name, he who dared to smile, or was it whistle, at a white woman.

Land sakes alive.

"He's dead, Daddy." I begin to blink, thinking of the poor kid.

Emmett Till had been found in the Tallahatchie River with his face bashed in, a seventy-four-pound fan tied to his ankles, in 1955, the year after the school desegregation law, Brown vs. the Board of Education, was passed.

You think you're as good as us? the two white men asked Emmett Till over and over again.

Yeah, he answered over and over again. Yeah. Yeah. They had to kill him, they said. They just had to.

"You sow what you reap, Zoe."

"You sew what you rip," I whispered.

"What's that?"

"You sow what you reap, Daddy."

"Look, a spot over there." It is as if he spied a roach, a piece of vermin. "You can never be too sure, too clean. You are known by the company you keep. Are you listening to me, Zoe?"

[**M A R G O W A S** the company I kept.

Margo pronounced Negro knee grow, like a knee grows in Brooklyn, and the hip bone is connected to the thigh bone, and would you knead that bread for me, honey.

Margo didn't know where she came from, so she told stories:

She said she was just floating down or up the Nile in a basket, or maybe it was the Mississippi or even the Amazon. The pharaoh's adopted Jew son found her in the bulrushes, taking her to his convert Egyptian brother. In this version, cattails grow out of Margo's hair. She cries: I was born in slavery and do not want to die on any cross.

Then there is the Brazilian memory:

"It is very hot. A man has come down the hill to beg for money to bury his wife. My adoptive mother, Judy, gave him the money, and the dead woman was put in a long box. The sharp smell of pine comes back. The dead woman looks like a wax doll. At the funeral, I am wearing a beautiful white dress, a First Communion dress, a wedding dress, a dream dress. It is flimsy, with panels of gauze like sewed-together bandages.

"My adoptive mother is sitting in a chair because she cannot stand anymore without difficulty. She has stiff metal braces on her legs.

" 'Why does everybody have to die?' I ask in Portuguese. '*Por quê todo mundo tem quê morrer?*'

"My adoptive mother starts down the hill, and the bereaved husband rushes forward and insists that she take the only thing he has to offer, me."

Aaron, Margo's adoptive father, is full of stories, too.

In the days before the revolution, when there was a pogrom, the cossacks split open the bellies of the Jewish women and stuffed live cats inside. Aaron's grandfather had seen that happen to his mother. Aaron's great-grandfather, a harmless musician who had traveled from village to village playing for weddings and bar mitzvahs, went crazy after his wife's death and hanged himself from the scorched rafter of what had once been his house. Like Aaron years and another continent later, this man, as a suicide, could not be buried in an Orthodox cemetery, hallowed ground, and so Aaron's grandfather packed up what little was left and with his young sister, traveled by cart, by foot, by train, and then by boat to America, to america, to a-mer-i-ca.

When they arrived at Ellis Island, the girl had to have her head shaved, not because she was getting married but because of the lice. The Salvation Army got them new clothes and sent them to Milwaukee. There they grew vegetables in an area called Pigsville, under one of the Milwaukee bridges, and from a cart, pulled by an old nag, Stravinsky, they sold their crops.

When Aaron's father wanted to go to medical school, as a practicality he picked from the phone book the most Anglo name he could find. In turn, Aaron became a wiz kid at the University of Chicago, where he learned about worldwide injustice and went to Spain in 1936. All the young intellectuals were doing it, joining the ragtag army defending the democratically elected socialist government, fighting Franco and Fascism. Aaron, since he could speak five languages, was a translator and interpreter for the International Brigades. The commander of the Lincoln Brigade, the American troops, while Aaron was there was a Negro. It was the first time in the history of the world, Aaron informed me, that a Negro led integrated troops, unless perhaps you want to count Othello.

Judy, Aaron's wife and Margo's mother, was crippled. Polio, like President Roosevelt, and in a wheelchair. Sometimes she walked, but she had heavy casts on her legs and it was very hard. At first I felt awkward around her, but I got used to her legs and wheelchair. When Aaron played the piano, she danced by wheeling around in circles, and sometimes we girls would form a conga line behind her. Other times

Margo sat in her lap as she had as a young child, and they tootled around together.

Judy could not have babies, and that was why Margo was adopted.

This is Judy's story: "Margo came at a time of deep despair."   **47**

And all the pictures of them together show Judy hugging Margo to her for dear life.

I see Margo and Judy in front of a large, low white house, palm trees in the background. There are Margo and Aaron on a sidewalk with mosaic swirls. There are Margo and Judy on a ledge overlooking Sugarloaf Mountain. There are Margo, Aaron, and Judy at a table in a fancy restaurant. There are Margo and Judy in a beautiful tropical garden. Judy is in her wheelchair and Margo is tiny. There are people in carnival costumes sometimes, sometimes lazy clouds in the sky. It always looks like Sunday.

[**MARGO'S PARENTS** met at the University of Chicago in a John Reed reading group. When Aaron first told me, I thought of it as a kind of knitting club with Great Books. Later I found out it was based on John Reed's book *Ten Days That Shook the World*, which is about Lenin's return to Russia from Finland. Then I found out the John Reed reading group meant earnest young men and bespectacled girls who had a big picture of Father Marx on their club wall.

Judy could walk when she was in college; she was perfectly fine. There is a photo of her and Aaron on some city street in Chicago leaning into each other luminous with love as the wind tries to rip away their pathetic overcoats. They are in front of some modernistic Midwest piece of architecture. The Future. Brave New World. Judy and Aaron.

"We smoked like chimneys at school," Judy said, cheeks aglow. "We made thin soup for dinner on our hot plates, and argued politics all night."

"We spent days writing leaflets and newspaper articles," Aaron added.

They would go out on strike for the cafeteria workers, just organize, like the song said.

They would support janitors for higher wages and nurses for better status and truck drivers for safer roads and cannery workers for fifteen-minute breaks every two hours. They believed in the rights of workers and the sentiments of the masses.

My evenings with Aaron and Judy and Margo went like this:

Aaron, Judy, Margo, and I sitting around their long dinner table, made out of a door, drinking beer and eating artichokes dipped in melted butter. Their huge bookshelf crammed with books rises before us like **49** the Ten Commandments. Thou Shalt Read. The damp night fog presses in at their floor-to-ceiling windows, jealous of our warmth and righteous glow. Judy would put on some Dave Brubeck and "dance." Aaron smiles his lopsided, half-sad, so very pretty smile. Yes, the world, the weight of the world.

At my house, I knew my mother was probably in bed with her bunched blankets clutched to her chest, and my father would be busy finding smudges on the wall, cuff marks on the woodwork, blotches of mud on the linoleum, the inevitable march of filth into our pristine domain. Keeping up appearances. Cleanliness is next to godliness. And *where* have *you* been? I said I had a friend. She was in my class, a Protestant, a pretty Presbyterian who was considering conversion.

And then, as the evening goes on at the Robinsons', which is essentially a chronology of Aaron's life, we get to the Spanish Civil War of 1936.

Aaron's Spain is the Spain of García Lorca, the playwright and poet. Aaron's Spain is the Spain of Pablo Casals, the cellist who left his country, and of Picasso, who went to France.

"We were there from all over the world, Zoe," Aaron would tell me, leaning across the table, sometimes touching my hand, "there from all over the world in 1936, defending the democratically elected government, which happened to be left. Dress rehearsal for the Second World War. Franco and the Fascists staged an insurrection. Freedom-loving men from everywhere responded, came to the defense of the republic."

I had an image of young men getting onto trains, hopping in cars, swimming the channel in tight bathing caps, greased for the cold, going by boat, by air, by sheer willpower. Droves of them. Like a herd of seals. Like the sea gulls rescuing the Mormons, the air thick with mercy on errand.

"There were three hundred of us when we reached Le Havre. The U.S. consul came aboard telling us that we still had a chance to go back. The U.S., of course, had a nonintervention policy. Nobody turned back. The French customs people would have let us go through without even a check. But the French government wouldn't let us through. We had to cross the Pyrenees, sneak in."

I thought of the mountains at night, the moon close, bobbing behind their shoulders like a balloon, Fascists hiding under every rock like the snakes they were. From the distance came the rat-a-tat-tat of gunfire. At the pass was a kindly Basque in a beret.

Salut.

They did not teach us Aaron's war in school. My imagination could only go so far. Dress rehearsal for World War II, an army of intellectuals—leftists and anarchists versus the artillery of Hitler and Mussolini? Picasso's painting *Guernica*, a reproduction which Margo showed me, made me feel sorry for the horse in it, and I liked the light bulb, which was a comic-book trick. The rest of it I didn't understand. Bombs away, that's what it was. Bombs were the things that would get us *all* in the end.

"There was a man who had betrayed us."

I began to blink.

Aaron was up on his feet now, pacing, lecturing like the professor he was. Sometimes he let his fingers run over my shoulder. His face was lean and intense like Kafka's, and he was very tall, very skinny. He wore blue jeans even then, when only sharecroppers would be seen in them. I felt, around Aaron, in touch with the world, in touch with history, not the official version written by the winners, not the underground history of gossip and guess, but the elemental, undeniable heart of the matter, the real people, the strong-faced, muscular people of Soviet Realism. And he touched me, not just my hands, my shoulders, my lips, sometimes my hair, but also my heart.

And so what was he doing in this remote corner of California teaching in a community college, I wondered. This man who had seen so much? This Aaron? One of his cousins had dug his way out of a concentration camp with a spoon. His great-uncle had left the Ukraine because of the cossacks. How could Aaron *stand* Pacific Grove? Why wasn't he at Harvard University or the Sorbonne or Oxford or someplace grand and famous? Why was he talking to *me*, of all people, and carelessly but cautiously letting his hands rest all over me?

"The man who betrayed us . . ."

"Maybe the girls aren't ready to hear this, Aaron."

"Judy, they must know the world."

"But Aaron . . ."

"He was a spy for the Franco forces and we found out. Hitler and Mussolini sent troops to help Franco, you know that," Aaron said.

I had seen a photo of Mussolini and his mistress hanging. It was only a picture, but it had impressed me. People looked so different then, so white and pasty in the photographs. Aaron had photographs of World War II, the piled bodies, the big eyes. Dachau, Auschwitz, Buchenwald, Belsen. I was fascinated, repelled, guilty.

Later I was to see a movie about the Negro troops which liberated some of the concentration camps. A black soldier before assembled German people of the town lifted a frail little Jewish boy to his shoulders.

"This is your enemy," he said.

Aaron, needless to say, also had photo collections of lynched men. Mississippi, Alabama. Margo said she was sick of them. Aaron told her she must stand up and be a Jew *and* a Negro.

"Does that mean lynching *and* the concentration camp, oh boy oh joy, aren't we lucky."

"Margo." Actually I did think she was lucky.

"My father," she complained in her bedroom, our little pink womb of rebirth. "Why do I always feel so guilty for just being alive?"

"Maybe because he does." It was relatively easy being a Mormon and being white, I knew. I wished I was somebody interesting.

"What am I supposed to do," Margo complained, "stop chewing bubble gum, not wear earrings?"

"I should feel guilty, Margo, not you. I haven't suffered at all."

"Don't worry," Margo consoled. "You will."

Aaron liked to quote La Pasionaria, grande dame of the Spanish Republicans: "It is better to die on your feet than live on your knees."

To me that was like being Red *and* dead.

"What is the point?" I'd whisper to Margo in her bedroom.

"Living on your knees could mean slavery," Margo explained, "if you are willing to endure anything just to live."

"I'm not advocating slavery, but if that is the only choice over death . . . I mean, God, Margo."

"Slavery was not like *Gone with the Wind*, dummy."

"I know, but it was life, it's living." I almost said, it's *a* living.

"Yeah, and what's so great about just living on the lowest possible terms?"

"It's not great. It's life." Slaves, I thought, could kiss each other.

When I was over at Margo's hearing Aaron talk, I knew I had to go to college. I wanted to learn more. I wanted to have the wherewithal to really be able to say something to Aaron. I wanted to live on the best possible terms—yes, on my feet. And I wanted to kiss Aaron. I even fixed dreams about him before going to sleep.

Aaron is in a house in the forest with two thousand daffodils growing amid the trees. He is wearing tights, I, a tutu. He is Petrouchka and I the Ballerina, and the Moor is Othello, except he is not jealous. He is not our servant either. He is our comrade. He is Paul Robeson.

"What happened to the traitor of the International Brigades?" I asked Aaron when he told his Spanish Civil War story. As if I didn't know. As if all traitors, anywhere, everywhere, are treated with humanity and not shot at dawn after their last cigarette against a forlorn wall.

I had learned the lingo. Fascist pigs. Traitors. The People's Army, the Four Insurgent Generals, the Scabs.

"We stripped the skin off him piece by piece."

"But . . ."

"We were idealists," Aaron said.

"What is ideal about torture?" I asked, confused.

[**SOMETIMES WHEN** I went to the bathroom at Margo's house, I would peek into her parents' room. They had double single beds just like my parents, and just like everybody married in the movies. I imagined Aaron helping Judy take off her braces, undoing the metal clamps, massaging the twisted feet, and gently lifting her into bed. She wore grandmother shoes, and I wondered if they were really a camouflage for feet as scrunched and small as Chinese women's feet or if the feet were clubbed or hopelessly twisted.

When she walked, Judy used canes and her legs swung out stiff and straight. So without the braces were her legs wet noodles? Slivery question marks? She wore thick stockings. Did they have a distinct odor? Must her feet be massaged?

The only decoration in their bedroom was a Japanese print—a woman in a red kimono, her back turned. She had the eyes of a ferret. Instead of having chenille or velvet or soft silk, the textured fabrics my mother favored despite the Mormonness of our household, Judy and Aaron had bedspreads of a rather rough and faded cotton fabric. It was a very plain room. A squat paper lamp on metal legs cast a cold glow. There was one chair, canvas on loins of black metal, a butterfly chair. I imagined Aaron sitting on that chair, his legs crossed, reading Thomas Wolfe's *Look Homeward, Angel*, a book he thought I would like.

My parents' bedroom was done in gold and white. Their walls were paneled in what my mother called a warm walnut brown. There was a flicker of gold in the white bedspread and drapes, and the gold theme was carried out in the brass lamps, and the doorknobs of clear Plexiglas were laminated with flecks of gold leaf between the layers of plastic. Of course the room was only large enough to hold their beds, two bedside tables, a chest of drawers, and my mother's makeup table. You had to slide sideways in between things. Yet the mirror of her makeup table was bordered by light bulbs, as if she were a movie star. Five minutes, Mrs. McLaren. And she favored Elizabeth Arden cosmetics, although she would waste hours of the Avon ladies' time, "testing" colors. I would come home from school sometimes, and they would be in the midst of a session on the living room L, my mother somewhere between sober and drunk.

"What do you think, Zoe, fashion-black mascara or career blue?"

I thought she looked like a schizophrenic. "The blue is definitely you, Mother."

Besides our section sofa in the shape of an L, our living room had my father's rocker-lounger-ottoman. The advertisement of it said it had the "bounce of pure latex rubber and a solid backbone of pure curled animal hairs." I dared not ask what animal. Of course, we didn't have a dog, but if we did, I know it would never be able to get up on the furniture, so what, then, I wondered, was my dad doing sitting on "pure curled animal hairs"?

The Robinsons' dining table was a long door on metal legs. All their furniture was basically something else. Their end tables were really wood boxes, their couches were mere pieces of foam rubber covered in boat canvas, and the fireplace, a dramatic circular structure in the middle of the living room, was wrought iron made by welders in a machine shop. And, actually, their house was designed like a bridge, that is, suspended between beams.

Margo's bedroom was where we listened to Margo's teenage-girl record player and, if softly, the radio. She was not allowed popular music, just classical and real jazz. But the station band of the radio beeped in the dark, and the radio had a life of its own. "The Glow Worm." It was the pulsating heart of Margo's room, pink and plastic. Around us huddled dolls from throughout the world—the Brazilian doll in kerchief and carnival beads, the Scottish doll in kilt, the Chinese lady, the Spanish señorita—and a scatter-pin collection on velvet, her china animal collection, an old microscope which had been Aaron's father's, jars with stinking pond water to look at through the microscope, and books. The Modern Library editions of Marcel Proust's *Remembrance of Things Past* and Freud's *Collected Works.*

My room at my house could have been in Winesburg, Ohio. I had **55** a chest of drawers, a rag rug my mother had made me. My bed was iron-framed like a hospital bed, but it had two gold knobs, and sometimes I pretended it was a flying carpet out of *The Arabian Nights.* Other than that, the only ornaments were a flowered lamp shade, a gift of Aunt Pearl, and my jewelry box, which was also a music box with a twirling ballerina on it. Under my mattress were my love comic books, my library books, an issue of *Mad* magazine, Alfred E. Neuman smiling an idiotic smile, and a photo of my mother and aunt when they were young. They both have long legs and silly grins and, except for their clothing, look like what I imagined Jo in *Little Women* to look like. Tomboys, tough cookies, smarty-pants.

In Aunt Pearl's house my favorite room was the Mexican room, full of mosaics and terra cotta, little earthen pots and bright ceramics, serapes thrown across straw chairs. That was where my aunt kept her Tito Puente records.

The Turkish room had brass-plate tables held up by elephant statues, fringed lamp shades, an Oriental rug, gold tassels at the windows in the shape of little pineapples.

And once, when my mother was quite drunk, she revealed to me that it was in the Turkish room that she got pregnant with me, and thus had to marry my father.

"If it were not for you . . ." she said.

If it were not for me, what? She would be a famous costume designer? Not a Mormon? Not married to my father? A happy woman?

The Mormon Temple is where sacred covenants with the Lord are honored, such as marriage and ordinances on behalf of the ancestors, for instance, vicarious proxy baptisms. Only Mormons in good standing, with letters of recommendation from their bishop, can enter. The first Mormon temples, which had been built in Missouri and Illinois, were destroyed by angry mobs.

When the pioneers entered the Salt Lake Basin in 1847, one of the first things Brigham Young did was set the site for the Temple. The cornerstone of the Salt Lake Temple was laid in 1853. When work began, the granite was quarried and then dragged by oxen, a four-day trip.

Then, in 1858, when President Buchanan, believing that there was seditious activity in Utah, sent troops to destroy the Temple, the Mormons got wind of the plan and buried the foundation. When the troops left, the foundation was exhumed, and work went on until 1862, when it was found that the foundation was cracking. At that point, the old stones had to be dug up, and work started afresh. The new stones were set without mortar. Blacksmiths, stonecutters, masons, foundry workers, and skilled craftsmen were employed. The Temple was a beehive of activity.

Then in 1868, on the advice of Brigham Young, the Mormons stopped work on the Temple and helped lay tracks for the Union Pacific. After the railroad was completed, sixty pounds of granite for the Temple could be hauled in one day. In 1892, the capstone was laid and the golden angel, Moroni, was erected, and in 1893 the interior was finished. It had taken forty years.

[**I BEGAN TAKING** the bus out to the Monterey Peninsula Community College campus, just happening to be using the library. Aaron shared his office in the English department with a couple of other people, so we'd go for a walk or even a little drive. He drove very fast in his jade Plymouth, and inevitably we'd end up at the Carmel beach, sitting in the sand and looking out toward the ocean. I would dig my feet in to the ankles, take handfuls of sand, squeeze hard (this is time, I would say to myself, letting the grains curtain down gritty rain; this is my life).

"I . . ."

I'd swallow hard.

"Yes," he answered, understanding.

Or we'd pace around Carmel, he with his hands in his pockets, looking down at the ground, and me with my head up shining, happy as a lark. If it was raining, we'd go to the Sancho Panza Coffee Shop in Monterey.

"Zoe."

"Yes."

I'd look up expectantly from my espresso. The coffee shop was in an old adobe building and had a soft wooden floor, the original old wide boards, and they played flamenco guitar music on the record player.

"Segovia," Aaron would say.

"Ah." How could anybody know so much.

Or:

"Zoe?"

"Yes."

"Did you know that Zoe means life in Greek?"

"No, I didn't." And I couldn't imagine how my parents had stumbled onto such a fortuitous appellation. If nothing else, they gave me a name worth having, worth Aaron.

So it was a chilly January afternoon in 1957. The fog had lifted. The boats in the boat works looked like dinosaur skeletons, museum replicas in the making. Now that the sardines were fished out, there was no hurry. Boats stood on their risers whole months, rotted. Cannery Row was a ghost town. Dora, the famous madam, had fled with all her girls. Doc Ricketts, the eccentric biologist who lived on Cannery Row, who had predicted the end of the sardines and the demise of the fleet, was dead and immortalized by John Steinbeck. Our area, Our Town, was changing. People driving by on Ocean Avenue in their finned cars looked like Q-tips. Haircuts were that close.

Sometimes on night rambles, climbing out my window, escaping my mother's snores, my father's scrubbing, I would walk all the way down to Cannery Row just to survey the ruins. This meant creeping down Companion Way (our street) to Asilomar Avenue. I would pass Shell Avenue and could see the red tile roof of the Stanford Hopkins Marine Laboratory. I passed Siren Drive, Sea Palm Avenue. On the left, oceanside, were clusters of aloelike cactus. I'd pass Fountain Avenue, the P. G. Pool. On and on. It seemed that I lived in a seaside resort, in paradise, until I hit Cannery Row.

Climbing into the empty factories was a little like being in a dark department store after closing, with all the little cables that ran overhead carrying receipts and money in torpedo capsules to the main office stopped. But in the nighttime canneries, there were no bells ringing the overhead route of money, no mannequins, only the echoing of my footsteps. Fe, Fie, Foe, Fum. Crates, chutes, conveyor belts limp as licorice set out in the sun, and everywhere the smell of fish.

This expedition was different. It was not a mere exploration, a childish ramble. It was a January afternoon and I was intent. In the morning I had looked through my father's *National Geographic* hoping to see naked breasts. No such luck.

My mother's *Saturday Evening Post* featured a cover of a group of girls in a homemaking class setting a table. On the blackboard was a diagram of where each thing should go, and Dinner #2:

MEAT LOAF

CORN PUDDING

STEWED TOMATOES

PINEAPPLE UPSIDE-DOWN CAKE

I couldn't concentrate. In my heart of hearts and in my bones of bones and deep down in the pit of my stomach, everywhere, all over, I knew it was wrong. But I was going to do it anyway. I had to do it. I thought of the insistence of my mother's black hair, which would not stay yellow, and the pungent smell of the limes she loved in her gin and tonics.

There you go, I said to myself. Precedence. The Bad Seed.

You'll do anything, won't you, Margo said.

For a laugh?

Don't ask me why.

I don't know why.

Except that on the other side of daring-do and devil-may-care was the sallow, bland life I led—*Lawrence Welk's Top Tunes and New Talent*, Campbell's Chicken Noodle Soup, *The Red Skelton Show*. Did you know that the founder of the Boy Scouts, Robert Baden-Powell, could touch his toes twenty-one times at age seventy-nine? Do you have tired blood?

I had walked along the railroad tracks from Lovers' Point past the Pacific Grove pool, past the public beach, and all around the Hopkins Marine Station Laboratory area, where the scientists busied themselves over Bunsen burners and bubbling pots. Outside their windows, the cypress-tree branches, thick and fuzzed, looked like Negro hair, Margo hair. Go back, little girl, they pointed with their branches, obvious as the signs in *Pilgrim's Progress*. I tramped forward, stepping on the succulents that grew near the beach—ice plant, they were called—and I broke their stems open. A milky substance oozed out. Take that, I said, and that, and that.

"There are three openings," Margo told me that night, after I admitted I didn't know a thing. I was painting her fingernails and toenails with fuchsia pink. We were trying on makeup, too. I gave her dog, Trotsky, a pedicure, and Margo dared me to kiss him on his beagle lips.

"You'll do anything," Margo said to me when I did.

The picture she drew of the womb and fallopian tubes and ovaries looked like a flowering tree or an ox head.

I had long ago confessed to the gumming, the false teeth that occasionally appeared in the sky over the bay in a wide leer enlarged a thousand times.

"This is the tunnel of love," she pointed out, then drawing a man's thing for me. She gave it a little eye, which at times spurted not just water like a fountain but a thick milk like the ice-plant goo. The milk of human kindness, she said with a sneer. "Penis, that's what it's called."

"Yuck." What an ugly word. Penis. At school there was a poor girl named Ennis, and another girl named Regina.

"It stands up, fills with blood," Margo continued.

"Don't tell me," I giggled into the pillow.

"I'm telling you this for your own good, woman to woman, Negro woman to white woman."

"Can we forget it a second, Margo?"

"My color?"

"Well?"

"Have you looked in the mirror lately?"

"Do you mean to tell me?"

"Yes," she said seriously. "Some has rubbed off."

For a second, I think I felt a tad of panic. It must have shown.

"Got you going, didn't I," Margo said.

The Stanford Hopkins Marine Laboratory buildings that fateful January afternoon looked like a college campus. It was all the sign I needed, so without any further qualm I walked up to Central Avenue and took a bus out to the college. I saw Aaron's Plymouth parked under the pine trees. Another sign. One and one made two.

Aaron's office was at the end of a long hallway near the school's science labs. I heard the jiggling of centrifuges, smelled the odor of solutions, poisons, formaldehyde, chemicals.

"Zoe, how nice to see you." Aaron was very courtly, nicely formal, as if he didn't know why I was there.

"I was just in the area. You know." I shrugged my shoulders, as if it were the most normal thing in the world for me to walk about four miles, take the bus, and just drop in.

He looked at me over his glasses, and I could feel his X-ray vision probing my brain, fingering my heart, handling my lungs, and penetrating my underpants to my little tuft of orange hair, which he tickled. Liar, liar, pants on fire.

"How is school?"

"Fine." I shrugged.

"A lab is empty this afternoon," he said. "Let's go down there."

He got up, and I could see that he was fumbling a little with his keys. His hands were shaking. So were mine.

I sat on a tall stool amid the glassware and Bunsen burners, the sink, and the trays and the slides and the microscopes on the black countertops.

He is forty, I thought.

I was almost eighteen.

When he talked to me I felt his emotions as he went through them. They were many and they changed in an instant. These changes and feelings were exciting and new to me. I wished I could draw his portrait, approach him, appease him. My mind had to run to keep pace with him.

"Don't be nervous," he said, taking my arms down from my chest.

"Aaron." I began to blink like mad.

"That's better, but don't blink, hold still."

The windows of the lab were tall, paned, very dusty.

"You have the luminosity of a sixteen-year-old girl," he said.

"I am going to be eighteen soon."

"Indeed you are." His smile was sad, of course, because he knew, I knew, that everything was impossible.

"I want to die," I said.

"No, you don't. You are precious," he said. "Precious and precocious."

"Precarious," I added.

"Yes, that, too."

I thought of my mother and her songs from musicals, making love sound wonderful. Only once had I seen my father touch her in tenderness, and that was when she came home from the doctor with a lump in her breast. I didn't understand. I thought it was something she might carry in her string grocery bag, something from the butcher. A lump, a cow's knuckle, a pig's snout, an ox's tail.

My father started to cry, and he hugged her.

"We have to go to church and pray," he said.

Apparently it worked, for she didn't have cancer after all. And I realized that he loved her. My father loved my mother. But it wasn't wonderful. His love for her was a tremendous ordeal, his life work, a dedication equal to hers for alcohol.

Aaron removed my glasses, put them on the black counter.

"My, my, my," he said.

I felt like Clark Kent, who in the phone booth shed his glasses and clothes. Revealed, he is Superman. The librarian in my pulp fiction throws away her glasses, takes down her prim bun. Lo and behold, she is beautiful.

"What about Margo, Aaron?" I said quietly, his face a blur.

"What *about* Margo?" He shrugged.

"And Judy?"

"Judy is not well. Let's leave Judy out of this." He shook his head a little as if ridding *himself* of the thought.

He was wearing corduroy trousers, of course, brown, with a beige shirt. His tweed coat had leather elbow patches. He wore penny loafers and white socks.

Nobody thinks of eyes as sex organs, but they are. Everything is in the looking, the locking. Aaron and I were Siamese twins connected by the eyes. And the measure of the breath, nobody thinks of that.

Expertly he unbuttoned my school blouse, button by button, looking me straight in the face, and he undid my bra far more expertly than any of my peers would do. This was no awkward fumbling in the back of a low-slung car at the drive-in movie. He held each breast like unspillable tea in a cup.

"Slow is best," he said, kissing them reverently.

The room was thick with time.

"I can only give you old-man love," he touched the tip of my ears with his forked tongue.

When I lay down on the laboratory floor, I found the tiles cold. For a second I thought he should have volunteered his sweater like Sir Walter Raleigh, but I let it pass. The glassware, the machines and paraphernalia of science, the periodic table on the wall seemed to belie what we were doing. Where was rationality? Where was the intellect? I lay very still, closed my eyes, pretended I was asleep because I did not want to believe it was happening, but I also wanted it to happen more than anything else in the world.

"You must look," he said.

I squinted my eyes open, could see him. His appendage was not bright pink like Margo's dog, Trotsky's; it was gray like an elephant's trunk, ugly and wrinkled, with a purplish tip, and when it lengthened, it got thick as a stick of rancid butter, the only fat thing on his body, and it dripped a little. His chest was sunken with little breasties. His thighs were only as large as his upper arms and they were smaller than mine. He had a huge scar down his abdomen from when he had half his stomach cut out for his ulcer. It was a red, angry line crisscrossed with small stitch lines like a railroad track. I was frightened, could imagine him coming undone, bursting apart all over me, a flood of guts.

It was a little like going to the doctor, and he telling me what he was going to do before he hurt me. Although in all his preliminaries, Aaron did not once kiss my lips. I had kissed Trotsky's doggy lips. What was the big deal? Or was this a final fidelity to Judy or the one thing, supposedly, that prostitutes never did? He never kissed me on the lips.

"Now, this will burn a little." He was going to insert it as if using a doctor's cold metal calipers.

I think I may have clenched my teeth, and I tried to be silent, and when I did scream, he put his hand over my mouth. The whole time he kept his eyes on my face, watching, watching.

Afterward, he wiped the blood up with a white lab coat, which hung on a hook on the door. The blotch on the floor was like a Rorschach blot, portending my career in crime. He washed me off very tenderly with the soft cheesecloths they kept around the lab for the glassware, and he took his socks off and fashioned a kind of sanitary napkin for me like the one my father found on the back of the toilet and beat me for, and the socks were also like diapers for Margo when she was a baby. Then I watched his bare feet. Oh God, but his ankles pierced my heart.

"Are you sorry?" he asked, lying back down beside me on the floor.

"No."

I was dazed.

He kissed me on the cheek.

"You will visit me again?"

I could feel the blood and his semen seep out, blending together in the nest of my pubis like sticky honey.

"Oh yes."

"You make me want to live," he said, getting up.

"What do you mean?"

"That's too much for you, isn't it? Sorry."

"I'm . . ."

I didn't know the term postcoital depression, how, after being so close, one must pull away and reassert independence. I didn't know then about Aaron's fondness for an unsophisticated audience—me, Margo, poor Judy, and apparently a bevy of beauties, nubile younguns newly hatched at the eggery.

That knowledge came later.

Then, at the moment, I felt flattered, perplexed, and overwhelmed.

"Nobody will find out, if that is what worries you," he said. "You look worried."

"No, not that." I was thinking more along the lines of some kind of cosmic retribution. Fornication would show on my face. People would be able to tell. People at church, Sunday school. My father. Everybody would know.

In the pulp fiction and romance comic books I bought with my allowance, like *My Secret Shame*, a girl paid for her indiscretions:

"You think I'm cheap?" she says, hurling a vase in his direction.

In a circle below: "I WANTED RESPECT."

"See," they would all say in Pacific Grove. "I told you she was no good. She's gone all the way. She's gone below the waist."

Aaron was hitching up his pants, rather expertly, and fitting his thin cowboy belt through its buckle with a quick snapping motion.

"No. Aaron, it's my fault, it's my nature to be somewhat . . ."

"Oedipal," he suggested.

"Electrical," I quipped.

"Taboos," he said, "are either as archaic as the Greek or of a biblical foundation. Tired humanistic relics not applicable to exceptional people."

"But that is what our society follows, that is how we live." I was lying on the floor, open to discovery at any second. He was standing above me. He was a teacher writing a book about *Othello*. I was a high school student. Were we exceptional people?

[**THE TERM** "love affair" makes it sound grown-up and glamorous. Trysts, clandestine kisses, close dancing, desperate phone calls, silken clothes, languorous afternoons in bed like movie stars. It was not like that at all. It was grubby, intense, as if our efforts were to dig into each other, rub off on each other, take hunks of flesh away, spoils of war.

Aaron:

The smooth slope of a nose with the edges of the nostrils reddened when he walked outside in long, loose strides and hair that sprung up so alive from his forehead that it seemed that his hair was the motion, the visualization of him thinking. Hands yellowed at the tips like old piano keys. Hardly any eyelashes, so the eyes seemed unprotected, at the mercy of all they looked upon.

Aaron was at the tip of my tongue and in the pit of my stomach. I walked about mentally hugging myself to myself. All the love songs applied to me. I wanted to kiss Elvis Presley. I kissed pages of books, the way in some churches the priest kisses the Bible. I wanted to kiss the world. I was not a virgin. I was a gloriously real woman. I was miserable. I was elated. It was both bizarre and beautiful.

Somebody, *somebody* was touching me.

Only when my mother was very drunk did she touch me. Like my father with his three o'clock scrubbing sessions, she, too, moved about in the night—a wraith from the gold-and-white bedroom down the hallway to my spartan girlroom. I would see her framed in my doorway like the witch of my worst nightmare, and without prelude or explanation she would throw herself over my sleeping body and, blurry and smelly and drunk out of her mind, would slur out: "I love you, I love you."

And I, how would I answer, pushing her off my body? My own mother? At that moment, I hated her.

When I was a baby, I slept in the living room, in a basket on the floor. My mother said I cried so much, they would have to put the basket in the back of the car and drive around all night.

"Why didn't you just pick me up?" I never asked, dreaming of my father holding me to his shoulder and pacing the floor, patting my little baby back. "There, there. There, there."

[**FOR MY EIGHTEENTH** birthday, my aunt took me to a Chinese restaurant on Alvarado Street.

"I like this red," she said, looking up at the dangling fringes of the rice-paper lanterns.

The aquarium in the restaurant looked like our bathroom.

"I might do a Chinese room," my aunt continued.

I could see it: red lacquered chests, blue pagoda chinaware, teapots, a parade of ivory elephants, jade Buddhas.

"You know, Zoe, darling, you are the apple of my eye."

I knew that as soon as she started to sound like my father, who had actually financed her ballet school, she had something unpleasant to say.

I smiled. For the occasion I was wearing the dress my mother had made for me recently, the buttercup number with the sash. I looked about ten, except, of course, that I was nearly six feet tall, an ostrich.

"I wanted to be able to give you money for Berkeley, or even the tuition for Monterey Peninsula College, but sweetie . . ."

"That's okay, Aunt Pearl."

". . . I'm broke."

The waitress brought over the small dish with our fortune cookies.

"Fortune cookies!" my aunt squealed. She always added the words "in bed" to the end of every fortune. Such as, "You will obtain your goal if you maintain your course—in bed."

"Good fortune will come your way—in bed."

Before I met Margo, I wondered if "in bed" meant sleeping on it. My dad, whenever I asked him for money, always said, I'll sleep on it. I'll sleep on it—in bed.

"Zowee," my aunt said, popping her cookie open.

"What does it say?"

"You are in for a period of financial stress—in bed."

I laughed.

"I wonder if that means you'll lose your bed, as one loses one's shirt?"

"Hah, hah, very funny, Zoe. What does yours say?"

"You will meet an exotic stranger—in bed."

"God, Zoe. Who could that be? There is nobody exotic in your dad's insurance office."

[**THE SLOW** unbuttoning, the careful rendering of the ancient rite, mere people transformed by ritual, our eyes peeled like bananas, our mouths monsters, our hands insects—this was love, I thought. Yet we never exchanged terms of endearment, we never talked of the future, what we would do next week, what we would see, where we would go, what we would eat. We never went anywhere together as a couple: no movies, no hamburgers, no milk shakes, nothing. We never kissed on the lips. It was difficult and solemn, and certainly a secret enactment, an initiation, separated from everything else I did.

When I visited his house, I was Margo's friend, and eyes stayed still. When we went anywhere, it was all of us together, as a family. When I was at his house, I was just a growing girl. But he knew I was changing not only from the talk but through a magical osmotic exchange, as if carnal knowledge was the ultimate knowledge and I was absorbing through my pores and atoms his essence and experience. I was getting older and wiser every day.

In fact, I was so smart, my period stopped.

Of course, I didn't tell anybody.

It was a day or so late, three days.

Panic set in.

I began jumping rope.

Nothing happened.

I ran around the block ten times.

Not a drop.

My father had always emphasized the power of prayer, and so I knelt on the hard floor in front of my bed, removing, for sincerity's sake, the rug. Let my knees bleed if it would bring on the other blood. Let my shins be scraped to shreds if it helped. Anything, anything at all.

I never did things the way you were supposed to, however. Not a pallid Dear Father, who art in heaven, please help me in my hour of need. Not Mormon prayers—I promise and pledge to you . . .

No. Excess was my path, Catholic saints my saviors. They were exotic and wonderful to me, the Catholic church lush and colorful.

I picked Saint Anthony from our local Saint Anthony's Catholic Church, who, despite an absolutely wretched life and temptations galore, lasted to 105. Living twenty of those years in a tomb, he did constant battle with the devil, who changed form as a beautiful woman and a Negro (I wondered if Margo minded). Saint Anthony is portrayed with a bell and a pig, is the saint of basket weavers, butchers, grave diggers, and is invoked against eczema. A favorite of Hieronymous Bosch, Saint Anthony is a laughable figure, but all the better, I thought, to induce my period.

For good measure, I also prayed to Saint Bernadette, of the movie *The Song of Bernadette*, and to Saint Bartholomew, since I also wanted to stop my nervous tic of blinking all the time, and

To Sweet Jesus.

Dear Jesus, grant me this one wish and I will worship you fiercely forever.

Quite frankly, *The Book of Mormon* left me cold. Like the Old Testament, it was full of battles and heroics, nothing warm or personal.

Sweet Jesus of the Stigmata, I begged, make blood come out of me like it came out of you.

Saint Anthony, do unto me, and I will take on pimples.

Saint Bernadette, I am not jealous of your beauty. I love you.

Saint Bartholomew, while you're at it, make me stop blinking.

Did I hear the rush of wings and feel the slow but necessary seepage of blood? Did my desperate piety gain me access to the secret of the universe, the control of nations, and governance over my own stupid body?

No. I continued to throw up night and day, and the pain in my stomach was like needles in a pincushion.

I didn't know what to do, but certainly I couldn't tell anybody. Who would I have told?

Margo? Margo, your father made me pregnant, so that makes me your stepmother.

My mother? Excuse me, could you sober up a moment so I could tell you something?

My father? Dad, I am filthy. Get out the scrub brush.

I had heard of people getting abortions in Tijuana, going down supposedly for bullfights, dog races, iguana matches . . . Somewhere there in the middle of cactus and sand, people got rid of babies. I imagined the fetuses planted all over the place, sprouting between tin shacks and old American cars and coffee cans and little green lizards. The baby hair would be cactus sprigs.

And well did I remember the girl in my school who had a baby in her bed one day when she stayed home from school, putting it in a shoe box and burying it in the sand dunes in Seaside. Boy, did she learn her lesson. A dog found it and they traced it back, found blood on her quilt. Quilt stands for guilt, I thought. Her name was Stella, as in the old movie *Stella Dallas*, and the play *A Streetcar Named Desire*. And nobody would marry poor Stella after that. Her whole life was ruined, as in the book *Diary Discoveries*, which detailed the demise of many a misled miss.

1. My reputation was on the line.
2. I was asking for trouble when I fell in love with a man who disdained conventions.
3. Nobody else would do what I did—only a love-starved girl.
4. There was nobody to help me.

It did not occur to me once, for even a tiny second, to tell Aaron. Obviously, my Aunt Pearl was the person to tell, but before I could do it, while I was watching *The Ed Sullivan Show* (I forget who was on; both my parents were at church, and I was worried they might walk in any minute and catch me watching television without permission) and drinking contraband tea, which, of course, Mormons don't do, I stood up a second, and the next thing I knew I was falling through the glass coffee table with the picture of the Mormon Tabernacle Choir on it.

My prayers were answered. I was dying.

In the hospital, they found out I was bleeding internally from a peptic ulcer, and I could very well have died.

Not a baby.

Not a sin.

I was delirious with happiness as I lay there getting transfusions through the wrist, bandages all over my face from the glass cuts, which fortunately were not going to scar me for life, and a dire prognosis that if this was the condition of my stomach at eighteen, well. As far as I was concerned, Alice had gone through the looking glass intact. In fact, I saw myself in a movie, the plucky heroine of one of my pulps, one who nearly died for love, but fought on, pale, valiant, beautiful. The hospital was like the snow in Milwaukee Aaron talked about. I felt adrift in all the white, and the hygienically chilly air forbade glooms and germs. I was in a room alone at the end of a long hall. People (nurses) for the first time in my life were asking how I was feeling. Somebody was taking care of me. I was safe.

My aunt was the first to come, dragging along my mother.

"Zoe, Zoe, how could you?" my aunt asked, as if guessing at an indiscretion. "How could you do this to us?"

They did not think I had the temperament for an ulcer. I did not bite my nails or pace the floor or worry unnecessarily over school tests.

"I didn't mean to," I said, thinking for the first time of the expense of the hospital.

My mother eyed me suspiciously. She was wearing a black cotton dress with a striped bolero. My aunt was in capri pants, and they both carried purses like little straw suitcases. They looked as if they were bound for the Riviera.

"And why?" My mother seemed angry. Did she think I wished to take over her place as the Family Problem? Her breath was suspicious. She must have stopped somewhere. I was in Carmel Community Hospital, and Carmel was not a dry town. My aunt would be angry with my mother after she got drunk, but she never did anything to keep her sober. On the contrary.

"Am I my sister's keeper?"

My dad came later, looked at me, shook his head. He was going to tell me about the money for the hospital. This was worse than college, I knew. Did I sow this, did I reap that. Would an apple a day keep the doctor away. I had fainted on the table, broken the coffee table. A stitch in time saves nine? I wasn't sure what he could say. I knew I was a very bad girl, much worse than he could dream. I began to blink.

77

"Zoe." He stood straight but uncomfortably in his blue church suit, white shirt, tie, black shoes. He looked across the room. "Zoe, I love you."

"What?"

"I love you. I want you to get better."

He took my hand, squeezed it.

I didn't know what to say.

"I mean it," and then he seemed too caught up to continue, for his face was moving around in the funny way faces do before people cry, and his nose was prickling all red. "Well, be back tomorrow," and he walked very quickly out of my room.

My goodness, I thought, my father loves me, what a well-kept secret. I didn't know what to do. Did that mean that he truly believed that everything he did or didn't do for me was for my own good? Was I not a disappointment to him? I tried to get my mind around it. My father loves me. It was like a storybook thing, not a true romance or even quite a fairy tale but something, if not fictitious, suspect. My father loves me. Well, well, well.

I thought about it for a whole hour. And little by little, like stepping in water, first my toes, I got used to the idea. There was nothing on the walls or in the halls to distract me, so I could give it my full attention. My father loves me.

"I heard you were sickeroo," Margo said, popping her burly head into my doorway.

"My father told me he loves me," I said.

"What is this, *Death of a Salesman*?"

"You are being cruel."

"Dads are supposed to love their daughters, Zoe."

"Well, you know . . . he never acted as if he did."

"Maybe he's the kind of guy that loves you when you are down. You have to be sick and in bad need before . . . Isn't that the way he is with your mother? You have to cripple yourself first. What's wrong with you anyway?"

Margo had her arms folded around her chest. She was in red, which matched the blood I had lost and the new blood I was getting. She had dotted her frizzy hair with tiny red ribbons. She looked strangely festive, as did my aunt and mother, and she was scrutinizing me up and down.

"An ulcer?" She shrugged her shoulders. "How come?"

"Maybe, Margo, my father just loves me."

"Maybe he just does. But the thing is, you are not exactly, how should I phrase this, in the best shape? So tell me, are you pregnant? Is this all a ruse for an abortion?"

"Margo." So she guessed it. I turned over.

"Just kidding. You can't take a joke?"

I pretended to be in pain, clutched my stomach.

"Are you okay, Zoe? I'm sorry. I didn't mean it."

"I'm in the hospital, Margo," I squeaked out. Actually I was rather sedated. In addition to the transfusion, they had given me something for pain, which made my tongue huge and my mouth dry. I hoped it was morphine or opium. I fancied the life of an addict. *So* romantic.

"I'm sorry. Maybe I don't understand you. You seem so carefree. I thought only grown-ups got ulcers. I mean, I don't want you to be sick, Zoe. Did you know my dad has one, an ulcer, that is?"

I groaned.

"And businessmen, but a kid?"

"It's true."

"No lie? Miss Daredevil herself? I never thought you worried about a thing."

"No lie, Margo, they did an X ray. I had to swallow barium, really bad stuff."

"So tell me the lurid details." She leaned forward, accidentally pulled at my transfusion tube. "Oops, sorry. Listen, did you know that it was a Kneegrow, Charles Drew, who found out about blood types? And then he died on some lonesome Southern country road, bled to death because the white hospital would not accept him. Just in case you wanted to know whom to be beholden to—I mean, in the long run, who is going to save your life, a white person or a Negro? If you were on a desert island and had to survive, which would you pick, a Negro Marine or a white car salesman in plaid pants?"

"How about a Negro college professor in plaid pants or a white Marine? I fell through our glass coffee table."

"I thought Mormons didn't drink coffee."

"We don't. It's just a table."

Margo had never seen it, of course, or anything else in our house, although on a drive once with her dad, we went by the Pacific Grove Golf Course. Oh, that's my house, I said, pointing in the distance, hoping my mother could not be detected weaving around the living room, lurching through the window, peeing in the yard, which she had actually done once when she couldn't hold it a second more.

"But how come you didn't let me know you had a stomachache? Ulcers are very high on the pain totem pole."

"Do tell."

I really didn't want to talk to her, and I was afraid if Aaron showed up, it would be obvious that . . .

"You don't have to say anything," Margo said, "but the retakes of the SATs are in a week."

"Thanks for letting me know." I turned back toward the wall. I needed to improve my scores to qualify for second semester matriculation and future scholarships.

"So if this is a way of getting out of them . . ."

"It isn't."

And, finally, the last fifteen minutes of visiting hour, I heard his long steps coming down the hall. Kafka was visiting the Hunger Artist.

"I thought I was pregnant," I whispered when he bent to squeeze my hand.

"You got this from me," he said. "Guilt by association," he said. "Ulcers run in the family."

"Aaron, please." Quilts, guilts. No wonder I was sick.

"Just teasing."

"If it was a baby, I would have it," I said theatrically, swishing my unneedled hand like Hamlet to-be-or-not. "No Tijuana dog races for me." But I knew I really didn't mean it if I was thinking of jumping out the window.

"You are confused," he said.

"I don't dispute that." I wanted it and didn't want it. I wanted . . . I don't know what I wanted. I began to blink.

"I want something, Aaron," I said.

"Don't be silly," he said. "You want attention, but a baby? That is so silly, and listen, that nervous tic of yours has got to go. Very unattractive. It makes you look unsure of yourself, Zoe."

"It's not silly that I want something, a baby."

"It is."

"I want . . . something," I said again.

"What do you mean?"

I looked around the room. There was nobody else there, and the white walls, clean without my scrubbing, gave me courage. White, white, save us from blight. Yellow, yellow, be a bright fellow.

"Is a baby the refuge of a lonely girl? Maybe that's what I want, Aaron, a friend for life. Want a friend? Make your friend. You figure it out."

"Stop it, Zoe."

Aaron was in his teaching clothes, a white shirt, a tie. He had never looked so beautiful to me, but something was gone. Like in the dentist's office, the little kids' book *Jack and Jill*. What's wrong with this picture? I felt, after months of our so-called intimacy, removed from him, as if I were seeing him through a telescope, not my glasses. I saw him as if he had never been inside of me, in my skin, under my skin. I saw him very distinctly and definitely as not a part of me. Or maybe, in some way, I had become equal to him by being sick. On one level, I could now deal with him. On another level, I knew suddenly and instinctively that I couldn't deal with him, and that I should stop trying.

"You know," he said, "I was precocious too, and it all caught up. It catches up and then you have to watch it."

"And who is talking?"

"Somebody older, wiser, somebody who cares for you."

"A baby would *love* me. I would love it. It would be a somebody who would *love* me *all* the time."

"Zoe."

And it would have settled the question of my life, what to do about it. Take care of the baby. Twenty years decided.

"Don't be so crazy," he said. "You are going to college soon."

I started to cry.

"Don't cry."

"I can't help it. I'm not going anywhere."

"So getting pregnant is the solution? Don't be childish."

"Aaron, I *am* a child. I don't know what I'm doing. You are the grown-up. Why aren't we practicing birth control? I can't go to a doctor and get a diaphragm. How can I keep from getting pregnant?"

"Why not get a diaphragm?"

"Without my parents' permission? Do you think any doctor in this town would outfit an eighteen-year-old unmarried high school girl? Why aren't you taking care of me?"

"I am not your father."

"I know, but . . . you could wear a condom."

"I can't help that your family . . . I hate condoms."

"I know. But, but somebody has to help me." I began to weep a little. It wasn't crying. It was more like soft sweeping. I didn't have the strength to really cry. I remembered how I used to be scared of the bomb, a bomb coming to get me from faraway. It seemed that everything close up was quite bad enough.

"I want you right now," Aaron whispered, drawing the curtains about my bed. Tears made him amorous.

"Aaron." We would have made shadows like praying mantises at their final work. "I don't feel well, remember?" Not to mention that one of my arms was hooked up to intravenous equipment, and I had bandages all over my face. If I had to urinate or anything, they had to bring a bedpan. The situation was ridiculous.

"Let me just see you," he said.

"The nurses come in all the time."

"Sh," he said. "Be my beautiful girl."

"I'm not beautiful. I have a hole punched in my stomach, cuts on my face." My hair was twisted ropes, sausages of grease.

"Sh," he said, pressing my hand to his rock-hard crotch. Somewhere within all the tweed was a stick of dynamite ready to go off. And he unzipped himself, yes, and rummaged within the overlapping folds of his shorts, and brought out what he considered a Sugar Daddy for the little girl. He wagged it at me playfully.

"Aaron, I'm in the goddamned hospital. Can you get that straight?"

He kissed my forehead, the lids of my eyes, the tip of my nose, my knees and elbows, my breasts, my belly button. Usually that worked, but I wasn't feeling a thing for him but an irritated disgust. Maybe my ulcer *was* a kind of abortion. I had rid myself of his baby, and things between us would never be the same. Meanwhile, as foreign blood was pumping into my veins, he had taken my free hand and was making me do it.

"That's a good girl," he said, closing his eyes and letting himself rock back on his penny-loafer heels. "A very good girl."

That night, before I knew Grey, I had my first coyote dream. I did not yet live in Big Sur, but, of course, we in California knew the coyote. I dreamt that Bad Luck was pursuing me in the form of a pack of coyotes. They ate our dogs on the ranch and destroyed our fences. As an example, my father caught one and chopped off its head, put it on a stake for the others to see, like Thomas More's head was placed on a stake by Henry VIII. Be forewarned.

But the coyote head after a few days on the stake began to move from side to side. It was like a mask, or, rather, a glove with a large cuff, a musketeer's glove. It moved like a puppet, as if a hand had been placed in it. We put it on the ground and it grew a body.

[**K E R O U A C** drank like a fish. Ginsberg took off his clothes at the drop of a hat. Pollock died in a car wreck with two young girls. Franz Kline died at fifty-two. Thelonious Monk went crazy and was silent the last years of his life. Charlie Parker drank iodine. Billie Holiday hooked. Dorothy Parker lived with a homosexual. Margo's dog, Trotsky, got cancer and had to be put down. I got out of the hospital, and before school was out that year, Aaron killed himself, but not over me. I was sure of that, pretty sure. Why would he kill himself over a kid?

[**THE SATURDAY** I took my SATs it was raining tigers and sheep. And though it had been a dry year, the rain made me feel abysmal. The top ten percent of our class, very important people, were all there in the algebra classroom of Monterey Union High, the site of many failures since I was not good in math, and though I got good grades in other subjects, people never expected anything to come of me. Damp chalk dust clogged my nose. A formula was on the board, the unknown *x*. Spare me, I thought.

From across the room, Margo winked. She, among others, was taking the College Qualification Test. I was just on the plain old SATs *again.*

Our health teacher, Mr. Beter, whom everybody called Masturbator, was the proctor for the SATs. He was the one who had told us that if a bomb fell, we must curl up and protect our "lower parts." Duck, fold, cover, those were his instructions in that order.

Duck.

Fold.

Cover.

Now, he walked up and down the rows making sure we were not cheating.

Cheating, I thought.

Cheat.

Beat.

Weep.

"Ten minutes," he would call out with glee.

"Five minutes."

"Time's up."

How he relished saying that.

"Pencils down."

My number 2 pencil was blunted to a nub. I couldn't think without a sharp pencil. Oh, well. The math I had skimmed, picking out problems here and there. I already had the grade point average necessary for Berkeley anyway. Not that I would get to go.

There had been a little scene at dinner. I had made macaroni and cheese, a kind of peace offering for going to the hospital and taking the SATs. Velveeta, little snail-shell macaroni, lots of milk, which was what I was supposed to drink for my ulcer. I could see that the stove had not been touched since I'd gone to the hospital. And the refrigerator smelled sour, though I could not find the source. Something was dead in it. Dead or alive. If anything was alive in the kitchen, it was the water heater, which had its own buzzy song, and the stove, which snapped and crackled where stuff had bubbled over and burned. When the fridge was opened, its hideous breath jumped out in our faces, and the toaster, which shorted and sparked, rested on a thick bed of crumbs interlaced with ants.

"Going to college would be a waste of your time," my father said for the umpteenth time.

"But it is my time to waste," I replied.

My mother sat silent and sullen.

"Don't you think you owe your family something?" my father continued. This was the man who had told me a bare week ago he loved me.

I blinked.

"Eighteen years of supporting you."

"I am your child," I said.

"Indeed you are, and all the more reason."

"I think I need to get to bed early." I was hoping that he would not wake up. "Get my beauty sleep." I was worried, and for a reason: the kitchen had not been scrubbed the whole time I was in the hospital.

I did not feel strong enough for a session at the floorboards. Yet, fortunately, whether out of altruism or indifference, he did not wake me.

Margo told me she "aced" the College Qualification Test, and asked if I wanted to go to the music store and listen to records. Since she was already a National Merit Scholar, I wondered what else she was aiming for, if she was trying for what was considered empirically impossible on the SATs, 100 in every category.

"I have to go home," I lied.

"Well, at least you're better," Margo said.

"Yeah."

I could walk. I could talk. I was up again, going to school, doing all the usual junk. I took phenobarbital and drank jugs of milk like Aaron. He carried his in a paper bag like booze. I put mine in my school thermos.

"It is going to be fine," I said to Margo, putting up my umbrella and thinking: fat chance.

That Saturday I felt too weak for intercourse, and for once Aaron respected my condition, so we drove around in his jade Plymouth Fury in the rain while he smoked and masturbated himself and played *Aida* live from the Met on the car radio.

By the time we got back to town, the rain had stopped, and I walked home; he let me walk all the way home from downtown. I used my umbrella as a walking stick, poking the ground of the path along the bay, right below the railroad tracks, as if I were making claim to territory.

I wondered: If I stay in Pacific Grove, I will have to have a job somewhere, at a gift store or as a waitress.

I did not relish standing on my feet all day.

If I went to college, I would probably have to work also, not only during the summer but while going to school. I could read fast, but . . . And then when I graduated, unless I became a teacher, then what? I did not really think I could become a lawyer. I knew of only one woman who had a Ph.D., and that was Margaret Mead. How impossible it all seemed.

"Hello." It was a man, not a ghost, but he seemed to have materialized out of the air, for I had not seen him in front or behind me. "Taking a walk?"

"Yes." He was shorter than I, and very compact. There did not seem to be a wasted bone or muscle in his body. No vestigial flesh, everything knitted together very tightly. He wore his shiny crow-black hair in a long braid down his back, tied with a red rag. His face already had deep lines, as if the man had looked straight up at the sun like you are not supposed to and said: Do your worst. He was wearing a flannel shirt, blue jeans, and heavy work boots.

"Where have you been? I haven't seen you around."

"Seen me around?"

"Sometimes I see you walking here in the afternoon. I've seen you at night crawl into the old canneries," he said.

"Really?"

How come I never saw him? A spy.

"Are you in the FBI?"

He laughed. It was a slow, deep laugh, a good laugh.

"I was in the hospital."

"Your parents? Where are they?"

Actually, a Saturday afternoon meant my father was at the hardware store. Not that he was such a big fix-up person, but he usually spent every Saturday afternoon "running errands" and "going to the hardware store." And my mother was at my Aunt Pearl's.

"Why were you in the hospital?"

"An ulcer."

"Really?" He seemed interested. "In my culture you would not need to go to the hospital." His eyes were very dark, heavily lashed, but narrow, so that when he smiled his eyes disappeared within the folds of his face. He had his hands in his pockets.

"What culture is that?"

"I'm a Hopi and maybe Sioux. I'm a wild Indian."

"Oh, that's nice."

"Nice?"

"I mean nice to be somebody interesting."

Later I found out that what he declared himself to be wasn't exactly true. He was Navajo, Sioux, but mostly white. The Sioux were Plains people. The Hopis, from the Southwest. The Sioux were hunters, nomadic. The Hopi farmed corn. The Hopi were idealists, the People of Peace, and made room in their theology for the white, the black, the red, and the yellow. Desert people, they believed the ancestors lived below the earth and that spirits (kachinas) inhabited the bodies of living people during certain times. The Sioux were concerned with animal transformations. It seemed unlikely that two such different peoples from such widely separated geographical areas would get together. However, with Grey, everything was unlikely.

"It *is* nice being Indian. Herbs, dancing, chasing away evil spirits, magic mushrooms which purify one."

"I think in your culture I would have bled to death."

"In my culture you would not have gotten that particular sickness."

"I don't live in your culture."

"Too bad."

"And you don't either. This is the twentieth century."

"And well?"

"Well, we have modern medicine."

"But still you get sick."

I sighed. I blinked.

He laughed. I laughed. And of course, then I knew. The Motorcycle Man, the resurrected coyote. My dreams were prophetic.

[**I SAW THIS** masked stranger a second time at a poetry reading the night of the prom.

"Boy, am I heartbroken," Margo said of not being invited, of not wearing a formal, of not dancing the night away at a country club.

Actually, secretly, in the corner of my bedroom, I *was* heartbroken, and cried nearly a whole night. Yet what did I expect, that Aaron would take me to the prom?

So instead of the prom Margo and I went to a poetry reading, not the famous Gallery Six, with Jack Kerouac collecting dimes and nickels for the wine, and Ginsberg coming out with his famous *Howl*, and Gary Snyder there and Bob Kaufman, and all their beat girlfriends, everybody hip and hep and with it and cool, man. Dig it.

Our poetry reading was a hometown thing they had at Ring's Restaurant in its courtyard. It was the exact time of the junior-senior prom, but what did we care, Margo and I told ourselves, whistling in the dark. My stomach was killing me despite the phenobarbital I took, and my hands were a wreck from scrubbing. And my eyes were throbbing.

Actually, all the town's bohemians were at the poetry reading, I mean, en masse. Every last tattered one of them had crawled out of his fringed hole—the women in their peasant skirts and big earrings, the men in turtlenecks. We saw one of our teachers, Mr. Elkhart, with his wife, of all things. Mrs. Elkhart was not much to look at. She looked rather old, we thought, maybe even thirty-five. Mr. Elkhart nodded at us. Where the hell was Mr. Watkins, the teacher of our dreams? But, of course, he was home *writing* poetry. See, that was the difference.

The poet of the night, like mine of old, the one with the portable teeth, wore the standard uniform: a black beret, the requisite goatee.

"He looks like a goat," I whispered to Margo.

Margo agreed. "He's a goat and doesn't know it."

Let it be noted that when I was with Margo, I *tried* to put Aaron out of my mind, and I never thought of Judy at all. But there they were, over in the corner, she in her wheelchair, he dutifully behind her. My dad would not be caught alive at a poetry reading. But my aunt was there, Aunt Pearl, in her dangling earrings and swishy skirt. I could tell she was on the prowl. She had just broken up with her last boyfriend, a pastry chef at a fancy Carmel restaurant, Chez something.

"Hi," she waved.

"Hi."

"Are you listening?" Margo asked me, elbowing me in the ribs.

"I don't know. I don't think I like poetry readings all that much, Margo."

"You act like you've been to hundreds."

The poet was reading something from D. H. Lawrence.

> *You, you don't know me.*
> *When have your knees ever nipped me*
> *like fire-tongs a live coal*
> *for a minute?*

Without warning, somebody stood up on his bench. He was part of the audience. There was a sudden mass intake of breath, as everybody realized there was going to be a scene. I braced myself.

"You can't read poetry that way," the man boomed out at the poet so all could hear. "Poetry is a living thing."

I gasped. It was the man I had seen on the path, the Indian man, Grey.

Margo nudged me.

"I want, I want," she whispered, like the Blake drawing of the guy with the ladder to the moon. I want, I want.

[**THE THIRD TIME** I saw Grey before Aaron died was not quite so dramatic. It was at a wedding in a stone church in Carmel. From the flagstone terrace we could hear the ocean roar, and the wind went through the pines like chimes. I felt that I was in a dwarf house or one of those magical places children find in the woods, where they are taken in and either baked in the oven or rescued from cruel step-mothers. The bride and groom were plain and boring. People in clear-framed glasses—a colorless biologist and a beaky teacher of Latin at Monterey Peninsula Community College. Mere figures on a cake. And the cake did not say "Down with Fascism," as Aaron and Judy's cake had. And Paul Robeson was not there, nor was Sigmund Freud. But the Wolfman, little did I know, *was* there. The bride wore a long white dress which fit her like a Halloween ghost costume, and the groom looked as if he had gone to a taxidermist to be fitted into his tuxedo. Margo and I hated weddings. How bourgeois could one get.

Aaron stood between Margo and me. He brushed my dress with his little finger, nobody the wiser. Then, shortly before the ceremony, somebody came out and asked if anyone could loan the best man a tie.

It was the Indian who needed a tie and Aaron who gave up his.

I saw it for what it was: the King is dead, long live the King.

[**"YOU ARE IAGO,"** Aaron said, not turning from his book. "You are not what you are."

We were in his office. Alone. I knew this was going to be a major scene. I hadn't visited in a week. All I could think about was the Indian. The Indian in war paint, the Indian in buckskins.

"Come on. Nobody is what they are, Aaron. Who are you?"

"Your lover."

"Only that? Are you not Judy's husband, Margo's father, a scholar, a teacher, and God knows what else?"

"I have seen you walking about with that Indian."

"Yes."

"He is at least ten years older than you are."

"You are at least twenty years older."

"Do you think of me as a pederast?"

"What is that?"

"One who molests children?"

"I am not a child. In other countries women my age marry, have children, assume full adult responsibilities."

"I thought you told me you were a child." He turned around and without his glasses looked defenseless. He was, indeed, forty, my father's age. He looked faded and defeated. I wasn't thinking of Oedipus, but of Methuselah. I couldn't believe it. The great Aaron Robinson was just a man, no more, no less. The disillusionment which had set in during my stay in the hospital had grown to disinterest. It was as if I had changed prescriptions and was seeing things very clearly for the first time. Aaron was my best friend's father, the only man who had ever paid any attention to me, but . . . but . . .

I was wearing my school clothes, my mother's sash dress, butter-cups all over me. But . . . but I held my eyes wide open, did not blink.

"Well, sometimes I am a child and sometimes I'm not, Aaron. I'm not perfect." How could I explain myself?

But I didn't love him anymore, *that* was the difference.

"You're fickle."

"Fickle?"

"Inconsistent."

"I want to be consistent." What I meant was, I wanted to be all of a piece, whole, and at peace. It had been five months of Aaron. I felt worn out.

"Inconstant."

"And you, you are married, remember?"

"Judy is incapable." He threw his hands up in despair, tipped back his office chair. I could see that his heels were worn out. Down at the heels, I thought, remembering the famous picture of Adlai Stevenson with a hole in his shoe when he was running for President.

"Is she? Is Judy really incapable? Not in any way?" I found it strange that we were having this discussion. All of this should have been said long ago.

"People can make love with their eyebrows, Aaron."

"Don't give me that, Zoe. Judy does not care to anymore."

"Maybe because you make her feel undesirable."

"Judy," he sighed, turned back to his book.

"Zoe is my name." I stamped my foot.

"I know. I mean Judy and I have not been close, close in that way for years. Why are we talking like this?"

"Isn't it about time, and I have a feeling that what you are telling me is standard for men who cheat." Cheat, beat, weep.

"Do you think this is cheating?"

"Yes. I think you are cheating both of us, all of us, yourself most of all." I pulled one of the chairs to me, sat down. On the wall was a picture of James Joyce, who looked very prissy in his stiff straw hat and little glasses.

"Why?"

"Because, because," and I couldn't put my finger on it. "Because you cannot be wholehearted anywhere."

"What do you know of a whole heart?"

"Apparently more than you."

"It is because it is inappropriate," Aaron said. "Our affair is inappropriate."

"Inappropriate? I would use the word unkind."

"It is not."

"In some ways you *are* like my father. If I take care of my mother enough, be the dutiful daughter, clean up the mess, everything will be normal, right, whatever. You want me to make your life complete, to remedy in my girl way something I have nothing to do with. You *are* unkind."

"I am not your father." He shook his head in distaste, as if he knew my father. "Why do we always go back to that?"

"You are *like* a father to me, a bad one."

"Maybe you are looking for a father."

"Maybe I am looking for a mother."

As soon as I said it, I knew I had hit it, but I rushed on, frightened of what I had stumbled against. My mother.

"Maybe I've given up, Aaron. Let's give it up."

"Maybe I am not what you want me to be," Aaron persisted.

"So *you* are Iago?"

"Who is what he is, Zoe, after all."

"God, God—when Moses asked him in the bushes, remember—said, 'I am that I am,' Aaron, you who are Moses' brother. Who else can answer with such assurance but God? The rest of us have to prove ourselves."

"You are prattling the Old Testament to me, Zoe?"

"Are you getting literary on *me*, Aaron?"

"Zoe."

"Maybe, Aaron, I am taking affection wherever I can, simple as that, and you, too." For I had never met any of Aaron's friends, and I wondered, now, if he had any.

"Maybe you are a desperate, crazy little girl."

"Maybe you are a desperate, mixed-up old man."

"Maybe you like to be told what to do. Does your wooden Indian tell you what to do?"

"No, and why suddenly the pejorative? Aren't Indians part of the Great Oppressed?" I got up from his office chair. One of the professors he shared his office with had a picture of his family on the desk. They looked so damned vulnerable huddled before the camera, getting shot.

"I'm sure he does tell you what to do. And he is a beatnik. Yes, I have heard of him. Seen him around, a self-styled poet. Antisocial. Kerouac is actually a political conservative, did you know that? Your great apostle of freedom is a Catholic Republican."

"Ginsberg is more my ilk." He was a better writer, that was for sure. I don't know how we got onto this, though, Kerouac, Ginsberg.

"Do you know what Ginsberg is, Zoe?"

"A Jewish Buddhist?"

"No, a homo."

"I read his poems, Aaron, I don't want to have sexual intercourse with the man. And if Grey is a poet, let us hope that he is self-styled. Anyway, it doesn't matter."

"Why?"

"Because."

"How so?"

"This is weird love if it is love," I said, taking a chance.

"All love is weird."

"More is at stake than just somebody else. What we are doing is not right, Aaron."

"What you call ethics is talk, Mar . . . Zoe, just talk."

"Zoe, yes, Zoe, my name is Zoe, and how dare you tell me ethics is just talk? All the time you are telling me what is wrong with the world. You tell me concentration camps are evil, lynching is evil. You have lists of evil, and now, now where is your fancy talk getting you? You are talking yourself out of business."

He flinched a little. Had I said more than I intended?

"What business?" he asked quietly.

"The business of me. And this, this between us *is* incestuous, not because incest is mother/son, father/daughter, brother/sister, cousin cuddling, but because the ultimate incest is Oedipus/Oedipus for his own pride, his own self-love. For all your humanitarian babble, you are using me."

"For what?"

"Consolation." *I* had to use the bathroom. I had to get out of there.

"Well, so are you. What is it all *but* consolation. At best, Zoe, at best. At worst, that Indian will ruin your life. You will regret him. You want babies? He will give you babies. He will weigh you down with babies, babies will be stones in your belly, a stone around your neck. He will put you in a prison of his making. He will—"

"Aaron, *you* weigh me down, you don't give me babies. You give me your ulcer. That is my baby from you, a hole in my stomach as big as a fist through a wall."

"What about the life of the mind, your life? What about college?"

"I am going to college."

"And who thought you could? Who gave you the idea? Who saved your limited Mormon life? You are biting the hand that feeds you."

"Oh, stop. Didn't you bite the hands that fed you? Isn't that what growing up is all about?"

I had reached the door. Somehow, I had managed to get up from my chair, and soon, I thought, I would be down the hallway and out the door, and on the grass, and in the bus, and going home, and leaving all this behind.

"Do you love me?"

"God, Aaron, I did. I did so much." I thought my heart was going to drop down the stairwell of my rib cage, get caught in my stomach, squeeze through my intestines, that I would void it.

"Then what?"

"I don't know. This is killing me." I held my stomach. "I worshipped you, but what was the nature of our interaction? Sex, just sex, and then you lectured. 'Lie down, spread your legs, open your mouth, stand up. I was in the Spanish Civil War. Hurrah for me.' I mean, what happened? What did it mean? We are not a couple." I was flinging my hands around.

"You're very emotional," he said.

"Yeah, so finally you noticed."

"I do love you," he said. "I want you more than my life, Zoe, my dear girl. This is a beautiful thing we have together."

"No, it isn't. I can't stand the way people use the word beautiful.

I can't stand the limitations of our so-called relationship, even if I am a limited Mormon."

"What else?"

"What about the rest of your life? You don't share anything with
me. You don't share your regular life with me. That is everything else."

"Everything else, my dear, is falling down all around me. You don't know."

"Tell me."

"I live in ruins, and I breathe poison. My life is a failure. The child prodigy grew up to be a disappointed man. The world is an awful place."

"Tell me."

"Oh my dear, my dear, dear girl. Just go. Just go. Go fast."

[**IT WAS NOT YET** dark when the ambulance came that night. I could hear it from my bed. One a.m. I knew immediately, throwing on my raincoat and tiptoeing through the darkened house. I grabbed my father's car keys off the front table, and though I did not yet have my license and could not drive very well, I backed the car out of the driveway and turned it around, heading for the whine of the siren. In driver ed, Mr. Healy would say, Kick it, kick it. That is what I did. I cannot count the time, but very soon I was out of the car and bounding over the railroad tracks and onto the succulents, which broke under my feet, making a milky mess. I had come down Central Avenue, taken a left to Ocean View Boulevard, and I saw across the marine laboratory the ambulance and the fire truck. The engine was still on, and it looked like a huge red insect wheezing asthmatically under the cypress trees. Dark figures were hastening down to the beach, where once the Chinese had their settlement, the one that was burned down.

Can we say that in the history of things, truth is not necessarily absolute, or even relative, or even secret, but perhaps various? After the earthquakes heaved up the land mass from the sea, after the dinosaurs died and the mammals took over, and then after the great diaspora of Asians from the north who were perhaps the Ohlone Indians, Aaron claimed the same land for his death. Once, women and children had spread out nets to gather shellfish—mussels, clams, oysters, olivellas, crabs, gooseneck barnacles, and abalones. Beached whales meant days of feasting. In 1848, the Gold Rush started up north. Leland Stanford opened a dry goods store in Sacramento which catered to the miners. Then there was the Chinese settlement—the men who remained after laying the tracks for the Central Pacific Railroad. One night a fire took it all down. They say it was set by whites in Pacific Grove. Later came the Hopkins Marine Laboratory of Stanford University, and then there was Aaron on the beach. All of it seemed contained in that one moment of awful truth. Earthquakes, dinosaurs, Indians, Chinese, Stanford scientists, Aaron. Red men, yellow men, blue men. Policemen. Chinamen. Red fire truck. The green fuzz of the cypress trees, and all the time the tide was rising, getting higher on the beach, with little hermit crabs scuttling among the large polyps of the seaweed, nature's floats, Aaron's death.

He was dressed in his familiar khakis, yet with a theatrical reporter's raincoat, the kind of coat Humphrey Bogart wore in *Casablanca*. There was a nice big bottle of whiskey (empty) by his side, and he had decorated the outline of his body with pretty stones and shells, feathers, a lace fringe of seaweed, and pill bottles. How whimsical, I thought, and how extravagant.

He looked, in the sand, like a snow angel. I had never seen snow, but he had described to me and Margo how as a kid in Milwaukee, he would lie down in the snow and make wings with his arms, leaving the imprint of an angel. There was a popular song at the time called "Earth Angel." And another song, "Mr. Sandman." That's what I thought: Aaron in a sand castle, prince of the realm, angel of dreams, my dead lover.

His profile faced the sky. Stupidly a priest from Saint Anthony's galumphed forward in the sand, awkwardly managing his skirts.

"He's Jewish," I shouted.

"You know who he is?" A policeman.

I think I may have laughed. "He's Dr. Robinson."

"You know where he lives?"

"Excuse me."

I had to throw up.

I turned, began to retch into the sand. People busied themselves about me.

"Is there a letter?" somebody asked.

"Didn't find anything, no note," a policeman replied.

There was somebody from *The Monterey Herald*, a photographer, a bunch of nuns flapping in their habits—old bats from the Catholic school on Central Avenue—kids on bicycles in the middle of the night.

"Are you all right?" the priest asked me.

"In a minute." I was alive. How bad could I be?

But I did retch until it became the dry heaves. Meanwhile, Aaron, with his feathers and sea shells, little rocks and whiskey bottles, totemic gestures framing his body, was asleep at his post, not witness to this, my degradation on his behalf.

"Aaron," I hissed through my sour breath. "Aaron. How could you? God damn you. Don't you know suicide is a stupid capitalistic gesture? The rest of us have to live."

There had been no attempt to pump or massage his heart. It was 1957 and there were none of those clamping machines that resurrected the dead with a great jolt of electricity. There was not even mouth-to-mouth. It was all hopeless. When you died, you died.

"He's been dead a good while," the doctor said. Lucky for him. Nothing to fumble over.

And Aaron had a little smile on his face, as if he had outwitted us all. Very funny, Aaron, I thought, very funny.

"You know where he lives?" the main policeman said.

"They live in the glass house," I said, wiping my mouth with my sweater sleeve.

"Oh, the glass house."

There was no other name for it. Everybody knew what I meant.

"He has a family?" the policeman asked.

"Oh yes." I began to blink.

There was Margo and there was Judy.

"They have the colored kid," the priest said, "the adopted one."

"Negro," I corrected, although Margo hated that, too.

"And the wife, she has polio," the priest volunteered. "She wears braces."

Then the ambulance was there, and two hearty men in starched white pants and shirt trotted down with a stretcher.

"Alioop," they said, lifting Aaron up. He was stiff already. A stiff. And I imagined him not going to the hospital and later to the mortuary but being set out to sea, in a boat of his own, an old Viking warrior set afloat. And after a year and a day, his body would wash up on a

South Seas beach and he would awaken. The sun would be hitting his eyes, telling him his journey to the next world was over. And he would shake off his slumber like a latter-day Rip van Winkle and marvel, as Gauguin had done, at the lovely island-brown ladies. Fragrance and frangipani would be his. Oh God, I thought, it's not going to be like that. I had seen a dead squirrel once having flesh eaten up day by day until only the skull and spine remained. It would be like *that*.

Sand was sticking to my shoes. My hands were sticky, too. I had been crying and I had to go to the bathroom. I found myself crouching behind a rock down on the lower end of the beach and voiding everything in my intestines, stomach. It wouldn't stop. My dumb body had taken over. I was putrid. I disgusted myself.

And then they were gone, wailing through Monterey to the hospital in Carmel. They had put a little rope fence around Aaron's last rites. The shells and rocks, feathers, and empty bottle of whiskey. He had gone, along with all his heroes: Tom Paine, Joe Hill, John Brown, Sacco and Vanzetti, the Rosenbergs, the members of the German resistance, the White Rose, and all of them, all of them in slavery and camps and jails and all who worked in fields and factories and cafeterias and in mines and bathrooms and other people's houses. From each according to his ability to each according to his need. The big pie in the sky.

[**T H E N E X T D A Y** *The Monterey Herald* reported that:

A Monterey Peninsula College professor, who was scheduled to testify before the House Un-American Activities Committee in San Francisco tomorrow, apparently committed suicide with sleeping pills.

A spokesman for the House committee, which is investigating Communist "intellectual infiltration," said Aaron Robinson was to have been questioned about information "which would have been significant to the security of this country."

The spokesman said that Robinson's possible testimony was considered so "very valuable" that he was to have been offered immunity from prosecution in return for it.

Robinson was called before the House Un-American Activities hearings in San Francisco because it was pursuing a lead arising from a 1955 hearing at which Robinson was alleged to have been a "contact man" for a "Marxist discussion group" in 1938. A few months prior to his subpoena he had declined on three occasions to cooperate with the FBI.

It seems that his appearance would have been a reprisal of his refusal to identify left-wing associates. Fifteen years earlier Robinson had been interrogated by the FBI and cleared of "security risk" charges inspired by the fact that in 1934 he had worked in Paris as an expediter of medical supply shipments to the Spanish loyalists. By not answering questions or by pleading the Fifth Amendment, he could have been charged with contempt of Congress and put in jail like the Hollywood writers.

Ironically on the same page, the Supreme Court had ordered the release of five convicted Communists jailed under the Smith Act. The **103** Supreme Court questioned the supposition implicit in the Smith Act that membership in the Communist Party was tantamount to advocating the violent overthrow of the government.

1934? The newspaper said he expedited medical supplies in 1934? The Civil War started in 1936. And 1938? What did he do then? Un-American activities? Had he deliberately confused me?

[**W H A T I F I** had been nicer, kinder, better, prettier, smarter, more alert, more sympathetic?

What if I had listened more, been less selfish?

What if I had simply said: What is the matter?

What if I had said: Aaron, I love you, live. Live, Aaron, live.

What if I had followed my intuition, that creepy feeling I had had at about eleven o'clock, and gone down to the beach near the laboratory? My parents were asleep. I could have made my way warily through the house, going past the dark face of the television and the still furniture—the empty table I had fallen through was repaired and polished now to a gleaming sheen—seen the shadowy reflection of my face, and whispered to the curtains: swish, swish lipstick.

What if I had gotten in the family Oldsmobile then, turned the ignition on, and quickly backed up and crept through the neighborhood, each mailbox a silver sentinel in a war against nonconformity, and gotten out, found him on the beach, rushed to a phone, helped him into the ambulance, given him artificial respiration and genuine genuflection. Then he would be alive.

What if I had called on the God of the Mormons, even though by Mormon definition Aaron was a Gentile. What if?

When I went over to Margo's house, nobody was answering the phone, but the door was open. I stepped in.

"Hello," I said.

I made my way down the front hall, and there they were, the two of them at the table where we had so many conversations, the four of us. Judy, Margo, Aaron, me. The two women were sitting in front of piles of food. Macaroni-and-cheese casseroles, each noodle a festering cocoon—roasts, carcasses—mounds of stew, turds—spaghetti with red sauce flowing off it, blood—grapes and shiny apples, salads, wavery Jell-O, cakes, muffins.

Judy, the widow, looked at me. Her face seemed to have shriveled down to the size of a prune. Her hands lay inert on her lap. Her wheelchair, so much a part of her body, looked wilted too.

"Judy . . ." I began.

"I remember his beautiful kisses," she said.

"Kisses?"

"I remember his beautiful kisses. God, how am I going to live?"

Kisses, I thought. But of course. He saved his kisses.

"Judy, I am so sorry." I was blinking tears. If I could have cried blood, I would have.

"It's not your fault," she said.

"But . . ." It *was* my fault, more my fault than anybody else's.

"Can you go with Margo to make the arrangements?" she asked me blankly.

"Me?" I wondered if it was okay, two kids doing it. "Me?" Where were the relatives, the friends? Who would help with Judy? Had people just dumped off food and run away? "Me?"

"Yes, you."

"Let's go right now," Margo said.

"Sure." My eyes were blinking so much that the tears seemed tangled like hair, and my "Sure" was like a slur, a bumbling, rumbling, topsy-turvy somersault into a gray, misty world, a grown-up world, a world I didn't know. There we were, two kids, June 1957. Suddenly we were asked on that day, less than a month before our graduation from high school, to be grown up, to make decisions. Make funeral arrangements. Make like we knew something. Wasn't that for grandmothers, old women in black kerchiefs? The kin of the deceased? Where the hell *was* everybody?

If it was just the two of us, would that mean that everything which came our way would be that unprepared for? Would our life be a series of "making arrangements," canceling appointments, looking up the way on a map, calling ahead, not being the first to arrive or the last to leave, missing kisses, and never knowing what to do or how to do it?

We trudged up the hill to Lighthouse Avenue. There was hardly anybody about. Just little kids.

"Why didn't anybody tell me about this stuff, Margo?"

"What's to tell?"

"That he was to appear before the Committee. What is an un-American activity? What is the Committee?"

Aaron himself had told me nothing of it, and yet, neglecting my mother, I made love with him after school as often as I could; and when we were not making love, he was pacing in front of me at his house, telling me and his daughter, my best friend in high school, about dying on our feet, not living on our knees. He had died on his back. Why had he omitted the most important thing?

"It is a Congressional committee, Zoe, initially set up by Senator McCarthy, from Wisconsin. They investigate so-called subversive activities, that is, who belonged to the Communist Party and the like, during the thirties mostly. They got Hollywood and they came north to get academics."

"What could they have done?"

"Well, he could have been put in jail for contempt of Congress for not answering the questions, for not naming names, for using the Fifth Amendment, for saying that he refused to incriminate himself, and I do believe he signed a loyalty oath to keep his job, get his *Othello* grant, and although he is loyal to this country, perhaps that signature could be considered perjury, and I don't know how long you stay in jail for that. Not that he had done anything except have a few discussions, and go to Spain."

"Maybe he knew people who did . . ."

"Zoe. Who did he know?"

I shuddered.

"He just knew us, Zoe."

"His students, Margo, his colleagues."

"A bunch of college kids, that's who he knew, the little girls he had sex with."

"What?"

"His students. But that's not a crime."

"Oh." It *was* a crime, a crime against humanity. Me.

"A new one every semester, each one more of a dope than the last. It didn't mean anything."

"Oh." Each one a dope?

"What's to tell about that? How could he inform? Common knowl- **107** edge. Everybody knew."

"Oh." I *was* a dope.

"The discussion group? What a farce. All of them already told on him, and the others died in Spain, I don't know. They were all crazy kids together. Is that what he was supposed to say? We distributed leaflets, me and Joe Schmo, for the cafeteria workers of the world?"

"Oh." What was the relationship about? Was I an oppressed high school girl?

"But he didn't want to overthrow the government, violently or nonviolently. That was crazy. Could you imagine Aaron being violent?"

I couldn't help it, but I thought of the traitor and his flayed skin. *My* skin stung.

"Zoe, are you still here? Knock, knock."

"He wasn't a Communist, was he?" I said quickly.

"I don't know."

"A card-carrying Communist?"

"Come on, Zoe, don't be so ridiculous. Card-carrying? You sound like old Joe McCarthy yourself."

"Sorry."

We walked without saying anything for a while. His students. Sex. One a semester. Common knowledge. This is a beautiful thing we have, Zoe. Drop dead, Aaron. But he was dead. Was I just another coed or was I the One? Was I an idiot or a murderer?

"Are you still going to college, Margo?" It wasn't just my medi- cation for the ulcer that made my mouth dry. I didn't know what to say. I didn't know what I was feeling. I didn't know anything. Was I sorry or glad?

Margo shrugged. "I don't know what else to do," she answered. Then she went on: "Actually, he didn't have to kill himself. The irony is that this whole thing, this whole McCarthy thing, is coming to an end. McCarthy himself is dead, and now the Supreme Court has ruled against the Smith Act, and actual membership in the Communist Party is not treasonous. I mean, couldn't he wait a day, one more day? God, what rotten timing."

Margo and I had linked hands from old habit. Her skin was dry and very smooth. Once, just once, I had gone for a walk with my mother, and she had put a stone in my hand. You can't say, she said, I never gave you anything.

"Anyway, what if he had gone to jail?" Margo continued. "Plenty of people go to jail, what's jail?" Margo shrugged her shoulders just like Aaron.

"Living on your knees, that's jail?" I offered, looking at her. Her skin was ashy and her eyes circled. "Instead of living on your feet?"

"It's not that simple," Margo said. "He would have lost his grant. It's a government grant, I think."

"A government grant?"

"Weren't you listening? That's what I said before, to do work on *Othello*."

"He had to sign a loyalty oath to get the *Othello* thing?"

"I don't know. I think so."

I thought of Othello, the Moorish general in Italy who was sent to Venetian Cyprus to repel Turkish attacks. It made perfect sense. Othello was the outsider, hired to do the dirty work, to refute and defeat himself. Loyalty oath? How loyal do you have to be? I am that I am. Prove it, Othello, kill your people, your kin, yourself. Aaron had told me that the Rosenbergs were put to death by Roy Cohn, a Jew, and that the judge was a Jew. Hey, we ain't anti-Semitic, we're just Americans. Who are you? We're Americans. Who are you? Louder now. Give me an A.

"But dead, Margo, he doesn't have his grant or a chance of a grant."

"It's not that simple."

"So tell me, explain. How hard is it?"

Margo looked at me. Did she know? Did she know about Aaron and me?

"Margo." I wanted to tell her I was infinitely sorry, that I . . . We were almost at the mortuary. We passed the Lutheran church, its pointy roof, where I had gotten stuck climbing and they had to call the fire department. Margo had dared me.

"What was it, then? Why?"

"He is the one who killed himself and wrecked us all." Now she was angry. "What gives him the right? Remember when he told us what

great blood flowed in our veins. His relatives dug their way out of concentration camps with spoons, played in two-bit bar-mitzvah bands, sold
vegetables from a cart, went to medical school, all so he could be born.
So *he* could be born," she hissed at me, "and then he chooses to die. I **109**
mean, so melodramatically. I mean, Jesus Christ, what's a little jail? My
people were shackled to this country in slavery. They survived slavery so
I could be born, go on, do better. And now, now they are letting people
out of jail, real Commies out of jail. The very same day he dies. The
utter waste. What a stupid waste. Yeah, I'm going to college. You bet
I am. What gives him the right to die right before I go to college, to not
see me graduate?" She started to cry. "I'll show him."

How could she show him? He couldn't see anymore. But I remembered the song he liked so much, and I began to sing it, the one
about Joe Hill, the Union organizer not being dead.

"That's a stupid song and you know it," Margo spat. "Joe Hill
was framed by the Utah mine owners, just like Sacco and Vanzetti.
Utah, your state, Zoe."

"It's not *my* state."

"I know. I'm sorry."

"Who died to save *me*, Margo?"

"What do you mean?"

"Like you said, Aaron's people dug their way out of concentration
camps and your people survived slavery."

"Shit, Zoe, if you don't know, you are in trouble."

"Jesus? Jesus' blood?"

"Jesus? Jesus? Are you kidding? Those Mormon pioneer women
following the covered wagons to the west, that's who. You told me they
had to walk behind the wagons. Jesus? No, Zoe, women in heavy men's
boots, faded housedresses. And all those Armenians who managed to
not get themselves raped and mutilated by the Turks and everyone else
who came along. I mean, they survived."

I didn't say anything. I was thinking about what Aaron had said
about living on your knees.

"But if living involves . . ."

"Listen, for all his intelligence, Aaron didn't know the first thing.
Life is . . . Life is a gift, Zoe."

"But, Margo, remember that Emily Dickinson poem: 'I have to go
on living, but I forget just why.' Maybe it was something like that?"

I so much wanted to understand why, why he did it, and then approve. Good going, Aaron. Hats off to you, buddy. I'm glad it's nothing I did or didn't do. I hate you for it, but I can live with it.

"It was nothing like that, not at all, and I have always hated Emily Dickinson and the whole lot of sensitive, suffering, poetic females," Margo said.

We were there. Mitchell's Mortuary advertised that they had served the Monterey Bay area for twenty-five years. Since 1932, they had had arrangements for:

FUNERAL SERVICES

BURIAL

MAUSOLEUM ENTOMBMENTS

CREMATION

WORLDWIDE SHIPPING SERVICES

Margo chose cremation.

"Your mother, a relative . . ." the man was in a tasteful gray suit. He peaked his hands together like a Christmas tree.

"My mother is crippled," Margo said. "She can't come."

Judy could have come, but it would have been difficult. And I realized quite suddenly that despite all the food brought in, the Robinsons really didn't have any friends. I was their friend and their betrayer.

The funeral man wanted us to choose an urn, so we followed him down a long gray hallway whorled like a cocoon; but it was cool, almost windy, a wind tunnel, and we mere paper airplanes or maybe moths, emptying tattered and tired into a room filled with coffins of every expense and material—oak, pine, redwood, even mahogany—and, along a wall on a shelf, urns. In school, we had read Keats's "Ode on a Grecian Urn." Aaron had told me that he had seen Grecian urns in the British Museum and that the figures that ringed the urn were men chasing each other with big erections.

"A cardboard box will be fine," Margo said.

Since Aaron had committed suicide, his ashes could not be buried in a religious cemetery, just like his great-grandfather's; and so a week later we returned to Mitchell's, which, ranch style with a red-tile roof, was something like the last roundup at the old corral. We carried his ashes back to their house.

"Let's listen to some Chuck Berry," Margo said, "loudly."

She turned her little portable record player on, and while the 45 spun "Maybellene," she placed the cardboard box full of ashes in her chest of drawers.

"I've got you where I want you now," she told her father.

"He's not there," I said.

"Where is he, in heaven?"

"I don't know, Margo."

Years and years later, I saw him at a Grateful Dead concert in the midst of the corn fields of Indiana. He was dancing amid the tie-dyed T-shirts, haloed or helixed, pure energy.

"See, Aaron, see what you have missed?"

"I have missed nothing," he replied.

And once I saw him in Chicago getting on the El with a candelabra dripping red wax.

"Where are you going, Aaron?"

"To Clark Street," he said, and then he was gone.

[**I HATED MYSELF**. I hated myself because I was myself and I hated myself because I was sorry for myself and I hated myself because I thought I had made Aaron die and I hated myself because I was relieved he was dead and hated myself because I had had sex and hated myself because I wasn't going to have sex anymore and hated myself for hating him for his promiscuity and because maybe he didn't kill himself over me and I hated everything else too, and everybody and on and on forever and ever. I just hated.

I hated myself so much that a few days after Aaron's death I was out on the back porch of my aunt's house cutting a man's hair. Grey sat in a rickety wooden kitchen chair with his shirt off. Beside us were the sour-smelling mop, several brooms, Coca-Cola bottles in their cardboard to take back for deposit. I used my mother's large, heavy sewing shears. He had to unbraid his hair. It was a glorious Sunday afternoon. My aunt had gone out with somebody she met at a poetry reading, a potter.

With his hair down, Grey looked like Jesus. I couldn't help but think of my loincloth dream: when the Jesus on the Catholic cross drops his loincloth and proves He *is* a man.

I was too scared to cut off more than an eighth of an inch.

I snipped quickly.

The hair fell like ashes.

"Samson and Delilah," he said.

He was smoking a joint, which I thought was a regular cigarette, and he offered a few puffs to me. I had smoked a cigarette once and gotten sick. This was worse—acrid and damp. Yet I was under a spell of some sort, as if I were the person getting the haircut. God help me, but I was purring like a cat.

"Well," I said after a few minutes. "All done."

He had sat dutifully, stoically, like a statue, erect, motionless.

"Thank you." He stood up and pressed my body to his chest and put his hands on my breasts. Laid them flat on like oyster shells. I thought of my Aunt Pearl's ballet school, The World Is Your Oyster.

"Wait," I said, my breath catching. I smelled like Aaron, faintly laboratoryish, floorish. My very fingertips smelled of him. But my engine was running, that's for sure.

Grey unbuttoned my dress very quickly, pushed down my slip roughly and my bra so that he hurt my nipples.

"You're so innocent," he said.

"Not really."

"Relax," he said. "Do you have something in your eye? Why do you blink so much?"

I tried to relax. "It's a nervous habit."

"Does this make you nervous?" He put his hand between my legs.

I closed my eyes, felt that strange but familiar sensation in my thighs, a shiver at the base of my spine.

"I want to marry you," he said.

I groaned.

He licked my nipple quickly, his tongue darting back and forth like a little snake.

"We are going to get married," he said.

"But I can't," I said.

"Why not?"

I pulled back. "I, I, I, I can't cook."

"*I* will cook." He said this laughingly.

"But I don't even know you."

"You will."

"I am going to college."

A hope and a wish. Berkeley had accepted me, but I did not have the money to send them to even ensure me a place.

I opened my eyes. Greylen Cloud had hairs growing out of his neck, little spikes, and the creases in his neck were brown with dirt. Aaron had a neck like a swan.

"No," I said, pushing him away, coming back to myself.

Quickly I tucked my breasts back in my bra, hiked up my slip and dress, buttoned. I felt dizzy, a little sick to my stomach.

Greylen was rough and ready. Aaron had been gentle and slow.

"I want to marry you this very afternoon."

"Stop," I giggled, and ran into the house, and slapped up the stairs to the Italian room, locked the door. He followed me slowly, knocked on the door softly. I looked at my aunt's statue of Romulus and Remus sucking at the wolf's teats. Cute, I thought, very cute.

"Tomorrow, the path," Greylen said, as if he meant more, like the Path, the One True Path.

And so it was that we met every day down by the Hopkins Marine Laboratory, going up to a tall group of rocks where in a clump of cypresses they had their water tank, which stored the salt water used for ocean life in the lab.

Grey told me he was Greylen Cloud, an orphan raised on a bleak, snowy reservation in Minnesota. He was taught by angry red-faced nuns who threatened to cut out his tongue and roast it in the fire on a sharp stick.

They said, If you don't understand your lessons, jump out the window.

"Who are the barbarians?" Grey asked me. "What is civilization?"

Grey's fingers bled from biting his nails too short, like Margo's. In school, he said, sometimes he could barely hold his pencil. Yet he learned to play the organ and the piano. His handwriting was calligraphy. And despite those nuns, he went back to the practices of his forefathers, and like every hipster in San Francisco and on the coast he considered himself something of a Zen Buddhist.

Not only that. Greylen had been in jail. He had robbed grocery stores, going in an hour before closing and hiding until all the customers were gone.

"Cool," I said, my heart quaking as I imagined his brown body folded up like a tobacco leaf underneath the cornflakes boxes, the last customer paying, the bang of the screen door, the yawn of the owner behind the counter, the lights being turned off one by one.

"I didn't use a gun," Grey said.

"What did you use?"

"A hunting knife."

Somehow that seemed worse, but more thrilling.

And if that were not recommendation enough, he had also, when **115** he worked as a printer, forged paychecks. He still had that money. Over two thousand dollars. For the stone house.

It was there in the cluster of rocks by the marine laboratory looking out over the two little beaches, that Grey told me about Kelly's land.

"It was raining like hell, Zoe." He acted as if he were relaying this on a World War II radio microphone. "Thursday night, North Beach, San Francisco. This cat comes into the coffeehouse, like, soaked. I offered my jacket as a towel. The cat seemed genuinely grateful. I made him sit down next to me, got him an espresso. So it turns out he's some kind of land baron and wants to make restitution to the world and the Indian nation by giving me 160 acres of land thirty miles south of Big Sur."

"Wow."

"I'll say wow."

Grey described Kelly as a cowboy, for he wore cowboy boots and a cowboy hat. A baron, like the Red Baron?

The land was undeveloped, sixty miles from Monterey, with a spring, a rugged road, that was all. Grey wanted to build a house on it, a stone house, five-sided, like a peyote house.

I didn't know what peyote meant, so I asked: "What about other people?"

"Other people? What other people?"

"You mean you are going to live on 160 acres all by yourself?"

"With my wife, with you."

"But it would be so lonely."

Grey spit.

"Please don't do that," I asked.

"Why not?"

"It's nasty."

He rolled his eyes.

"It's offensive to other people, Grey."

"Fuck other people. What have other people ever done for me?"

"What if you need something Grey, from people?"

"Ah, I will have you."

"Me?"

"We will be an island unto ourselves."

"I am not sure of that, Grey."

"I am. I know I am not what the white man wants me to be."

"What is that?"

"Dead. The only good Indian is a dead Indian."

"Not all white men."

"Many, most. I don't need their schools and jobs, their books, their medicine, their technology, their ideas and institutions. I reject their way of life."

"But your life, how will that be different?"

"I wish to live like my ancestors, part of the earth."

When Grey kissed my body he made me feel like one of those redwood burrows with sprouts growing up here and there, each kiss a seedling. And sometimes he made marks with his mouth along my neck that looked like little batwings, shadowy, in a few days turning to green, like kiwis, with little black seeds in the middle, and then brown, fading off my skin forever. There were necklaces of them around my shoulders and a little flurry of them behind my knees. I had scratches on my breasts, as if a little cat had suckled.

One day he put his finger inside me. At first it felt uncomfortable, like a sharp pencil pricking me.

He said, "It is warm and wet, very pretty and quite ready."

Thus I found myself one June Saturday, barely two weeks after Aaron's death, telling my father I was sleeping overnight with my Protestant friend, a masquerade, this friend, that I had used for visiting Margo, an invented friend along with her invented family, the father an accountant, the brother an athlete, and even a pet dog, a collie like Lassie named Nathaniel, who could fetch, roll over, and shake paws. They were all thinking, I told my father, of converting to Mormonism.

Grey and I drove down the coast in Grey's truck to his friend Hans's cabin in Big Sur. Hans was a sandalmaker, and his cabin held one huge table with cutting implements and stacks of leather, and along the walls tacked on nails were hides.

Grey opened the back door so that the moon shone in on our bed and we could see each other. Grey's penis hung long like a pointer, and when it grew hard as a stiff stick, the testicles were drawn into it. In fact, his own body seemed to be pulled forward into that one thing,

disappearing into the power of that one thing, his penis. It yearned
towards me with its little black eye.

He had me kneel, my back to him, and as I held my hands over
my ears, as I always did in scary parts of movies, he pushed and pushed
against me until I felt it give. I was terribly embarrassed. He was facing
my bottom, looking at my rectum, holding the cheeks of my buttocks
in his hands as he entered my vagina from behind.

"You are not a virgin?" He seemed shocked.

"No."

I felt like one of the hides hanging up. Take off your skin, make
yourself uncomfortable. I couldn't see his face, but at the moment of
climax, he cried out as if he was in much pain. That was one of the
rare times he ejaculated, since he practiced kundalini.

And we always did it the same way. Doggy style. The other he
called the missionary position. Disdained it.

I didn't think that missionaries made love, so, of course, I was
utterly baffled, though I knew how much Grey hated missionaries for
all the harm they had wrought in the New World. However, it seemed
nice to be able to see a person's face at a particular moment in time.
Not that I mentioned it.

That night of my initiation into womanhood, as Grey wanted to
call it (despite the fact I was not a virgin), we did mushrooms. During
my initiation into hallucinogens, I walked through a screen door, broke
my glasses, made grunting sounds like a pig and got little scratches
around my mouth, and thought I saw Aaron hiding in the bushes.

Grey said when we came down from our hallucinations, "Too
much. You were too much, Zoe."

"But I need my glasses, Grey."

"You can see without white man's medicine," he said. "Do not
get new glasses. Do not wear glasses around me. I want you to see
through my eyes. I will make you stop blinking."

I think what I saw without my glasses is what is called in the Tibetan
Book of the Dead the magic theater, or, in some circles, the living theater.
The living theater, of course, was also where the Stravinsky-Nijinsky
ballet-puppet Petrouchka performed and became real, not a puppet, not
just a clown, but a real man.

[**IN SAN FRANCISCO,** on one rainy Saturday of our brief courtship before my graduation from high school, sitting across from Grey in the Old Spaghetti Factory, I listened to him describe what our lives would be like. Our courtship seemed like an invitation to something utterly foreign to me, although that is what ultimately attracted me, the opportunity for escape.

Remember:

Get on the motorcycle; it has no handlebars, no brakes.

Climb the church roof.

Go to a strange apartment with a strange man without teeth and let him gum you.

Have a love affair with your best friend's father.

Is there anything you won't do? Margo had asked.

"We'll get stoned in the stone house," Grey said.

I didn't know what stoned was then, and to me the term "stone house" connoted jail, like the French penal colony on Devil's Island, in French Guiana. Hardened criminals wept like babies, called for their mothers when they heard the name.

Furthermore, stoned was to be stoned. As were adulteresses and prostitutes, witches of old. Casting stones. Mary Magdalene. Billie Holiday.

"It sounds like jail."

"Jail? A stone jail? No, my wife and my children will roam the hills picking blue lupine and wild poppies."

"Grey."

"You will swim in the stream and have wonderful picnics. There is a grove of bay trees, cool and pretty, right below where I am going to build the house. In the afternoons, we can sleep there under the trees, which smell like spaghetti."

During this conversation, we were eating spaghetti and garlic bread in San Francisco. Our tablecloth was checkered red-and-white. I felt gloriously grown up. Here was a man, not somebody's father, talking to me. This was a date, I thought, a real date.

"We will have birthdays with brown cakes seeded with raisins soaked in orange juice from oranges from our own trees. I will hold your toes on cold nights. Our daughters will be married looking out over the ocean. Our sons will become strong. In our bed, my dear, I will whisper to you every night until we grow too old and must die. We will be buried in the Bay Grove, side by side. Roots will entwine themselves around our bones and our seed will continue."

"Grey."

I had to get up, go to the bathroom. I wove my way among the tables, reached the back. The graffiti above the toilet said:

God is dead—Nietzsche

Somebody had written underneath:

Nietzsche is dead—God.

I peed, washed my hands. In the mirror, I saw a tall thin girl with orange hair every which way. God, Nietzsche, all will die, I thought. No longer did I believe (how could I) in the Mormon heaven, with secret passwords and magic underwear. But cakes seeded with raisins, now that was something.

"What about radios, newspapers, the news of the world," I asked him when I got back to the table.

"We will make our own world, our world, Zoe, our own self-contained, perfect world."

"I am not sure that is possible, that it is even right."

"What do we care that they are killing themselves all over the globe."

"But other people, Grey?" They were all about us, enjoying their spaghetti dinner, no harm to us. I liked to eat out. I wanted to eat out every day.

"We will visit them from time to time. But, of course, it will not be like the city, where you look out your window and see the beggars and filth."

"But what if there is an emergency? With no phone, and miles away from a doctor . . ."

"We don't need doctors."

"Grey, one never knows when one needs a doctor. You talk of all these children. Yes, I want a baby, babies. But how are they going to get born, and then they need immunizations, checkups. Kids fall, hurt themselves. They have accidents, any number of things can happen. They have to go to school."

"We will have our own medicine. We will teach them ourselves. Immunization is a city thing. The white man brought smallpox in his blankets. We don't need white, Western medicine."

"People die for lack of white, Western medicine."

"In my country, on my land, people won't be sick, because there will be nothing to sicken them."

"Your country? Who will you be, the dictator?"

"I will be king of the mountain, and you, you, my dear, will be queen of the universe."

"The coast highway to Big Sur was built with convict labor, Grey, highway 1," I said. "They packed the convicts into little shacks at night, locked them in. Later, when Henry Miller first came down the coast, he lived in one of the shacks."

"So?"

"Everything is connected and complicated and we are all implicated. I mean, to escape civilization, you will use your truck made by Ford Motor Company and fill it with gasoline involving us with gas stations and we will go along a road built by convicts. You can't get away, even if you want to. I mean, you drive a truck down the coast. It was made in a factory. Technology isn't evil in itself. I mean, we will

have to build a fire to cook our food, Grey. Your ancestors used bows
and arrows. That was modern technology in its time."

"That doesn't say we have to work for the Defense Department,
get a Sears and Roebuck washing machine, go to the electric chair.   **121**
There are many approaches to reality, that's all I'm saying."

"I think you are saying more." I was now having a latte, he a
baklava, and he pulled each crusty, sticky layer of dough off one by
one, with the nuts nesting below, waiting for the fatal swoop of the
spoon. "Running away is not the solution, Grey."

"Are you sure it is running away and not going back to one's
essential self? To what is real? To get in touch again with our roots, to
be who we were/are?"

"God, Grey, whatever philosophy we hold, we need to eat, be
well. Margo's father, Aaron, told me a joke about philosophy. He said
that if you want to know what is real, just don't eat for four days, then
you'll know. Your stomach will tell you."

"So he was a cook?"

"A Marxist."

"A crook, then. Like Stalin."

"No, not Stalin." But I thought of the Spanish traitor who was
flayed alive.

"And isn't this guy with all the answers dead now?"

"That doesn't make him wrong. Everybody dies."

"You said he killed himself. That is different. You said he was an
intellectual, that he believed in ideas, in civilization. But isn't that exactly
what got him into trouble?"

"What got him into trouble was . . . was a loss of faith in his
ideas." I was the one who got him into trouble, and now I was putting
Grey, Grey's body, as a wall between memory and myself.

"Are you sure?"

I sighed. "I'm not sure what got him into trouble."

"Listen, Zoe, what good is an idea if you can't live by it? He had
to eat his words or he couldn't eat his words, something like that. If
food was so real to him, why didn't he grow his own?"

"Grey, you don't understand." I was the kiss of death.

"What's the point of being a Marxist? Or anything else? It's just
talk. Schoolboy talk."

"Grey. He didn't want to go to jail."

"Why is jail the end of the world? Good people go to jail. Three hots and a cot. There are worse things. I was in jail."

"Do you want to go back?"

"I'd rather die."

"Well, there you have it."

"But I put in my time, served my American apprenticeship. All poor colored Indian American boys either go to jail or go to the army. Take your pick. Warrior or caged animal."

"Aaron didn't want to betray anybody. Naming names, that's what they wanted him to do."

"Exactly. Keep quiet. That's the Indian way. So he goes to jail. I think the man wanted to die and this was an excuse. I think there is more to the story that you don't know." He was stroking between my fingers.

"Maybe." I remembered Margo saying, It's not that simple.

[**G R A D U A T I O N** night, Margo gave one of the speeches. Sure enough, it was about bombs, the need for disarmament. The word was that the principal, our pal, had tried to dissuade her from the topic. Mr. Neils was a Swedish immigrant. America had been good to him, he explained to her.

When we were all assembled in the gym, putting on our caps and gowns, Margo came up to me.

"New glasses," she said. We hadn't talked much since her dad, since Aaron.

"Yeah."

"The University of Chicago rejected me," she said. "At the last minute."

"How could they? My God, Margo, there must be some mistake."

"The letter from one of the teachers was not good."

"Because of your father?"

She shrugged.

"Because of everything, I suppose. I have a feeling it is kind of political. I think Mr. Appleton in his recommendation letter said I was troubled or confused." Mr. Appleton was one of our English teachers. I could imagine his letter: What is black and white and red all over?

"And everybody else in college is not confused?"

"I don't know."

We were supposed to be getting in line to file out two by two.

The graduation was on the football field, which was wet and soggy.

"How about Oberlin?"

"I'm not going to go to a place where they 'let in' Negroes," Margo said. "I'm going to Howard."

"Really?" I lost my breath for a second. "That's all Negroes, isn't it?"

"Right. Like every place else is all white."

I thought of how the Negro kids in our school did not associate with Margo. But the white kids didn't either.

"You're going to Berkeley, right?" she asked.

I shrugged. "I don't know. I guess." I wasn't quite tuned in. "I was thinking of it. I mean, I had started to think of it when . . ." I didn't want to say: when your father was alive. I didn't want to say that I had not reserved my place at Berkeley because I did not send in a deposit because nobody would pay it and because I had to watch my mother after school and therefore could not get a job and yet I had time to see Grey as I had for Aaron. So I messed up all around.

The graduates who were to sit in the back rows had already left the gym. There were just a few of us now, and the gym seemed more like the gym again. I was aware of the smell of sweat and dirty socks. The basketball hoops sagged.

"E. Franklin Frazier, the Negro scholar, is at Howard. I am going to study with him."

"That's nice." I didn't have the slightest idea who he was.

It was drizzling, and the parents, sitting on the stone bleachers made by the workers of the WPA, huddled together under umbrellas. Margo and I had eaten lunch there for the whole year, until her dad died. Now I looked for my aunt and mother, but I couldn't see them. Margo got several awards, one for best music student and one for best language student. The principal gave a speech about how we were all on the threshold of our lives. My feet hurt, my stomach ached, and my hair was flat and stringy. We all wore white shoes, which were ruined. Margo was in her tennis shoes. Her speech was short and bitter. Two boys fell off the back bleachers because they were so drunk.

And afterward, since my father was out of town, my mother gave me a party. All my so-called friends, people I had dragged up at the last minute who had no other party to go to, sat around in our house. Margo had declined the invitation.

The minute before everybody arrived, I was aware of the smallness of our house, the paltriness of our lives. I feared nobody would come and that somebody, everybody, would. A few people did come. My mother wondered why we didn't dance, and she put on a record. It was an old 78—a big-band swing record, Glenn Miller's "Little Brown Jug."

"Why isn't anybody dancing?" my mother asked blearily. God, I thought, she's drunk already. Her lipstick was smudged, and her zipper was half down her back.

"Come on," she said, grabbing at one of the boys, Jim Zim, who was going to West Point. "Let's dance."

"Mom." I got up off the couch to whisper in her ear. "Mom."

"What?"

"People are shy."

"Well, if that's how you feel about it, I'll dance by myself."

She twirled around with her arms in the air and fell on the floor.

"God," I said, squeezing my eyes shut. "Get me out of here."

But nothing happened. I didn't drop through the floor to the other side of the world. I was still there, it was still all happening.

"Saint Anthony," I intoned, and this time I jumped up, skipped a bit, gained a little momentum, and, breaking through inertia as thick as glue, dashed out of the house.

"Wait," my mother called out. "Wait, Zoe, wait for me."

I ran toward the P.G. pool. I kept running, going past all the little streets named after cute ocean things, shells and seahorses, ran past Lover's Point and toward Cannery Row. The air was crisp. I could breathe. I'm eighteen, I thought. I can do whatever I want. I turned up on Foam Avenue and headed toward a group of small shacks. That's where Grey lived. He was sitting in his one chair at his table, rolling cigarettes on his cigarette rolling machine. Behind him was his print of the Botticelli *Venus*, and his radio was playing some baroque music, an oboe concerto.

"Talk about white-man culture," I said.

He laughed.

It looked as if he had just bathed. His shiny black hair was wet and flat on his head. Behind him was his iron bed carefully made up with clean white sheets and an army blanket. He looked very dear. I thought of how we go through life meeting people and having such moments. What do they come to, I wondered. What do we make of them. I wanted to fix him there at the spot forever, so that even after he died, it would be him sitting there in his chair, not filled with despair, as in the Billie Holiday song, but filled with himself at his best, with his great containment, his Indianness and his Greyness, his hisness.

"You are in green."

I looked down. "Yes." My dress, in my favorite color, made by my mother, was different shades of green, which faded into each other. I had a thin green ribbon holding back my hair. I thought of a poem by the Spanish poet García Lorca, Aaron's martyr to a misunderstood cause. Aaron said Lorca was taken out on a lonely road by the Franco people and shot. The poem, "Romance sonámbulo," goes: *Verde que te quiero verde. / Verde viento. Verdes ramas.*

Green oh how I love you green. / Green wind. Green boughs.

"Green is the color of growth," I said.

"Naïveté," he countered.

"Newness, innocence, Grey."

"Jealousy, Zoe."

"How does it feel to be a survivor of a vanquished people, Grey?" I broke in, something I always wanted to ask my mother.

"Angry."

"Let's get married, Grey," I said. "Let's get married and get the hell out of here."

This is how Grey's telling would go:

One day when the sun was high in the sky, Coyote decided he would leave the animal people and go down the hill.

"Why are you cleaning your whiskers?" his wife, Mole, asked.

"Never you mind, Mole."

It was true that Coyote kept many secrets. He could change shape, be a man or a woman, an animal or a man, or half and half, and sometimes he spoke in riddles. In fact, he often spoke to his penis.

"Penis, do you wish to do this?"

"Yes," Penis answered in a deep, sonorous voice that belied his eager nature.

So Coyote, in his best snakeskin leggings, took Penis down the hill. The woman was there grinding acorns (these are Esselens, Big Sur Indians) in a large stone bowl. She greeted Coyote kindly. Her hair was long and silky. Coyote entered her ears and eyes, her mouth and her ass, and the tunnel to her womb. He planted worms in her heart and trees in her brain.

The man was not so compliant.

His skin knit together in resistance. Coyote could enter him in only one place, which bled like a tomato spitting seeds. And Coyote, nibbling the man's intestines and tonguing his liver, left a green sickness, a trail of tears, bitter as bile. Thus it was that Coyote impregnated woman and man with his knowledge of life and love and great grief, and planted their future with death, the worst trick of them all.

Although some say it was not death but knowledge, and still others say that

Coyote fashioned the world in the first place, putting poison within easy reach.
The real secret is that Coyote can assume not only the form of the son of man
but that of the son of God Himself, and as such Coyote is his own father, changing
into smoke and rain, all things of earth circling back, ass in mouth, hole to hole.

[**WE GOT MARRIED** in North Beach, San Francisco, on a crystal-clear Saturday morning in July 1957. The church, a kind of beat pad, a basement room with mattresses and pillows, was decorated with felt appliqué signs.

Jesus Christ, that's Who.

I am become a fool in glorying

and

For Christ's Sake.

He is my refuge.

Done in banners of red, green, and white, they contrasted sharply with the subdued tones of the room and people. Reverend Paul wore a gray sweatshirt with a stretched collar. A large wooden cross on a shoelace dangled against his narrow chest. Reverend Paul's wife, Marianne, sported a faded housecoat with a sagging hem. She looked tired of the selfless life. The witnesses were two runaway girls, one in her nightgown, the flannel worn to threads, and the other in what appeared to be a big black sack, redeemed only by its in-fashion turtleneck. Both girls were very pregnant. One strummed the guitar during the "ceremony." I believe the tune was "Amazing Grace." The other hummed in a high, beautifully eerie voice that frightened me. We had encountered an angel in rags. Surely she could approach the celestial realms without benefit of husband and secret name. Her voice alone should gain her admittance.

Meanwhile, I was the radiant and indulged bride in a wonderful skirt Grey had bought me. It was heather and beige-yellow, with a matching vest of gold buttons with thistles in the middle. My hair had gotten longer by then and curls clustered below my ears, and Grey insisted that I not wear my glasses. Grey was in new blue jeans, a new black-and-red-checkered flannel shirt. His hair, at my request, was unbraided and flowed long down his back. You could say that we were a handsome couple, if an unusual one, as was the wedding.

Needless to say, I was very aware that this was not a Mormon Temple with a baptismal tub in the basement or where I would get magic underwear for life and a secret name to get into heaven. Everything had happened so fast. I could not quite believe I was even getting married. Grey looked shell-shocked, too. I had to keep insisting to myself that this was the most important day in my life, that ritual effected transformation, for was not wine made into blood and bread into flesh and that marriage was marriage and I had better watch my step.

Instead, my gaze wandered in and out of the street-level window. This is your wedding, Zoe, pull yourself together. Girl magazines, starting in April, always had articles about: Planning Your Wedding. Color Schemes. Handling Bridesmaids. Should you wear a full-length veil? I had no cedar chest, no trousseau. There was to be no honeymoon, no champagne. I saw a dog.

"And the dog trots freely in the street," I recited to myself. Ferlinghetti's poem.

It reminded me of way back in June, mood indigo, San Francisco, at Buena Vista Park on Haight Street. A foggy Saturday, people letting their dogs run down the hill in the damp grass. We couldn't sit on the grass because it was so wet. Instead, we hovered under the gloomy cypresses by the stone stairway.

"I don't know, Grey." I shook my head a little to clear the cobwebs. In those days, I always felt muzzy and disconnected. Aaron had just died but still seemed very much with me. I saw him out of the corner of my eye, his narrow face, springy hair, the way he walked with his hands in his pockets, shoulders slumped, kicking his heels forward. Before I went to sleep at night, I sometimes could hear him walking toward me. We would meet in the hallway by the light.

I would circle Aaron's house, see his Plymouth Fury in their carport, as if it were a relic from an ancient past. Nobody was using it. In time the jade green would rust red, sink down into the earth, and get covered with a tall stand of grass. I have seen cars like that in the Midwest, hunkered down, tireless in their own grave of weeds, squared off, the field shorn around them.

When Berkeley wrote me another letter wanting to know if they should keep a place open for me, I had nobody to tell. My aunt was looking for a job, only teaching at night the few faithful students who hung on. She had cut down on expenses, and after class she kept only one light on in the Gatehouse, the room she was in. I could see her hunched over a book, Nijinsky sulking in the background. In the old days, the place had been lit up from top to bottom, from Italy to Turkey, an international extravaganza of lights.

I had applied for a few waitress jobs, but nothing came of them. One boss explained that most men did not like to be served by a person who towered over them.

"I can cut off my knees and calves," I said.

"Get out of here."

"Just kidding."

Men didn't like a smarty-pants either.

After I refused to go to work in his office, my father started nagging me, saying every day when he came home from work, "Have you got a job yet?"

Not only that, but a few days before graduation my father began talking about sending my mother somewhere, if we could afford it. Where? Downstate to a funny farm? I pictured her in a place of hallways with many doors, and I don't mean doors of perception. I pictured others like her in faded smocks and fuzzy slippers, nobody to comb their hair, shuffling listlessly down to the rec room. No, I thought, no. But would I stay home to take care of her? No, not ever.

"You can visit me in Berkeley, Grey," I even said in Buena Vista Park to Grey that gray, damp Saturday shortly before I decided to marry him. "It'll be fun. Weekends."

"Are you talking about football games?" Grey sneered.

"No." I didn't know what I was talking about. I was confused. Only a miracle would get me to Berkeley.

"If you ever leave me, I will kill you," he said.

"What?" Did I hear that right? A black dog, his fur in wet peaks, streaked by us. Faust's devil, I thought. Get behind me.

"You heard."

"I don't want to hear. You scare me."

As I walked away from him, he grabbed my wrist.

"When we are married," he spat, "you won't be able to run away from me anymore, you understand what I'm saying?"

"I have to be back in Monterey by five. Okay?"

"I'm dead serious."

"Don't be *dead* serious."

"Why not?"

"I tend to take what I am told seriously." Aaron had taught me that lesson. He was seriously dead.

"You *should* take me seriously, Zoe."

"I'm just a high school girl, Grey."

"You *are* marrying me, you understand what I'm saying?"

That meant not walking freely in the street like the dog in Ferlinghetti's poem.

Beats walked freely in the street. They were not in the Haight then, but in North Beach, the Italian neighborhood with pasta and espresso, where the sailors in their tight white pants and jaunty caps, docking in the bay, would come for their girlie shows, where later I would dance, my ballet lessons finally of some use.

The beats walked loosely in the street with their thin shoulders hunched, hands in their pockets. They drank Gallo wine, smoked Camels. They got on the road. They got drunk on the road. They got laid on the road and left their beds unmade, made their adieux unceremoniously, and came and went as they pleased. They trotted freely in the street, talked fast on the phone, ate anchovies on ice cream cones, recited poetry on the run, moved as the spirit moved, and didn't care what people thought.

"I do," I said to the minister when Grey nudged me.

We were pronounced man and wife.

"I present Mr. and Mrs. Greylen Cloud," Reverend Paul said to the poor runaway girls who had sought haven in his church.

Grey did not have a ring, but he gave me a piece of Elk Horn, polished to a shiny gray sheen with a stone in the middle, hung on twine.

"The stone," he said, "was picked up on the Trail of Tears, you know what I mean?"

He was referring to the long march of the Indians, the Cherokees, who were forced to walk from Georgia, Tennessee, and North Carolina to what was to become Oklahoma. I had the feeling the so-called stones picked from that trek were like relics of the Crucifixion, that is, false, and therefore desecrations.

"Trail of Tears?" I wasn't sure that was the best omen, but Grey grabbed my hand, as if it belonged to him.

"Come on," he said, taking me down the street to have espresso and sweet buns in a coffee shop.

"I think I should call home, let them know," I said, looking down at the small white tile octagons on the coffeehouse floor and thinking of the milky way at home.

"Right, I know what you mean."

I didn't feel married at the moment. I didn't feel any different at all, but I would have to say something.

"Do you have change?" I asked.

"Sure."

I called home from a pay phone on Vallejo and Columbus.

It rang a long time. I could visualize the hallway, the table, the chair, the mirror on the wall.

"Hello." It was only eleven-thirty on a summer Saturday morning. I had sneaked out of the house early in the morning, caught the seven-thirty Monterey express to San Francisco. A mere three-hour ride, but eons, light-years away. I had crossed over borders, international time zones; I could have been on the moon.

"Hello, Mom. I won't be home tonight."

"Zoe, is that you?" My father had grabbed the phone.

"Dad." The San Francisco air smelled of French bread, oregano. A light breeze was blowing. Oh God, what a clear, beautifully blue day, and how happy I felt. Across the street, on the steps to the Catholic church, under the carved words "To Almighty God Under the Invocation of Saint Francis of Assisi," I saw a real bride. She stood a minute on the steps, looking as fragile as the ballerina on my jewelry box.

"Zoe, where are you?"

"Listen, Dad, I won't be home tonight."

"Why not, have you gone mad?"

"I've gotten married."

There was, of course, an immediate and significant silence on the other end, an audible intake of breath. It was so quiet, I could almost hear the mold growing on the kitchen baseboards two rooms away from the telephone.

"I am married and moving to Big Sur, actually south of Big Sur, Gorda. You can address my mail to Zoe Cloud."

"Cloud? What kind of name is that?"

"An Indian name. Grey Cloud is my husband." Grey was holding my hand as I spoke and pressing it to his penis. He was getting hard right there on the street. Gadzooks, I giggled.

"Zoe." It was my mother on the phone again.

"What?"

"Zoe," and there was a long pause. "Zoe, I'm sorry."

"For what?"

"Everything."

I was going to cry. I didn't want to, there in the street, on my wedding day.

"Are you still there?"

"Yes, Mom."

"Be happy."

"I will," I said. "I will try."

Then my father was on again.

"You make your bed, you sleep in it," my father said, and hung up.

I turned to Grey. "You make your bed, you sleep in it."

"Let's fuck first," he whispered wetly in my ear.

On the ferry to Sausalito, we necked like high school kids at a drive-in. The boat churned by Alcatraz, the prison of no escape, and we stayed the night in an old-fashioned hotel which had a huge canopied bed and a chunky chest of drawers. The whole place was hung with lace, which somehow reminded me of fishnets, the kind they used in Monterey to catch sardines.

Maybe I was delirious, maybe I was a little drunk, for we were drinking wine straight from the bottle, as Aaron had done in Paris. Then after we had made love, I kneeling on the floor and he withdrawing his sperm almost successfully, as you are supposed to do in kundalini, that is, not let it out but bring it up to the head through all the chakras of the body, the seven centers—the sex chakra, the belly chakra, the solar-plexus chakra, the heart chakra, the throat chakra, the forehead chakra, and, finally, the crown chakra, where there occurs a burst of white-light ecstasy far surpassing an ordinary, occidental orgasm—and the bottle was empty and the street quiet and the whole world asleep, Grey got me a glass of water, held my head in his arms, and told me a story about Coyote, the Eternal Trickster.

"Very interesting, Grey."

Then I told him my version.

This is my version:

"Who goes there? Who goes there?" Papa God asks, for He is walking in the garden in the cool of the evening.

"It is I, Coyote's wife, Mole."

In the beatitudes, it is the pure of heart who see God, but moles are practically blind. Without my glasses, I am blind.

"Come, my child," says Papa God.

We feel our way toward each other. God lifts my small paws, which are like little claws, to his face, which is hairy like mine with a black, wet nose like mine. God has whiskers, too, and He is Mother of all Moles, King of Kings.

"I forgive you, little Mole."

"So you know."

"Yes," Papa God says, "I know."

Of course he knows. He knows about Aaron. He knows about my mother. He has seen me scrubbing the wallboards in the kitchen and hating my father. But mostly Aaron, how I left him, the sin of omission.

"I know, little Mole, and I forgive you."

I feel happy.

"But can you forgive Me?" Papa God asks.

"For what?"

"For the world."

This is the eighth day, when the universe catches up to itself and the price for all that we have seen and heard and tasted and smelled and touched is paid. We must begin to break our way out from the walled garden; we must begin to think.

[**OUR LAND** in Gorda, some thirty miles south of Big Sur, still surveyed in the 160-acre bundle given to homesteaders after the Civil War, was traded to us by Kelly Bannon for a piano, a flock of geese, and a pack of cigarettes.

The piano was an old red upright with bright green leaves painted on it from a Mexican bar in San Francisco, and Grey bought the geese in Salinas Valley. We tied the piano to the back of his truck, which had a homemade bed of boards, no railings, and placed the geese in dog cages and headed on down the coast, the keys of the piano jiggling a crazy, modern ragtime, and the geese snaking their necks out of their cage bars and honking their heads off. I sang Little Richard's song "Tutti Frutti," leaving my window open for the wind to blow in my face and ruffle my hair. God, did I feel glorious.

We barreled past beaches violently divided in two by curved estuaries from mountain streams. We went by the lighthouse, which was on an island but connected to the mainland during low tide by a long damp beach. We went by beaches full of driftwood, gray and gnarled, trees become fierce old faces. The meadowlands and yellow hills of the cattle ranches were gentle in comparison. We snaked between the passages of tall redwoods, zipping by River Inn, Pfeiffer State Park, the Post Ranch, and Deetjen's Big Sur Inn, where Dutch, Mr. Deetjen, sat on a bench outside all day and Mrs. Deetjen, too obese to move much, had her bed installed in the guest dining room so she could keep her eye on things. We whizzed past the restaurant Nepenthe, where you could folk-dance on a large terrace under the stars, and Slade's Hot Springs, with mineral baths on a ledge overlooking the ocean for fifty cents. We flew past Naciemento Road, Mill Creek, Jade Beach, Pacific Valley.

We traveled deeper, no houses to be seen, to the end of the steady march of the telephone poles, which looked like crucifixes on the way to Rome. Then we were at the point of no return. We had only the sea, the rocky coast, the hills—now getting dryer—and the tiny ribbon of highway which strung everything together. It was the day after our wedding, the first day of my life.

It was all going to be great, I knew, even though I was feeling a little queasy. I had made the right decision, I was sure. Thinking of Margo stuck in a classroom for the next four years, I felt sorry for her. My mother at home; my aunt at her paltry ballet school, her pupils getting fewer and farther between, their tutus sagging; Judy, Margo's mother, a widow in a wheelchair: they were all to be pitied. I did pity them. I was the luckiest woman alive. I was loved by a man. Our life together was going to have meaning, be a grand adventure.

But way in the back of my brain, in a tiny, dingy room with a concrete floor and walls that sweated, there sat a small man on a small chair, and beside him was a tin plate of beans, a crust of bread. A tin cup, tepid water. Rats scuttled in the background. He was a prisoner of my brain, perhaps inherited from the foreboding character of my father, the ancestral tortures of my mother, Aaron guilt, for this miserable person said: If you feel this good, the other shoe is about to drop.

[**WE DROVE** the three more hours from Monterey, after the three hours from San Francisco, stopping before going up to our land to see our benefactor, who lived on the coast side of the highway. Kelly Bannon was squat, red-faced, elfin, eyes the color of leaves—not at all the cowboy or land baron I expected.

"Kelly," Grey said, "this is my wife, Zoe."

"My man, Grey." They clasped their hands together like long-lost brothers. I was the wife. Wife. I let the word echo.

"Pleased," Kelly said, graciously extending his hand to me. "It will be so nice to have neighbors."

We were on the deck of one of Kelly's yurts. On one side of us was the ocean, which, of course, was endless, at least all the way to Japan, and below the yurts were his fields, Kelly's crops.

"What are you growing?" I asked.

"Cash," Kelly said with a smile.

"Greenbacks," Grey elaborated.

"Oh." I guess I was supposed to know what they were talking about, so I laughed, hah hah, money that grew on trees.

"And that is the Big Rock Candy Mountain." Kelly pointed to the hill, our hill, which rose up across the highway with the impudence of a youngster, as if just emerged from the sea in a recent geological upheaval. However, behind our cocky little hill rose the Los Padres

National Forest, where the redwoods were reputed to be hundreds of years old.

"Wow," I said. "I own a tree? We own trees? Rocks? Land?"

I hadn't quite realized what Grey meant when he talked about the Land. My father owned our tiny little house, and my aunt owned the Gatehouse, but this, this was . . . enormous, overpowering, magnificent.

"Home sweet home." Grey nuzzled my neck and, putting his arm around my waist, said, "I knew you would love it."

"It's ours? One hundred and sixty acres?"

"With a spring on it," Kelly said. "Very important."

"All yours, baby," Grey answered. He was easing his hand down to my hip, when he dropped it quickly.

"Oak," Kelly said. "Where were you? This is Grey. I think I told you about the land, right? Look, they brought us the piano and geese, the tobacco smokes. Hey, his wife, Zoe. My woman, Oak."

Oak.

The other shoe.

How to begin:

Tall and thin.

I was tall and thin, too.

But she was graceful, and not as tall as I was. She was decently tall, and there was a lyrical quality to her height. She swayed to one side like a willow tree. Her posture had a note of inquiry about it. Her torso, with the haunches of a racehorse, was one smooth stalk up to a set of big, full breasts.

I had the grace of a stork picking her way through a muddy marsh. I loped along awkwardly, and hunched to appear shorter.

She was pale.

I was pale if you didn't count the freckles and assorted blemishes.

Her pale was spun sugar at a fair. She brought to mind the Ferris wheel, one of the few rides I had ever been on at all, and with my father at that, one of the few times we had ever been happy together. There we were up there in the heavens, while below us rivers of people walked and hawked. Hey, this is something, my father had said. I was happy that day.

Oak was blond, of course, so blond as to be almost white-haired, but not in an old way. No, her hair was exotic, Scandinavian. It hung

141

down her back to her hips in a curtain of silver rain. Should I go on? Torture myself? Her eyes were a deep brown, the brown of the forest and all its secrets.

My eyes were dirt-poor in comparison.

Oak was, in fact, simply the most beautiful woman I had ever seen.

I, I with my flat chest and pear hips, gawked at her.

She extended her hand like a princess to Grey, looking him straight in the eyes.

"Delighted," she said, her lips at half-pout, "to like, uh, meet you."

Grey looked pretty damn delighted himself.

"Hello," I said brusquely, worried as hell.

Yet driving up the hill on the homemade road to our property, Grey put his hand on my knee.

"I love *you*," he said, as if reading my mind. "Does that make sense?"

"Really?"

"Really."

"Really and truly?"

He gave me a hard look. "You belong to me. You are my wife, okay?"

"Okay." I took a deep breath.

We set up camp in a small valley below a huge rock, which rose like a tomahawk from the edge of the top of the cut road. Tooth rock. It was there that I later discovered the shell mounds, irrefutable evidence that Indians had lived there, the ones that had been massacred the century before by the white people. Thus, Grey was indeed to be the restitution of former abuses.

Our equipment was meager. We had a small green canvas tent, World War II issue, which you could not stand up in, a double sleeping bag, pots and pans, two guns. In a clear spot in front of the tent Grey set up the cooking area. A pile of stones against the hill, a slab of rock for the pots. Simple in design, difficult in practice, because I did not even know how to cook on a regular stove.

In San Francisco we had bought a fifty-pound bag of rice, a fifty-pound bag of flour, five pounds of sugar, twenty pounds each of pinto, red, navy, and dried lima beans, a pound of salt, a bag of onions, potatoes, a slab of salt pork, a chunk of lard, yeast, pepper, a sack of oranges, apples, dried figs and apricots, dates, raisins, a tin of honey, a couple of pounds of carrots, bullets, matches, tin plates and cups, our pans. **143** We had shovels, picks, an ax, a wheelbarrow, and bags of cement mix. Grey was to build our house, stone by stone, from the little quarry on our hill, rolling them into place, mixing and pouring concrete by hand.

Our dirt road from the highway was cut by a pickax and a jeep with a scraper on the front. Later we heard that Kelly did the road one winter in the pelting rain, wildly drunk and cursing to high heaven, daring the lightning to blast him down. It didn't. The road was rammed, chopped, hacked, cleared. Supposedly, Kelly was mad at his mother, whom he lived with down on the coast, and he planned to build on the mountain himself. Then she died, but not before living her last crazy days in a tin lean-to in the woods. She had turned into a spitfire, a cat with tangled hair who spat at intruders. They said it happened sometimes, that the coast could turn one crazy.

Yet gossip had it that in her glory days, Kelly's mother had been a favorite hairdresser of the mistress at Hearst Castle, in San Simeon. The castle was twenty miles south, which is how Kelly's mom got the land to give to Kelly to give to Grey.

Kelly had remodeled his mother's plain cabin into a series of low round houses with grass planted on the roofs. The yurts were connected by a series of stepping-stone decks. He kept a little herd of goats, who munched the roofs trim. He also had a big pig, a bunch of chickens and ducks, a Japanese garden of raked gravel, a stone garden full of exotic succulents, a little stream wending its way under the decks so that you felt you were on a bridge when you were on the decks between the yurts, and he had a marvelous flower garden. Kelly called himself a farmer, and he did grow vegetables in quantity, but his cash crop, as I was to realize, was the hemp plant. The marijuana was interspersed with weeds and baby tomato plants. Foolproof.

Thus, with their homegrown, Kelly and his woman, Oak, were always high or low or in between or just ready to light up, up and away.

"Hi," Oak would say dreamily. "Would you like to burn one?"

I could imagine Grey saying, I'll smoke you any day.

For Oak soared higher than anybody, and sometimes when she was way up there in the clouds, she lifted her dress and we could see a fuzzy patch of blond hair, light as frothing bubbles, for she did not wear underpants, and disdained false modesty.

I felt it was only a matter of time.

[**O N E   D A Y ,** soon after we had moved to the coast, we were walking up the hill from Kelly's after a little smoke.

"Did you get a buzz?" Grey asked me.

"Yeah."

It was still bright afternoon, but I felt sleepy and settled. I wished that we hadn't left the truck on top of the hill. I wished we had a magic carpet.

"Oak is a fine-looking woman," Grey said.

"Tell me about it."

"Don't be that way."

"What way? I'm just human."

Then I saw it.

"Grey." I grabbed his arm, scuttled behind his back.

"A real rattler," he said.

"I nearly stepped on it."

Stretched across our path taking a sun bath was a fat, long, ugly rattlesnake. The king snake, though large and ugly, black with white bands, is harmless to humans. The garter snake has a yellow stripe, and it, too, is harmless. The gopher snake is big, but all he goes after are gophers. But for the rattlesnake we had a kit with a razor in it and a tourniquet and suction cup. I was worried that if it came to it, I would not be able to save Grey, or that in trying to suck the venom out I would swallow it myself and die.

I was about to run back down the hill, when Grey said, "Shh," and he let the ax, which he always carried over his shoulder, fall across the rattlesnake's neck, or the upper body anyway, close to the head. The head immediately slid off into the sagebrush and the body began to wiggle like mad.

"Get it, hold it," Grey said. "Hold the body."

"No. You get it."

"What kind of mountain woman are you?"

"Scared."

But I took the tail, he the front. It was not so slimy as crusty, and he put it in his gunnysack, slung it behind his back, and the damned thing, without a head, wobbled all the way up the hill.

"Grey," I squeaked, walking a safe distance behind him, "it's still alive."

"Naw. The head is gone."

"Where is the head?"

"It went in the bushes."

I could imagine the head sneaking out of the bushes, following us along the road, ducking back in the bushes when I turned around, and taking little leaps forward behind our heels, coming after its rightful body.

"Have you ever heard of the expression 'a head on your shoulders,' Grey? A head of one's own. The head is going to get us," I said. "It wants its body back, Grey."

"It's dead, Zoe. D-E-A-D."

"But the body, it's still, like, moving."

"Nerves, Zoe, just nerves."

At camp, Grey tied one end of the snake to the crossed poles we had for game, the skinning poles. It wiggled all the while, and when Grey held it down for me to chop it up, it writhed as though in pain. I threw the pieces into a paper bag filled with flour and salt and pepper. It jumped in the bag. Grey built the fire, and even twenty minutes later when I dropped the pieces into the hot fat in the frying pan, the snake pieces bounced and spattered, hopped right out of the pan onto the ground, and skipped away.

"My God." I felt sick. Not that I was going to eat any of it. "It's going to hunt for its head, Grey, I just know it."

"Sh."

"No, no. Why did it keep moving like that? It's so creepy." I looked up. The sky seemed to darken.

"Let's forget dinner. Snake medicine," Grey explained, "is very powerful. It means transmutation in First People language."

"Just what I wanted to hear. It's going to rain. I'm going in the tent."

"There is something else you do not want to hear, but I must tell you," Grey said. "The truth. In the Bay Grove."

The Bay Grove was a group of bay trees below our camp. It was cool there because of the shade, and there was a quality to the area much different from the dusty hot flats or the field area. Compared with Redwood Gulch, the huge forest that crowded the mountain gorge above us with trees, the Bay Grove was tame, quiet, a good place to rest in the hot afternoon.

"Why now, Grey? I don't know if I want to hear the truth. The snake has been enough truth for today." I was afraid. In my experience, the truth has never set me free. On the contrary.

But the snake had set him off. When Grey talked in the ponderous, deliberate way of Indians in cowboy and Indian movies, I knew it was confession time.

So we left the empty frying pan and walked down to the Bay Grove, sitting down next to each other on a large rock.

"This is the truth," Grey said, passing me the peace pipe. "A smoke?"

"No, thanks." Somehow I thought I should have my wits intact. Nerves, Grey had said of the snake, just nerves. But he, too, I could tell, was unnerved by the snake experience.

"You must understand," Grey began. "Now that you are my wife."

"I will try." I was sitting on a stone, trying to keep my balance. I was afraid he was going to say something about Oak. The truth is, I am in love with Oak, and she loves me, and, well, Zoe, you just don't cut the mustard; bye, nice knowing you.

"I hope you can handle this."

"I hope so, too, Grey."

I hadn't used a flush toilet in a week or taken a bath or had a decent meal. My hair was matted, and my feet, properly attired in beatnik sandals, were filthy and sore. The last thing I wanted to hear was what I thought he was going to tell me.

"I haven't seen many snakes in my lifetime, Zoe."

"But you were raised in the pueblo or reservation or . . . out in the country. That's what you told me."

"I am second-generation city, Zoe, not from the mesa, not from a teepee, not from the pueblo, not from a reservation in Minnesota even."

"You were raised in a city?"

No one city, it seemed. Once he had been in Seattle, where it rained, hailed, snowed, and was sunny in one day. Portland was dreary. Needles, California, was hot. In Santa Fe there was an evening and a morning breeze. Atlanta was beautiful in early spring, and all the streets were Peach this and Peach that. Kansas City, Missouri, had a famous hamburger place. And although his mother was perhaps part Hopi or part Sioux, tribal purity was a thing of the past, and Grey didn't know who his father was or even exactly when or in what city he was born. His birth certificate was an approximation, something sent for before he presented himself to the draft board; for Grey was born where he was conceived and where he lived—in the back of a car—and he was actually twenty-five, he thought, not twenty-eight.

"Oh," I said, remembering that we had to show our birth certificates when we got our marriage license. The man at City Hall had not believed I was eighteen, but I was, my birth certificate proved it. Was Grey's certificate a forgery, like his paychecks? What happened to those three years?

"Mostly we traveled through the Southwest, me and my big brother, a little nest of rats in the backseat with all the dirty and clean clothes. In the front seat of the car was our little camp stove and pots and pans." His mother drove from city to city, working here and there, cleaning up rest rooms in railroad stations, picking fruit and vegetables, and selling beads on the sidewalk. "Who knows what else."

"Oh, Grey."

"I learned to read staring hard at a comic book. I spent hours and hours in libraries. That was where I could go in the day and be in a large room and stretch out my legs, sit on a real chair at a real table. And sometimes I spent the day in a church. They were cool and restful. In the Southwest, the churches have tall, whitewashed ceilings, rafters of oak. Inevitably the main figure in back of the altar is a statue of the padre, the one who founded the church, in his long black robe and bald head with its rim of hair. Rosy cheeked, plump, he looks like the owner of a hacienda. To his side, emaciated, carved in rough wood, almost pagan in its simpleness, certainly not more than a stick figure with a pointy little diablo beard, is Christ crucified. I have nothing against Him."

"So you were never in a mission school, never tortured by nuns."

I thought of the beheaded snake, the idea of being whole, the search for self. Grey passed me the pipe. I needed it now. It was ceramic, white with blue designs, Dutch- or Japanese-looking, not at all rustic. I took a long drag, looked up through the leaves of the bay trees. The sun was sparkling like diamonds, fake diamonds, cut glass.

"And stealing from grocery stores, is that true?" Was his whole account before we were married a fraud, then?

"Yes, that part is true, and the forgery."

"Oh, Grey," I said, putting my hand on his knee. "You poor, poor baby." But I was relieved. It was not Oak, not something about how he felt about Oak.

"I have four distinct memories of childhood," he said.

There was a time, long ago, when he lived in a house, or maybe it was an apartment, but the floor was solid and the rooms spilled into each other. You could walk through them, one foot after another, pound, pound, pound on a real floor. Maybe it was just a dream.

In another memory he is in the car, an ancient jalopy packed in the back with his brother and the clothes and toilet paper, hardly room to stretch out, and they are parked outside of a town, under a tree. He wakes up, and in the dark, crouching beside the car, the front door open like a big metal wing, his mother is going peepee.

The third memory is the last time he was in a regular church. He was twelve or thirteen, maybe fourteen, when the priest took him in back of the altar to a little room, and throwing him over a large polished desk and holding his hands down so his wrists hurt, he pushed his big, hard penis in Grey's asshole until it tore and bled. The priest spanked Grey's bottom right, left, right, left, all the while telling him that God would kill him if he told.

The fourth memory is when Grey was fifteen, and his mother had finally moved to a trailer. One night after a furious fight in which he and his brother were pushed down to the floor by big cowboy boots and made to beg for mercy by one of the mother's boyfriends—a big

Apache with a feather in his cowboy hat—Grey left for San Francisco, where, after turning a few tricks, he got a job in a printshop and learned how to be a printer and forger of checks.

"Do you still love me?" Grey asked, when he was finished with his story.

"Of course," I replied, giving him the pipe and drawing him to me, taking his head in my lap, stroking his hair. "I love you more." He needed me.

"Very few people in America," he continued, "live in houses, houses as you know them. They live in cars and old trains, trailers, boxes and shanties, abandoned school buses, under a piece of tin. They wash in public bathrooms and eat out of garbage cans. We used to pull up to campgrounds after the ranger had left for the day and use the showers."

I sighed.

"Zoe, we are so lucky that we have all this land, and our house will be of stone, strong as a fortress, and it will be rooted, clawed, part of the ground. Ten bulldozers will not be able to move it."

What could I say?

"I understand." I was thinking of a little boy in the backseat, roaming the country, wondering, as children do, Are we there, are we there yet? And never quite being there.

And I was also thinking that, as very few people have houses, very few people have beds. We did not have a bed. Except for our wedding night and the first time in that cabin, we had never made love in a big white bed.

"Your brother, Grey, where are your brother and mother now?"

"I don't know."

"Hmm." As much as I had wanted to be adopted and even though I had apparently been disowned by my family, at least I knew where they were, and, of course, they were mine, as bad as they were, they were mine.

"So you see how much I love this land, and how much I want to build this house, you see what I'm saying?"

"Yes." And here I thought he wanted to tell me that he was in love with Oak. What a fool I was.

"And you must forgive me sometimes," he continued. "I have had
a hard time in your country."

"Surely, it is as much yours, Grey."

"That's not how I feel, and you know it."

"Sorry."

"You forgive me then?"

Forgive *him*? I was thinking, If Aaron was Ichabod Crane, skinny
and scared, then you, Grey, in a sense are the headless horseman.

"There is nothing to forgive you for, Grey." Except that he wasn't
who he said he was. I am not what I am, he should have said, when
we were standing up in front of Reverend Paul, and he asked, if you,
do *you* take this woman?

"The earth is my mother, Zoe; we are all migrants on the road
of life. But the Hopi are people of peace, and I wish to rest here. I
want to live and die here."

"You are a long way from dying, Grey."

"And if, if there is. I mean, if, if I ever stay, I mean stray . . ."

He *was* talking about Oak. Oh God, I knew it. I knew it would
come to that.

"What are you telling me?" I moved slightly. My body became
rigid. He had to lift his head off my lap. I covered my ears with the
palms of my hands.

He moved them gently to my lap, held them down, looked me in
the face.

"You are my wife, Zoe. *You*, I love."

"Grey, you are my husband. We have made vows." Although I
distinctly remembered how distracted I was at our so-called wedding.
However, I knew I must choose my words carefully. I knew I must be
careful. *Cuidado*, the Spanish said, *cuidado*.

"We are each other's kin, each other's tribe, Grey, and particularly
since our other kin, yours, mine, are not accessible. Our loyalty must
be strong and fierce." I was speaking the way he did, giving weight to
each word. I inhaled, held the smoke in, let it infuse my lungs. God of
Marijuana, I thought, remembering my childhood saints, God of Marijuana, give me wisdom. Actually, I was confused. I knew if I had been
given a map at that moment to save my life, I would not have been
able to find my way home.

"But what if . . ."

"What if?" I shook my head sadly. How long were we married? A week, a little over a week? "But if, Grey, if for a moment one should forget the True Path and who we are, let us hope that we are strong enough to overcome that obstacle as a pair."

I had spoken.

July 30, 1957

Dear Margo,

Do you remember your father's work on Othello? *Iago said: I am not what I am. Who are we, onions who reveal layer after layer who we are/are not, Russian dolls within dolls? Is deception merely misunderstanding and lack of knowledge on the part of the deceived and confusion and unhappiness on the part of the deceiver?*

Dear Margo, do you remember telling me that things are not as simple as they appear? What you see is not *what you get. That's what you said. What I said was that things were simple.*

I wanted: everything I saw.

Do you remember looking at Grey that first time at the poetry reading and saying, I want, I want.

I wanted him, too.

We wanted the moon.

What did we get? I don't even know if you are getting this letter. Are you still in Pacific Grove, or have you gone East to your Negro school, Howard University, where my voice sounds foreign and white and not delightsome.

Margo, marriage is fraught with peril. I thought I would be safely enfolded by official sanction, a cocoon of comfort spinning a golden web of soft days. I thought: Married. That settles it.

So, get this: our first day here we meet a sex goddess, my luck, and her generous consort. The point in all the fairy stories is to get married, but what then? Am I not the princess, the queen for a day? Is this a homosexual dream? Do we not live happily ever after? Instead of marriage settling things, I find it is a Pandora's box.

The $64,000 question is, who is cheating this week, the college professor or the kid from Brooklyn? My Mormon ancestors were polygamists and, according to all accounts, quite happy with the arrangement. Kerouac said: Don't talk to me about essence, but show me what's happening. Dig it or dump it. But I don't know what is happening. I don't know what I am doing. And I cannot talk it, because to talk it makes it happen, fulfills the prophecy. And the denial is the confirmation. I am between a heart and a heart place.

Are you in love with Oak, I want to ask him. Her name is Oak, if you can imagine. It used to be Joy. If your name was Joy, would you change it to Oak? Poison Oak is what I think, or else I conjure something Druidical, for there is something indeed sinister about this woman who baby-talks and pouts like Marilyn Monroe. People change their name at the drop of a hat here, realign themselves, redefine, rediscover. Me, I, you would say, I want to be reupholstered. Is that too much to ask? A new skin, please, and while you're at it, can you work on my brain a little? Rewire.

I dream that there will be years in which nobody says, I love you. I have dreams of animals wearing muzzles and walking around indistinctly, shrouded in fog. I am blind and there is no foghorn to guide me.

Grey says Nature just is. Good and bad do not enter into it. Good is a white, Christian idea. Sometimes he sounds like Aaron, your father, but he is coming to the same conclusions from another direction. Grey wants me to accept the duality and profusion of existence. But sometimes I think what he says is his own obstinate Indian blanket of rationalization.

This is what people do, Margo, get married. I have done the normal thing, the right thing you are supposed to do, the natural progression of life. Girl, woman, wife, mother, grandmother. I think of myself as old, an old woman someday. The squaw. Old Mother Hubbard. My children, "Mommy, Mommy"; my grandchildren, "Nana, Nana," a chain of love. In time, Grey will have a million wrinkles crisscrossing his face like the Indians of the old wild West, Chief So-and-So, Medicine Man Cloud, the shaman, the hunter, the brave. Me Minnie Ha-Ha. Pocahontas. And, yes, the papoose. I will wear a leather-fringed jacket, beads, and moccasins. Words like Pachaco Pass, Paso Robles, palomino ponies, sagebrush would be like straw in the broom sweeping across the floor of my life until it was all clean, all gone. All love, Zoe Cloud.

[**THESE WERE** the things I didn't write to Margo:

In the day, it was snakes. They sunned themselves across the path, and Grey would ax with his ax, ask me no questions. And when they held still, we ate them.

In the day, without the protection of sleep, I realized second by second that our great life of living in nature was plain old camping. Everything was sooty all the time. All my clothes smelled of smoke. Since the water was hauled from the spring, one bucket would be used for washing our faces and necks and, afterward, the dishes and for watering the few tomato plants we had started. Water was poured from receptacle to receptacle, from the bowl to the pot, where the spoons and forks and knives were soaking in yesterday's clothes water, and, lastly, back to the ground, which was parched and grateful.

I was sticky and grungy, had an animal, musky odor, and between my legs I itched and burned. Sometimes I didn't change, going for days in the same pants and shirt. What did it matter? Who cared? Who was there to see me? No matter what I did, could I ever be as beautiful as Oak?

A meal often took hours to prepare and half the night to clean up. I couldn't find things. Mosquitoes hovered in little clouds over any uncovered food; they dipped in on the little cuts and sores which were spotting my face, and came to rest on the mounds of earth covering my shit. Everything took so long. I was hot and tired all the time.

Sometimes I felt sick to my stomach. I wondered if my ulcer was being agitated.

What I really wanted, though, more than anything, was to be cool, that old beat pledge, but actually, on Gorda mountain in Big Sur those first weeks of marriage, at night I was freezing. The days on the hill were like thick meat, the nights thin cold milk. Our green canvas tent was frail protection against all the sounds and possibilities. Our sleeping bag was lumpy and uncomfortable. As soon as the sun set, thick black bat clouds swept across Redwood Gulch like no movie I ever saw. I knew they were headed for my hair. And owls would start up hoot-t-who, while their prey scuttled through the sagebrush making their way zigzag to the stream, a shiny silver strip in the moonlight. There was an owl as large as a boy, which perched near our tent and watched me when I had to pee, cocking his head from side to side. Grey said it *was* a boy, and not to listen to him. He was an Indian boy who had died on the mountain, Grey said. Below us, if the winds were moving west to east, I could hear the waves crashing on the rocks. It was the Pacific Ocean trying to pull the California coast back down to the depths, Grey said. And if the wind was coming from the east, King City, it was the souls of the Indians massacred on the mountain. And always the coyotes, whatever the wind.

The Big Sur coyotes hunted in packs, like Russian wolves—not like the bad wolf in *Peter and the Wolf* but like the wolves Freud's famous patient the Wolfman feared. Once, as we were walking up the hill to our tent, a deer jumped out in front of us, followed by a run of coyotes. The animals were so close we saw the coyotes' black inner lips ridged like wet tires and the deer's eyes blazed with panic.

These are things I didn't write Margo:

When we got high on mushrooms with Kelly and Oak on the deck, the deep, chewy fungus among us, and I watched Oak and Grey like a hawk—trying to intercept glances, prevent accidental touching; reminding Grey with terms of endearment (honey, darling, dear, sweetheart) that he was *my* husband—that was when I knew Grey *was* Coyote. Just for an instant I knew it and felt sick to my stomach, and then it was as frightening as in the story when the bride peeks in on her husband in a secret room and finds that he *is* a monster and all those boxes are actually bridal coffins and everybody was right about him, even her mother.

And these are the things I did not write Margo:

In the tent, using the flashlight, if I could find it, I watched Grey take his clothes off. I flashed the light on his knobby knees, delicate ankles, hair as black as tar, and his long hatchet face and thin purple lips that ran like a slash across his cruel face. We didn't have all that much sex, because it was so uncomfortable in the tent. Yet when we did, Grey wove a spell over me, whispered to me in a language (wetting my ear and shoulder) I did not understand. Secrets, everything a secret. Or he said nothing.

"Am I too quiet for you?" he asked. "If you know what I mean?"

How would I know? I only knew Aaron, who groaned as if in great pain.

For kundalini, Grey had to concentrate. Furthermore, according to Grey, to lose sperm was to lose a year of life. He needed to keep it all.

However, he couldn't always manage it, and when he did ejaculate he said, "Damn."

And I said, "Sorry."

For I had just shortened his life span by at least a year.

My father would call it the wages of sin.

[**WE DID NOT GET** mail at the end of the road down by the highway as the people in Big Sur did. We were too far south and had to go to the gas station in Gorda to pick up deliveries, which came daily on the mail truck from Monterey. Grey and I went to the gas station about once a week, not really to pick up mail but just to see people other than Kelly and Oak. Grey was friends with Narcissus, who pumped gas, wrote poetry (who didn't in Big Sur?), and had once been a philosophy major at Brooklyn College.

Since I had written Margo in care of her mother in Pacific Grove, I assumed she had received my letter and would respond immediately.

"You don't understand," Grey would tell me. "You left the world behind, you understand what I'm saying?"

Narcissus nodded. "That's right," he said. "You left the world behind." Narcissus had a British accent, had moved to New York from somewhere in the Caribbean, got fed up, and came west.

"Okay, guys, I get it." I left the world behind and yet I wanted a letter.

These profound conversations were held while we drank decadent, imperialistic Coca-Cola in the little store near the gas station. They sold stamps, postcards, things for tourists, who, in their sneakers, Bermuda shorts, and visored hats, would stare at us, the locals, the locos with our dirty feet. The pop was kept in a large red bin of ice. The gas station had its own generator, and was a mecca of civilization compared to our tent.

"Yeah." Grey tilted his head way back to drink in long gulps. He thought the Coke was wonderful, too. I knew that. Just being inside a store was marvelous to me.

Then finally one day, I did get a letter. I looked at the handwriting. "It's my aunt," I said. Grey read over my shoulder on one side, Narcissus on the other.

> *August 12, 1957*
>
> *Dear Zoe,*
>
> *I heard you got married. I didn't even know you were pregnant.*

"My aunt is a card," I explained to Grey. "She's nuts, she tells jokes."

"Well, it is about time you were pregnant." He put his hand on my stomach. I *was* getting fat. Actually I might have missed a period, but hygiene on Gorda Mountain cast all bodily functions into doubt and confusion. I had lost track.

> *I know that love is love and youth is youth and age is wisdom and never the twain shall meet, but your parents had other hopes for you.*

"Hah," I said. "Like work in the dime store?"

"Work in the dime store," Narcissus said.

> *Well, there are many changes in my life. Sorry to say the World Is Your Oyster Ballet School had to close its doors after eighteen consecutive years of successful operation.*

I thought of the rectangular room which was her dance studio, one whole wall mirror, the long barre we held on to when we were doing our barre work. The floor was oak, and at one end was the resin box to rub your ballet slippers in so you did not slip. In the reception room was a free schedule attached to the bulletin board and a pyramid of paper apples with the names of the girls who had done the splits.

"Brush, brush, brush," my aunt would shout out, banging her long pole on the floor to match the rhythm and inspire fear, as we stood at the barre. "Half point, close, full point, close, tendue, press, piqué, piqué, arms in fifth. Shoulders back. Shoulders, shoulders."

The music would stop.

"Ladies and gentlemen, you must stand with your shoulders back."

When I was taking lessons, she still had a piano player. He was a young man, a piano student with a great bunch of hair that fell in his eyes and who smoked cigarettes dribbling out of his mouth until all the keys were gray with fallen ash. The smell in the room was of sweat, smoke, resin, and wood. Recitals once a year. Sometimes, just sometimes, we would be transformed by the music and the tradition into something resembling dance.

I trained a generation of dancers and am proud of it. But, as your father would say: onward and upward. I am now employed in the ready-to-wear department of JCPenney's in Monterey on Alvarado Street. Trying to make the best of it, but least said.

If I had ever been cast in a ballet, it would have been in the role that the famous American Indian prima ballerina, Maria Tallchief, took, that is, the Firebird in *The Firebird*, with music by Stravinsky. The Firebird is not a romantic lead but a part for a tall, solitary woman. The golden orange bird, a woman aflame, is actually a sorceress who saves a prince and his princess from an evil magician, who has erected a wall to the clouds and turned many worthy princes into stone simply by touch. The Firebird helps the one heroic prince defeat the monster with many heads (actually the evil magician) by finding the secret keys for rooms which open into rooms, until, of course, the sanctum sanctorum is reached, and the magician is destroyed. Each key bears the same words:

> *I open the casket in the golden room*
> *That hides the secret of Kastchei's doom.*

In the end, the Firebird flies to the sun, leaving behind a feather, which becomes the prince and princess's dearest possession.

Your mother and father are not at all happy about your marriage.

"Do tell."

They suggest you get an annulment. Actually, in the Mormon Church, you are not really married.

I think my aunt was wrong there.

"Annulment?" Grey asked. "Why does she say that?"

"Oh, it's just family, Grey. You know . . ."

"I'm your family. Didn't you say we were kin?"

"Well."

"We are kin, doesn't that make sense?"

"I don't know why you always ask me if stuff makes sense, Grey. Much of what you say doesn't make sense, is *not* logical."

"White-man sense is not what I mean. What I mean is, we are one and the same. Together."

He took my hand. He kissed the palm. "What I mean is, you are mine, all mine."

"My aunt, I don't know. It doesn't mean anything."

"Your family hates me, and yet I am your husband."

"But . . ."

"Don't you want to be fully human?" Grey asked.

"Oh, yes."

"Well then. I don't think we need letters, do you? You are my wife and that is that."

Narcissus giving me a strange look, whispered to me: "You *are* human, Zoe."

"He means a complete human being, Nars. You know, our other half, the whole hermaphrodite thing, as in Plato."

Narcissus told me once that in an ethics class he had taken, they were hunting for the Good. Thus, they went through the pre-Socratics, Plato, Kant, Wittgenstein, Ayer; and on the last day of class, their teacher (at Brooklyn College) had said, Good Schmood, and taken off with a student he had been doing some good with on his kitchen table, where he also graded their papers. They sped off on a motorcycle, just like Marlon Brando in *The Wild One.*

"Remember," Narcissus said, "*The Wild One*, where the girl asks Brando what he's rebelling against and he says, 'Waddya got?' "

I didn't remember.

"Well," Narcissus says, "that is why I am here at this station, pumping gas at the ends of the earth."

"Hunting the Good?"

"Guess again."

"Rebelling?"

"No, I am here pumping gas."

"You want to do good, huh, Nars? When Grey is not looking, slip it to me. Slip any letter I get to me."

"You mean deceive your husband? Is that a good thing to do?"

"I mean, we don't have to advertise is all I mean."

"All you mean, Zoe, is more than you say, and you just might get both you and me killed."

"Narcissus."

"Yaw?"

"Look in the mirror. I am not your echo."

"Who is asking you to be Echo? Not me, girl."

Narcissus had skin like Margo's, but his hair lay on his head like a pile of little black O's.

[**FOR MY NEXT** letter, I had to sit in the bathroom of the gas station. Actually sitting on a real toilet was a luxury. Even Oak and Kelly with all their gadgets did not have a flush toilet.

I read:

September 30, 1957

Allen Ginsberg is passé. Kerouac is a bad writer. Khrushchev exposed Stalin for the fascist he was in 1956. The Little Rock Nine, now that's where it's at, Zoe.

The Little Rock Nine, Margo? I asked myself. What is that? A musical group? I've never heard of them.

God, Zoe, where are you? On Mars?

Yes, I'm on Mars.

The Little Rock Nine are high school students who insist on going to a white high school in Little Rock, Arkansas, following the letter of the law (Brown vs. the Board of Education, 1954, honeychild) *that states that separate are not equal schools. Have you ever heard of Rosa Parks, the Montgomery bus boycott, Martin Luther King?*

Margo.

I knew you hadn't. You don't read newspapers, right?

I read it, but forgot.

Rather than sit in segregated seating on the bus, the Negro people walked, Zoe. Rosa Parks started it by refusing to leave her seat and go into the colored section. The person who led the boycott, which, by the way, was successful, was Martin Luther King, an articulate young minister.

Where was I when all this happened, Margo?

In never-never land, Zoe, California.

My eyes smart and nose prickles. I can't help it. I look up at the rusted door of my booth. The graffiti are not philosophical.

Oh, Margo, forgive my ignorance.

Listen, I met James Baldwin when he came to Howard for a reading. He is not my spokesman. A fairy, but a Negro one. With huge frog eyes and wonderful hands.
Zoe, are you there? Come in, Zoe. Zoe.

Margo. I am here on the mountain. (Actually in a gas station bathroom with a backed up septic tank.) We live in a tent, bathe in a stream sometimes, cook over a fire. My husband hunts deer and we eat rattlesnakes.

Whatever for? Do you like rattlesnake?

It's like chicken, if you forget what it is.

Why not just eat chicken, then? Isn't that easier?

That's not the point.

What is the point?

Self-sufficiency.

I'm not sure I get it, but why is it more self-sufficient to eat rattlesnake?

You have to live in town, have a drone job, be part of the system to eat chicken.

Well, I could win this quarrel, but let's drop it. What else is new? Why don't you just raise chickens?

I miss you, Margo. When I think of Ginsberg's revelation of the beauty of the world through Blake's poem "Ah, Sunflower," I think Marigold, Margo.

> *Ah, Marigold, weary of time*
> *Who countest the steps of the sun;*
> *Seeking after that sweet golden clime*
> *Where the traveller's journey is done.*

That's nice, but I am not weary of time, Zoe. I am discovering my time, my culture, my generation. Those kids in Little Rock who bravely go to school each day amid threats and shouts have inspired me to be myself.

I am on a wheel of meals, Margo. I'm a campfire girl.

Don't you watch the news, read the newspaper, know what is going on?

No, we don't have electricity.

Why not?

It's the principle.

Of what? Darkness?

Margo.

Sorry. Grey thinks I should lose the shackles of ego, as is prescribed in the Tibetan Book of the Dead, Margo.

Lose your ego? You are just a kid. I am trying, with my compadres, to develop an ego. Book of the Dead? Remember Emmett Till, killed in 1955?

"You think you're as good as we are?" they asked Emmett Till.

Not No, sir, not Yes, sir, not I am a human being created equal, sir, in the eyes of God. But such a simple, casual Yeah. Yeah, I think I'm as good as you are. And so they had to dredge the muddy Tallahatchie for his body. Yeah. Zoe, one must have ego. As an eighteen-year-old, are you ready to throw off the shackles of ego? It sounds like mumbo jumbo to me. In fact, it sounds like brainwashing. How are you to define yourself except through ego? People that ask you to lose the shackles of ego usually have very big ones themselves, Zoe. I'd look out.

"Who is that letter from?" Grey asks through the door. "I know you are reading a letter in there."

"My best friend."

"I am your best friend."

"You are my husband."

Suddenly the door is wrenched open.

"Do you want me to pull you off the pot?"

"God, Grey!" I cry.

"Pull up your pants and let's get out of here."

"It is just a letter. Close the door please."

Narcissus loomed behind him like a shadow.

"Close the door, man," Narcissus said.

"Tell her to get out here, then."

"I'm coming, Grey." I pull my pants up, flush the toilet like I'm using it, run the water in the sink like I'm washing my hands, stuff the letter in my pocket like a magician doing a disappearing act, and step out of the bathroom like I was entitled to be there.

"What's up, man?" Narcissus put his hands on Grey's shoulder.

"My wife is deceiving me."

"It's my best friend, Grey. It's not a deception," I say.

"*I* am your best friend."

"From high school."

"Why don't you read it out in the open?"

"Because the last letter I got upset you so much you didn't want me to get letters, and I think I am entitled to a letter when I get one. It is addressed to *me*, has meaning for *me*. It is my letter, Grey."

"Come on, man." Narcissus tried to pull Grey around and take him to the little store. "Want a Coke? It's on me."

"It's a conspiracy," Grey said, "and I gave you my name, my protection, my whole life."

"Grey, it's just a letter."

I pressed my hand to my pocket. How had it gotten to this? It was *just* a letter.

"Give it to me." He grabbed at my hip.

"No, it's mine." I shielded my pocket with my hands.

"Let the woman have a little privacy, man."

Some tourists who have pulled up to the gas station are looking at us. This is a show.

"Privacy, privacy? I am going to build her a whole stone house," Grey said, "five-sided, like an Indian peyote house. And she wants privacy? That's a white idea. In the tribe everybody got together to dig the ground with digging sticks, scooping the earth with their hands and piling it up into a low wall. Then they erected a center pole as big as a tree."

"That's great, man. Let's just take it easy, huh?"

"Give me the letter, Zoe." I bunched it up inside my pocket, held on to it with my fist. It was like a crumpled gardenia now, and I could remember—was it a hundred years ago?—that I wanted a boy, a man, somebody to give me a corsage, take me to the prom. Margo and I used to buy a gardenia every month in honor of Billie Holiday, consigning it to gardenia Valhalla (her pop-up garbage pail in the Robinsons' très suave kitchen) when the edges of the petals got brown and curly.

"I have a right to have a letter," I said, cringing. "What has gotten into you? Why are you so mad? I have never seen you like this."

As Margo would say, the Big Switcheroo. Husbands are dads and dads are husbands, and in the end they were men. In fact, Grey's fist was clenched, and his jaw rigid.

"Here," I said, shoving the crumpled letter into his hand like a bunch of Kleenex to wipe his nose. "I've already read it. You can't take it away from me unless you cut my head off."

"That's a dangerous line, Zoe. Are you going to say, Over my dead body?"

The look on his face terrified me. So much hate. How could he hate me so much, so suddenly? We had come down to the gas station peacefully. The night before we had done a few mushrooms. We had had coffee, and Kelly had given us some eggs, so we actually had fried eggs for breakfast. I had cleaned the camp up. The sun was shining. Fall was the best time on the coast, the days full of warmth and softness, the nights cool. We had made love the night before, made love. Was it the mushrooms?

"And your shit stinks, Zoe."

I burst into tears. "All shit stinks, what a thing to say." I began to sob.

"It's the septic tank, Grey, man," Narcissus said softly. "Leave the lady be, man."

"Isn't it your job to clean up the female crap, Narcissus?"

"Naw, man, they got a woman."

"What are you going to do with my letter?" I moaned. I had planned to fold it neatly and put it in my jewelry box, the one thing I brought from home, my little box with the twirling ballerina. The actual letter *did* mean something to me. It was in green ink, of course, and in Margo's lovely handwriting, and it was fragile and beautiful, like cloth, like a handkerchief, and reminded me of Desdemona's handkerchief that had first belonged to Othello's mother. I'm talking about the actual thin airmail paper. As an object, that letter was precious, precocious, and precarious to me. I wanted to press out the wrinkles I had made, unfold the pages, reread, kiss it like the priest does the Bible in the Catholic Church. Suddenly I loved my letter.

"Watch." Grey walked across the highway, and, ripping the letter into little triangles and squares, he threw the pieces over the cliff.

"Ah." I put my hand on my heart. My letter was not a sea gull or a handkerchief, but confetti, the year's end.

"Get in the truck before I beat the shit out of you."

"Grey, you don't have to talk to me like that."

"Hey, man, take it easy, you don't have to talk like that to the woman."

The tourists were watching us avidly, confirming all their fondly held notions about Big Sur. It was the fifties everywhere else.

"Don't put yourself between man and wife, Narcissus."

"Grey, man, I just don't want to see anybody hurt is all, man."

"Get in the truck, Zoe, or I will beat the shit out of you."

I stood by the road, hoping to die, but not wanting to be beaten.

"You don't believe me?" he said, glaring in my face. "You don't think I could hurt you?"

I got in the truck, closed the door, stared straight ahead.

"Someday you are going to be fat," Grey said, slamming his door.

"Oh, yeah, is that so? You, too." I regretted it the moment I said it, but, God, I had to say it.

He slapped me hard.

I didn't turn my face. I didn't cry.

"Grey, man. You don't have to do that to the lady, man."

"Go clean the shit," Grey said out the window as we took off.

I didn't turn to look back. I kept staring straight ahead.

"So let's have no more letters, Zoe. Indians don't write letters." He put his hand on my thigh.

"Margo lives too far for smoke signals, Grey." Again, my mouth was acting on its own.

He tightened his grip.

"When are you going to learn?"

"Ouch, Grey, you are hurting me."

"Yeah, well, don't make fun of my people, you hear."

"I'm not."

"Zoe, you want to find yourself out on the street? I took you out of the gutter, you know that?"

"No, you didn't."

"Listen, Zoe, when I met you, you didn't know which end was up."

"That's not the gutter."

"It's not exactly the street either."

"I was . . . young." We had been married almost three months. I was eighteen years old, and it occurred to me that I had made a terrible mistake in marrying Grey and coming down the coast.

"I don't know what it takes to put the fear of God into you, Zoe, but . . ."

"You are not God, and the real ones do not require fear."

"Don't give me that, Zoe. Do you want to turn the other cheek and get another slap?"

We had started back down the highway. The beauty of the landscape betrayed me every inch of the way. How could it be so lovely yet so indifferent, the hills, the cliffs, the trees, the ocean. Why didn't the flowers shrivel up and die, and the foam on the tips of the waves be rabies.

Sometimes, Margo, I said to her in my mind, the beauty of the natural world is too much. Sometimes we can't handle all this beauty, which we didn't make. Is that it? I have yet to understand my relationship to it, but it overwhelms me and haunts me. I know it cares not a whit whether I live or die.

"You know I love you," Grey said as we drove along. "You know this is for your own good, Zoe." His tone of voice had changed. "Zoe, talk to me, baby."

Baby. The magic word.

"I am thinking about dinner, Grey." I turned to him.

"Zoe, give me a smile?" He was coaxing.

"Please?"

"Please." His demeanor had softened.

"Pretty please with sugar on it?"

"Pretty please with sugar on it."

"And I am sorry, Zoe, and will never hit you again?"

"And I am sorry, Zoe, and will never, never hit you again."

I smiled.

"You want a hamburger, a real hamburger at Slade's Hot Springs, and after that, we can go for a hot mineral bath? How about that?"

He patted my knee.

"A real hamburger, Grey?"

"Sure, anything for my girl," and he turned the truck around and headed north toward the hot springs, the wonderful tubs of mineral water on the open ledge overlooking the ocean.

"The door, Grey?"

"What door?"

"The door in the stone house."

"The door will be a smoke hole in the middle of the room."

"So you have to go through fire to get out?"

That was the idea, Margo, I continued in my head, walk on coals. We don't own a mirror either, though I sneak glimpses in the truck mirror. Just checking, I explain to Grey, just checking to see if I'm still here. Sometimes I don't know anymore, and, staring at Grey, I see myself. It is a weird narcissism, speaking of Narcissus. Grey's stern face is more familiar than my own. Yet sometimes I hate him. I hate his teeth and his nose, his fingernails and his penis. I hate him. I hate him. But after that, after I get rid of the hate, I realize he is just a man, not a monster, not an animal, but simply a man trying to exist, and I feel sorry for him, for me, for all of us. Dear Margo, I am filled with pity for all of us.

That night when we returned from the hot springs and crawled into our sleeping bag, I had a strange dream. It was in black-and-white, no colors.

I dreamt that the stone house was built, that there were stone walls that went up into the clouds. I was outside, right in front, and two birds, two large black crows, fell from the sky. I looked inside the house and it was full of birds, not pretty twittery birds but a huge wild turkey and big gray owls and lots of crows. They all held smaller birds in their beaks.

[**THE OLDEST**, biggest stones Grey called the Grandfathers. He carried those in the wheelbarrow. I hauled the babies, dragging them in a cloth behind me. We ate watercress from the stream, brewed tea from the yarrow flowers, made salad from the mustard greens that grew wild along the coast highway. We ate berries and abalones and mussels, fish, rattlesnake, and, yes, Grey hunted deer with an old secondhand rifle.

Before going on the hunt, he would pray to the Great Spirit, and to the spirit of the deer he would ask for forgiveness. And it was very important that every part of the deer be used, not just the meat, but the teeth, the hooves, and the bones. The viscera were buried in our new vegetable garden, the eyes under flower seeds. I imagined the flowers looking up at me, their eyes lashed in petals.

Grey used an old .30-30 caliber Winchester with level action to kill deer and a .22 for rabbits. As soon as the deer's eyes glazed over in death, he would field-dress it where it lay, not let it get cold. Using his hunting knife, he would slit a long line from the asshole to the neck, being careful not to cut too far below the surface of the skin. He did not want to cut the bladder or any internal organs that would taint the meat. Then he would split the rib cage and cut the windpipe and a small membrane between the lungs and the intestines so that he could pull all the internal organs out of the body cavity in one piece. While it was still warm, he would urinate on the skin to keep it soft and would scrape the fat away. There was an old oak stump near our tent which had been collecting rainwater for God knows how long. Grey used the water, which had absorbed tannic acid from the stump, to work over the skin so that it would stay soft and usable. He had made a kind of tepee of long sticks, and on this he hung the skinned carcass for butchering. Soon, he said, we would have a smoke hut, where we would keep a smoldering fire going in order to smoke the meat. But as it was, we could hang thin strips in the trees to dry for jerky, and other pieces we wrapped in burlap sacking and hung up in the Bay Grove.

173

Once, twin babies had fallen out of their dead mother, white silk amniotic filaments twisted around their perfect bodies. I was reminded of my mother and aunt. Their mother had died in childbirth, and that is why their father came from Armenia to America. He died long before I was born.

"Get away," Grey said, brandishing his machete. "This is not Bambi."

The pieces of wrapped deer flesh dangling from the tree limbs in the cool Bay Grove seemed grotesque to me, and also magical, as if bestowing on the grove some sort of dangerous power, like that of the burial ground the Donner Party had supposedly walked through, thus incurring the retribution of the spirits. I wouldn't go down there. Grey would have to fetch the roast, the stew meat. Walking back up to me in his sandals with his gunnysack package tied in twine, he looked like something out of the early days of Christianity, when sorcerers and magicians, snake charmers and miracle workers, and rabbis claiming heavenly hereditary rights walked the Middle East. Grey, of course, would be a Gnostic, one of those who believed the world was created by a cruel demiurge, the trickster himself, Coyote, and that all institutions, the Church especially, were corruptions of the original enlightenment.

"Ah, yes," he would tell me at night, when we sat together staring into the campfire, mesmerized by the color and dance of flame.

"Coyote, spent and weary from his work in the garden, tucked tired Penis between his legs and climbed back up the hill on his four paws, clawing the earth for a foothold, his tongue hanging out long and dangly in the heat, his snake suit shed in the bush. That night he lifted his head, howled in the wilderness. I am Coyote. I am Coyote."

Coyote and his penis reminded me of the little boxes kids carried around, with a hidden hole in the bottom and a supposedly dismembered thumb resting in cotton. Or Van Gogh's ear. Later, I was to hear of strings of ears brought back from Vietnam. And later than that, I was to read of one of Carl Jung's dreams in which the penis was enthroned, a crown on his head.

[**K E L L Y ,** our benefactor, said that when his mother had been a hairdresser of the Hearst mistress in San Simeon, the basement of the castle had a beauty parlor and a wardrobe department, as in a movie set. To me, the whole castle was like a movie set. It rose up twenty miles south of us like a mirage. I imagined William Randolph Hearst as played by Orson Welles in *Citizen Kane*, that is, dashing and relentless, the king and his retinue. I conjectured a Great Dane, and several eunuchs for the castle. The king's falcons would be kept in a royal aviary, and the king himself with a heavy crown and in a voice of gold would pace and mumble on the ramparts of his palace. I imagined a printing press in the basement, where the Hearst newspapers would be printed and then taken by Piper Cub to L.A., thrown like pamphlets over the Los Angeles flatlands. The angels.

Rosebuds.

Capitalism forever.

The Hearst castle was built on what was called the Enchanted Hill, with balconies, grills, columns, a Greek portico, an indoor and outdoor pool, a mile-long pergola walk, a twelfth-century Cistercian cloister, the Four Ages of Man (a tapestry cycle), sixty-six Attic vases, a French Renaissance chimney piece, the Methuen cup, to name but a few.

Meanwhile Kelly's mother did
pompadours and

twists and
soft curls and
pageboys and rolls and
French braids and
shags and bobs
and Cleopatra,
roaring twenties
Bad Girl bangs
in the basement.

"Oh, the farmer in the dell," Kelly sang.

"The farmer takes a wife." Oak's voice. "Heigh-ho, the derry-oh."

Oak's grandmother was a silent-film actress, like Gloria Swanson in *Sunset Boulevard*. They had tons of money in that family and the women lounged about in evening gowns, holding long cigarette holders between their perfect teeth, their eyes rimmed in kohl.

"And the wife takes, like, a child," Kelly continued.

Oak smiled cryptically, running her tongue over her lips.

I had to concentrate to get it all straight, the chain of inheritance, the chain reaction resulting in the A-bomb, which would destroy my life.

Hearst; his mistress; Kelly's mother, who was dead now, but who, when old and crazy, lived in a tin lean-to; and Oak's grandmother, who made her mark before the talkies, rolling her eyes wildly and clutching her handsome chest; and Oak herself, sitting in L.A. in Pershing Square, where all the bums hung out and crazies crooned and the beggars spat, sitting there stoned out of her mind; and Kelly, passing by, saw Oak, a.k.a. Joy, the most beautiful woman in the world, sitting silently without shoes. He sat across from her speaking the language of eyes for six whole hours, until darkness sliced across the dirty, dingy palm trees.

Finally, he approached her. This is what he said:

I want to bathe your feet like bad, like mad.

He wanted to show in one symbolic gesture that he was her humble servant and that, if she let him, he would bring her to his yurts, like crazy, man.

No doubt, as in the household staffs of old when the mistress was brought home, the yurt goats lined up on the main roof, the chickens stopped pecking, the marijuana fields held steady, and even the ocean itself paused at polite arrest.

"This is the kitchen yurt, the meditation yurt, the bathhouse yurt, the bed yurt, and the main yurt."

A row of mushroom houses, all painted differently in rainbow pastels. All yours.

"Stay with me, sweet Oak, and I will make yurt high, 150 percent Dizzy Gillespie, no jive."

And then on a trip to San Francisco one rainy night, ducking into the Cafe Trieste, around the corner from the Hungry I and up the street from City Lights Books—the Cafe Trieste, which had an ancient copper ceiling with long hanging green light fixtures and a wall plastered with photographs of patrons and patron saints, Joe DiMaggio for one—he met an Indian.

The watchword was How. The password was Solid, man.

And it was fine.

[**SATURDAY**. I think it was a Saturday. I had lost count of days. Was it October still or November yet? We had stopped visiting the gas station. No more letters. I hadn't seen Narcissus in I don't know how long. Once, Grey and I had been to Slade's Hot Springs for a mineral bath, smoking a little, sitting together on the men's side in a large tub in an open room overlooking the ocean. The waves, high that night, had flooded the floor, while the hot steam of the bath met the cold air of the ocean.

But otherwise we stayed stoned up in the camp or would go down to Kelly's. The rains were going to start soon, and only two walls of the stone house had gone up. Grey was talking about getting a trailer if we could haul it up. He had one thousand dollars left of the forged paychecks.

"You think we should get a trailer?" Grey asked Kelly that Saturday when we found a lot of activity going on in Yurtland.

For one, Kelly and Oak were up and about, and the two Mexican men who helped were cleaning and their wives were cooking in the kitchen yurt.

"A trailer, cool, man."

"WeeWee and PeePee had, like, a headless chicken race," Oak said.

"I thought you were vegetarians," I said. In fact, they made a very big deal of it.

"Guests," Kelly said. "Mucho guests. The harvest festival, that's why the chickens had to go, a goat or two, and Porky, a kind of luau thing."

"The geese we gave you?"

"Yup. The geese had to go."

Oak arched her well-placed eyebrows. She was wearing a beautiful sky-blue dress, flannel, red trim, seeded with little red hearts, a Lanz original.

"It's going to be like a party," she told me. "Like stay, like come."

"I look terrible, I can't go to a party."

"You look," Oak stepped back, tried to focus, "like you need a good bath."

"Could I use your mirror?"

I saw a sunburned skinny-tall waif with a pot belly in a pair of Grey's jeans and flannel shirt. Her hair was a nest for spiders, and her skinny white arms were crisscrossed with scars. Her glasses were dirty and scratched. Her thick lips were cracked and puffy. I looked wild and slightly mad, as if just found in the forest; perhaps I was a feral child or a wood nymph gone astray. I could not remember when I last saw myself in a mirror, for, of course, Grey didn't allow them. We were to look at each other and nature alone. Early on, I sneaked looks in the truck mirror, but lately I had become afraid of how I might look. Rightly so.

"Let me," she said, taking a comb. "Sit, like, be still, and I will contend with that mop of hair."

"Why are the guests coming?"

"Well." Oak's concentration floated off for a minute. "Ah, the consummation ceremony, that's why."

"Did you really have a headless chicken race?" I asked.

"Well"—Oak cocked her head to one side, gave me a little smile—"I think so. Yes, I think we did, and I was the one to chop off their heads." She made a little karate chop motion. "Kelly couldn't, like, do it. We are having, like, a big celebration tonight, the harvest festival *and* consummation ceremony. Did I tell you? Well, it will be quite the thing." She got up off her bed, did a little twirl.

"Oh."

Harvest of what? Consummation of what? I knew I was naïve and should know what everybody was talking about. But, frankly, I couldn't even inhale well. Embarrassingly, I had not known my astrological sign when I moved to Big Sur. I had only read the word *Zen* in poems, never heard it come from people's lips. I thought only crazy people and poets had hallucinations. India, to me, was a place where people starved to death. I didn't know about the writer Hermann Hesse, although Thomas Mann's *The Magic Mountain* was one of my favorite books. In fact, I had betrayed my ignorance in a hundred stupid ways. But I didn't care. Yet, sitting next to Oak while she combed my hair was to enter a different state of being. It was a low, buzzing, sensuous dream-state. I was in her hands. I wished she would never stop brushing my hair ever, ever. If that were not enough, she took me to the outdoor showers they had on a little hill behind the main yurt facing the ocean. Taking off her dress, too, she washed me with her sea sponges and soaps made of pressed fruit oil—apricot, green apple, avocado, cucumber. She lathered and rinsed me. Everywhere. Even Grey did not touch me there, even I did not touch me in those places. It was a shock. In fact, I had a little spasm or tremor. Frightening, yes, but also very pleasurable.

"Grey doesn't, like, go down on you?" Oak asked.

"Like, down?"

"You know." She looked out at sea, turned back to me, stuck her tongue out, wiggled it. "Zoe, you look, like, has your period come?"

"I don't know."

"I mean, well, you know, your monthly."

"I've lost track."

It was easy to lose track. For instance, I knew it was September. No, it was October. I think it was. But the day, the day of the week? Saturday.

"You are, like, out of it."

"Out of what?"

"Well, let me see, just about, like, everything."

"We have lots of supplies."

"Zoe, you don't know your own body, do you?"

"I do," I insisted.

"Is he, and don't take this wrong, good?"

"What do you mean by good?"

"In the sack?"

"Sack?"

"Rack?"

"As in torture?"

"Like sex? Do you know what sex is?"

"Oh, that?"

"Yes, that."

"Well, he practices kundalini, you know, withdrawal of the sperm, so that when it's time to ejaculate, he sucks it back in and up his spine and into his head where it, well, the Big Bang."

"Hmmm, really? Always?"

"Well, sometimes some leaks out."

"I think, like, some did. Look at yourself."

"You think?"

"You are definitely pregnant, Zoe, maybe five months."

That was the most emphatic thing I had ever heard Oak say, and when I looked at myself I realized that it might, like, be true. My breasts were large and sensitive. And a dark line ran between my belly button and my pubis. My stomach was rounded. The wife takes a child?

"So, does he, like, attain it?"

"Attain what?" Pregnant, a child.

"Satori, enlightenment?"

"Oh, sure." I didn't know, of course. Grey and his mysterious ways. Sometimes he said he almost had it, almost got there. Unlike him and all the authorities on the subject which he quoted, Chinese and Indian from India, I did not think that kundalini was good for him. I thought it might lead to prostate cancer or impotence. I didn't think withheld sperm added years to your life, although I could have been very wrong. Sometimes I had to stroke his PC muscle, his pubococcygeus muscle, between the penis and anus, to get the sperm going up so he could have his High Sex. While he was at the zenith, I was at the nadir. Oh well.

"What are you going to do?"

"Do?"

I was thinking about it.

"I am, too."

I wasn't listening to Oak. I was listening to: pregnant. Not a hole in my stomach, not a negative, an ulcer, but a positive, something growing there, not a cancer, runaway bad cells which eat you alive, not the stomach, rather, the uterus, or was it womb, a warm, cozy room of a place. Well, come on in, make yourself comfortable. Knee grows, or did the toes come first, connecting with the ankle bone. I had seen pictures of the transparent, veined head of a growing fetus. It looked like a space child, something otherworldly. I felt wonderful, absolutely full of wonder. I suddenly wished Aaron could know.

"You're a twin?" We were outside, naked, and having a conversation crucial to my life, another life. I looked down at my stomach. I could see my toes. And I could see the little tuft of red pubic hair, the beard on my chinny-chin-chin.

"Pregnant," Oak said. "I am pregnant also. We *are* twins. Twins in pregnancy. I am six months."

"Maybe I'm not, not really."

"Come on, Zoe, who are you, like, kidding?"

Oak had real towels, sumptuous and huge. She spread one out on the rock next to the showers and rubbed me down with her perfumed oils. I thought of the Three Wise Men—gold, frankincense, myrrh. Myrrh was like purr.

She dressed me in a long filmy shirt, the color of saffron, and pants a deep brown. In my hair she wove poppies and mustard flowers, and she put gold earrings in my ears. They were thin hoops filled in with a crosshatch of gold, a web of golden filaments. I looked like a harem girl, a princess, a Greek nymph. I think I looked beautiful. For the first time since my wedding, I felt beautiful.

"Does Grey, well, know, like, you're pregnant?"

"No."

"Well. Maybe, you know, perhaps, it might work out well that you tell him tonight."

"I don't know." She made it sound like something to announce over the radio. Request time, dedicated to the one I love. From Zoe to Grey, "Dream, Dream, Dream."

"And I am going to do my own birthing at home," she continued.

Something clicked in. The smoke screen cleared. I was suddenly rather lucid.

"Isn't that a little dangerous, Oak?"

"I, like, hate hospitals, don't you?"

"No, I don't. I was in one once. It was okay."

"Not my style. Cold, serial."

"You mean sterile, but for a reason. Bacteria doesn't grow in cold."

"Impersonal."

"Actually, I would have died without a hospital."

"Technology all over the place, metal and clamps."

"Yeah, but sometimes you need it."

"Not me. Like, natural, Zoe, natural all the way."

"Babies often die naturally."

"They die, like, in hospitals, too. It's, like, a matter of principle."

"Is it? I think it's a matter of practicality."

"The body has its reasons . . ."

"You mean the heart."

"To each his own," she said.

"To each *her* own," I said.

"Oh, Zoe, always the little sufferjette."

"Suffragette."

She led me out on the deck, where Kelly and Grey were sitting cross-legged. Plates of milk formed a circle around them.

"This," Kelly said, "this we offer you, Erzulie."

He held up a weed. Bunches of them were being dried on the rafters underneath the yurt, the winter stash. He then handed me what looked to be a cigar.

"Smoke, little mole," Grey commanded. "It's been a good harvest."

"Who is Erzulie?" I asked Oak. But her eyes were closed and her hands were open at her knees.

"Erzulie is the voodoo moon goddess," Kelly said. "The goddess of love."

"Oh."

"There is a little hash mixed in," Kelly said.

"You look," and Grey hesitated, sought the word, "just wonderful, Zoe. Do you hear what I'm saying?"

"Oak made me beautiful." I closed my eyes and I felt that I was back up the hill in the tent and could hear everything around me, all the animals, and the sky itself had a sound. It was a *hmm*, an endless, low hum, the hum of the heart of the world, like the beautiful voice which came out of the girl's mouth on our wedding day. Grey was unbuttoning my shirt. The tent flap was open and the moonlight spilled on my breasts. Milk, the nights are milk, the day is meat. His clothes were off and he was kneeling in front of me. I remembered in *Lady*

Chatterley's Lover the gardener's pubic hair. Was it aflame? Did Lady Chatterley worship at its shrine, like the little stone phalluses in Greek gardens?

"Your totem pole," I said to Grey.

He smiled. "Yours, Delta Queen."

Was it then? Had a little leaked out that night?

Or was it from the very first time when he had let himself spill out to me in a great torrent at the leather house, skinned alive? It *was* then, way back before we were married, right after Aaron died.

"Perhaps many people might be here, sometime soon," Oak said.

"They will converge from all points of the compass."

Kelly was now drawing pictures on the deck with colored sand. He was actually dropping pictures between his fingers.

"I don't know about those pictures," Grey said. "Who taught you?"

"An Indian."

"Not supposed to. Those are Hopi sandpainting, and they are made only by medicine people, made in the morning and erased by night, used for healing, and are not to be seen by just anybody."

"We are not anybody, Grey."

"You are doing the twins, the God of War and the God of Recreation. The pranksters. They are only to be used in ceremonies, sacred ceremonies or . . ."

"Or what, man?"

Oak said, "The gods will descend tonight all right. But until then, let us nap."

Grey seemed uneasy, but the four of us went into their bedroom and lay down on their bed. It was boy, girl, boy, girl. We held hands like children at a kindergarten nap. I didn't think I could fall asleep, but the next thing I knew I had awakened and the new moon was showing between the diaphanous curtains which framed the doorway. Oak, Grey, and Kelly were gone, but I could hear sounds of laughter and music.

I stepped out on the deck.

And I could have stepped out into another world.

A caravan of cars rounded the point from Gorda gas station, looking like a string of Christmas lights. And people, as if springing from the hills and roots, swarmed down on to the compound, the yurts. Each

circular building was lit up. On the bottom, kitchen yurt, Kelly's three
goats were grazing on the grass top. A group of Haitians, it looked like,
with their tall drums had already assembled on the main deck and were
beating a slow even rhythm. Flute players in medieval gear were tuning
up by the bathhouse. More people converged from the highway. I felt
I was at a king's feast or an Oriental bazaar. There were minstrels and
a snake charmer with what looked like a python wrapped around her
shoulder, only she was a man shaved and made up, and jugglers and
acrobats, men in women's dresses and women in men's suits and work
boots, girls in tiaras and men with long, flowing beards. There was a
man with a monkey on his back, and a tall woman on stilts in a bunny
costume with holes cut out for her breasts and pubis.

Where was Grey in this costume ball?

Oak had vanished, too.

The line of lit bug eyes wound around the highway. The caravan
of cars was still coming.

I went down to the gardens, up to the bathhouse, past the open,
filmy curtains of the meditation yurt. Just Kelly in a full lotus. I found
a gaggle of women in the kitchen cooking a curry. There was a couple
copulating in the Japanese garden very politely. Oh, excuse me.

I could hear the drums again, and the faint breathy notes of
instruments, as if tuning up before the symphony concert. By the bathhouse some people were standing on their heads humming *ommmmmm*.

I wondered where Grey was.

In the shadows a group of men formed what looked like a cha-
cha line. Somebody snickered back in a girl's voice: "Little Bo-Peep has
lost her sheep."

And then, finally, among the melon vines, the baby cantaloupes,
I found Grey. He and Oak were sitting knee to knee, passing the pipe
silently. The peace pipe.

"What is the consummation ceremony?" I asked.

Grey looked annoyed. "Sh."

"Ask, like, one of the L.A. people," Oak said. She turned back to
Grey, put a flat hand on his cheek.

"You're, like, so, so . . ." she said.

I felt confused. What was going on? But, of course, I had been
drinking wine and smoking, and the air was thick with incense and
hash.

I stumbled back up to the deck. A group of people in identical Mexican garments were weaving back and forth, chanting in a line.

"La cucaracha."

"Who are they?" I asked a brown man, standing next to the door in a serape. It was Narcissus.

"The chorus line," he said.

"Oh. What is a consummation ceremony?"

He turned to look at me, and I could see painted on his brown forehead a black spade.

"Long time, no see," he said.

"Is it like an Alice tea party?"

"Alice B. Toklas?" he asked.

"Wonderland. You know, the cards."

"Ah yes, yes. The Mad Hatter will be here soon."

"He is to officiate?"

"Oh no, Cupid officiates. Cupid and Psyche."

"Who are you supposed to be?"

"I am Narcissus, of course. Black Narcissus."

I looked up in the sky.

"Yes," Narcissus said. "The full moon, and the stars do come down, each constellation. We can almost touch them. Orion. The Bear. Follow the drinking gourd, my dear."

A woman in a long peasant skirt, no blouse, and Indian bracelets on her ankles was going about with a tray of dates with coconut shreds and slivered almonds. Figs. Cashew nuts dipped in honey. Seeds and raisins.

"Sweetmeats for the consummation ceremony, tasties and savories, food of the spheres," she called out. "Get your sweetmeats."

The peyote buttons being passed around were rubbery and dark green. The Baja. They were dried out and hard to chew.

The mushrooms had little lungs, accordion pleats. There were pills, too, like the ones my aunt kept in her antique pillbox of bright mosaic chips.

"Nice breasts," Narcissus said. "I hear she was Miss Clear Lake 1956."

Another woman followed her, a Negro woman, with a silver tray of rolled cigarettes. She was dressed like a cigarette girl in a bar, with a sequined front, tutu net skirt, and a perky little pillbox hat perched to one side of her head. She could have been in a fancy nightclub in a big city, so I asked her.

"A consummation ceremony," the cigarette woman said looking up at the sky, "is doing the nasty."

"Fragmento delicioso," another woman chirped in.

"Flagrante delicto, you mean." It was Narcissus.

"They make love in front of us so we can see," the sweetmeat woman explained.

"Why?" I thought of my father's vision of Sodom and Gomorrah.

"Why? Why, you ask?" Narcissus spread his cape. "In the olden days, my dear, at the time of the pagans and the Druids, when there were men in long beards and women in rough clothes, the ceremony would take place in the fields, the priest and his wife in the furrows, the prince and his princess on the mounds and in the valley, by moonlight, in the spring of the year, to consecrate the ground, make it fertile. Seed for seed, I say unto you."

"They did it last year when they got together," the cigarette lady said, "and it was such a success they wanted to do it again."

I imagined one of the bishops of the church of Latter-day Saints in Salinas with his wife, a frumpy, grumpy woman, out in the lettuce fields, which always smelled of fertilizer. Or maybe in Gilroy, garlic capital of the world, or Castroville, the artichoke capital of the world.

Consummation ceremony. Come one, come all. I visualized the Mormon man, stepping out of his trousers awkwardly, having to hold on to his wife's shoulder, his sorry, pallid, pale wobble of a penis shriveled like a little peanut above his dingdangly longdaddy balls. His wife would slip out of her flowered silk dress and rayon slip the color of cantaloupe meat, undo her garters, roll down her stockings, unfasten her girdle. Her flesh would pucker and puff, have little blotches of veins and pockets of bruises. Maybe she would belch at the moon. Maybe he would fart from nervousness. The congregation would be lined up at the sidelines ready to cheer them on. The wife would have breasts like pears and a stomach like the Venus of Willendorf. The sidelines would be chanting something from Carl Orff's *Carmina Burana*, and at the moment of consummation there would be an eclipse of the moon, a total eclipse. And then the heavens would crack open, and the gods and the goddesses would march down, a ghost train, a Jacob's ladder, like the angels in the opera *Hansel and Gretel*, and bless the fields and the orchards.

"Let the consummation ceremony begin," a small woman dressed as a king's herald announced.

The deck was cleared with a heavy sigh. Everybody pushed back under the eaves of the yurt. I felt like a worm under the ledge of a mushroom.

"Let the drummers step forth."

The drummers stepped forth and set up a cadence.

"They're Jamaicans," Narcissus said. "And the drums are imported from Haiti."

"Gee whiz."

Narcissus looked at me strangely.

"Are you from there, Narcissus?" He was a Negro, yes, but definitely not American.

"Trinidad. Calypso, the land of the scarlet ibis, yes, dear."

"Let the flute players begin tootling."

The flute players appeared. Less disciplined than the drummers, they had to tune up again.

"Give me an A," somebody said.

A flat, A sharp, and B flat. I think there was even a G.

Around the deck, as in the first theater in California, in Monterey, they had candles shielded in tin cans. When the drums crescendoed and the flute players struck their assorted A's in unison, all the animals, the remaining chickens, ducks, dogs, and cats in the pens below the bottom yurt, set up a howl and a wail. One of their members, poor Porky Pig, was being roasted underground Hawaiian style, and the geese were gone, their long necks twisted, their honking throats stilled.

A short woman in a sari and thongs stepped forth, rang a little bell.

"Let the revelry begin."

I thought of the midsummer night's eve, all the reversals, the people with animal heads, the fairies, the confusion as to who was what. I shivered, remembering that I was pregnant.

A man in motley stepped forth with a long trumpet. He played something that sounded like the call at the beginning of the horse races. Then a guitar began a slow flamenco. Above it were the shrill, out-of-tune notes of the flutes.

"In the beginning," a low voice began, "there was the goddess."

"Oh, brother," Narcissus said. "Not that old chestnut."

Oak stepped forth out of the darkness. She was draped in veils. Her handmaidens lifted them one by one until Oak was naked. The candlelight flickered up, illuminated her large, rounded stomach, the knots of her buttocks, her hair, her taut, full breasts.

I felt like throwing up.

"She has the neck of a swan, the back of a ballerina, the tits of Aphrodite, the ass of Helen, and the heart of a villain," Narcissus said.

"What?"

"Oh, I know these people," he said softly to me. "Big time. They wheel, they deal. Oak has the heart of a pineapple."

"Does a pineapple have a heart?"

"What do you think?"

"What is Kelly's heart?"

"A saint or a coward, take your pick. But he manages to make a bundle."

"He gave Grey the land," I defended.

"Yes, I know. But listen, sweetie, you can't do anything with that land without more water. You can't farm it. You can't even have livestock. There is maybe enough water for one household. You think if it was worth anything, people would not have developed it?"

"We live there."

"I know. But what if somebody has to go to work, where are they going to work without driving for a good two or more hours? When the rains come, the highway will fill up with rock slides, and the road up to the house will be completely washed away. You'll be trapped. Always look a gift horse in the mouth."

"Narcissus."

"Yeah, I know, shut up."

The snake charmer stepped forth and put the snake across Oak's shoulders. As Oak danced, it streamed down between her breasts and her legs.

"Behold Isis," the voice said.

Oak kissed the snake on the tongue.

"Behold the snake."

"It's a python," Narcissus said. "They can be nasty."

Oak straddled the snake, rubbed herself against the dry scales.

"But the goddess was lonely," the voice said. "And so out of clay and her own wetness she created man, the Green Man."

"I wonder if they have some cold beer," Narcissus said.

And then suddenly there was Kelly. Kelly was already naked, and small rings of flowers decorated his erect penis and streamed out of his anus, and leaves fell from his mouth, and he was painted green. When he kissed Oak, the snake embraced them both.

And then, without announcement, coming up from the shadows, was Grey, Grey also naked except for his boots, and, either invited or not, he became part of the drama. He knelt in front of Oak and holding her legs, pulled her toward his face.

"What is he going to do?" I gripped Narcissus. My heart climbed my throat. I was going to choke on it.

"Looks like going down or going up. One or the other."

"It's Grey, Narcissus, can't you tell. It's my husband."

"Oh dear, trouble in paradise."

"Wait . . ." Kelly said. "Wait a minute. You can't . . ."

I felt ill, truly ill. I pushed my way forward through the crowd of people.

"Grey."

Then Oak was flat on the ground and Kelly was over her. She curled her legs around his back. Grey came around to kiss her face.

"Grey," I grabbed at him. "Grey."

"What are you doing here?" He plucked my glasses off my face. "You don't need those." He flung them over the deck into the garden.

"Grey, Grey, I can't see."

"Go home, go home, little girl," he said.

"Grey, it's me, it's Zoe."

He pushed me so that I fell back.

"Grey!" I screamed.

He was coming at me to throttle my neck.

"Grey, don't."

Suddenly Narcissus was there between us.

"Come on," he said to Grey. "Don't push the lady, man."

"She's my wife," Grey said.

"Settle down, man."

Narcissus put his arm around me, led me away.

"Grey!" I shrieked.

"Calm yourself," Narcissus said. He took me down to the garden, lifted me up, and sat me on a large flat rock. The ocean was below, but all I saw was solid black. I could hear it, but I could not see it. I was shaking all over.

"He can't . . ."

"Sh, let it go, just let it go, disconnect. You're a big girl."

"I can't see." I was crying, and so my vision was not only blurred but flooded.

Above us was the party, the sounds of people shouting, a shriek. What had happened? Did they have to pull Grey off her? Were they entwined fragrantly, delectably?

"They are just playing," Narcissus said. "It doesn't mean anything."

"It means something."

"It means itself, but it has nothing to do with how your husband is with you. It's an orgy. A bacchanal? You've never been to one of those? It's like carnival. People take off their wedding rings and for two days there are no rules. But it doesn't mean anything."

"It doesn't?"

"Naw."

"But why do it then?"

"Men are like that."

"Like what?"

"There is sex and there is love. Sometimes they go together, sometimes they don't." He looked at me.

"No."

"And remember this: Father Peyote is singing the tune. You cannot disobey Father Peyote. If Father Peyote says kneel, you kneel, man, unless you want to get messed up. It's not logical. It's something else."

"But . . ."

He handed me a reefer.

"Just breathe in, take it easy. I'll tell you a story. Lean back, close your eyes."

Narcissus began:

"The very first people in Big Sur were the Esselen Indians, and they lived all the way down to the Monterey Bay. They ate acorns, shellfish, venison, deer, rabbit, and quail. Legend has it that they came from the north after a great tragedy involving sheets of ice, famine.

"After centuries of peaceful living, the Esselens spotted strange birdlike things floating on the sea. They must have been as exotic as spaceships. Then some manlike creatures with hair on their face and absurd heavy clothing hanging all over their bodies landed on the beach. They put a cross-stick of wood in the ground, knelt before it. How curious they were. They had other long sticks with them, not arrows, and they had long knives, sharper than any flint.

"The Esselens made the best arrows of any tribe in America, but they were peaceful. So, except for an imprint or painting of Esselen hands in a cave at the Tassajara Hot Springs, the California Esselens were obliterated in a few decades. Those not killed were rounded up by the Spanish missionaries and put in a missionary school in Carmel, a prison to people used to wandering free and naked in forests of redwood. There at the mission, the remaining ones languished and died. Those that tried to escape to Big Sur were hunted down, brought back to the mission in Carmel.

"After the Indians and the Spanish, the Post family came to the Big Sur area over the mountains from King City, then the Pfeiffers, the Trotters, the Harlans, the Newells. Some raised cattle and hogs and hunted sea otters, and there were industries such as tanbark, lumber. At Bixby Creek there was a limekiln. In the early days, supplies came by steamer and landed once a year at the mouth of the Big Sur River. The first wagon road was completed in 1881, so that people could make the two-day trip into Monterey."

"Narcissus, that is very interesting, but Grey and Oak . . ." I was feeling very, very sleepy. His story had lulled me, calmed me.

"Easy does it, Zoe, easy does it."

"But . . . why are you telling me all this?"

"Because history, the bigger picture, makes you realize that your own pain is not solitary. You are not alone."

"A community of sufferers? That's supposed to console me?"

"Yes."

I noticed lots of stars. It *was* actually a rather lovely night.

"I'm pregnant," I told Narcissus. In the dark he looked like a panther, a beautiful glossy cat. "I'm pregnant," I told him again.

"That's nice."

"Really. I think I really am, you know, quite pregnant."

"I believe you."

"But what is going to happen to me?"

"Egypt," Narcissus murmured. "Look."

It seemed like a funeral procession. A blurry but definite procession.

Huge and powerful figures came across the sky, outlined in stars. They moved slowly and solemnly. Osiris, his wife, Isis. They trod the horizon and then dropped down one by one into the underworld at the other side of the ocean. Mars with shield and saber, Babylonian winged lions with men's faces and curled manes, a parade of chariots. And a large coyote upright on two legs moved with difficulty, like a trained circus animal, first one leg, then the next. Was it the Magic Theater or the Tibetan World of the Dead coming to bless the crop?

[**GREY CAME** into the tent at dawn after the consummation ceremony, lifting the flap of the tent to a cold triangle of gray. It was crisscrossed with pine branches and reminded me of a Japanese painting, not like the one on Oak's screen, which was lewd with angry eyes, or the one in Aaron's bedroom, but a soft Japanese landscape in blues and grays, pine trees in the distance. I pretended to be asleep, so I was just peeping through a narrow slit in my eyelids, and anyway I no longer had my glasses.

"I have to get out of here. I want to go home," I said just as he was getting into the sleeping bag.

"Zoe, Zoe," Grey said, cradling my head in his arms. He smelled of wine and peyote. That was his breath. His skin was smoky, as if he had been in a bar or had actually smoked himself in a smokehouse. He smelled of sex, too.

"I want to leave you, Grey," I said.

"You can't. We are married."

"I can. I am unhappy. It's no good."

"You have a roof over your head, your belly is full . . ."

"You call this canvas a roof?" I poked the top of the tent with my finger.

"But you want for nothing, you see what I'm saying."

"Sure enough, and I am not crippled or blind. I *am* blind, come to think of it. And no, I don't *see* what you're saying."

"You're not starving."

"I still have the right to be unhappy." I was not sure that Margo would agree, but she was thousands of miles away, and Aaron was dead, and it was just me, me and Grey, and I was miserable.

"And you have a husband who loves you."

"That's a laugh."

"What do you mean?"

"I mean you copulate with another woman in front of a bunch of people. I believe it is called adultery to begin with and maybe exhibitionism, blatant betrayal, humiliation upon humiliation to end with. A husband who loves me, no, I don't hear what you are saying and I'm not seeing it, and it doesn't make sense, okay?"

"It was Father Peyote."

"Don't give me that crap."

"But it was only part of the ceremony."

"I want to go home, Grey."

"To what?"

"To my mother and my aunt."

"Isn't your mother a lush?"

"She's not mean."

"But your father is."

"Not as mean as you."

"I am not mean."

"I want to go to college, Grey."

"You can read here, at home."

"At home? At tent? I need glasses."

"I can train your eyes through meditation. I can make you see. Anyway, I told you knowledge is not to be found in books."

"Books are written by people, Grey, and short of meeting and talking at length with everybody in the world for all of written time, reading is the next best thing. Books are people, don't you understand that? And they are even more than that, they are themselves. To me it is not abstract. It's not a luxury. I need that kind of life. Anyway, where did you get *your* ideas? The Tibetan Book of the Dead is a book, goddamn it, and so is all that Zen Buddhism mush you subscribe to. You didn't go to Japan to get hit on the head. You can't discard civilization, Western, Eastern, what have you. Kundalini is not your idea. You can't act like the rest of the world doesn't exist. At least I can't."

"Since when?"

"Since, since Margo and Aaron. Since before. Since I got my goddamn library card. Since I was six and learned to read. God, I don't know. I'm not a Girl Scout. I don't even like to camp. I don't like to spend three hours making a meal—the wood, the fire, on and on. I can only appreciate nature so much. Jesus Christ, Grey, there are other things."

"What about the land, your body?"

"This wasteland?"

"Your body?"

"My body? When has my body been anything to you?"

"My body, Zoe. My body."

"Your body. Your body has . . ."

"My body speaks to your body."

"No, it doesn't. Your body speaks to Oak's body. Your body speaks all over the place."

"It was obligation, ceremony and ritual. Father Peyote had infused me, so that I was obeying it. You cannot disobey Peyote."

"What are you talking about? I'm sick of Father Peyote and Mother Marijuana, and cousin mushrooms and the whole goddamn pantheon of poisonous plants. It would be easier if you just drank beer, got drunk like an ordinary man, and went bowling on Thursday night with the boys. Fall is almost over. I'm even losing track of the months, let alone the days of the week. I'm getting as dizzy as you and dumb as Oak. We can't live in this tent all winter. The land you love so much is full of snakes and spiders. Our garden didn't grow and now winter is coming. We haven't built anything, cultivated anything; we've done nothing. I feel like I'm wandering in some desert. We're drifting, Grey, can't you see that, farther and farther away from reality. Soon I'll be like Oak, like, like, like where did my mind go?"

"That's good. That's what gurus do. And if you do not surrender to Father Peyote, you can go crazy."

"You *were* crazy. Father Peyote is not Father Christmas, believe me. *He* makes you crazy. You don't even know what crazy is or isn't. I feel like I'm in an endless knot."

"Wow, Zoe. The endless knot in Buddhism means the interrelatedness of all things and the endless interaction between wisdom and compassion. Remember what Thoreau said about not wanting to die without having lived and getting in touch with himself."

"So you've read Thoreau. See, a book. But I hate Thoreau. *Walden* is the most boring book I've ever read. Margo knows this guy that was **197** swimming in Walden Pond, and you know what came down his way, floating pretty as you please, a big turd."

"That's perfect."

"Grey, you're crazy. The stuff you are taking is altering your brain. You can't tell what is real anymore."

"For the good. I am not crazy at all. Crazy is leaping off cliffs, that sort of thing. And tell me, what's so great about real?"

There was a story of a young woman who had leaped off a cliff in the early days of homesteading. She was very religious, and had stood up during a family dinner and announced, "Jesus is calling to me." She had run out of the house, down through the meadow, and, as if she thought she could walk on air, stepped out. She did not scream, they said, but went silently, slowly, head over heels in love, over the cliff.

"Nothing is great about real, but it's what we have to contend with, it's the world, it's our job."

"You make your world, Zoe."

"Objective reality exists. Objects exist. I bump into things at night when I can't see. I can't see now, yet I am going to get up," I said. "You were out all night. For me the day is real, you get up to it."

"And make some coffee?"

I stepped out of the tent. It was early, but the fog had started to lift. We kept a bundle of kindling and sticks of wood dry under a heavy tarpaulin. I gathered a bunch, put them in a pyramid on the ashes of the morning before. The matches were kept in a covered tin. I crumpled some paper, stuffed it between the kindling. I struck a match on the stone, poured some water from the pail into the coffeepot. I extracted the coffee sock from the shelf we had made out of two boards suspended over two rocks.

I walked some ways from the camp to pee. Even though there was nobody there, I did not like to do it in the open and sought some cover. As I turned to squat down, I saw a deer, but barely, fuzzily. It was small, maybe an adolescent. Its fur looked soft, and was a soft gray color, tipped in blue. She looked at me curiously, and she was tame as a dog. She turned her head to the side a little, as if asking to be petted.

"Little deer, mood indigo," I said. "What should I do? Am I seeing you or imagining you?"

The deer bent her neck, went back to eating something on the ground.

"I thought you had leaped over the cliff," Grey said when I got back. He had put the sock of coffee in the pan and put out two cups.

"Not me. I'm not the type."

"Glad to hear it. Cheers," he said, lifting his cup.

"I keep seeing deer," I said.

"Maybe the deer is your animal totem. Very good medicine."

"You kill deer, Grey. And I'm not in the mood for this. I don't believe in all that totem-pole stuff."

"So you believe that a man named Christ cured the sick, raised the dead, converted prostitutes, pushed aside a huge boulder when he was dead, and ascended to heaven? If that is not fantastic, I don't know what is."

"There is a historical Christ."

"Immaculately conceived? That he had no brothers and sisters? You see what I mean? And you said the Mormons believe he returned after death."

"I believe . . . I believe that we, as humans, have a special destiny. We have responsibilities to each other."

"Who told you that special-destiny garbage?"

"My aunt, okay?"

"The Mormon?"

"No, the Armenian. She said I was destined and not to forget it."

"The salesclerk?"

"I am going for a walk, Grey, and when I come back, I am going to get my things together and you are going to drive me to town."

I walked away from camp toward the forest, which loomed up beyond the spring. There was a little path of sorts, and I followed it carefully. I wanted to compose myself, get away from Grey so he could not persuade me to stay. I was counting on nature, not the nature that Grey used to counter rationality but nature as a means of seeing order and beauty in the world, an objective world out there, real and unhampered with moods, something beyond my own whirling brain. Sometimes I thought Grey was not the only one going crazy.

But as I walked along, it seemed that trees swept down at me. Bushes leaped up. I saw the blue deer luminously blue, with trails of bright neon gold trailing from her nostrils.

Oh God, I thought, I was still high from something the night before. What had I taken? Why was it cropping up now? Or was my brain, like Grey's, so saturated that everything had been rearranged?

Then I saw menacing geometrics. Octagons and trapezoids, polyhedrons in bright colors. My skin came off from my skull, and I knew I was nothing and never would be anything and my life was a paltry and stupid thing. I pictured droves of forest rangers, forming by their green-clad bodies a living, crawling comb, a phalanx of soldiers sifting through the brush of Los Padres National Forest. Zoe, Zoe.

Everything I thought was a landmark in the forest was betraying me. The stump was a fat log. The redwood sapling was a thin person. The branches of the fir tree were hands reaching to grab me. I saw a grave. It heaved and breathed. Time stretched and contorted, compressed and zigzagged, rolling back in on itself. I was done for, done in, done. I plunged deeper and deeper where the ferns grew in torrential profusion, and I could imagine night coming on, the birds calling to one another in a lonely end-of-the-day way. I could see leaves curling at the edges, tucking up, receding from me. They were scared. I was scared. And then I knew I was being followed. Aaron was following me. He wanted to tell me something. You won't get away so easily, he was saying, and if he touched me, if I turned around, I knew I would have to go with him to the underworld, just like in the myths. And then I rounded a corner and I could see our clearing. I could see the tent, Grey.

"Peace?" he asked.

"I'm having a baby, Grey."

"Thank you, Zoe. Thank you, my wife." And he bowed low before me, kissed my feet.

[**MARGO,** you can't be jealous all the time or it will destroy you. I spoke to Margo in my head, telepathed across the continent.

We got a dog.

We got cats.

We got chickens.

We got a trailer.

Grey bought it in Cambria and dragged it up the hill on a hitch attached to the truck. It took all day. It was an old trailer, turquoise, streaked with silver, more spaceship than house, shards of metal tacked to struts of steel. We placed it on cinder blocks. In one end was a wraparound bench and table, and in the other we put a real mattress. In between was the kitchen. We could not use the bathroom, of course, and stored the broom and mop there. Grey fixed up a hose from the stream, so we actually had running water in the kitchen sink. No electricity though. Kerosene lanterns were used at night. The smell in that confined area made me sick.

Jealousy will defeat you, Margo, I wrote in my mind.

We got a butane stove.

That smell made me sick, too.

Everything made me sick.

Meat made me especially sick. Cooking, frying, roasting, boiling meat. And Grey had to eat a lot of meat.

It *had* been an aberration, Margo, Grey's lapse with Oak, a sad mistake brought about by external substances such as peyote, wine, the fact of the harvest, and the idea of a consummation ceremony. Does that make sense?

In the day, Margo, Grey works on the stone house, which is situated **201** on a plateau below the trailer and concealed by rocks. I straighten the trailer, can finally cook on a real stove. Once a week I bake bread. I feed the animals. The chickens sleep at night in a wire cage under the trailer. One chicken, Chicken, thinks she is a dog and sleeps in front of the trailer on the welcome mat, her legs stretched out.

One night Grey and I were tucked into our sleeping bag at the back of the trailer when we heard a great ruckus. Chicken was being carried off by a huge raccoon.

Another night, there was a great screeching, and bobcats came down and ate up the cats.

And this is the part I do not write Margo in my mind:

And then Crazy Dog—we did not know how it happened, except of course, she was not inoculated—got distemper.

"We are going to have to kill her," Grey said.

The animal had fits.

"We can take her to the vet, Grey."

Grey laughed.

"And he can cure her, okay?"

"She is too far gone, you know what I mean."

"We can have her put to sleep, Grey." I felt sick. I should have taken her for her shots.

"Travel all the way into town, pay money to have somebody else do what we should do?"

He was going to shoot her. That's what people did, did they not, in the old days. Shot lame horses, put cows out of their misery, walked about with guns like angels of mercy.

"You are going to shoot her with your .22 rifle?"

"And waste a bullet on a dog?"

He lay her down, held her, and as she looked up at him, he smashed her head in with a rock. She had been trying to lick him.

Margo did not know that the cash crop loomed large down the hill. It seemed as if it was steadily advancing when our backs were turned. Surely if it was discovered, Kelly would go to jail. If we were sitting there, would we go to jail, too? Had Kelly and Oak never seen the old-time movie *Reefer Madness?*

And although Grey emphasized the "naturalness" of peyote and mushrooms, I wondered, remembering Frank Sinatra's uncontrollable craving for heroin in *The Man with the Golden Arm.*

Sometimes I worried that we would see a car coming up the road and it would be the sheriff coming to get Grey for forgery of those payroll checks.

We were in the main yurt among the pillows. It was raining outside, not hard, but a drizzle that had kept up all day. Oak was baking spaghetti squash, a large yellow squash whose meat was stringy and soft like spaghetti. You ate it with butter and brown sugar. We were having that with red enchiladas and cream of sorrel soup. Oak was a marvelous cook. Somehow her hazy, drifty manner and careless measuring translated into ambrosia. I could not begrudge her that.

"There are stories of gold," Kelly said. "Pass the bowl."

"Oh yes, gold in California," said Oak. Sometimes she took gold dust and theatrically outlined her eyes and made scrolls and paisleys on her cheeks.

"The Indians would come up with gold dust to the mission. Naturally the padres were anxious to find the mine. But it was a secret. The white men looked for it in the Santa Lucias, the Ventana Wilderness, but they didn't find it. It was said that the padres tortured the Indians, but the Indians had been sworn to an oath of secrecy. It was called the Lost Mine of the Padres. Then, when Robert Louis Stevenson visited the ruins of Carmel Mission in 1879, he looked for it, too. Later he wrote *Treasure Island.*"

"An old Chinese, Sing Fat, who used to collect seaweed on the coast, was said, like, to know the secret of the gold mine."

"A spirit held the gold," Grey added. "She was split down the middle, and if you saw the other half you would go crazy. Only Indians could get near her. She lived in the waterfalls."

"Old man Clarke, this crazy guy who wandered the coast but was really an anthropologist from U.C. Berkeley, knew the secret, that's what people say," Kelly put in.

"He stole it from the Indians." Grey looked at me as if I had done it. Oh yes, he was up on all the abuses the Indians suffered, and though he disdained current news, the kind of current event we had to talk about in school, he did know about what *had* happened. And somehow, as an accidentally born white woman, I carried a big bad bag of what-happened on my back. It was the same way I felt with Aaron—Aaron and history. If I was not a Jew, I could be a Nazi. If I was not a Negro, I could have held slaves and been in the Ku Klux Klan. If I was not an Indian, I was, as an Anglo-Saxon, a survivor benefiting from what my people had done to others.

And supposedly all the American Indian tribes were sitting around smoking the peace pipe together, never killing, never going on the warpath, never even saying a discouraging word to each other before the bad white men came.

"Lilies of the field, they toil not," Kelly pronounced when other people came, people from L.A., San Francisco, and sat around and smoked with us.

Furthermore, Kelly and Oak had an electric refrigerator powered by a generator. And a butane stove. Two Mexican helpers came on the mail truck twice a week and were picked up at the Gorda gas station by Kelly. They did the housework, yard work.

Oak bought her soaps and oils in L.A. Her nightgowns were from Lanz. Lots of her clothes were in the particular shade of blue the sky takes on just before sunset and mauve and the off-white of raw silk and the texture of real linen. Regularly, she made expeditions into San Francisco for Ghirardelli chocolates.

Oak was obviously, bloomingly pregnant. I was still pretty thin, as if that honeydew melon I was carrying around was a tumor and not a baby.

"It seems, like, the least I could do," Oak said, "having a, like, a baby for Kelly." This was our girl-talk time on her mattress. She liked to pull me in between the curtains, finger my breasts.

"It seems a lot, Oak, having a baby."

"Kelly, like, lost a baby here, you know, with his last woman."

"I didn't know."

"They say when the east wind blows from the hill, it's an evil wind. The baby was six months. Tara."

"Her name was Tara?"

"Something like that."

"Well, it's *Howdy Doody* time," Kelly said, coming through the curtains into the bedroom, where he kept the peyote stash, Grey following. "A button for you and a button for you," he said, handing them out.

"I'll pass," I said.

"Why?"

"I don't think it's good for the baby, the baby heart, the baby brain."

"Why not? Indians in Mexico give it to their six-month-old infants. It's a natural substance, Zoe," Grey insisted.

"So are foxglove and hemlock, Grey."

"Suit yourself."

"I am."

Margo had just sent me a letter, which Narcissus sneaked to me through Kelly.

So you are pregnant. Go see a doctor immediately. Don't smoke, don't drink, don't even drink coffee, and between the lines I can tell you are indulging in mind-changing experiences. None of that is good for the development of a child. You have a real responsibility now, Zoe, to yourself and to her. And listen, get some new glasses. I know you're as blind as a bat. What utter bullshit. I feel scared for you. You say you are an hour and a half from town? What if you should go into labor and your husband isn't at home with the car?

I had blabbed about the glasses, not having them anymore, but since my letter, Narcissus, going into town, had gotten me a new pair with the old prescription from my eye doctor's. I sneaked them on when Grey was not around.

[**N E P E N T H E** was a restaurant and bar on a hill, thirty miles north of us in Big Sur. It sat on a plateau which jutted out to sea, offering a magnificent view. The actor Orson Welles, who played Kane in *Citizen Kane* and Othello in his own *Othello*, originally bought the land, which had a cabin on it, for Rita Hayworth.

Not a castle, but a cabin. The real Hearst castle lay like a mirage some thirty or so miles south. The original Orson Welles cabin was now used for the family quarters of the restaurant owners, and a separate building was erected below—a huge room, not unlike Margo's house in Pacific Grove.

Grey and I were on a kind of date. It was warm for November. I was supposed to be feeling very good. I was pregnant and with my husband. We had our truck, our trailer, our land, and we had money, enough money to go to a restaurant. I preened in front of the car window, actually untangled my hair and drew it back from my face with a piece of twine, and put on a clean shirt of Grey's. I was making an effort. But I had a feeling of dread. It was like distrusting Christmas, knowing in your heart of hearts that you are not going to get what you want, because nobody understands you, and that the greatest day of the year was going to be something of an ordeal. Oak and Kelly were going with us. So it was kind of a double date. And since I couldn't wear my glasses in front of Grey, for me it was a blind date.

Nepenthe, the restaurant, was all scaffolding and glass and a huge round terrace with a bonfire in the middle overlooking the ocean. It was both elegant and rustic. People folk-danced on the terrace. They had horoscope parties. Virgo Night, Gemini Night. Like-minded astrologers cast their dice. Henry Miller went there, real artists, successful writers. It was a fancy place, arty, very fun. Anything could happen. Grey was in a very good mood. And I, I was scared.

Kelly sat next to me, Oak next to Grey. Oak and I were pregnant, of course, but she, she was, if anything, more beautiful than ever. She was dressed like Heidi that night, with a scooping neckline, her breasts pushed up under cotton lace like warm red apples. Nice, I thought, very nice.

"I am going to have the baby, like, at home on the deck." She had said this often enough.

"In, like, the rain?" I teased, for her baby was due in January. As far as I could determine, my baby would arrive in February. "In, like, the cold, Oak, have your baby in the cold?"

Grey jabbed me in the side.

"It's a legitimate question, Grey," I whispered.

I hadn't told Grey yet, but I was going to have my baby in, like, the hospital, no doubt about it, with all the equipment and nurses and doctors, and I was going to be completely knocked out. I was going to be rolled into a sterile operating room totally unaware of the world and unable to feel every little pang and pain. I did not want to experience my womanhood to its maximum. I did not want to feel ripped apart, drawn and quartered. I did not want to scream and moan, call for my mother, pant like a dog, crouch like an Indian squaw, or be part of a continuity of women through all of time giving birth naturally, i.e., painfully. If I called for my mother, who would come? I could remember as a kid wanting to call for a glass of water. If I proved a point to Grey, would it carry me through my life? What did the women of history care how I gave birth? If I gave birth in Gorda and something went wrong with me or the baby, what good would all the right thoughts and home-brewed tea and hocus-pocus do? No, I was going to the hospital.

I knew Grey wouldn't like it, the hospital thing. I knew that he admired Oak's decision. He didn't like me to mock Oak, and I didn't mean to, but perhaps, despite all my rationalization, I had never gotten

over the consummation ceremony, that little drug-induced incident a
month ago in celebration of the harvest.

On the deck of the restaurant, they were playing an Israeli song, "Maya,
Maya, Maya." A woman in an anklet and long skirts was leading the line. The
dancers seemed like characters out of the Old Testament, worshipping a God
who spoke to them on a daily basis. Do this. Don't do that. Bow low, brush,
brush, heel toe, heel toe. Or like students in my aunt's dance class, arabesque,
arabesque, her long pole beating out the time.

"This is such a cool place," Oak said, giggling a little, and tugging
at her bodice, revealing still a little more cleavage.

We ordered french fries. The men drank scotch. Oak had beer. I
was drinking orange juice. Grey had a silly grin on his face. I could feel
the baby kicking. It seemed to be a secret signal, tap, tap, Morse code.
I am alive, I am alive. Over and out.

"I'm driving back down the coast," Kelly said after a while, "before
I get too drunk."

"I'm not ready to go home yet," Oak said.

"Can I get you folks something else?" the bartender asked.

"I'll have another of the same," Grey said.

"I'm just not ready to, like, you know, go back down the, uh,
coast."

"You can go back with us," Grey offered.

"That would be cool," Oak replied.

"When are we going back?" I asked.

"Soon."

"I feel tired, Grey. Maybe we should go now, too."

"You can go back with Kelly."

"I want to go back with you."

"Why don't you nap in the truck. It's a warm night."

"I don't want to take a nap, Grey. Then I won't be able to sleep
tonight."

"Stop being such a baby, Zoe."

"I'm not *being* a baby. I'm having a baby."

"Zoe." Grey raised a finger at me.

"I'll walk you down to the parking lot," Kelly said.

"Go on, I'll be down in a little while." Grey held up his drink.
"Soon as I finish this."

"I'll be down, too." Oak giggled a little.

"Really?"

"Ten minutes at the most." Grey patted my bottom. "Go on."

Kelly and I walked through the restaurant and out onto the terrace, down the steps, and to the parking lot. It was an extraordinarily clear night. Soon it would be Christmas, I thought. Of course, we had not celebrated Thanksgiving. But I wanted to decorate the trailer for Christmas. We couldn't have lights, but I could cut ornaments and we could put boughs at the windows. I wanted to buy Grey a new shirt.

"Zoe," Kelly said when we got to Grey's truck. "How old are you?"

"Eighteen."

We were standing next to Grey's truck. Kelly was tipsy, I knew. Why was it that I could be tolerant of other people when they were drunk, but my mother made my flesh crawl? As soon as I heard the gin splash into her glass, I would find myself in a rage. I put my hand on Kelly's cheek.

"Be careful driving back," I said.

"*You* be careful."

"What do you mean?" That word again. Careful. *Cuidado.*

"Maybe you're in over your head."

"What do you mean?" I asked again.

"Oh, Zoe." Kelly looked at me sadly, his chin slack, his eyes droopy.

"What is it, Kelly?"

He shook his head.

"You're tired," I said.

"That's not it."

"What *is* it then?"

Below us, the sea was black and the great cliffs that circled the ocean were shadows of giant hunchbacks. The cypress trees were fuzzy and indistinct, like Balinese dancers in strange positions behind dimly lit screens.

"You are so innocent, Zoe, so, so innocent."

"No, I'm not." And even if I was, what was wrong with it?

"Why don't you go home, Zoe, to your mother?"

"To my mother? Are you crazy? Grey is my husband."

Go home and sit on my bed, wondering what mood my parents

were in? Go home so I could get up at three to scrub the kitchen? Go home to pick my mother up off the floor? Go home to Aaron, who was not only married but now dead?

"What do you mean, Kelly, go home? I have nothing there. Grey is my home."

"Grey is difficult."

"I know. So what? I made my bed, and now I have to sleep in it."

"That's bullshit. Where did you get that from?"

"My father." It was funny, but I knew I was hearing my father as soon as I said it.

"Don't you know you should never listen to your parents?"

"I didn't, that's why I married Grey."

"Oh, well . . ." Kelly shook his head.

He got in his truck.

"You're sure," he said, sticking his head out the window.

"Yes," I laughed. "I'm sure. You're the one who gave him all that land."

He laughed.

"Don't you have any confidence in any of your decisions, Kelly?"

"Nope. They are all disasters."

"You're drunk."

"Not really."

"I like you, Kelly."

"I like you, too, Zoe, and Narcissus and I, well, we've been discussing you, that's why . . . Oh well."

I stood by awkwardly as he got into his truck.

"I wouldn't want you to get hurt," he said.

"I don't know what you mean."

But I did. I did. And though I could see Kelly's truck navigate the curves—because, of course, I did put on my glasses—I took his leave-taking with a sense of foreboding.

"He'll be all right, I'll be all right," I said to the sky in a kind of prayer. Kelly's truck was like an old horse that knew its way home on its own. I was tough, too.

I got into the cab of Grey's truck, pulled the blanket over me. They would be down in a few minutes, and I would go home to the little capsule, the cocoon of turquoise, our silver streamlined trailer.

Totally alien to the countryside, it looked as if it had just landed from a Buck Rogers movie.

"Blast-off time," Grey would say before popping something.

Inside, our spaceship, I must say, was cozy: the table, the bed, the stove, everything compact, efficient, safe. Yet once, twin snakes had come up the water pipe and done a duet over the sink through the faucet, entwining themselves like a doctor's aegis. I had screamed and Grey had run up from the house to see what the matter was. The snakes had dropped down into the sink and slithered down the drain. Just garter snakes. You dreamed them, Grey said.

Nowadays when I dreamed, I could not remember my dreams. When Margo and I had been in high school, we made a pact to wake up every time we had a dream and note it down in the dream books we kept. During lunch hour on the stone bleachers made by the WPA people, we would go over them together, I eating the peanut-butter sandwich I had fixed in the morning and Margo being surprised by something Judy had concocted—liverwurst and cheese, tomatoes and chicken, sliced apples and pineapple. Then we would walk along the school grounds to see if any of the boys looked good.

That night in the truck I did dream. I dreamed of my baby. Or maybe I was simply aware of it, in me, growing. When I was a kid, I stayed up at night, trying to catch my legs lengthening. Now I felt I was consciously bringing into being toes and tiny toenails, lips and a baby bottom. It seemed an act of will, *good* will, as in a story I had read about a man who dreamed up a man. Was that God's dream? It was as if the dream had hands of its own and, like the biblical account of Adam, could fashion life from mere clay. Spawned in a swamp. The baby, this baby of mine, seemed more of my own making than of Grey's. It was to be the company of a lonely woman, as I told Aaron the time I had the ulcer. The outsider's insider, the outsider from inside, like turning myself inside out and showing all the seams, and what do we have here—a girl's best friend is her kid.

I no longer have an ulcer, I prayed to Aaron. I have a child. I am happy.

I don't know how long I was sleeping, but when I woke up it was still dark, not the dense dark of night but rather the dark that begins to lighten up, the short time between night and day. The sky lifted bit by bit, as the thick curtain of black revealed first a rim and then a band of thin gray light. My God, I thought, I had been in the truck all night. Where was Grey? Where was Oak?

And then I saw them, as I put my glasses on, in the rearview mirror, coming down the road not from the restaurant but from Deetjen's Inn, the bed-and-breakfast place where the obese Mrs. Deetjen slept in the dining room.

I felt my stomach spasm, freeze.

"Zoe," Grey said when he opened the car door. "Oak got sick. I had to take her to Deetjen's for the night."

Oak got in. I moved over. I couldn't say a word. Nobody said a word. Grey had a stupid grin on his face. He kept it there the whole hour down to Gorda, dropping Oak off at Kelly's, and on up the hill he continued to grin like a damned Cheshire cat. He stopped the truck in front of the trailer, looked at me.

"What's the matter with you?"

"I waited the whole night."

"Well, you don't seem to be any the worse for wear." He got out. "I told you Oak was ill."

"I am ill, and I'm not coming out."

"Suit yourself. The animals need to be fed."

"What animals? Everything is dead. Crazy Dog is dead. The cats are gone. Chicken is dead."

He went into the trailer, let out the remaining chickens from underneath. I stared straight ahead, literally saw red. Red sky, red bushes, red earth, red chickens, the red bark of the eucalyptus, blood flowers.

There was a knock at my window.

"Are you coming in?" Grey asked.

"Never."

"I asked you nicely, Zoe."

I didn't say anything.

"Either you come in here and fix me breakfast, or I'll pull you out of there."

I stared straight ahead. Maybe I had broken a blood vessel in my eye. That's what the red was, real blood.

The door wrenched open.

"Grey!" I shrieked.

He grabbed my arm.

"Don't touch me!" I screamed.

"You are my wife," and with that, he pulled me out to the ground. "Talk to me."

I could now taste blood, blood mixed with earth.

"You answer when I talk to you," he said.

He kicked my stomach.

Instinctively I folded my arms over my knees, protected my stomach and my genitals, as we had been taught in bomb drills.

Duck.

Fold.

Cover.

The bomb was dropping. He kicked me at the base of my back, and I felt a little trickle of something come out between my legs. He kicked my pocket. I felt my glasses break against my legs.

"Grey!" I screamed. "Be careful. The baby."

He moved forward. Something contracted in me.

"Don't touch me. I'm going to lose the baby," I said.

Moisture was seeping onto my pants, Grey's jeans.

Grey knelt down.

"Oh God," he said.

"Get me to town, Grey. I need a doctor."

I tried to get up.

"You have new glasses," he said lamely.

"Yes, Grey, yes. For God's sake, for the sake of the baby, our baby, help me up. I need to get to town."

He put his hand out, took my arm, tried to help me. I wasn't heavy, but with my long legs, my feet, I couldn't get up.

"Help me."

He pulled me up.

"I'm going to lose the baby," I said, leaning against the side of the truck.

"No, no."

"Help me in, Grey." I kept my legs pressed together. My pants felt more moist.

"Zoe, I'm sorry. I'm so fucking sorry."

He got the door open, pulled me head first, then my feet, then he wrapped the blanket around me.

"Hurry," I said. I was holding my legs together very tightly. "Take me to Carmel Hospital."

"Doctors . . ."

But he had started the truck and we were bumping down the hill, skirting around the curves, and then we were on the highway again, going north, back up the way we had just been, heading this time all the way to the hospital in Carmel. Trees, cliffs, the coast, the white rims of waves, beaches. There were no other cars on the road. It was early Sunday morning. We passed Nepenthe, Deetjen's, River Inn, the meadow, the lighthouse, the flatlands. My legs were clamped together.

"Sweet Jesus." I was bleeding. "Saint Anthony, you're all I have. Save my baby. Stop the blood." I remembered praying for blood when I had the ulcer and wanted my period. Little had I known that my body was full of blood, that I was bleeding internally. "Blood." I remembered what Margo had told me about blood, Aaron's blood. Think of the people, all his people, the ones who used spoons to dig their way out of concentration camps, and the other one who sold vegetables from a cart on the streets of Milwaukee. What gave him the right to decide to die? That's what Margo had said. And I thought of the people who struggled against slavery so that Margo, beautiful, brilliant Margo, could make her mark on this planet of ours.

"I want a child. I want this child, Grey. This is my child."

"Oh, Zoe," he moaned. "Me, too. I want this, too."

My pants, his pants that I wore, were wet.

"I love you so much," Grey said. "Do you understand?"

"No, no I don't. I'm going to have a miscarriage."

"No, you're not."

"I'm bleeding, Grey, I'm bleeding."

"I love you so much it's killing me. Don't you understand, I have to break it, break it in, tame it, dilute it, spread it. It is too much, too much." He was crying. "I can't stand it, I love you so much."

"I don't believe that, Grey. If you loved me, you would be kind and good. You would be faithful. You would want nobody else."

"I want nobody else." He took my hand; I pulled it away.

"It all seems silly to me, I mean, in the face of a child." I looked out the window. The coast, I thought. My coast.

"I only love you, the baby, only you." He picked up my hand

again. "Please," he said, "please. I am going to take care of you. I am, Zoe. I promise I am."

My stomach was contracting.

"I'll do anything for you, Zoe, you know that. I would walk through snow barefoot for you."

I crossed my legs, closed my eyes, sucked in my breath. Please, I prayed, please. Please, please, please Saint Anthony, saint of basket weavers, brush makers, butchers, domestic animals, gravediggers, swine, please save my baby.

I knew my attachment to saints was childish and irrational, but I couldn't help it. Whom did I have to help me but an invisible collection of fanatics and misfits? And my idea of God was a paradox. Not male / female or power / love, but is / is not. If you are there, Papa God, I prayed, help me, and, if not, help me anyway.

By the time we hit Garapata Creek, the cramps let up and the blood stopped.

I said, "I'm not going to miscarry, but I want to keep going on to the hospital."

Grey sighed, put his hand on my knee.

"I am sorry," he said. "Never again."

"But Grey, this is the second time, the second time with Oak. I can't take it. I want to go home."

"You really want to go back to your parents' house? Pregnant?"

I closed my eyes.

"I promise." Grey stopped the truck, turned to me. "I promise. Give me another chance, one more chance."

[FROGMAN

Little Dog Face
Crooked Nose
Old Man
He Who Runs Fast
were all snoring up a storm on top of Gorda Mountain, in the sweathouse,
the hot grandfather stones long grown cold, when the band of drunken
white men got there. It was about 1896, summer, early morning, and
overhead the fog had not risen, but you could hear the shrill cry of
hawks. The white men were drunk from the night before, and they had
been driving cattle all week over the mountains from King City.

"Let's get us some Indians," Billy Whiteman said, as he raised the
deerskin door of the sweat lodge with the barrel of his Winchester.
"Come on out, you filthy Indians, and face the music."

Below, the ocean roared and yawned. Hundreds of tiny animals
and plants were swept out with the tide—six different kinds of starfish,
three different kinds of sea urchins, snails and crabs, bristle worms,
giant flatworms, algaes, sponges. The double-crested cormorant dove
for fish.

"Out," he said.

The terrified Indians in the sweat lodge were not all Esselens, but
castoffs from various tribes—Rumsens, Ohlones, and a few misfit Esselens, outsiders—and they didn't have any weapons. All they had were

flint knives to scrape limpets and mussels and abalones, and stones to grind acorn mush. They didn't even have women. A few scrungy dogs is all that were sleeping with them in the sweathouse, and the dogs didn't bite, bark, *or* growl. The men didn't have a chance to pee or open their eyes. And all they left behind was a pile of shells. Yet their ghosts could be heard when the east wind blew.

[**I STARTED** to write to Margo again, sneaking letters through Narcissus.

December 1, 1957

Our house is beautiful, I wrote. *There are wooden benches around the stone wall and a fireplace in the middle, really a fire pit with a smoke hole and ladder over it, and a big woodstove in one corner. We have a terrace like a bridge connecting the house with the bathing area. Grey has also constructed a sweathouse up the hill of bent tree limbs and deerskins. Rocks are heated by fire at Tooth Rock and set in the house. Water thrown over the hot grand-father rocks creates the steam. There is also a chicken coop with cross beams, so that the entire structure is enclosed with chicken wire against coyotes, bobcats, and the chickens have their own little stone house.*

Our dining room table is a huge redwood slab on rocks. We have some nice wooden chairs and a large old-fashioned bed. I am married, yes, but not living in Levittown. This is *an adventure.*

I spoke to her about my life, as if to elicit a summer image of an English garden, me going about in a diaphanous dress and floppy straw-hat, shears and a basket in my hand. I didn't tell her that in the real summer I had to clear the land with a hoe and an ax and a shovel, and get down on my knees to dig out rocks twice my girth and "weeds" as tall as I was; that now I peed like a man or a horse standing up in the midst of brambles, because I couldn't crouch without getting poison oak up my ass. I didn't tell her that in the summer I gardened naked except for my tall boots sometimes because the sweat ran off my back in sheets, and that Grey had to inspect my body for ticks, making them come out by holding a flame very close to their bloated gray bodies and sometimes singeing the fine hair off my skin in the process. And that in the end rabbits and deer had destroyed the whole garden.

Dear Margo, (I had written, anticipating spring) *the flowers along the coast will be exquisite, the Indian paintbrush, the manzanita, the California goldenrod, the larkspur, the buttercup, the lupines. Yesterday we sighted a sperm whale when we went fishing, and otters floating on their backs in the sea kelp. I saw a shooting star. It is easy to see the stars because there are no lights here. Celestial light brings everything we do into a different perspective.*

I didn't tell her that Oak had her baby by herself, on the deck, prematurely—a boy with straight blond hair. They named him Redwood. He was never away from Oak, and was held to her back by a little sling and sometimes strapped to her stomach, so that she looked like a many-armed goddess or a kind of turtle or sloth.

I didn't tell her that Grey was beginning to act strange, stranger than ever, that sometimes he babbled incoherently and laughed when things were not funny.

[**IN FACT**, Grey laughed when I cut myself prying an abalone loose from its shell. I had to insert the ab iron, given to us by Kelly, putting it beneath the abalone's mantle at the head and working it under the muscle.

"*You* can pound it tender," I said, handing him the wooden mallet and practically throwing him the abalone.

He laughed.

He laughed when we made love. He still approached me from the back, of course, but the kundalini had been abandoned entirely. And yet, even though in the scheme of things he *could* ejaculate, which to my mind made everything easier, he seemed to lose interest, could not complete. Withdrawing after a half-hearted entrance, he would say silly things like, A hard man is hard to find.

Grey laughed over his split-pea soup. He laughed when it rained and when the sun came out.

Then one day we were sitting outside on top of the hill. I was feeling sleepy and very contented, and Grey was sitting next to me, looking at a hawk soaring above us. Suddenly he jumped up, grabbed my hand.

"Grey, what is it?" I widened my eyes, looked up.

I thought that the hawk which was floating above had dived and that Grey wanted to trace it to its prey, a mouse or small rabbit.

"I am dangerous," Grey said.

He wasn't doing any peyote.

"Wait a minute, Grey, calm down."

"I need to get you away from here," he said.

And with that, he dragged me the whole way down the hill to the highway. He stopped a car by jumping out, standing in front of it.

"Take her, take her away," he cried.

"Grey, are you insane?"

"What is going on?" The man in the car drove around us, skittered away like a frightened insect on all legs.

Grey laughed. "Let's go visit Oak and Kelly," he said, as if nothing had happened.

They were relaxing as usual in the main yurt.

"I think," I whispered to Kelly when Grey went to the outhouse, "that something is wrong with Grey. He laughs all the time."

"He's happy." He passed me the pipe.

"No, thank you. No. That's not it. Grey laughs when it's inappropriate."

"What's, like, inappropriate?" Oak put in. "Can't somebody laugh when they want?"

"It's a silly laugh. And just now, he dragged me down the hill to send me away because he thought he was dangerous."

Sometimes I came upon Grey giggling to himself. Then he would be silent for hours, not even talk. Once, I had come upon him sitting under the tree near the tepeelike construction he had built to skin deer, and he had been masturbating and continued to do so as I watched him.

"Grey, what are you doing?"

He started to laugh.

Sometimes he walked about with his penis out of his pants. At night, I lay in the bed, looking up at the darkness of the ceiling—in the day raw pine beams, at night a black peak, the night coming through the smoke hole and the rough ladder leaning against it as if we were somewhere underground and the ladder led to light, the surface, civilization, a hope, a face.

Grey had intended the stone house to be a sacred place, like a kiva. The Hopis built tall structures, towers with ladders to the top. The bottom was the kiva, the sacred ceremonial chamber. In the center was the snake altar, where they did the snake dance, the prayer for rain. Around the altar they sprinkled naturally colored sands. Red was the south, white the east, green the west, black the north. They had twin gods. The God of War and the God of Recreation. I thought of Narcissus and his brother, my mother and her sister. I thought of myself and Grey. Grey? Were we two halves of the same seed? I used to think so, but now, now I was remembering Tom Sawyer stuck in the cave with Injun Joe, how scary that was, and I was scared, too.

Sometimes Grey had accidents in his pants. He would giggle about it like a bad schoolboy.

"I think he needs to see a psychiatrist," I said to Kelly the next time we were down there.

Oak, overhearing, leaned over. "And, like, have his head shrunk? You can't, like, be, like, serious, Zoe."

"I am very, like, serious, Oak. I am dead serious."

Those words again. Dead serious.

When Grey was bathing in the stream or hunting quail in the woods, I began driving the truck on the large flat area by the trailer. Once I drove all the way down the hill.

The last time I had done peyote, before I knew I was pregnant, I had had an experience that made me doubt my own sanity, and now I tried to use it to understand Grey's mind.

This is the way it went:

It was a dream. Grey and I were children. We had pets, freak pets. His pet was a rabbit with tusks. Mine was a lizard, a huge, iguanalike reptile. It crept up my coat and inside my sleeve and started to bite me. I told Grey, and he stared at me straight in the eyes, seeming to understand, but he moved very slowly. The lizard was sick with convulsions and held on to me with its teeth. It held on to me with its teeth biting me as it died. What was it? What did it mean?

The vision vanished, but I was still high, very high. I wanted one lucid moment, just one, before I died. I tried to walk off the disorientation, but it would not go. We were down at Kelly's, as usual, and I looked in Oak's mirror to banish the buzzing cloud which seemed to encircle my head, but I didn't see anything, not even myself. I walked back out on the deck. Oak was winding cloth around her body like bandages, like bondage, like badinage.

"She puts new meaning in the word bondage," Kelly said, pulling her toward him, exposing her, her pubic hair a blond Russian muff.

I went back into Oak's room and looked in the mirror. The stuff hadn't cleared my head yet, for my mind was not back in its home, my skull. I knew that. But it was getting better. I had not seen myself the first time I looked in the mirror. This time I began to see myself. I wavered up like a mirage or something underwater, barely below the surface.

It was wearing off.

I walked out on the deck, happy to be seeing myself.

The ocean was calm, smooth. But that was deceptive, for when I went fishing I could see from my rock perch the great force of the waves. There were whorls of deep danger. You could get sucked down to the bottom.

I went back to the mirror a third time and not only saw myself but was worried about how I looked. If I was worried about how I looked, I was myself. I was coming out of it. A tall girl with wild red hair, freckled, disheveled, but it was I, Zoe.

Now I wondered if that confusion, that rush of chaos, was what was happening to Grey constantly these days or had been happening all the time or was creeping up on him like a silent, light-footed brave from the east wind, first a foot, then an ankle, a whole leg, a body of madness come to settle in, stretch out, make itself at home in Grey's brain.

Or maybe it just stayed there, the peyote madness stuck in his brain buzz to buzz, a permanent rearrangement of nerve cells. They called pot smokers potheads. Maybe peyote eaters turned into peyotes, little buttons of insanity, whirling dervishes of disarray, flinging off a piece of rationality here, another there, doing a madcap, prickly hokey-pokey in the old cranium tonight. Maybe I had not seen it in him before, but it was there, growing like a silent cancer. Or maybe there had been mere spurts of it, which I had missed. Even now he would surface after silence, and, after crazy giggling, and fiddling with himself, and twitching and nodding, he would be the old Grey, fine. What's for dinner? So that I would think his dazed behavior was willful, deliberate disobedience, a kind of private and pointed rebellion aimed at punishing me.

"I am losing my desire for you," he said one night. "It is no good."

"No," I would cry. "You can't."

"Is it a crime? I can't help it," he would reply, giggling stupidly.

"You want to suck my lifeblood away. You are a damned succubus."

"I believe they feed on the dead, Grey." I began to blink very hard.

"Oh God, Zoe, would you hold your eyes still for just one moment.   **223**
And I'm supposed to be the crazy one?"

"I think you should see somebody," I said. "A doctor."

"Under no circumstances."

"Why?" I asked.

"You know I am not crazy, that the word *crazy* is a white-man term and that I do not believe in that."

"I am saying you need help."

"I am Coyote."

"You are not. You are a man, an ordinary man."

"No, no," and he clutched my throat.

"Coyote incarnate? You are having religious delusions." He made me think of my mad saints, and of course in my church we were considered Latter-day Saints. Where *was* the line between piety and insanity? Surely Saint Anthony was bizarre. Yet I hung on to the rational, ordinary side of things. I was not inclined at the moment to argue over semantics or ethnic differences. I knew something was wrong.

"This is the twentieth century, Grey," I said. I almost said, And God is dead. But it was silly to have a theological discussion with somebody who obviously not only was not himself but had assumed a self that destroyed the idea of selfhood, that is, of a human identity. The coyote he fancied himself to be was both the slack-jawed, flea-ridden animal that lived to hunt and eat and had a mind the size of a walnut and also a Coyote clever enough to fashion a world. He was a god *and* a dog.

Furthermore, we were running out of money. And thus, in his more lucid moments, Grey talked of grocery stores, grocery stores with cereal boxes and shelves and cash registers.

And I was thinking, How do you get a psychiatrist? They had them in Carmel, but they were so expensive, so many dollars an hour, and he would not see one anyway, and if he saw one would he get cured, and what actually was he sick with, and who could help me get him seated in some office? Who could help me? There was certainly nobody in Big Sur.

Big Sur people would say:

Psychiatrists wear suits and ties.

They have desks and offices, charge fees for jargon. What do they know of the soul?

The world is hostile, and to perceive it as such is not paranoia but keeping your eyes open.

Psychiatrists are part of the establishment conspiracy.

Psychiatry is:

> Lobotomies.
> Shock treatment.
> Sterilization.
> Hysterectomies.
> Throwing away the key.

Had there been a medicine man in the vicinity, I would have tried that, have Grey, like the ancient Hopis, cured with sand paintings and chanting. But there wasn't anybody, or anything.

Another night I made sorrel soup, venison scaloppine, cabbage salad. Everything was ours—the sorrel picked on the hillside, the deer killed in Redwood Gulch, the cabbage left from the destroyed garden. I cooked for comfort now. Comfort for myself and comfort for Grey, for I didn't know what else I could do.

I rubbed his back with olive oil.

Had he had the interest, I would have sucked him not like a succubus, but like a seasoned sex goddess at his service.

I told him stories.

"There was once a beautiful girl growing up on the coast. She had long red hair."

"Like yours?" he asked, smiling.

"No, long and straight, or wavy at the most. Not these corkscrews."

I pulled a curl down, but it sprang back up. Little springs, copper wires, a mechanical head of hair.

"And she had a lover. He was an Indian, an Esselen. This was one of the last left, a secret one, a forgotten one, an Esselen who had escaped massacre and mission school. He showed her how to make acorn bread out of ground acorns. He showed her how to shell and pound and leach the tannic acid out of acorns. He lived in a little wooden lean-to in a canyon by a stream, and he gathered herbs and plants—the coffeeberry and the manzanita—and he knew a hundred natural remedies for poison oak, including the coyote brush, yarrow, and chia."

"It sounds like this was quite an Indian. Somebody told you all this, right, Zoe?"

"A little bird."

"A big bird."

"Yes, you told me this story, but it is not over yet. This was the problem: the beautiful redhead's mother was jealous. She was jealous of her daughter's youth and her love, and the mother had no love; so one day, when the daughter was on her way to visit her secret Indian, the mother killed her, stabbing her in the back. Then she made a wooden coffin for her and buried her in the yard so nobody would know, and that was fine; and after many years, the old woman died. But the new owners of the property were digging one day to make a foundation for an addition to the house, and their shovel struck something hard. It was the coffin. And when they excavated it, out from between the boards, long as a sail, grew beautiful red hair."

Grey began to cry. "Oh, Zoe," he sobbed. "Help me."

"I am trying to, Grey." It was the wrong story.

Meanwhile, I was cooking my heart out. I was straightening up all the time. I was sleeping half-awake. I was worried sick. I was sick with fatigue. I was gray with fatigue. I was crazy with fatigue. I prattled stories to Grey to keep him with me, singing for my supper, *his* supper, his head, our life.

"Tell me, what is the matter, Grey?"

"I just want to be alone," he said.

"Is it . . . ?" I was being a little girl again in my parents' house and waking up to wonder what my parents' moods were so I would know how to feel. I had tried to be a good girl, and to love them enough that they would love me back, to scrub enough, to help enough. But love is not something earned; you cannot gain it by being a good girl, by cooking a hundred meals and telling a hundred stories. You cannot earn it by acquiescing, by lying down obediently on a cold tile floor, legs apart. You cannot keep people alive and sane with love.

At night I would wash myself from the sink we had hooked up to the hose from the spring, get into my flannel nightgown, which had roses all across it. My mother had made it for me, my poor mother. I would prepare for the night as carefully as a priest his table of wine and bread, which would turn into blood and flesh. My ablutions, my absolution. Ritual was all. If I did it right, got it right, Grey would turn to me for love, and the stars would rain down from the sky like baptismal water shedding grace.

Grey would turn away. And looking up at the ceiling, I would see not stars, but dry, stolen pinewood from the lumber store in Cambria, a midnight expedition. Our nights were long and sleepless. Days were barren, without hope or help. My life was without mercy. Because from the second Grey opened his eyes and stretched his arms, I could tell what kind of day it would be. Just like with my parents, I could tell if he was going to be silent and angry or laughing ridiculously, or if he wanted to be alone, or, rarity of all rarities, just be a person, a regular husband who gave his wife a kiss, whistled while he worked, and came in saying: It is going to be hot today.

December 10, 1957

Wright has to live in Paris in order to breathe freely. I will not make mention of Josephine Baker, and all the musicians. Was my father a card-carrying Communist? No. And even if not, did not the Khrushchev revelations about Stalin atrocities, Siberia, etc. in 1956 send a chill through the liberal establishment and scare members, the workers' paradise being one big hell of a concentration camp, the socialist experiment a big failure.

Nonconformists were sent to mental asylums.

Jews were executed.

Poets and writers were detained in the night.

Better Red than dead?

The color of death, dear girl, is red.

Do you remember the big discussion we had in my home about La Pasionaria, the Spanish Civil War woman, who popularized, "It is better to die on your feet than live on your knees"? You said it would be better to live on your knees. Do you still feel that way? How do you live?

December 20, 1957

Dear Margo,

You must come to California. I need your help. Desperately. My husband, I truly believe, is going insane. He laughs uncontrollably and at all the wrong times. He giggles in corners, exhibits himself, and strokes himself. Once, he stopped a car on the highway and asked them to take me away before he killed me. Once, I was driving to town and he opened the door to jump out. Jump out on the highway. The problem is that whenever I talk to anybody about it here, they all think I want to commit him to a hospital to get rid of him, that is, to lock him away forever, to punish him for his nonconformity. Doctors? Hospitals? How uncool, how uncouth. But tell me, what else is there?

I have heard of this place in San Francisco. It is part of the University of California hospital. It is called the Langley Porter Clinic. It is free if you can get in, and they are very advanced and unique in their approach to psychiatric problems. If I could get him in there—but how? How do I begin? You are good at things like that. Remember how together we made the arrangements for your father? You are good at arrangements. I cannot ask my family, for they would not help to begin with and would say I told you so to end with. I love Grey, but cannot cope with him. When are you coming? Don't you get Christmas vacation? Sometimes there are rock slides and the highway is not cleared for days. I'm scared.

[**IT WAS A STRANGE DAY** on the hill for late December. It was hot. The air was thick with menace. Yet I made bread in the morning, as I always did when I was out of sorts. While I measured the flour by handfuls, the bits of sugar and salt, and set the yeast to rise, Grey went out to meditate.

In my memory of that day, what is notable was not the heavy, hot silence of the morning, or maybe it was *because* of the silence that the sound of the car engine was so distinctive. You could always tell what part of the road the car was on by the sound. Slow at dangerous turns, and bumping over potholes, and in one place having to back up and then go at the incline with a roar. I could also tell if it was a familiar car, and whose it was.

"Who the hell is that?" Grey said in his old voice.

I was heartened. Grey was fine. And the car was Kelly's truck. I wondered what he wanted so early in the day, not yet noon, the time he usually rose, he and Oak, from their bed draped like a pasha's tent.

"It's Kelly," I said needlessly. Overhead a hawk careened in the still blue of the sky. It was hunting and would soon take a deep dive.

"Kelly." I waved when he made it around the final corner, but he looked angry and did not move his gaze from the road. Then he came to a stop. For a minute he sat in the car, stared straight ahead.

"What's wrong with Kelly?"

Grey shrugged.

Then Kelly got out of the car, looked at us.

"Want some coffee?" I asked pleasantly.

"No. I came to talk to Grey."

"Is something wrong?" I felt Grey tense beside me.

"Leave my woman alone," Kelly said.

"What?" I clutched my chest.

"This doesn't concern you, Zoe," Grey said. "Go inside."

"Yes, it does. What is going on?"

I saw that Grey was sweating, and an acrid odor came from his body. It was the scent of fear. But he also seemed unusually lucid.

"Grey, Grey, what is this about?"

Kelly moved up closer. "I've had it," he said through clenched teeth. "If you don't leave Oak alone, I'll kill you."

"Bullshit," Grey said, spitting in the dust, and then laughing.

"Bullshit nothing. I don't want to be raising another man's bastard."

"What?"

"I haven't touched Oak," Grey said.

"What, in an hour, a night?"

"You are still seeing Oak?" I began blinking tears.

"Kelly is lying."

"No." He shook his head. "You are lying."

"Are you calling me a liar?"

"Yes, I am."

"Why don't we all go into the Bay Grove and sit down," I said desperately. "I can make some lemonade. We can have some bread." I didn't know what to do. "This is all a mistake of some sort."

"I am not a liar," Grey said.

And then I heard another sound, another car, the soft put-put of Oak's classy gray Volvo barreling up the hill in first gear.

"I'm going to kill you," Kelly said.

For a second I wondered if an east wind was blowing, the one that boded ill, the one that brought on the stupid Indian ghosts, the kind that possessed your body and made you crazy with grief and anguish and killed babies.

"I want you off my land," Kelly said.

"No, you're going to get in your truck and go back down the hill and ask your God for forgiveness," Grey said seriously, but then started to laugh.

"Are you nuts?" Kelly asked.

"Grey hasn't been too well lately," I said. "I think I told you."

"Yeah, she's getting ready to commit me to a state hospital, throw
away the key."

"No, I'm not."

"*She* thinks I'm crazy just because I don't fuck her brains out every
night."

"Probably," said Kelly, "because you're doing it with Oak."

"The hell I am."

Oak had arrived with the baby, Redwood, in her arms.

"Kelly," she shouted. "Like, stop this nonsense."

"You call this nonsense? How do I even know about Woody?"

"He is yours, like, all yours, Kelly."

"Are you pregnant again?" Grey asked her.

"Oh." I felt the arrow go through my heart, for I saw the look
between the two.

"It's like . . . this." She threw up her hands. "Cool."

"No, it isn't."

"Babies are, like, God's gifts."

Grey was advancing on Kelly.

"Grey," I cautioned.

Kelly had knotted his fists, raised them up.

"Kelly," Oak called out too late, for Kelly just walked up to Grey
and punched him in the face.

"Grey, you ingrate, you bastard."

Grey stumbled back, gained his footing, and picked up a long board
left over from the roof.

"Grey!" I screamed. "Don't."

Grey lifted the board over his head as Kelly approached him.

"Go ahead," Kelly said. "Just you try."

"Please, Grey," Oak said. "Don't, like, hurt him."

And then he lowered the board onto Kelly's head.

"Stop!" I screeched.

And he lifted it again, and again hit Kelly, who just kept advancing
toward him.

"No, no."

Grey lifted the board again and again, and finally Kelly fell. He
slumped down to the ground. Blood began to seep out of his nose.

"Oh no!" I screamed.

Rivulets of blood like Fourth of July streamers flowed from his nostrils.

"You've killed him," I said.

"No, I haven't."

Oak did not move.

"What do you want to do?" she asked Grey.

"Let's get out," he said.

"Where are you going?" I screeched. "What is going on?"

"I'm not going to any damned mental hospital, that's for sure. I know what you've been plotting."

"I'm not going to put you in a hospital against your will, Grey."

"Like hell, I read that letter you wrote."

"What letter?"

"To your friend."

"That's as an outpatient, a good place, a place you can get help."

"I'm leaving you."

"You can't. You're my husband."

"Come on," Oak said. "Don't, like, listen to her."

"I'll drive," Grey said to Oak, and got in the driver's seat. She came over to the other side, holding Redwood, and climbed in.

"You can't!" I screamed.

Grey backed up the car and turned it around.

"You can't leave me." I stood in front of the car.

"Zoe, move, or I'll run you over," Grey shouted.

"No."

"Zoe," Grey said, "you bitch. You won't get me." His head was out the window, the car inching forward, and he was laughing like a hyena.

"No."

"Zoe."

He came a little closer.

"I don't love you," Grey said out the window. "I've never loved you, never wanted you. You coerced me into sex, into marriage, into the pregnancy. You want to put me in prison. I'm never coming back."

"No," I screamed so the whole Gorda hill, the ghosts, the snakes, and the coyotes could hear me. "No, no, no," I echoed. "You need me."

"Like a bullet in the head." Grey began to laugh uproariously.

"You are crazy, Grey," I said. "You need medical attention."

Grey looked at Oak. I saw Oak nod her head, and slowly the car moved forward. I knew then that he *would* run me over, that he would do anything, anything at all.

The car came within two feet of me before I jumped aside, scraping and bruising myself.

I watched the cloud of dust all the way down the hill, and saw that they did not turn into Kelly's circle of yurts but headed the car out, south, toward L.A.

"Oh God." I felt my body coming apart, my face loosening, my limbs wobbling in their sockets, my eyes, my eyelids, my lashes, my eyebrows . . . I felt like a brick building falling apart brick by brick.

"Zoe." Kelly was moving.

"They left," I wailed. I fell to the ground.

"Zoe."

"I tried to stop them," I said, maneuvering myself to my elbows. My heart fluttered, a bird escaped from the cage of my ribs. Then my chest gaped open and the wind was rushing through the cavity like a wind tunnel. My hands were shaking like mad. "I feel, I feel, oh Kelly, I feel so terrible."

Kelly crawled over beside me, shook his head slowly.

"I actually put myself in front of the car." I felt as I had when Aaron died and Margo and I were at Mitchell's mortuary and we were going down the hallway to look at receptacles for his ashes. Ashes, ashes, we all fall down. I felt then like a moth with only one day to live, caught in the gray tunnel of that brief life.

"Zoe, stop blinking like some confused little girl. You're pregnant. You are going to be a mother."

I looked down at my melon of a belly.

"You would put Grey over your baby?" His face was streaked with blood. "You would do *that*?"

"No."

"But you did. You risked your life, the baby's life, to stop Grey, to do anything to keep Grey."

I shook my head. "I don't know what I did, Kelly. I don't know anything."

"Get up and get away from here, woman."

"Oh, Kelly, Grey is gone."

"Zoe," he said, taking my arms and threading them around my stomach. "This is your life, this child. Don't put anything ahead of that.

Don't put some crazy coot ahead of that."

"But Grey . . ."

"Oh, he'll be back, they'll be back. Give them a few hours. Shit, man, I'm going down to take a bath. When she comes back, tell her I don't want her anymore, the whore, the high-class L.A. fuck-ass whore, the vegetarian, holier-than-thou whore, movie-bitch whore. Tell the whore to go fuck herself, will you. And if you know what's good for you, dump that bastard. Leave him. What does it take? God Almighty. I want him off my land. You can stay, but he has got to go. Let them both go."

"Do you really think they're coming back?"

"Unfortunately. But you, you . . . I thought you were the one with a level head around here. He's a dangerous guy, can't you see that? He tried to kill us both."

"Are you hurt?" It dawned on me that he had been pounded by a board.

"Yes, I'm hurt."

He got up and walked to his truck, got in, backed up the little incline, turned around, and headed down the hill.

I gave Grey the rest of the day. I put the bread away, cleaned the house. Everything made me cry.

Loss feels like this, I thought, it must. People were right when they said you felt that a part of you was gone. It was not just the heart but lower too, as if intestines had been scooped out, as it was done in hara-kari. I had to rock myself, hug myself, keep everything held together. I was a person, after all. Yes, yes, I was. But I had been through this before. Grey had betrayed me before. I knew what it was about. But that thought didn't make me feel better, yet I knew what to do. Just hold it together, I said to myself. Keep moving. Keep busy. Keep going.

I couldn't sleep that night, and I got up and went outside. I thought I heard voices, the slow beat of the drum. Was it the phantom Indians, a ghost dance, a peace-pipe-smoke dream, a grisly powwow of the dead, the Hill of the Misfits come alive in the dark to taunt me, daring me to live on their burial ground? Or was it my saints, my guardian angels come down Jacob's ladder, as in the opera *Hansel and Gretel*, to keep watch over me all night.

The moon was full. Thin clouds went across it like fingers stroking and tickling, gichi-gichi-goo. The pine trees, the needle-leaves tinkled like silver. There was the owl as large as a small man. Maybe *it* was Saint Anthony and not an owl and not a boy. Maybe *I* was having religious delusions. Maybe it was the ghost of Aaron Robinson. The Indians believe that after a man dies his spirit continues, and so it was with Wakantanka, their Great Spirit. They believed he was everywhere and also in the spirits of friends whose voices we cannot hear.

I heard the howl of the first coyote.

That sent me back inside. I went to sleep, fitfully, with dreams of disaster.

The next morning, there was a dense fog surrounding the house, and for a few minutes I thought I heard voices in the fog, as I had that night. The braves. But it was nothing. The day went by. I spent it on the bed crying. Later that afternoon, I heard a car, but it was not the Volvo. It was Kelly. I did not go out of the house to greet him. I did not respond when he knocked on the door.

"Zoe," he called, pushing the door a little way.

I didn't reply.

He came in.

"Let me take you to town. Can you stay with anybody?"

"This is my home."

"It is not safe for you to be here alone."

"Grey is coming back."

"No, no, he's not."

"How do you know?"

"I got a telegram at the gas station."

"Oh." I didn't ask what it said, I didn't dare.

"You know what it said?"

"No, no, I don't want to know."

I started to cry.

"You are not blinking," Kelly said.

"No," I admitted. "I am beyond blinking."

"Don't cry. You know it was no good. It's over, Zoe, over. It's over."

I could barely move, but I began to collect my belongings. Kelly helped me get things together, the few clothes I owned. Our old sleeping bag had so many patches on it, it looked like a quilt. I took that, the books. Kelly carried everything to his truck, put them in the back.

"Goodbye, house," I said before leaving. I looked around. The woodstove, the bed, the stone walls, the hole with the ladder, the shelves holding pots and pans, and the redwood slab, a small round wood table made from a spool for telephone cable we had found along the road. There were some rocks from the beach, some feathers and shells. A deer skull, a small wooden cross. Grey's red-and-black flannel shirt, his wedding shirt, was tossed across the chair.

If people came in, they would say: They disappeared in the night.

This is what loss feels like, I said to myself. This ashy taste, this rumbling in the bowels, this hole in the wall, this evisceration. It was a familiar feeling.

I imagined the chopped-up rattlesnake that had gotten away becoming whole again, and the deer and rabbits Grey had killed growing up from the floor, the dog whose head was pounded to a pulp resurrecting, the chickens eaten by hawks and foxes being disgorged, and the cats eaten by bobcats, and the bobcats, all coming alive again, the curse lifted. And in time, plants would come through the floorboards, and rocks from the quarry by the spring would roll over and cave in through the roof, and the dead Indians on the hill—transparent, insubstantial—would sit around the fire, and the animals ranged behind them, would say: Heap big trouble way back then.

Nature would be restored to herself. The only remnant of Grey or myself would be a few rocks in a falling-down, haphazard wall. And maybe there would be stories. But I had been through this before, this nostalgia, and I hated it, just hated it. I picked up my ballerina jewelry box, and, as hard as I could, I threw it against the stone wall. It shattered into pieces, and the little notched cylinder rotated one last time, getting slower and slower, "The Teddy Bear Picnic" come to an end.

I got in Kelly's truck, and we drove to Pacific Grove, completely silent the whole way.

When we arrived in front of my aunt's, I asked Kelly, "What am I going to do?"

"I don't know, Zoe." He reached in his pocket, pulled out a hundred-dollar bill. "For you."

"Will you let me know if they are coming back?"

"They are not coming back," he said.

"How do you know?"

"They are driving to New York. Oak called the Gorda gas station to have me send her things there. They are already on the road." **237**

"On the road? A highway? A modern highway? To New York? But Grey hates the city."

"Zoe, you can't . . ."

"But why did he go?"

"Maybe he was frightened."

"Of the hospital? I wasn't going to commit him."

"Maybe he was frightened of you, of being married."

"But he was the one who wanted it. I don't understand."

"Let me help you get your stuff out," Kelly said.

When I knocked on the door, my aunt opened it, looked in my face, said nothing, but took me straight into her arms.

"He left me," I sobbed.

"Oh, my poor baby," she said, "my poor, poor baby."

"I want to die, Aunt Pearl."

"No, no, it just feels that way."

"I feel," I looked up to the sky. It was gray, chilly, and reminded me of my forlorn youth, lonely trips to the library, dreams of Nijinsky, hopes for delivery. "I feel, Aunt Pearl, that I keep spiraling down, that I have gone in circles, come back to where I was many times. I feel like I'm nowhere and I'm nothing."

"Sh," my aunt whispered. Kelly stood behind me. Had my aunt been tall enough, she would have signaled over my shoulder with her eyes: "Leave her, she'll be taken care of here. Don't worry."

And his eyes would have said back to her eyes: "But I am worried. I am worried for her, for me, for all of us."

And if any of us were Catholics, our eyes would have said, Lamb of God, take away the sins of the world, take away our sins.

Lamb of God, take away the world.

Margo's father, Aaron, told us he slept with Judy Garland when they were both kids, on a train in a Pullman car going west. Of course, the dates were all wrong. Aaron was lying through his teeth.

He said he and Judy Garland went top bunk, a metaphysical experience. By then I knew what sleeping with somebody meant, and I was embarrassed in front of Judy, his wife. What was going on?

I made love with Aaron on the floor at his school. That was true.

Aaron had been a cook on a Mississippi riverboat. So he said.

And a jazz pianist when he went to law school. I believe.

The Renaissance man.

And did Aaron know cities? That man knew cities. He said he knew the Village in New York like the roof of his mouth; and, yes, the fountains in Madrid quenched his thirst when he was tired from battle; and at three o'clock in the morning in Paris, the City of Light, a green bottle of wine in his hand, he had sung at the top of his voice the songs from Paul Robeson's record Songs of Free Men. In San Francisco it was the bread, and in Seattle the rain, and in Chicago the bold American architecture, Carl Sandburg's Chicago, hog butcher of the world.

One Christmas Aaron had stayed in Chicago in an old and elegant hotel, aristocratic, all oak and brass, with real pink roses and real candles on the Christmas tree. Then it started to snow.

I had never seen snow. Aaron said it was beautiful, and I dreamed that one day I would find myself in a large American eastern city, walking on its diamond streets knowing the second before snow, snow. And, looking up, I would be the first person in the whole city to catch the first flake. Then more would come, tumbling like feathers from a burst pillow. I would have to duck into a Chock Full o'Nuts coffee shop. We would all be there, huddled in our bulky winter coats, the steam rising from our cups, the waitress looking out the window.

"Supposed to get five inches before night," she would say.

That night, in the snow, I would go to the opera The Magic Flute. My date would hold my elbow as he escorted me from the apartment building to the waiting cab. I would be wearing a red coat with a leopard-trimmed collar. We would hear somebody practicing the piano, scales. My cheeks would glow, and the city would be vast and quiet under the sparkling hood of snow.

"The first cities, Zoe," Aaron had said, "grew up along rivers. The Nile, the Tigris, the Euphrates, the Ganges, the Hudson."

When he said cities and the growth of civilization, I envisioned shoots of bamboo, a hut here, a skyscraper there, hanging gardens, soon a marketplace, and then a symphony orchestra, the ballet. The children go to schools, and at night everyone is tucked into an apartment next to someone else's apartment. Density, cohesion. People can buy newspapers on the street. Extra, extra, read all about it. From a humble hut on the Ganges to Rockefeller Center.

[**MY AUNT SAID** I could stay with her as long as I wanted, and if that was forever, that was just fine with her. I was given the Italian room, replete with Chianti bottles hung crisscross on the wall, painted lamps with rotund, rosy-cheeked, black-haired women, a red-and-white-checkered tablecloth on the dressing table, the statue of Romulus and Remus taking suck, a whole stack of Mario Lanza records, and a fern. The ornate wrought-iron furniture made me feel that I was living in a restaurant, but the bed, thank God, was canopied, and I could pull the curtains—maroon silk, gold-tasseled—around me and pretend I was somewhere else, somebody else. I was a Juliet in her bedroom, or I was a courtesan during the time of the Borgias, or I was Audrey Hepburn in *Roman Holiday*. Anything but a pregnant American girl stuck at the end of the fifties in a rinky-dink California town.

After seeing the doctor and getting settled in, the next thing I did was file for divorce. The day I did it, I thought I might die, the little that was left of me.

"You have to do it, Zoe," my aunt said. "You have to sever the tie formally, so that he has nothing to do with you anymore. Don't you see?"

My aunt and mother hated Grey not, as my father did, because he was an Indian; rather, they hated him because he had taken me away and then hurt me. I had to explain my face, my bruises. Yet, as a few days went by and then weeks, I began to regret the case I had made against him, and when my bruises healed, I began to forget the bad parts of our relationship. I was getting lonely, and I felt that my aunt and mother were not quite fair in their assessment. They didn't know how Grey had tried to rescue me from a meaningless life, and how much I truly loved him. What could they know of love? My aunt's infrequent and maladjusted boyfriends were not noted for their attentiveness, and my mother barely tolerated my father. They didn't know that I was so lost without Grey that I didn't know what to do from one moment to the next. How could they?

On the other hand, it would occur to me that Grey, life with Grey, was impossible, that he was unfaithful, vicious, self-pitying, self-indulgent, selfish, egotistical, rather crazy, and probably copulating with Oak every minute I was away. I had committed myself, said I was going to get a divorce, and there I was in the lawyer's office, no going back.

I was scared of Grey, there was that, too, and I had only really been afraid of one other person. My father was stern and eccentric, and, once, he had beaten me, the time I left the sanitary napkin on the back of the toilet without wrapping it in toilet paper. He humiliated me on that occasion, and I hated him for it, but I wasn't afraid of him. Aaron I should have been afraid for or of or something, for he proved dangerous, at least to himself. He would stop at nothing, I realized, to make a point. But even in death, he was not a monster. For him I felt anger, sorrow, regret, guilt, not fear. Margo's disapproval could hurt me. That, however, wasn't fear.

I *was* afraid of my mother, of how her personality could flip right over into something which I couldn't cope with. I understood her, I think, or had a glimmer of her sense of frustration, but that did not lessen my fear. In my dreams, she came at me with all the fury of a spurned witch. And once, in a dream, her hair had blackened as she stood there, the roots growing out with the speed of fire, only the tips remaining blond—and those sizzling and crackling like popcorn. She scared me to death.

With Grey, my fear was different. I was afraid that he might hurt me, not just by being unfaithful, which made me feel as if all the fishhooks lodged in my heart were twisted with pliers, but by simply breaking my bones. And however much I dallied with the idea of death and wanting to die, I didn't really want to die. I wanted to feel good, to live well, to be happy. I wanted him, but I wanted to live. When people say they love each other more than life, I suppose that means even if they go down in death together. Not I. I did not want to die for love. Marriage, I felt, was not a license to kill. And I had given up, without remembering when, the Mormon idea of heaven.

So there I was in the lawyer's office. It was in a large building in downtown Monterey, the halls with red-and-black block linoleum flooring and the walls a dull gray. His office had a rippled glass-topped door, like the ones in detective films, and inside was his secretary, who, true to form, wore tight skirts and chain-smoked.

The lawyer himself, Mr. Creesom, had the cheery demeanor and rosy complexion of a born alcoholic. And when it came to the grounds for divorce, and I described the beating when I was pregnant, the consummation ceremony, the car inching forward, he rumpled his tomato-red forehead, put his beet-red hand up to his cheek, poked his red fox nose forward at me, and stuck out his red carpet tongue.

"My dear, that sounds just absolutely terrible," and he filled in where it said:

> and the court having determined, upon the facts adduced, that the plaintiff is entitled to a divorce from the defendant upon the ground of
> EXTREME CRUELTY.
> *It is Ordered, Adjudged and Decreed* that plaintiff above-named is entitled to a divorce from said defendant upon the ground of
> EXTREME CRUELTY.

I think I must have turned a little pale at that, for Mr. Creesom then told me about a reservation he had been on in Arizona, where the Indians dropped their pants at the slightest excuse, the women as well as the men. Somehow the vision of people dropping their pants reminded me of my false-teeth experience and my most embarrassing moment at school, when I jumped so hard at jump rope—double-Dutch red-hot peppers—that my pants fell down. I had to laugh.

"That's more like it," he said.

"But it's very hard," I admitted. "The thing is, I love my husband."

"How about the past tense, dearie."

"No, not yet."

"There are many fish in the sea."

"I don't think so."

"The trouble is, you've been fishing in murky waters."

"Are there any other kind?"

The thought of another man or of men in general was, at the moment, beyond my comprehension. Each night in my canopied Italian bed, as if encased in the Eternal City, I remembered Grey's smell, the feel of his hands on my rump.

After going to the lawyer, I felt at fault. That always happened to me. I was schooled in doubt. If, for a moment, I thought I was right, that feeling immediately flip-flopped into the reverse. Then I would feel I was wrong all along or that wrongness or failure resided in me like perennial plants in perpetual bloom.

I can't do anything right, I would say to myself. I killed Aaron, I didn't go to college, I couldn't stay married. I was the kiss of death, a femme fatale. Those were the facts.

Wandering through the empty house when my aunt was not home, I realized for the first time that her decorating scheme—her international rooms—was her way of traveling, that since she had left Armenia, she had only gone, like the rest of us on the Del Monte Express, to San Francisco. Yet it seemed all right, a good solution, decorating your house with objects from around the world, not a real deprivation. As my mother had a capacity for grief, Aunt Pearl seemed to have a capacity for happiness. She was always excited about something, somebody, and I could see her going through her whole life the same way. And although it did not seem at that moment that I would ever be happy again, I knew that I was more like Aunt Pearl than like my mother. I could conjure up whole blocks of happiness, buildings, alleyways, places I had visited and would find again, a happy this, a happy that.

[**PREGNANT AS I WAS,** I got a job in a garment factory in Monterey, because at least with a sewing machine in front of me I could sit down. I am sure the boss didn't care if I was about to deliver on the floor, the wages were so low. I didn't really know how to sew, thanks to my mother's having done my sewing for me, but my job was so repetitive that it hardly felt like sewing. Marx was right. The modern assembly line and production factory alienated the worker from his work. I was an automaton in the service of blue-jean capitalism.

"Do you know," I asked a fellow worker, "that we are all being exploited?"

"Are you from the union?"

"No."

"What's your name?"

"Zoe."

"Well, Zoe, if you want to keep working, just keep your hat over your head, kid. You talk union, you lose your job."

"Really?"

"Yeah, really."

Aaron and Joe Hill said: Just organize. My supervisor said: Just shut up, or we'll all be out of a job.

Clothing Classics was in new Monterey, on Central Avenue. We did contract work for bigger garment firms, such as Levi-Strauss in San

Francisco and Talbott Ties in Carmel. My job was to sew on pockets, butt pockets. The trousers came to me not whole but each leg separate, and I was paid not hourly but by the piece. Ten cents a pocket. Piles

and piles of pockets.

There were about fifty of us in the warehouse, with our sewing machines lined up on either side of a long cutting table and the cutting knife hanging on cables above it. The cutter could cut a hundred or so legs at one time—the cloth stacked up and outlined in chalk—just like a buzz saw going through wood. We had a lunchroom, and a bathroom with a couch in it, as required by law, so that if we got our period we could lie down. Somebody was always on the couch—cramps, nervousness, female troubles; legs, fingers, something was always hurting —and I nearly gave birth on it.

All of us at Clothing Classics, a.k.a. the Armpit of the World, were pretty much in the same bad boat. The rowboat, a leaky one at that. We were poor. We had no men. And most of us were raising kids. We were Negroes, Asians right off the boat, and a couple of white people like me. Our boss called all of us women broads and bitches to our faces, and the cutter, a deaf homosexual, the boss called a faggot-fly to his back (Thomas could read lips). Mary Ellen, my Negro supervisor, had a wooden leg. I thought she had been a victim of racism.

"No, baby. I lost my leg when I was a kid hiking in the Sierras, frostbite." She owned her own house in Seaside and was, at age fifty-four, on the verge of her sixth marriage. She hung her wedding dress up in the lunchroom on the cage protecting the spokes of the fan, and when the fan was on, the dress looked like a ghost blowing out at us in the sewing room. We were all envious.

"And you. What happened to you?" Mary Ellen asked me. "How did you land in this hellhole?" Our conversations were in the lunchroom at the wooden picnic table under the time clock with all the time cards and a poster that said: ACCIDENTS DON'T JUST HAPPEN.

"Lovesickness."

"Lovesickness," Mary Ellen repeated so that the Asian women and Thomas could get it. She put her hand over her heart. It seemed they understood, for they shook their heads sadly, tsked, tsked.

"I'm getting a divorce," I said.

"Ah, the Big D."

I flinched a little.

"Olive Oyl is getting a divorce." Mary Ellen dusted her hands off. "Gone," she said to the women. They sighed like weeping willows in a strong breeze.

"I know how that is, honey, but you just got to ride it out, keep up," another woman said. Ida was her name.

"I'm trying."

"She's trying, girls," Ida repeated.

The Asians, in their restrained way, patted my hands. Yes, yes, yes.

"Need I ask," Mary Ellen inquired, "was he good to you?"

"No, not always, and when he was bad, he . . ."

"Gracious. The man hit her," Ida announced.

Mary Ellen pretended to slap Ida.

"That's right, the man is a beast, a living beast," Ida reaffirmed to the Asian ladies and Thomas, who drew back in horror.

"That's why I'm getting a divorce."

"Very well and good, but sometimes these things turn up again, like a bad penny."

"I hate him."

"Well, it sounds intense, Olive Oyl, and complex. You say you hate him, which means you probably still love him. I bet you do?"

I nodded, looking down at my jeans. They were Grey's. At Clothing Classics, we did not get discounts on jeans. The boss said that if God himself walked in off the street, He would not get a discount. I did not button my jeans to the top, and I wore JCPenney smocks, bought by my aunt with her employee discount. My shoes were rubber flip-flops.

"What would it take for you to really hate him? What does he have to do? What would be enough? If he came to the doorway right now . . ."

I looked at the door expectantly. Then I looked back at Mary Ellen. I was eating a peanut-butter-and-jelly sandwich, just as I had every lunch of high school.

"See, now that is bad, real bad, Olive. You should run the other way. Enough is enough." Mary Ellen was disappointed in me. She wasn't the only one.

"Don't you have any pride?" Ida asked.

I shook my head.

"This is a sad case," Mary Ellen told the Asians. Her floating wedding dress, hooked on the fan, wove about, in and out, back and forth, the angel of our expectations.

Actually, I thought of Mary Ellen's wedding dress as a swan costume, a swan song, anything but happiness forever. But for her, it was liberation. No more Armpit of the World, Clothing Classics.

"You do not honor yourself?" she pressed on.

I shrugged. "He told me I was beautiful." I tried to remember when that was exactly. Was it in the Spaghetti Factory before we were married?

Mary Ellen looked at her wooden leg, looked up again.

"They all say that; that's standard, Olive Oyl. Isn't your life worth something more to you than somebody feeding you some line?"

I shrugged.

"Don't take me wrong. You *are* beautiful."

"I am?"

"Sure you are. Didn't your parents ever mention it? You're a knockout. With that red hair and those big brown eyes, my, my, my."

I didn't say anything.

"But beauty is cheap, honey. Beauty is neither here nor there, but everywhere. The point of this tale is, and I'm getting to the big picture show, this hyena on two legs from nowhere tells you what you've never heard before and suddenly he is Mr. Wonderful. Come on, child, grow up. You have a baby on the way. So he says you're beautiful. Others will tell you that. Burnell, now, he tells me every night. And he is beautiful, too, and we are going to have one beautiful wedding. I can't believe a cute white girl like you is so dependent on beautiful. Flattery, Olive Oyl, is skin-deep."

The Asian women fluttered their hands like fans in rapid agreement. Thomas nodded his head.

"The man got her wrapped around his little finger," Ida said.

The Asians looked puzzled. Thomas understood.

"Beats her, too. I mean, this is pathetic. You mean to tell me, that is all you have going for yourself, somebody telling you you are beautiful?"

"Easy, Ida, easy," Mary Ellen cautioned.

Thomas got up, fluttered through our ranks to the ladies' room. We didn't care.

"She going to have a baby, that's what she got going," Ida insisted.

"The baby?" Of course I knew I was pregnant, intellectually that is, but my levels of cognition at that time, I suppose, were so thick that, deep inside, I didn't always know I was pregnant. Only sometimes, when I held very still or when I was going to sleep and told the baby good night, did it register, or when I was walking to work, which was less than a mile away from my aunt's, and the baby would kick and my legs would ache.

"There you go," Mary Ellen said. "Ida is right. Live for your baby. The man nearly beat the baby out of you. Now, is that the father you want for your child?"

"No."

"Of course not."

Thomas, back from the ladies' room, smiled sweetly.

"I say the man's lucky to be deaf," Ida said to his back. "Or whatever he is. Boy, girl, mineral, or rutabaga. The things you hear nowadays you're better off not hearing."

Sometimes I *did* wish I was deaf and mute like Thomas. Because I didn't know why I told everybody my troubles. That information, however, was on the tip of my tongue and practically my first words out. Hi, nice to meet you. I was married. He beat me. He tried to run me over.

I didn't know whether I was attempting to get rid of the event, of Grey, by spreading his misdeeds about, or whether by talking about my troubles I was holding on to them, to him, or whether I was using my misfortunes as a way of getting attention, a way of making myself interesting. Truly, I had nothing else to say. See my wound? *Watch me bleed.*

Inevitably it backfired and I ended up defending Grey. "He would never hurt the baby," I said.

"Oh, is that so?" Mary Ellen piped up. "It's perfectly acceptable to brutalize the mother when the baby is in the stomach and almost kill the baby? And it's fine with you if your baby becomes an orphan. What makes you think that he would not hurt the baby if he would hurt you? And what makes you hold your own life at such risk and yourself in such low esteem? Don't you count?"

The clock said ten. Our break was over.

"Four things you got to learn in this life," Mary Ellen concluded, holding up her fingers.

"Be
Good
To
Yourself."
I smiled.
"Sounds easy, huh?"
I continued to smile.
"It ain't easy," Ida said.
I shrugged.
"You got family here in town?" Ida continued.
"My mother and father. I live with my aunt."
"Now that's nice, real nice."
"It isn't always nice."
"Well, you know," Ida said. "I mean, what the hell. The thing is, you got to live somewhere, and if you feel sick or tired at work, curl up on the sofa. We got our sofa."

"Yeah," I said. "Our sofa."

I thought of it: a faded, itchy pink, a spring popping up in the middle, and generations of sweat stains on its arms.

[**MARY ELLEN** found me curled up on that sofa one day after a break.

"What's the matter, Olive Oyl? The world got you down? The cat got your tongue? Are you depressed?"

"I have a stomachache."

"Like cramps every ten or fifteen minutes?"

"Yes, I think so."

"That's not a stomachache. That's the baby, sweetie pie."

"It's too early for the baby."

"*You* think so."

The boss, Mr. Smith, took me, the pregnant broad, with Mary Ellen to the hospital in his car, and his secretary called my mother, and my mother called my aunt, and soon we were all there in the waiting room, and then, as in a dream, I was being led upstairs to a large white room with a bunch of beds filled with groaning women.

"Cloud," the woman said.

"Uh-huh," the nurse replied, brandishing a razor.

I began to blink hard.

"Everything has to be sanitary," she explained, as she shaved my pubic hair with such vigor that, had I known what it was, I would have feared a clitoridectomy. The enema was introduced with equal gusto. All the while a doctor watched, chewing gum.

As a walk-in patient, I had to take the doctor who was on duty. A resident, he needed a shave and some manners.

"Okay, get her up on the stirrups," he said.

Then he put his finger up my vagina and another one up my ass.

"Ouch," I said.

"You should have thought of that a little earlier when you were playing around," he said, looking at my ringless finger.

"I'm married."

"So you have trouble with intercourse," he pronounced.

"Is that a rhetorical question?"

"No, just wondering why you tense up so much. You have to relax."

I tried. I tried hard.

"You're not ready," he said after the third excruciating probe. "Go home."

"I think I'm ready."

"Put your clothes on, young lady."

"I'm ready."

"I'm the doctor."

I put my clothes on, went back downstairs to the waiting room.

"Well?" my aunt said.

"Well?" my mother said.

Standing side by side—even though my mother was in the current fashion and my aunt was in slouchy Bohemian gear, and my mother's hair was blond and my aunt's pitch-black—they were still identical. The way they moved their heads, held out their hands. Their voices, everything.

"Well?" said Mary Ellen.

"He says I'm not ready."

"Are you?" my aunt asked.

"Are you?" my mother echoed.

"Yes."

"Well, no point in going all the way home. Let's just wait here until we get a doctor who knows his business," Mary Ellen said.

So we sat down, all together, and waited. My mother hummed a song from *Annie Get Your Gun*. I must say that since I had been back in Pacific Grove, she was pretty much on good behavior. Although there were some I-told-you-sos in terms of my marriage, she refrained from daily commentary. She had not gotten drunk once, to my knowledge. My father had also been restrained and circumspect. I knew he had given up hope for me, for who would marry me now, certainly not a Mormon man. But perhaps because he had given up hope, some of the tension between us had been relieved.

"The baby *is* coming," I said, for it seemed that bands of pain were crisscrossing my stomach and forcing something to happen to my body over which I had no control.

"She's having her baby," Mary Ellen shouted out to a young man dressed in whites who was passing by in the hallway.

"Let's take her up and see." He looked about sixteen and wore braces on his teeth, but he was indeed a doctor, a resident or intern, somebody who could deliver babies.

Again the big room, the stirrups, the deep poke.

"You sure are." He winked. "Nurse, move my girl into the labor room."

I was so grateful, I almost forgot my pain. But only for a moment, for the next second I was wheeled into the Labor Room, the AFL-CIO baby factory. Everybody, lined up beside one another, was moaning and groaning, calling for her mother, her god, her anesthetic.

"I'm not going to be like that," I told the nurse.

"Of course not."

It took about ten minutes before I, too, was screaming my head off and begging without modesty for an anesthetic. And by the time I got into the delivery room—the doctor wheeling me in on a stretcher and calling out, "My girl is next"—I was a rack of pain, a wrung towel of pain, a vise of pain. I felt that I was being twisted and turned and that what Grey called thunder knives were poking me. I beseeched the nurse for a gas mask. I called upon Saint Anthony for divine interference. Not only would I serve him until the end of my days if he made the pain stop, but I would make my child serve, too. I told him that a torture had been devised for me, specifically, just like the one in *Brave New World*, or was it *1984*. A buzz saw was drawing and quartering me. My legs were strung up. Nobody had given me a clue about the pain. It was the world's best-kept secret. I didn't deserve this. And the worst thing was that everybody was going to get it. Nobody was going to get out without torture. Nobody was going to get out alive. I realized it was a deep and pervasive conspiracy. Life and death, hell and hell.

"Push," the doctor said, his voice a muffled hundred miles away.

Above me rose an angry red sun.

"Push."

The red disk was hot on my exposed parts. Clippers and scissors and other instruments, like the paraphernalia of Latin American torture, were lying on a white cloth. I was to be sliced, drawn, and quartered. They were going to eat my body, drink my blood.

"Push."

Masked strangers leaned in toward me.

"Push, goddamn it," the doctor said.

I began to push because I had no choice. My body was doing whatever it wanted without my permission.

"Push harder. You are going to get a baby out of this."

I began to push, although I knew my body was going to rip apart.

"Push down, sweetheart, push it all out. Just give it one big push."

I thought, on top of all the torture, I might humiliate myself and shit, but I couldn't help it, my body was turning inside out of its own volition, and suddenly there was some enormous thing (a bowel movement?) between my legs that wouldn't go away.

"Another big push. Atta girl. One more."

I pushed and reached higher and higher. I reached for the sun on the ceiling, and there, my wings melting, at the top of my pain, I knew why I was alive. I was no longer the outsider, better Red than dead, the white-girl nigger lover, the bookworm, the frog, the four-eyed creature, the adolescent lover of a political suicide, the dragon lady, the displaced squaw, the exploited garment worker, the kid alone on the asphalt playground waiting for the bomb to hit her over the head— no, I was at the center of the universe, doing, for once, what I was supposed to do.

An exquisite, trembling pleasure rippled through me, a little greenish worm with a lumpy head was put on my chest, and then I was thrown back down. Down, down into darkness.

[**I NAMED HER** Nadja, after André Breton's *Nadja*, the book Margo was reading at the City Lights bookstore the day I was gummed, a surreal Nadja, the Nadja who says, Who am I, the Nadja who inhabits a book, my Nadja.

She had lots of straight black hair and Grey's dark complexion. Her eyes were bluish but would change, I thought, to brown, my eyes. In the hospital, I had beautiful dreams. In those dreams, everybody wanted to hold her. Even my father. And, in fact, he did like to hold her, and would walk back and forth, reciting truisms like: "A penny saved is a penny earned." "A bird in the hand is worth two in the bush."

When I wrote Margo, she wrote back: "Rename her. Nadja is a ghost in the Breton book."

[**MY AUNT** baby-sat early in the morning before she went to work at JCPenney's, and then my mother came over. I had started nursing Nadja in the morning and at night, and she had the bottle during the day. I would walk to work with my little lunch box, which still smelled sour from grammar school, still had a picture of the Lone Ranger on it, and Tonto, which I thought appropriate, given everything.

My breasts, encased in two bras stuffed with cotton, hurt like hell and leaked continuously. My nipples were cracked, and I was sore between my legs. Yet I was happy with my baby. Was this it, I wondered. Did the drive for sex and mating and courtship and companionship and engagement rings and all the sighing and even the jealousy—were they just preludes to babies? Baby dreams and baby clothes, and baby books and little baby booties. I asked my mother if she had any of my old dolls. Did I have dolls? The only thing was my music box, which was broken to bits in Gorda.

What did it matter? I had my child. I would run home from work to see her. She could grab on to my finger. She held tight. She could follow sounds with her head when she was lying down in her crib. She could coo and gurgle. She even smiled, curling herself up like a little monkey first. I longed for her all day, made plans for her. She would have toys. She would have help with her homework. I would read her stories and take her to puppet shows. When she got to high school, I would not tell her she was cursed. No, we would have a warm discussion about how wonderful it was to be a woman. And she, she would go to college, become a lawyer or anthropologist, whatever was her heart's desire.

And I held her to me every minute I could and even slept with her in the large bed. I did everything my mother didn't, and didn't do what she had done and then some.

Yet, amazingly, my feelings for my mother mellowed, and I think hers for me underwent a change, too. It was not quite that I forgave her, but in *my* motherhood I was able to feel a distinct kinship with her. While she did not like to be considered old enough to be a grandmother, she seemed to like being a grandmother and would hold the baby, something, I understand, she never did with me; and she and my aunt, who would get out of her work clothes—her girdle and garters, stockings and high heels—and I would sit around and talk. We talked about everything, and one night we talked about Aaron, who had become a community legend through a series of newspaper articles, "Commies in Our Midst."

My aunt called it "Commies in the Mist." It was February, chilly and bleak. We sat around the fireplace in the Mexican room. My aunt made Mexican hot chocolate and powdery white cookies called Mexican wedding cakes. My mother sang "South of the Border."

"His wife is crippled, and his daughter, well, she is adopted." I left out the facts that, while my mother had snoozed and boozed, I had spent every waking minute I could over at their house, that I had done It, the dirty deed, with the father and even gone with Margo to have him cremated, his flesh turned to dust. Margo was the adopted one, yet I adopted them as my family and secret love. For a year I had thought of little else besides Aaron, Margo, the Robinsons.

"To think he had a family," my aunt uttered.

My mom was pasting Green Stamps in a booklet, saving up for patio furniture. Our "patio" was a square slab of cement.

"Right," I concurred. "They *chose* to have Margo. Surely that was a responsibility he should have honored. Why does everybody think of him as a martyr?" I don't know why I said that. Very few people thought of Aaron as a martyr. I even heard somebody say at school that he "didn't look like a Communist." Had they expected horns and a tail? I don't know why I was so hard on Aaron. Surely I had dishonored my relationship with him, although I could argue that the relationship itself was a dishonor to his family. Usually I didn't discuss my feelings with my mother and aunt or with anybody, but I noticed that, away from Grey, I liked to talk, and I went where my voice took me.

"Come to your auntie," Aunt Pearl said, asking me to pass Nadja to her. Unlike me, according to my mother, Nadja was a good baby. She didn't cry much and she didn't fidget and blink. She held you in a steady gaze, slept through the night, and was quiet and content. I had bought a camera, and already I had enough pictures of her to fill an album, for there were none of me as a baby.

"If homicide is a crime, so should suicide be a crime. It is. It's vengeful and irresponsible." This was my aunt again. I knew that was her attitude, yet she wasn't aware of the small ways people committed suicide, how her own sister was killing herself bit by bit with gin and tonics, although, in all fairness, my mother had been sober since I was back. She faithfully attended AA meetings, and she and her AA buddy would have lunch together, go shopping, and, if they got the urge, stop in at the drive-in for sodas and onion rings.

"I think sometimes very intelligent people do not think that ordinary rules apply to them. They think they are extraordinary people, above and beyond regular responsibilities." This was my mother. I wondered if she thought herself extraordinary. Aaron *had* thought of himself that way.

"For women," Aunt Pearl said dreamily, "love is everything."

"Is it?" I asked.

"Oh yes." She said this vaguely looking at the clock. She had a new boyfriend. We called him the Baron, for, like a McLaren, he had red hair. "Men are different." Her mind was not completely on our conversation apparently.

"What is it for men?" I asked, reaching for Nadja. I couldn't stand to have her out of my arms for too long. I unbuttoned my blouse, started to feed her. Even in front of my mother, I draped a blanket over me, so that I wasn't really exposed. I was afraid that they would think I was showing off my breasts. "Originally we were united," my aunt continued, "according to the Greeks, and we go about looking for our other half. Without our other half, we feel empty."

This reminded me of my words with Narcissus at the gas station.

Grey had asked me, Don't you want to be fully human?

Meaning married.

Narcissus countered, But you *are* fully human.

Meaning all by yourself.

"We feel empty only to be filled by a penis?" I asked. "Plugged
in?"

"Why so crude, Zoe?" my mother asked, breaking into "June Is
Bustin' Out All Over."

"June is not busting out all over," Aunt Pearl corrected. "It's only
February, and damned cold at that."

I had never used that—*pee-nis*—word in front of my mother, and
when I said it I thought of Grey, how hard he was all over, including
his bottom. He did not wear underwear, and the thought of him going
about like that, naked under his trousers, had both dismayed and excited
me at one time.

"I don't envy your penis," I said to him once.

"You don't?" he laughed. "Listen to you. Just listen to you."

I looked down at Nadja, who was sleeping in my arms. "I think
to a woman a child is everything." Her perfect little mouth was open,
and a little drool of milk made a thin white line on her tawny chin.
Her black hair was thickening and spiky. She looked vaguely Asian. But
she was mine, all mine.

"I wouldn't know about that," Pearl said. "I'm a woman and I
don't have a child."

"Frankly," my mother said, "I don't know what is the most important thing. I do think that when one is suicidal, things like love
become obscured. The thought of death takes over. It's an obsession."
My mother widened her eyes. In the firelight, she was very beautiful.

"I think this Aaron Robinson felt trapped, very trapped, in a way
he could not get out. Maybe it *is* a kind of insanity, a box you get into
and can't get out of, except one way, through death. You no longer see
what is the most important thing. Still, it's a crying shame, a crime
against humanity, his humanity, for doesn't he count?" This was my
theory.

"Zoe, I really think you should have gone to college."

"Too late now, Aunt Pearl. I can always read."

"Yeah, but then what?"

"Look at Aaron Robinson," I said, for now, more than ever before,

I could not go to college. And although I had discarded much of what Grey had told me, one thing he did convince me of was that there was life after high school, and it did not have to be college.

"It wasn't college that killed him, Zoe," my aunt said.

"It was something *like* college," I said, taking Grey's line.

It was that stupid John Reed reading group, I was thinking, playing with ideas like toys, yes, believing he was beyond good and evil, taking the powers that be for granted, seducing young girls. Isn't that what Margo had said? I remember how I was mesmerized by him, how I walked into it as though I were sleepwalking; and when he said, Open your eyes, it was not the pipes on the ceiling of the laboratory I really saw with my blurred vision but some kind of starry heaven housed in the white and delightsome column of his body.

"Surely, Zoe . . ."

"Isn't death a mystery, and suicide even a greater mystery?" my mother asked.

"I could never kill myself," I said. "Because of Nadja. Not only would she be helpless, but what kind of legacy is that? How can you as a child find meaning in life after your parent rejects life? The parent is there to show you how to live and then, then . . . then what?"

I looked at my baby. Dr. Spock said that babies reach out for things, for people. Well, there I was. She could see me, feel me. I held pretty colored objects in front of her, raised and lowered them, watched her eyes follow them. Soon she would be able to play with them. How could I ever think of dying?

[**" D O Y O U K N O W** the Fillmore?" Lucille asked over the phone, her voice loud enough to alert my aunt that I was making a long-distance call. The room advertised in the *San Francisco Chronicle* was the cheapest one listed.

"No."

"This room is in the Zone. It's the slums," Lucille shouted on the phone, so nobody ten feet away could misunderstand. "You sound like a white girl."

"Ah," I sighed. The fog was rolling in, bundles of it like the tumbleweeds I had seen on the mountain. "I *am* a white girl."

"Well."

"Well."

Lucille didn't know she was my great black hope. I had to get out of Pacific Grove. As sweet as my aunt was, I felt trapped at her house. The discussion about Aaron clinched it.

"My best friend," I began on the phone, "is . . ."

"Spare me," Lucille said, "the details. This is the Ghet-to, get it?"

"Yes." At least it wasn't part of my childhood, part of Aaron.

"Black face, honey, and we ain't Al Jolson singing 'My Mammy.' "

I remember Margo saying her knee grows in Brooklyn, and how much our legs had ached when they were growing, toes and knees, from the shinbone to the knee bone . . .

"Get the picture?"

"Yes, I do." It wasn't Pacific Grove.

"Get the drift?"

"Yep." I could get away.

It made sense. It was fated. Negroes were going to save my life.

"It's cool?" Lucille asked.

"It's cool."

I got to the Zone after disembarking at the Greyhound Station amid pimps, prostitutes, pickpockets, and pederasts and taking a trolley down Market Street, carrying Nadja in one arm, the old cardboard suitcase in another, and a diaper bag across the shoulder. I arrived at nine o'clock at night. Lucille opened the door.

"Hey, ain't you scared?"

"No."

"Why not?"

"I never worry about strangers jumping out of the bushes to get me. It's your friends and lovers you have to watch out for."

"I know what you mean," she said. "I know exactly what you mean. This ain't exactly the White House. But welcome, come on in." She opened the door.

There were a bunch of old Negro people sitting cross-legged in a circle in the living room with their eyes closed. We tiptoed through.

"They are getting in touch with the orishas," she explained.

"That's nice."

"You know what that is?"

"No."

"Then why did you say it's nice?"

"They look happy."

"They *are* happy."

She showed me my room and the bathroom, where there were stacks of toilet paper reaching to the ceiling snitched from various public rest rooms, and orchids growing from bark attached to the shower curtain. Every time we went out somewhere, we were instructed to go to the rest room and not return empty-handed.

"In case we get rained in and can't get to the store," she explained. "You can't be too prepared."

"Good idea." The orchids, unfortunately, had to be bought, a luxury in the midst of privation.

Lucille was a tiny woman whose grandfather had come from Cuba.

She had a poochy little ass, and her hair was pressed into a spurt on the top of her head. She wore big earrings and big jangly bracelets, and chewed Dentyne gum all day long, except when she was feeding her kids. She and Mitchell owned the house and rented rooms, but we shared the kitchen, and soon everything else.

Although their house was not Belle Rêve or the White House, they did name their big white 1940-something Oldsmobile Blanche. Every Sunday we would take a ride to Stinson Beach, in Marin County, with a big pot of beans and rice, passing cars treacherously close while the old people hung out the window shouting, "Get out of the way, get out of the way. We're coming through."

The Zone was actually the Fillmore District. Our house was wooden, pale yellow, and, like my grandmother's house in Bingham Canyon, Utah, it was mashed right between two other houses. Unemployed Negro men hung out down the street on Haight. And there were parts of the Fillmore full of half houses, so you could see, thanks to the wrecking ball, a sofa, a mirror on the wall; and you would expect life going on as usual (good old Dad reading the paper, Mama washing the dishes), except for jagged floors walking out into sheer empty space and, below, empty lots with men sitting on buckets, knocking concrete bits off bricks and piling them up for resale. And there were potholes in the street so big a car could fit in them. Parked cars disappeared, too, but not into the ground; rather, they were spirited away in the night by masked strangers, pig-men who wore gas masks shaped like snouts, repossession men. Oh yes, the Fillmore, 1958, before the whites moved back, was secondhand, second-rate, seconds, irregular, here today, gone tomorrow. I mean, everything was used: people putting dresses and sweaters on hangers on fences for resale, pots and pans lined up on the sidewalk for resale. And watches, rings, televisions you could get hot. The city of San Francisco did not bother with the Fillmore District. No, sir.

In our house, there was Lucille's husband, Mitchell, a carpenter who restored interiors in North Beach and the Castro, the up-and-coming areas—sporadic, uncertain work. Lucille and Mitchell had two little kids, Zulu and Zandra. Then there was Lucille's old mother and father and her uncle and aunt, and some extra old people who just hung around and got Social Security checks once a month, for which we all praised God and Country. Then there was Harry, who called himself a

New Negro and taught literature at San Francisco State, and his white wife, who read movie magazines all day, and a Turkish woman, Yasmin, and her Protestant American husband, who was a hemophiliac. They slept in a separate bed, in case she should scratch him accidentally in the middle of the night with her toenails. And I and my newborn baby, Nadja.

The old people played bridge all day. After a long life of working hard, they were entitled to take it easy, play a little game of bridge, Lucille said. Addicted, her husband countered. We had a scrubby back-yard, where Lucille would put the old people on sunny days under the clothes line with the card table and all the chairs and a jug of lemonade spiked with rum. Cold days was the living room, coffee with a tad of whiskey. The old people also baby-sat, told stories, cooked, bought booze, and kept everybody company. When we were gone, they guarded the house with brooms and old hoes and cooking utensils.

For my room, Lucille put down straw mats and covered the mattress with a blue cotton bedspread from Macy's, courtesy of one of her little trips. Later on, I became the main buyer, since I was white and innocent-looking. Lucille showed me how to carry whole hams between my legs; wear three dresses at once; stuff my pockets with blocks of cheese; fill my purse with sticks of butter, cans of Spam and corned beef, bottles of aspirin; and buy a pair of sunglasses at the checkout counter with a confident little smile on my face. I really took to it. There was not only the thrill of having things but of getting them for nothing; or, rather, the fact that they were ill-gotten gains added to their value in my eyes. Things they were. Things we needed. Things we didn't need. Initially, I was frightened to death of getting caught; yet as time went on, that fear lessened and I became braver and braver. More things. Sure enough, within a couple of months I got caught, which is why I took up exotic dancing.

I think one of the worst feelings when you are young, or really any age, is a sense of helplessness, that is, that there is nothing one can do in the face of fate or one's own weaknesses because one hasn't figured out the secret, the secret words or the key that will open the world. I can remember in the ballet *The Firebird*, how the firebird was able to open one room after another with the secret key with the secret word until she got to the heart of the mystery and freed the prince and princess.

I open the casket in the golden room
That hides the secret of Kastchei's doom.

Those were the words.

I wanted to be the firebird, but the secret of success seemed to elude me, and instead of opening doors and going forward, I seemed to go backward, to keep returning to old territory. It was like being a little child and being sent to stand in the corner.

At any rate, I was working at a respectable job when I got arrested for shoplifting. My job was at an insurance company on Montgomery Street in a marble and stone building of hard polished surfaces near the Wells Fargo Bank, in the financial district of San Francisco, where, to my naïve vision, buildings seemed so tall that, like Einstein's parallel lines, they might converge. Of course, I had never been to New York or any other city. In other words, going to work there reminded me of that awful book Margo and I read once, *Atlas Shrugged*, or was it *The Fountainhead*? Power, Money, Beautiful People, the angular lines of cubism and neofascism.

Except I wasn't a beautiful person. I was a file clerk, and as a result of my arrest in the baby department of Macy's one fat Saturday—the apprehending security guard ("Lady, could you come with me, please?"), the little trip in the back of the police car down to headquarters ("What's a nice girl like you doing shoplifting?"), finger-printing ("Let me take your finger and press it on an ink pad and hold it down on paper, so we can trace you forever"), photographing ("Say cheese"), putting me in a cage in the middle of the police room (this is what Grey went through, I thought, what Aaron was so afraid of), the booking, the charging (and I was living through it), the court date, the fine—I was fired.

Not only fired, but they were sorely disappointed in me at Arat Life. I lost my desk, my chair, my special stool for the high files, and my dignity.

"Young lady, your future has just gone down the drain."

I began to blink hard. My boss's words made me think of the bathtub, the water going out. When I was very young, I thought I would get sucked down, funneled, and later on I worried that a snake might come up and bite my bottom. My father had read an article in the newspaper about crocodiles living in the sewers of New York City.

"It just goes to show," my dad had said.

When my boss declared my future ruined—"We had big plans for you"—I hung my head, wanted to crawl into a hole, and I had

to wonder at the sudden efficiency of the San Francisco Police Department. They must have called the first thing in the morning or roller-skated over. Why couldn't they leave well enough alone? I was arrested, had to go to court. Wasn't that enough? Yet I was told that out of the great mercy of their hearts I was not jailed. All over a baby dress.

"The company would have taken care of you for life," my boss rubbed in. The Big Mother. "You had such a future ahead of you."

Because, somehow, the day I had taken the insurance test I had a great deal of concentration and scored well. They saw potential in me as an adjuster or evaluator or actuary, something. In fact, I could even become an insurance agent like my dad, even though I was a woman. There seemed to be no end to my possibilities with the company.

"Happy to have you on board," my boss said the first day, as if I were in fact boarding a cruise liner, and he hinted at my own office, an office with my own porthole; but until then, I filed, and cleared thirty-five dollars a week. I had to wear nylons, a decent skirt and blouse, and high heels. I had to take the bus, and I had to pay Lucille or the old people at least a little something for watching Nadja. Also I had to eat. And Nadja had supplementary formula bottles, and was beginning on cereals. I could nurse her only twice a day. Furthermore, she would need checkups, vaccinations, diapers, little T-shirts, sleepers and sweaters, little socks, soon those little white baby shoes, and her first dress. Need I say the shoplifted dress was for Easter? We were going to go to church, not the Mormon church but the storefront church on the corner, the Pentecostal Church of God in Christ. Lucille went there even though she was Catholic. So it was an Easter baby dress.

But no ordinary baby Easter dress, a baby-girl dress the color of summer, green with splotches of yellow, an abstract expressionistic baby dress, a dress so beautiful that I thought if Nadja wore it our lives would be transformed. In the dress we wouldn't live where we lived the life we lived. No, it would be like living in Aaron's house, with real art on the walls. Do you know, I wept more over the loss of that dress (privately) than over the so-called disgrace of being arrested (publicly). I didn't cry at all then.

In fact, not crying exacerbated everything. When I wouldn't cry (but I *was* blinking to beat the band), the arresting security officer declared me incorrigible, said that if I were his wife, he would beat me so hard I wouldn't be able to walk.

My fine was one hundred dollars.

When I smiled, the judge said, "Wipe that smile off your face."

When I couldn't stop smiling, he said I would never get a good job in the state of California.

Lucille, who went with me to court, wondered what had happened to everybody's sense of humor.

"Fuck them," she said. "Fuck them all in Fuckdom."

And when we went home, she put a spell on the judge. As follows:

At midnight she lit a funeral candle, and I called out my enemy's name, Judge Walker.

As I pronounced his name, I made small cuts and stabs on the candle. I repeated the procedure for three consecutive days.

Lucille was sure he was rendered impotent at the very least, and dead at best. We perused the obituaries every evening in vain, folded the borrowed paper nicely, and put it back on our neighbor's doorstep, nobody the wiser.

"Don't you worry none, Zoe, baby. He's going to get his."

But I still had to pay that hundred dollars.

Lucille said I should give up breast-feeding and get a factory job, be practical. Chinatown had lots of sweatshops, sewing jobs. I could get one easy.

"You should talk, Lucille," I said.

"Yeah, I do talk. You got a problem with that?"

"You stay home with *your* babies."

"Well, so what if I do. I got Mitchell. Who do you have?"

She had a point. Grey and I were separated, in a year to be officially divorced. Nadja was born prematurely on a blustery January day in Carmel Hospital. Only my mother and my aunt and a friend were there. My dad came later. That was it.

So Lucille and I talked strategy and revenge in the kitchen. Unlike the Formica on the milky way, this table was wooden and cluttered with jars of plants taking root. Tins of plants that had taken root sat on every available windowsill. It was like a jungle, Lucille's kitchen. Spores wafted across the ceiling at every slight breeze. I knew better than to ask if the green around the kitchen sink was being cultivated. It was the dawn of vegetation. And Lucille, dressed in an orange kimono with one of those little back scratchers as scepter, was the philosopher-queen.

Her kids, who were two and three, got their food chewed up, and she kissed it into their mouths like a mother bird feeding her nestlings.

"Give up breast-feeding or make them boobs pay their way, honey," she said. "You are a good-looking girl."

"I am?"

"Sure, and men would pay good money to see you naked."

"They would?"

"Sure."

Lucille had her *santería* altar there in the crowded kitchen. It was a big pot with a stone, pieces of coconut, feathers from a sacrificed chicken inside. The old people kept fresh yams around it. Little nips appeared in the morning. But I had a feeling it was not just spirits feeding.

This altar, Lucille informed me, ensured our continued good luck. I thought any more good luck and we would just die of bliss.

"North Beach, the Barbary Coast, sailors, tips, you'll make *mucho dinero*. Just take off those glasses. Didn't you tell me you studied ballet?"

I had never danced exotically, so to speak. My ballet lessons at my aunt's studio were rather highbrow, I explained to Lucille, and Margo and I stayed home together during high school dances, including (I did not care to remember) the prom.

"And you're very graceful," Lucille continued.

"Sure."

"Well, graceful enough for a tall girl. You have a very pretty smile. Just grin your head off. They'll love you at a club."

"Let's see your tits," the man at the Eagle's Nest said.

Up to that point, the only men who had ever seen my breasts

were Grey and Aaron. But where were *they*? And thanks to Nadja and breast-feeding, I had something to show.

I lifted my sweater, pulled down my bra.

"Not bad," the man said, moving his cigar around in his mouth. "Not bad at all. How old are you?"

"Twenty-one," I lied.

"Except for the tits, I'd say you were a tall twelve. You have one of those baby faces."

"Really?"

"Yeah, and your ass ain't bad either. You can start tomorrow night. It's a slow night, but you'll get the bang of it."

I looked around. Smoke. Men. The faint smell of semen. It was very dark. A woman on the runway was shaking her breasts to the tune of Ritchie Valens's "La Bamba." All she had on was a sombrero. I'll take the A train, I thought, express.

But there I was, between an arrest record and no job.

"I'll take the A train," I said aloud.

"What?"

"The job."

"Is it red?" he asked before I left.

"Yes."

"Great. We'll let a little come out of the G-string, okay?"

"Okay."

"Can you dance without your glasses?"

"Yes."

"Well, you got to get a shtick," he said.

"What do you mean?"

"An act, a role, something you just do. We provide the pasties and the G-string. You do the costume, the angle. We got ourselves a nurse. She has the hat and white uniform, even the shoes and stockings, and, of course, the rectal thermometer. We got Charlie Chaplin with a mustache, baggy pants, and a knockout in the buff. There is a schoolteacher with a ruler, and a bride. Either a bride or a First Communion, you got me on that one. She is all lace mantilla. Very blond, very young, from the Midwest. She comes on veiled and leaves on her garter, something blue. Guys love that. I suggest you do a little girl. You look like one, an overgrown little girl. You do your act, your dance, then you come down and hustle drinks. Get them to buy you a drink.

It's really water, but you get half the price and they go all the way up to the fifty-dollar champagne bottle. At ten dollars you got to go under the umbrella."

"The umbrella?"

He pointed to a picnic table in the corner with a big beach umbrella secluding the bench.

"What happens under the umbrella?"

"They can sit close to you, like that."

I must have looked a little dismayed, and I began to blink.

"You don't have to turn tricks, Zelda."

"Zoe."

"Zoe. That's your own business. If you do, not on these premises, that's all."

Lucille was the one who dreamed up my costume, picking it up in the girls' department of Macy's, my experience apparently no deterrent to crime. And while she was at it, she got the baby dress. My costume was a plaid skirt, schoolgirl pleats, white blouse, red Mary Janes, pinafore, a little slip, cotton pants and cotton bra, a jump rope, and, of course, chewing gum. I was to wear my glasses coming on, discard them as my first thing off.

Lucille taught me the bump and grind in the kitchen while all the kids watched from the communal playpen, and coffee bubbled up weak and watery behind us, and the spirits yawned as they invisibly nibbled at their yam offerings, and the old people clapped appreciatively. Mitchell and Harry, the New Negro, also thought I might have a career in show biz.

Harry was reading *The Sound and the Fury* for his class aloud to us, as I practiced bumping and grinding.

And Harry's wife was reading about a little tiff between Elizabeth Taylor and Mike Todd.

Lucille said, "You can have Liz Taylor and *National Velvet*."

The Turkish woman was filing her nails down to nubs.

"Don't forget your teeth," Lucille said.

They all knew I was going to be a big hit over at the Eagle's Nest and get lots of tips.

When I left for work, Lucille said, "Break a leg"—as if I were headed for Broadway. Actually Columbus Avenue did cut into Broadway,

and I was very near the apartment where I had been gummed by
the man with the false teeth. It seemed eons ago, but it was only
a year and a half. Margo and Zoe, two little girls at City Lights
Books contemplating jazz, that's what we were doing, contemplating
jazz.

[**I WAS A LITTLE** drunk the first time. I hoped to be very drunk, drunk as a skunk, drunk like my mother, but of course I had to be able to walk, dance even. We had to put our own nickels in the jukebox. The songs I used were "That'll Be the Day," with Buddy Holly and the Crickets; "Whole Lotta Shakin' Goin' On," with Jerry Lee Lewis; and "Bye Bye Love," with the Everly Brothers.

I was nervous, yet aware. It was the kind of edgy lucidity you get when you are very tired. I *was* tired the first time. Nadja would not take her nap that afternoon. I took her out for a walk in Lucille's carriage; then I nursed her, took her out for a walk again, let her play in her playpen, and, before I left for the night, nursed her again.

I drank too much coffee, too. Maybe that was why I couldn't get drunk. The way we made coffee in the house was the same way I had made it in Gorda, that is, we put it in a sock, knotted it, threw it in a tall pan of boiling water. Used two or three times, the grounds produced coffee pale as amber.

Well, anyway, I'm onstage. This is my big debut, but I'm barely aware of it. I just know I'm stripping. I'm not seeing things right.

For one, the girls in the "dressing rooms" have given me two shots of mescal, the kind of tequila with an ugly brown worm in the bottle.

Two, I didn't have my glasses on.

And three, you could not see past the first row anyway, it was so dark and so filled with cigarette smoke and ancient dust. I thought I was in the catacombs of some secret society, the Masons or Rosicrucians. The little red circles of the cigars looked like mystic signals, and the dark suits appeared as capes and sacred mantles.

Actually, I was numb. Ice. Not paralyzed, because I swayed and gyrated and put my hands on my knees and, bending down, showed my little-girl panties and, slowly removing them as I wiggled, knew to bend even lower. I used the jump rope so my breasts jiggled, and even sucked on a lollipop. I was every daddy's little girl.

I wasn't smiling, though, not because I was sad but because I wasn't seeing anything, and I wasn't feeling anything either, pain or pleasure. Sexy is probably the last thing on the list. I just wanted to make some money.

Somebody, when I bent low to let him put the dollar in my G-string, said, "Smile, honey."

And I did. I think I smiled for real.

I had not been able to wipe the false smile off my face when the judge wanted me to, but then, when I was up there onstage, by the second song, just little old me and the spotlight, the numbness which had taken over during the four months since Grey had left seemed to leave me inch by inch. I was thawing.

Up there onstage with my bottom hanging out and my breasts jouncing all around, I realized exotic dancing wasn't going to kill me if I didn't think about it too much. I thought of Nadja, the light of my life, and I started thinking everything else I could as fast as I could. Since I was wearing red shoes, I thought of the movie *The Red Shoes*. I had never seen a real ballet. That movie and *An American in Paris* with Gene Kelly were the closest I had been to the real ballet.

" 'Atta girl," somebody shouted.

"She likes you," somebody said.

In the movie *The Red Shoes*, Moira Shearer plays the part of a ballerina who covets and buys some beautiful red shoes. But once she puts them on, she cannot stop dancing until she dies. She falls in love with a composer and must choose between dancing and loving, that old chestnut, as Narcissus would say, the career-versus-family thing. She cannot make the choice and, in her red shoes, she jumps beneath a train. I shimmied the pole.

"Move it, baby."

I shimmied the pole, and I sat on a chair backward, like Marlene Dietrich in *The Blue Angel*. Dietrich was one of our heroes in the Robinson household. She had left Germany when Hitler came to power. Aaron had said that at the beginning of the war there had been German students opposed to Hitler who were called the Swing Kids. They listened to American jazz—wore their hair long. They danced in response to their impending death. I bent down. The guys hooted and howled. I was dancing in the face of life.

"Mamacita."

My breasts were big then, almost dripping. Yes, they had gone from fried eggs over hard to soft white dumplings. That was childbirth for you.

Up there onstage, I thought of everything I once was: the girl in glasses, the bookworm, the egghead, the girl who went to the Saturday matinee at the Grove theater for twenty-five cents, the girl who took ballet lessons, the serious, tall, strong girl, the Mormon girl from pioneer and Armenian stock.

And then the music stopped. And it was over.

I came home on the trolleybus that night, going across town with fifty dollars—more in one night than I'd cleared in one week of work at the insurance office—to my room and my baby. I could hardly wait to see her, and ran the last block. I would be able to buy her dresses, now that I took mine off. Now I would be able to buy her all the little jars of Gerber baby food in the store. I could get her toys and then little books. I could get her a mobile for her crib. I would be able to buy, actually *buy*, Lucille earrings, some brand-new earrings.

Exotic dancing, what was that? Just dancing. I wore red shoes like those Judy Garland wore in *The Wizard of Oz*. So I was a little naked. Just a body. Just dancing.

Indian tribes did rain dancing—the Eagle Dance, the Sun Dance, the Snake Dance—and the Sioux even did the deadly Ghost Dance, designed to raise the dead. Dancing. Dancing for rain, dancing in the rain.

"I'm rich," I shouted when I burst in the door.

"Oh, my baby," Lucille said, taking me in her small arms. "My poor, poor baby." The old people fluttered around us, patting our backs with their frail parchment hands, already turning into soft feathery wings. There, there, there, there. You did good, you did real good. There, there, there.

[**FRIDAY NIGHT :**

North Beach, at twelve midnight, April 1958, the smell of garlic and oregano and espresso, soy sauce drifting over from Chinatown, bebop pulsating from the Hungry I, pretty boy Chet Baker wooing with the crescendo of his golden horn or Miles Davis and his trumpet tonguing Milestones. The ting-a-lings of the trolley and cable cars, the people going home or going out, the Bay Bridge in sight, the Golden Gate out of sight but not out of mind, more beautiful to me than Hart Crane's Brooklyn Bridge, which I would not see until many years later.

I would be dressed, dressed in a dress, dressed in a jacket, dressed in stockings, shoes, the weight of clothes on me sheltering me, covering me after being naked. The comfort of clothes. I would count them— glasses, bra, panties, slip, dress, garter belt, stockings, shoes, and even, sometimes, a beret. All black, of course, but on me, nuns' wear. I was expressing it not abstractly but concretely, with the improvisational freedom of jazz, which lets the mind go and the notes follow. I was beat, beating it, deadbeat, downbeat, and the love I felt for my baby was straight out of the beatitudes. Nobody was going to beat me ever again.

A nightcap at Vesuvio's under the Tiffany lamps, bands of brown tile on the wall, cluttered, noisy, art-nouveau mirrors, a big black wooden cat with a raised tail and injured foot across the bar, the booth upstairs for lady psychiatrists, and the inscription

T'was a woman who
drove me to drink.
And I never had the decency to write
and thank her.

Glory, glory, San Francisco.

When I got home, there was a letter waiting for me.

"They tried to serve me the divorce papers," Grey wrote, April 23, 1958. "They did serve me the divorce papers. But, Zoe, you can't divorce me. We'll both be dead first."

The letter went on:

I know about the baby. Next time it will be a boy.

Do you remember when we were in Buena Vista Park together so long ago? We had some kind of argument. You started running off. I said that once we got to Gorda, we'd never be able to run away from each other, and so it is.

How can there be anything but each other?

This whole letter is prompted by the divorce papers. Was our whole life just a dream? Wasn't there any love? I don't think we were playacting. So, the divorce papers surprised me more than anything that has ever happened to me in my entire life. I can imagine losing you as my wife; as man and woman I can't imagine losing you.

Do you understand the distinction I'm making? You can go ahead and get a divorce if you want to, but we are more than paper. I love you. I think of the bread you make, of sleeping together. Certain things stand out in my mind. The day you got lost in the woods—you remember? I pretended to be worried, but I knew in my heart that nothing bad could ever happen to you. Lost in the woods. We are so afraid of the woods . . . And yet you must have felt as though you were lost in Wakantanka, alone, forever alone. As though you were in his hand, his providential hand.

I think back to the old days of our wedding. I remember, I was trying to be serious and you were laughing—not at the ceremony. I'm not accusing you of that, but rather as though you couldn't suppress your laughter. After all, that's what a marriage means. They say every man marries his mother, a fine theory. Actually, we are required to marry ourself. My wife, the man says

painfully, grimacing. It's himself. Jesus. You are me whether you like it or not.
It couldn't be any other way.

  So. Back to the day you were lost in the woods. Redwood Gulch, wasn't
it? You must have gone down into the canyon where there was only the faint
sound of water. It must have been like the jungle, where you become dimly
aware of your own somethingness. What that something is you do not know.
But it is you and you blend into the forest and disappear as finally as a leaf
falling from a tree.

  It was the prophetic life, something we had forgotten and wanted to find
together as man and wife. Are we getting a divorce or are we going to get lost
in the woods, darling . . .

I did remember Buena Vista Park, that foggy day, and the curved
set of steps, surrealistic, strange, scary, and I remembered getting lost
in the woods. I did *not* feel as in the Rilke poem that I was falling,
falling, with God's hands out to catch me. It was frightening. And the
day of the wedding, I hadn't laughed. I just did not pay attention. I
should have; I should have said at the point when they ask if anybody
has any objections, Yes, this wedding cannot go on. The husband is
mad, and the wife is too young and too stupid to know what she is
doing.

I didn't write back, but I felt like saying:

Dear Grey,

  Every word you write carries a rock. To be with you is to be in the
position of the man Aaron spoke about, the traitor, who in the Spanish Civil
War was flayed alive.

The city marked on the envelope in the little circle was New York
City.

[**BY THE END** of May, Nadja had started to laugh and giggle, could blow out saliva bubbles. Inheriting Zulu and Zandra's toys and equipment, she had a little sling chair with wheels. We gently pushed her around the kitchen, the bedroom. I thought: Grey is missing all this.

One Sunday, fighting my inertia and habitual waiting, I took Nadja to Playland on the bus, the number 38 Geary.

Playland was catercorner from the Cliff House, San Francisco's famous restaurant with a view. There was a funhouse and a merry-go-round, an airplane swing, the Whip, the Ferris wheel, and a metal roller coaster. In front was an eight-foot wooden puppet which, mechanically driven, bowed at the waist and emitted sounds.

Laughing Sal, who couldn't stop laughing. She had one tooth missing and freckles. Nadja cried when she saw her.

At one time, right across the street, the Sutro Baths were open. Under a conservatorylike roof were seven pools, toboggan slides, thirty swinging rings. Now, all that was left was Playland. But all Nadja and I did was go on the merry-go-round, buy pink spun sugar, and look at the row of mechanical games. For five cents you could watch wooden dolls do the hula in a little glass booth, or, if you had a friend, you could move levers and play a whole baseball game with wooden figures for ten cents. There were fortune-telling dummies that nodded their heads and a miniature train which went through a whole tiny city. That was what fascinated us. That, and the opium den which had tiny Chinese people layered on little toy benches puffing real smoke.

Nadja smiled at all these things. It was a sunny day and the sea gulls glided overhead and the sea lions barked on their white-tipped rocks. I was happy, too. For the first time in a while, I felt it was going to be all right. Nadja and I, together, would find our way. We didn't need Grey or anybody else. I didn't miss him. I had Lucille, a job, a place to live. San Francisco was becoming familiar.

But when we got home and one of the old people said someone had come by looking for me, my heart leaped to my throat.

"Who was it?"

"It was a man."

"Did he say where he was staying, if he would come back?"

"Nope."

I began to tremble.

"Put Nadja down for her nap," Lucille said, her hands on her hips. "Let me read your cards. Put the baby in her crib and come into the kitchen. We've got to get something straight. Let's see what the cards say."

"Oh, Lucille."

"It's time," she said.

I set Nadja down for her nap, and Lucille took her tarot deck from the bookcase, where it was wrapped in a silk kerchief in a little bundle that always looked ready for a trip.

Lucille shuffled. She asked me to cut the deck into three parts with my left hand and then put them back together. She had her own special way of laying the cards.

"This is where you are right now," Lucille said.

She slapped the card down in the middle of the kitchen table.

It was the Wheel of Fortune, like the Ferris wheel in Playland, except that people were falling off right and left.

"The Wheel of Fortune is your psychic house, Zoe. Don't be scared. It's not a bad card. Judgment. Renewal, birth, higher consciousness. When you're down, the only way is up."

The next card she placed on the left side of the first card. The Page of Wands.

"A message is coming." Lucille narrowed her eyes disapprovingly.

"Here is your recent past." She put this card under the Page of Wands, so it seemed that the message was creeping up.

The Devil.

"That is your bondage, Zoe."

I am not taking this seriously, but Lucille is very serious. Every time she slaps down a card, she studies it closely. She is even trembling a little as she draws the card out of the deck.

The Nine of Swords.

"Despair, anxiety. Don't look back."

Despair, of course, the worst sin. That was Aaron's failing, fall, hubris, end.

"Don't despair," Lucille said. "Remember what was left in Pandora's box after all the evils of the world escaped?"

"What?"

"Hope, Zoe. Hope."

I don't want to be but I feel myself getting caught up in this reading. Stop, I want to say, stop this game right now.

The Tower is next. Lightning bolts hit the tower, people are falling out of it as they did the Wheel of Fortune.

"Lightning, Zoe, is the cosmic force which breaks down false structures and ideas."

"Great, Lucille."

It is just paper, I tell myself, the random drawing of pictures from a medieval deck. We, we are in the twentieth century. But I have started to blink.

"Now, this will tell you what you can do to change."

We begin another row.

Lucille carefully laid down the Hermit.

"The Hermit: Ask and it shall be given."

The King of Wands.

"Strong and generous, can be impulsive."

Lucille laid down another card.

"And this, Zoe, is what you can't change: Five of Cups. You find it difficult to explain what is inside of you."

"Oh really?"

Once, on my way to work through Chinatown, I stopped in front of a fish store which had tanks of live fish on the street. I stood and stared at them, and they with their large, bulgy eyes stared back. We were the same, I realized—I on my stage being stared at, they in their tanks. But they didn't know it. Only I knew, yet who could I tell, who would care? How could I explain myself to silence?

The last card was the Fool.

Lucille smiled weakly.

In the Native American deck, the connection between the Fool and holiness is traditional. It is Coyote.

In the Native American deck, Coyote is like Prometheus, the bearer of fire, but he is also amoral, a trickster, a creator, and in one hand he keeps a lighted pipe, in which there is a hallucinogen.

In the Native American deck, Coyote is also the shaman.

"Does the Fool mean I am a fool, Lucille, or that the Fool is arriving?"

"Yes." She packed up her cards hastily, wrapping them in their silk scarf.

"Yes what?"

"Yes everything, anything. Pick a card, Zoe, any card."

"Don't be mad. They are just paper, Lucille."

"I know."

"I mean, why do you take it so seriously?"

"I'm not taking it seriously."

"You are."

"You want my advice, Zoe?"

"No."

"Well, I'm going to give it to you whether you like it or not, because if I don't, I will be standing by and letting something happen which I don't like."

I stood up. "Lucille, I respect your opinions. But you listen to me. Do you want me to spend the rest of my life, or rather until I get fat, dancing in front of a bunch of drunk men?"

"No. There are alternatives."

"Name one."

"You could baby-sit kids, a bunch of kids, start a little nursery school."

"I'd have to get a license to do it officially. And a school, I'd have to go to school in order to do that."

"So go to school."

"Yeah, with an arrest record?"

"Sure."

"And graduate in about a hundred years."

"The time is going to pass anyway, Zoe. You could have gotten a scholarship straight from high school."

"Are you kidding? Only certain people get those."

"You said you had good grades. Did you apply?"

"Listen, in high school you had to be a certain type. You had to be flashy, a favorite. My best friend was black, my parents were yellow, my ex-lover was a Red, my new lover was a red man, and I was as green as they come. No chance, no way."

"A regular rainbow."

"With no pot of gold."

"Oh, Zoe, you know what I mean. Just don't go back. Resist it. Isn't it better to be a nude dancer than a dead duck?"

"Lucille, I'm not blind."

"Oh, yeah. You sure do blink a lot, though."

"That's just nervousness."

"Well, maybe you have something to be nervous about."

[**SURE ENOUGH,** one night, when I was looking out across the audience—the usual blur of smoke and red circles, shadowed faces, bits of hair adhering to the tops, like Mr. Potato Head with his sprouts, sometimes an eye, a nose—I registered something familiar.

I was embarrassed for a second, and then he waved and I waved, and when I was finished with my dance and wearing just my pasties and G-string, I walked up to him.

"Narcissus," I said. "Nars."

He hugged me to him.

"You look . . ." he began.

"Don't say it."

"I won't say it."

"I look older, don't I?"

"You are, I mean, you are beautiful."

"We're in the dark, Nars."

"We are all in the dark, my dear, in the cave. We see but shadows."

"Not that again. How did you find me?"

"How did I find you? Well, your aunt. They gave me your address. They think you work in an insurance office. It's funny. I came to find you, but I was in North Beach, and I don't know. Usually I don't go in these places . . ."

"But the vibrations."

"Definite vibrations."

"And you never go in places like this? Come on, Nars, come clean."

"I never *do* go in places like this, not my taste, but how are you?"

"As you see. Fine. I have a baby girl. I can do 'This little piggy goes to market' with her, sing 'Row, row, row your boat,' play 'Peekaboo.' "

"A baby girl. Oh, that is fine."

"What are *you* doing?"

"I'm going back to school, Zoe. Remember that discussion we had about the Good, my philosophy teacher, and how we searched for the Good through all the books, and how the philosophy teacher left on a motorcycle?"

"Yeah, I remember you telling me. Good-Schmood, right?"

"Well, what I'm thinking is that the Good is doing good."

"Doing well."

"Doing good. Giving back to the community what I got out of it."

"What community?"

"Negro."

"American?"

"Maybe. Maybe Trinidad."

"So what did you get out of the community?"

"Myself, Zoe, myself."

"And what are you going to study?"

"Botany, plants, you know, farming techniques, agronomy. Feed the world."

"Really?"

"Yeah. But, Zoe, I'm here to talk to you about Grey. Can we go, can you get dressed?"

"I have to wait until closing." A feeling of dread swept over me.

"I'll be in the front in the truck at closing. We'll talk."

A truck. I laughed. Riding in a truck again. But as I watched him go through the door, I began to feel scared. Grey was sick or in the hospital or in trouble somewhere. Yet, I returned, walked through the bar smiling. A couple of guys bought me drinks, the fake drinks we were allowed, and finally two o'clock rolled around and I was in my jeans and shirt, regular sandals, getting into Narcissus's truck.

"Grey. What's happened to Grey?"

We barreled down Columbus, made a left at Broadway. The streets were pretty empty, and when we turned into the canyon of Montgomery Street, the old feeling came back, the Big Sur feeling—the bad one, the scary one. I was anxious, worried.

"Is Grey alive?"

"Grey is alive."

"Is he in trouble?"

"Trouble? Life is trouble, Zoe."

"In the hospital?"

"In the hospital? No. He's still in New York, but he is coming to get you. I am here to warn you."

"Warn me?"

"Warn you."

We turned right on Market and headed toward Haight.

"So you two are not friends anymore?"

"Friends? We were never really friends."

"Because he's an Indian?"

"Of course not. Anyway, he's not that much of an Indian, as far as I know. Maybe a quarter at most. He likes to play Indian and cowboy, put on the feathers, go on the warpath, that sort of thing."

"Are you a hundred per cent Negro?" Narcissus was only a little darker than Margo.

"No. That's not the point, ethnic authenticity. The thing is, I heard what happened on the hill. It's an isolated spot, Zoe. It's not good to be so far away from help if you need it. He's a fucking lunatic, and yet, when he's lucid, I know how persuasive the man can be. You are . . . what is the word?"

"Gullible."

"Gullible, vulnerable, naïve, and maybe just needy. You have this very trusting nature, Zoe. I like you a lot, but you have to be careful."

"When I thought Grey needed psychiatric help, nobody in Big Sur would believe me."

"I don't know if it's all the stuff he takes. The marijuana on its own is okay, but the peyote, the mushrooms, the pills."

"Get to the point, Narcissus."

"The point is, Grey is already a very volatile guy, to say the least. He already fancies himself Coyote or a shaman. Maybe he is crazy all on his own. Who knows? The guy has lost it."

"And Oak?"

"I hear she's out of the picture."

"Ah, we're here." He stopped in front of Lucille's.

"This is a Negro neighborhood, Zoe."

"I know, Narcissus."

"What is it with you and minorities, Zoe?"

"You can stay if you like," I said.

"I can stay? It's okay?"

"Everybody's cool."

We walked into the house. It looked like Lucille was having some kind of séance. The old people were gathered around the table, and the faculty wife and the Turkish woman were tiptoeing about with tiny cups of coffee. There was a red scarf over the lamp, and everybody looked vaguely pink and eerie. Somebody's dead wife was being summoned. I didn't dare interrupt, and Narcissus and I quietly went into my room.

"This is it," I whispered, holding my arms open to embrace the bamboo matting on the floor, the awkwardly placed curtain, the stolen bedspread, and, of course, Nadja.

Nadja was asleep. She slept until five in the morning, and in the blue light of that hour, I would bring her into my warm female bed, the mattress on the floor. She was now asleep in her crib like a big girl. She slept on her back a lot, which I found strange. She didn't fold, duck, cover. At this point in her life, she trusted the world.

"Sh," I said to Narcissus.

"She's a real honey, Zoe," he said, looking at her, and then he sat down on the floor, took off his shoes.

I went into the bathroom, changed into my pajamas.

When I came out, Narcissus was under the covers except for his head.

"Grey . . ."

"Grey is no good."

"Sh." I knew he was no good, but I missed him.

"Sh nothing, Zoe. You are going to have to leave town."

I got into bed. Grey, I thought. Grey.

"How can I leave town?"

"You can leave town because I can give you some money."

"Narcissus." I feared Grey, and feared for him.

"Narcissus nothing," he whispered.

"Oh, stop." My feelings were tangled, knotted.

Narcissus reached for me.

"No," I said. "Just friends, just friendly."

"You're so different, Zoe. Seeing you . . ."

"I'm the same."

"You are not the same. You were always wearing those baggy jeans and shirts."

"Grey's. And I was pregnant."

"I didn't know you had a body. And the glasses."

"Grey threw away my glasses, remember?"

He put his hand down between my legs.

"No, Narcissus."

I held my legs together.

"No."

"No?"

"No."

"Really no?"

I laughed. "Really no."

"Have it your way, Zoe. Have it your way."

"Narcissus," I asked, "how did you get your name?"

"Narcissus got his name from his parents, Zoe. You know how people of my complexion like to name their kids after heroes of the ancient world—Cassius, Ulysses, etcetera, etcetera—especially in the West Indies."

"But you are not in love with yourself?"

"My parents didn't know that part, but I *am* in love with myself, sure I am, as much as anybody else, I suppose. Every time I look in the mirror, I think, What a handsome fellow. At least I'm not sexually repressed like somebody I know."

"I'm not sexually repressed."

"Not much."

"I'm just not that interested in it, Narcissus."

"Not interested? Baby, you have a lot to learn."

Narcissus put his other hand on my breast.

"No."

"It's because I'm a Negro, isn't it? This is where you draw the line, isn't it?"

"No, it isn't."

At least I didn't think so.

"Any man, Narcissus."

Any other man besides Grey . . . And maybe I just wasn't attracted
to him, to Narcissus. How convenient for him to be able to say, It's
because I'm Negro, and to turn everything into race. Of course, *I* had
said, You don't trust Grey, because Grey is an Indian.

"I told you there was somebody else. That other person is dead.
He died after we had a fight. He died before I could say I was sorry
or that I forgave him." I was blinking in the dark. "Every time I get
with somebody, it's disaster. I feel like the Dragon Lady."

This was a big speech for me, but I was heeding Lucille's tarot
card reading and trying to explain myself to somebody.

"So guilt, Zoe. White guilt and sex guilt and you-name-it guilt. I
don't know, but I don't think it is your job to keep people alive, except
yourself and your child. So you've only had two lovers, this dead guy
and Grey. Great selections, Zoe, and if you're lucky, there will be others
even worse, if punishment is what you're looking for in this world."

"What others? Men who smoke cigars and go to girlie shows? Men
who roll their eyes at me and stuff dollars in my string?"

"Do you blink on stage?"

"No, I don't. I feel I'm wearing a mask."

"Did you know that I have a twin brother?"

"My God, Narcissus, my mother is a twin. Where is your brother?"

"Nicodemus is in the hospital, Zoe. That's why I can tell about
Grey. I know what I'm saying."

I took a deep breath.

"Why?"

"Why? He is a paranoid schizophrenic."

"You are identical?"

"Yes."

"But . . ."

"I don't know why. But I do know I am sane. Maybe I'm too
sane, Zoe. Maybe he's doing it for me, you know what I mean, acting
it out. Maybe he is freeing me. I want to be there with him, instead of
him, but I can't, Zoe. You can't do that for people, even your own twin
brother, and if you go down, if I let myself go down, I pull a whole
lot with me. So I have to stay away and stay strong. It's not easy, and
you want to tell me about love? Zoe, you cannot begin to tell me."

"Let's go to sleep, Nars."

"Yeah, I think that's a good idea."

Soon Narcissus had rolled over and begun to snore lightly, but I couldn't sleep. I tried to concentrate on his warning, but I couldn't be warned off. In fact, Narcissus's warning had the reverse effect on me. Instead of dreading Grey's return as I had been doing, I found myself weaving a net thread by thread, skein by skein, tying the little knots. I cast my net. It sparkled and shivered. He would come to me, I dreamed, like a baby, a baby covered in a placenta of silver gossamer threads.

[**N O T   A   W E E K** later, while I was dancing, I saw my father.

His eyes blazed a trail through the darkness. And then I said: No, I am just seeing things. I looked again and the apparition was still there. I thought of Christ. "Get thee behind me, Satan," I thought. Then I blinked. He wasn't there.

My father would not be in San Francisco. He would be at home. He didn't even read the San Francisco newspapers. Sin City. That was what he thought, as he made his lunch every day, a deviled-ham sandwich on soft white bread, which would be limp and moist by his lunchtime. He tied his shoes so tightly, the soft black leather would look to me like slick black bananas, rotten bananas, as if his feet were bound not to be short but to narrow and lengthen. His starched shirts from the laundry made a red mark on his neck. He had an Adam's apple, wore old-fashioned wire-framed glasses, parted his hair in the middle.

Such a man would not be at the Eagle's Nest.

"The funniest thing happened," I told Lucille in the morning. "I thought I saw my dad last night at the club."

"Guilt trip," she said. "Or old home week."

Nadja was sitting up and repeating sounds she heard. Nana. Baba.

"You can't see without your glasses anyway, right?"

"Right."

"I saw my father again," I told Lucille the next night. She was still up. There was a poker tournament with the old people.

"You are letting him haunt you," Lucille said, looking back at her cards.

But the following week, after I got off duty and was putting on my clothes in the room in the basement—really an old men's room, with urinals and rusted mirrors and the smell of ancient pee—I heard a knock, and I knew, I just knew.

"Are you trying to kill me, kill your mother?" he said as soon as I opened the door.

"What are you doing here, Daddy?"

"I am going to take you home. Cover up, make yourself decent."

I was actually in a dress, my street dress, one I had worn to the insurance company. His face was red and he seemed extremely nervous.

"How did you know I was here?" Actually I was furious. My eyes widened.

"Somebody we know saw you."

I couldn't imagine anybody they knew in the Eagle's Nest.

"How's Mom?"

"She's fine."

"Aunt Pearl?"

" 'Night, Zoe." One of the girls sauntered by, looked at my father as if he were my john.

"You have to get out of here," he said.

"I like it," I said. And for that moment, the smelly dressing room, the long dark hall with the concrete floor, the smoke of the club upstairs took on a warm glow, the warm glow of independence. "And I'm not coming home."

"Think of your child."

"I am. I'm feeding her."

"Think of the implications of what you're doing."

"I'm feeding myself, too."

"If you don't leave, I'll tell the owner that you're underage."

"I am not. Eighteen is the age." I was actually nineteen.

We were quarreling in the basement hallway. The bare light bulbs in the ceiling made my father look green, sick; his freckles looked like deformities, age spots, and his red hair was a layer of tarnished pennies.

"Zoe, I will cause a disturbance in the audience when you go onstage."

"The police will come and get you, put you in jail."

"And when I get out, I will do it again."

I groaned.

"I will do it again and again, until you get fired." He had his fist
balled up as if he were ready to fight.

"I won't come home, Daddy."

"You can go to Utah. Salt Lake, live with my aunts."

"Oh God."

"Exactly, God's own land."

I remembered what that was.

"No," I said.

"I know where you're living," my father said.

"Oh, you do?"

"That house is not zoned for multiple use. All residents must be
related."

"The Zone has no zoning laws. We *are* related." I was feeling sick
to my stomach.

"Related by blood, Zoe. I could close them down in a minute."

"Why persecute me, my friends, my everything?"

"You are doing the devil's work, Zoe, and living with Ham's
children."

"Oh, that."

"Do you think I am joking?"

"No, I don't." What I thought was, How could there have ever
been a moment of sympathy between us. He had bought me a rocking
chair. He said once, when I was in the hospital, that he loved me, and
he also said Nadja was beautiful. Couldn't he extend those words into
more words and feel differently about the world and others in it?
Couldn't his language extend and change his reality?

"I'm grown up, Daddy. I can do what I want."

Actually, I did feel old, older than anybody. I could feel my jaw
getting tight and my eyes dulling. My teeth hurt, and always my feet.
And my scalp was so tense, my hair felt like a wig. When I went to
Stinson Beach with the old people in the old white car Blanche, they
were the ones who frolicked about. I stayed seated on the sand, holding
Nadja to me as if she were my protection, rather than vice versa.

"You are not grown-up, and I am going to take you away from

all this, whether you like it or not. I may no longer have legal jurisdiction over you, but I can make your life so miserable, Zoe, that you will come along gratefully."

"My God."

"Not yours, Zoe."

We were still standing there in the basement by the so-called dressing room. I felt as though I was in our bomb shelter at home, and the bomb had fallen and I was trapped. It was a daydream or a nightmare, a real one. I could hear a tap dripping somewhere, and small skittering sounds, no doubt rats.

[**NADJA AND I** were put on the train. I thought of Aaron and Judy Garland. I thought of the seduction scene in the Mary McCarthy story "The Man in the Brooks Brothers Shirt," which Margo liked so much. Everybody on *my* train looked worn out, defeated, terminally ill, and ugly. Furthermore, I wish I could say that the name of my train was *The Spirit of St. Louis* or the Orient Express or the A Train. I didn't notice. A long, dull ride, Mood Indigo all the way. We went through scintillating downtown Stockton and whole miles of the Nevada desert with no name at all; and then finally the Great Salt Lake Desert, flat as a pancake and dry as a bone and about as boring as anything could be, loomed up ahead of us like a drunken man's mirage. My life is worth nothing, I thought; but then Nadja woke up, and, with a baby blanket thrown over me, I nursed her. She put her little hands on my breast, each finger perfect, each nail beautifully formed, the tucks in the skin where the fingers came out of the palms a row of symmetrical indentations.

I had to live. I had to keep going.

My dad's mother lived in Bingham Canyon, a copper-mining town. Her street was so narrow only one car could go up at a time, and all the houses were lined up against each other close as teeth. The mine was a big red hole in the ground, with graduated rows along the side like a coiled snake. My grandmother was so fat she could not leave her bed without the aid of a derrick, which lifted her to the toilet. Living with Grandmother Melba was out of the question.

Instead, I was shipped to my three great-aunts, who lived together in Salt Lake City, a.k.a. New Jerusalem, in a large house called the Henhouse by the rest of the family. They were waiting for me on the railroad platform, three plump white-haired ladies in black grandmother shoes and felt hats with little veils, dresses patterned in flowers and checks. It was June 1958, and hot as hell.

"Zoe, Zoe," one of them waved. She had a handkerchief in her hand, as if she were actually flagging down the train. This was Sister Mercy, the youngest of the Old Hens. She was a bit of a coquette, with her hat at a slight slant and the seam of her stockings a little off.

They cooed over Nadja, insisted on carrying my one suitcase, and we got into their 1950 black Lincoln Continental, which had enough grillwork on its mouth to fence a fort, and roared away.

"We fixed up your room for you," Sister Martha said.

Sister Martha was the oldest and the wisest. She had a long beaked nose, and I could tell she was not one to take no for an answer from anybody.

"And we will have a nice cup of tea." Sister Matilda was the clown. She was tall and lanky like Goofy, the crazy, buck-toothed dog in the Disney cartoon. Goofy in a white wig.

"Tea?" I exclaimed.

I thought tea was on the Mormon no-no list, since it had the stimulant caffeine in it.

"Sister Matilda made a cake for the baby, a little baby cake," Sister Martha said.

"So awful about your husband dying," Sister Mercy said.

"Yes," Sister Matilda chimed in. "You are so young to be a widow."

So that was what my father had told them.

"And the poor fatherless child."

I felt like somebody out of Dickens, as usual.

"But we'll manage," Sister Mercy said. "Won't we, darlings?"

Everybody said yes.

The Henhouse, I was surprised to see, was yellow, another yellow house. And I knew immediately that a yellow house could not be all bad. Yellow was the color of sunshine. Roses grew helter-skelter all up the front. The second floor had a kind of Louisiana porch with a wrought-iron railing, and a front awning of rusted tin was falling down on one side. The Hens roosted on the second floor, and Nadja and I got the top floor, really an attic, all to ourselves. We had a window that looked out from the peaked roof across the city, and you could see the golden angel Moroni with his long thin trumpet on top of the Temple. I could pretend I was in a pyramid of old, but something Aztec rather than Egyptian, for surely that was more in accord with *The Book of Mormon*, which talks of Jesus appearing after his death in the civilization of the Americas.

My great-aunts had fixed up my room as if I were still a little girl. The pink flouncy bedspread, the picture of a little lamb, the fluted lamp shade, and the furry pink rug were a bit startling, and the little girl had obviously let somebody go all the way, go below the waist, because there was a crib, a lovely crib filled with teddy bears.

"This is wonderful," I said. "You've gone to so much trouble."

"Oh, it was nothing," they said in chorus.

When they closed the door and I had set Nadja down for her nap, I sat down on the bed and cried softly. The sun, which had been shining in on me, went behind a cloud, and the room was suddenly in shadows. All sorts of doubts crossed my mind. What was I doing there? What did it all lead to? Pacific Grove, Big Sur, San Francisco, now Salt Lake? I wondered where Grey was, what he was doing. It was two hours later in New York, summer, too. Maybe Grey would stay through fall and winter, long enough to walk in the snow. That would feel like earth to him, much better than the sidewalk. This was the side of me that still loved him, still longed for him. I wasn't cured yet.

The other side hoped he had gotten in a fatal car accident, he and Oak and Redwood, the whole goddamned forest of them, smashed up, kindling for fire.

"Are you all right?" It was Sister Martha at the door. I could imagine her ear poised, hoping to hear a sound.

"Fine," I answered. "I'm fine."

"Why don't you come down for a bite of cake," Sister Matilda added.

"Yes," Sister Mercy agreed. "Cake."

"Oh, do," they all said.

I glanced over at Nadja. She was awake now.

"Cake?" I asked her.

Dreading the kitchen, thinking it would be like the one at home, I descended the stairs slowly. On the walls were photos going back nearly a century. There was one of the three sisters, my great-aunts, in their early twenties or late teens. Mercy was in a long white muslin dress with oversized pockets and a little pin in the shape of a bow at her collar. She had a kind of lazy, sexy smile on her face, and she had her hands on her hips. Martha, in the middle in something polka-dotted, was standing tall and straight. Matilda had a broad grin on her face. It was a little disconcerting because I had only known them as old, yet their posture was still the same. The older and wiser one, the funny girl, and the coquette.

The kitchen, I found, like the rest of the Henhouse, was comfortable. Each aunt had her own chair and place at the table, and, wonder of all wonders, they had a coffeepot, a huge double-decker that sat, in pride of place, on the stove for all to see. Only when the bishop visited did they put it away, along with the coffee cups, the teapots, the tea, and medicinal liquor. I could imagine them all scrambling to hide the evidence, although anybody with a discerning nose could tell what kind of house it was.

The table was wood, not Formica, not glittery, but a round heavy oak (dare I say the word) polished to look like the sun. All the potholders had brown hens on them, and running along the wall above the sink on wooden pegs was a row of shiny cookie cutters in the shapes of animals.

"I am partial to chocolate chip," Sister Martha declared.

"I'm an oatmeal girl," Sister Mercy announced.

Sister Matilda said she did not eat cookies, but asked me what my favorite was.

"I don't know," I said. "To tell the truth, I have not had many cookies in my life."

"Oh my, my," Sister Mercy said. "We bake every Friday, since Martha retired."

Sister Martha had been one of the first female graduates of Brigham Young University and had taught physical education to girls in high school for forty years. When she first started, she said, they wore knickers and white blouses with puffed sleeves. They did jumping jacks, touched their toes ten times.

When I went to the bathroom and stood looking at myself in the mirror a few minutes, just to register that I was there, there in that place, I heard a light knocking on the door.

"Are you all right?" Sister Martha asked through the crack in the door.

"I'll be out in a minute."

Had they been told I might kill myself?

"Oh, there you are," they all said when I opened the door.

Sister Mercy was a poet who had poems published in the *Deseret News* from time to time. She specialized in the seasons, I was told. When I read them, they sounded like the work of the poet laureate of Indiana, James Whitcomb Riley, when-the-frost-was-on-the-pumpkin sort of thing.

Sister Mercy's favorite food was a nice leg of lamb flavored with mint leaves, which we had every Sunday after church. She had been married once, but nobody talked about it. Something about the husband absconding and something about the husband and money, the shame of it all, and the husband had been disliked from the very beginning and they really didn't like to mention it, but if I must know, he was not worthy of her.

"Oh, that is too bad."

"Luckily, there were no children from the union," Sister Martha concluded, "and so all's ended that ends. No offense to Nadja."

"Could not agree more," Sister Matilda said. "Except you have the quote wrong."

"Well, my dear, we can't all be Shakespeare now, can we?"

"No. That is true."

Sister Matilda could tap-dance on occasion and used a pendulum, which she held over all her food, to determine what to eat. If it went left to right, it meant that the angel Moroni, the same angel who had given Joseph Smith the sacred Mormon tablets and the one I could see with a golden trumpet in his golden hand out my window, didn't want her to eat that food; but if it went backward and forward, she could eat it. The three months I was there, she ate oatmeal, until she was put into the hospital.

"We want you to think of this as your home," Sister Martha said.

"Your home away from home," Sister Mercy added.

"Your heart of a home," Sister Matilda went on.

We had had our cake and eaten it, too, and were now in the living room watching *I Love Lucy*, Sister Mercy's favorite program. The Philip Morris cigarette commercial was over, and it looked like Lucy and her sidekick, Ethel, were up to no good. They wanted jobs. I wanted to tell them work wasn't as great as they thought. On the other hand, staying home all day in an apartment didn't seem particularly interesting either.

"I've seen this one," Sister Martha said. "They work in a bakery. Soon it's a big mess."

"My husband is not dead," I said. "We're getting a divorce."

"We know, dear," Sister Mercy admitted.

"Mormons don't get divorced," Sister Martha added, "so we were in a quandary."

"They do so get divorced," Sister Mercy corrected.

"Well, where is he? The husband?" Sister Matilda asked me.

"He's, you might say, he's on the road."

"The yellow brick road?" Sister Mercy asked.

"Mercy."

"Well, I don't know, Matilda. I mean it as a metaphor. Oz is a metaphor," Sister Mercy, the poet, explained. "And there is no place like home."

"I don't know about *that*," Sister Matilda replied. "So what road is he on? Route 66? I would love to be on Route 66."

"It's like the book *On the Road*," I explained. "Traveling, moving."

"But to where? All roads do *not* lead to Rome, thank God," Sister Matilda piped up.

"He wanted to get away."

"From what, dear?" They were so solicitous.

"Me maybe."

"Oh no," Sister Mercy said. "Couldn't be, and not that sweet baby."

"Away from," I tried to think, "everything?"

"But it comes with you, doesn't it, dear, everything?"

"Away from *it*." I struggled. "He wanted to get away from it, I think. He wanted to . . ."

"From what?"

"He wants to be free."

"And you? What do you want?"

Hell, I didn't know. Did I want a job like Ethel and Lucy? No. But I did not want to feel like my heart was ripped out of my body anymore. "I want to get a good job to support myself and Nadja, and I never want to be in love again." Was that what I wanted?

"Ah, love," Sister Mercy, the poet, sighed, perhaps remembering something.

"I remember," Sister Matilda said, "when our brother was sick, our one brother. He was in bed, dying of tuberculosis, and he asked me for some popcorn and I said no. The next day he was dead. His last, simple request, and I denied it."

"Oh Matilda, please don't bring that up."

"Well, Mercy, dear, when I meet my maker I will have to account for that."

"But the rest of us will have to account for much worse."

"Could not be so."

"What do you think Heaven is like?" Sister Matilda asked me.

"I think . . ." I wasn't sure what they wanted to hear. Oak and Kelly believed in reincarnation. My parents believed in a kind of pantheon in the clouds, everybody walking about in togas or underwear, and somebody playing the harp. Did Grey believe it was the plains, a happy hunting ground full of buffalos and tepees? "I don't believe in Heaven," I said.

"Oh, you must, you just must," Sister Martha said.

"Because, well, you know. Grim," Sister Mercy added. "Otherwise prospects are grim." She pursed her lips as if she had tasted something tart.

"It is grim," I said. "But *I* don't mean to be grim."

"Don't tire her out with theology now," Sister Matilda said. "She needs to get to bed. We get up early, with the rooster, so to speak. Then we all go back up to bed with a nice cup of coffee, except for Matilda, take a little nap."

"Coffee? Caffeine? You're Mormons, aren't you?"

"Yes, we know. But who is perfect? I am sure God will overlook a few little mishaps, a bad habit or two, an omission," and here Sister Martha looked hard and long at Sister Mercy. "An error now and then, bad judgment in some cases. I mean, otherwise, what is the point of being God, if you take my meaning?"

"Exactly, my dear," Sister Mercy said.

"Truth is, I can't make heads or tails out of *The Book of Mormon*," Sister Matilda put in.

"I know what you mean," I said.

"But I don't drink coffee," Sister Matilda asserted.

"Of course, dear. But, on the other hand, if the pendulum said you could, you would."

"Mercy, you have it in a nutshell."

In my bed in my attic in my pyramid in my sleep in my dream, I was in a car that went fast down a hill. I was the driver. I was in the car of my dreams—a 1955 Mercedes 300 SL Gullwing. In the dream, my Mormon aunts approved. They were waving, except Aunt Matilda, who was holding Nadja in the passenger seat. I was the driver. The passengers were Nadja and Aunt Matilda.

"Birds of a feather flock together," Aunt Matilda was saying.

[**"D O   Y O U   B E L I E V E** in God?" Aunt Matilda whispered. "We were talking last night, and I was a little worried."

I was barely awake. She had gotten into bed with me.

"I put the coffee on for the others," she said. "Just warming my feet."

Nadja was there, too, nursing. It was a little crowded.

"I believe in saints," I answered. "People who have lived. Unusual people. I believe in the idea of good, somebody, something.

This was not a before-coffee talk. My mouth was glue.

"Oh dear, I have never heard of that. You mean Latter-day Saints, us?"

"No, or maybe, but mostly the old saints."

Her hair was down, and, despite the flowing white locks covering her shoulders, her front was bald. I felt as though I were in bed with Benjamin Franklin. Later on, she let me watch her push it up and over her whole head and fasten it with combs, so it looked like she had a full head of hair. It was a good trick.

"And Jesus, do you believe in him?"

I sighed. This was not what I wanted to talk about on that particularly gray morning, but, on the other hand, I knew my aunt was asking me a serious question, and one that she may have been asking herself.

"I love the son, the son who lived and claimed divine parentage,"

I answered. In the Mormon church, there is the tradition of testimony. People get up before the congregation and testify their faith, ending always with: "In the name of Jesus Christ, amen."

"Gracious, Zoe, you sound like a Catholic."

"I think we are all sons and daughters, Aunt Matilda, and can claim divine parentage when we need to do so." I should have said, and especially when earthly parentage fails us. It would have been hard to explain to her my beliefs. It was not like talking with Aaron, arguing about language and relativity versus ideas and absolutes. I did not believe that religion was the opium of the masses or merely a primitive way of coping with life. I thought most people needed a philosophic framework outside their lives, not as a stupor-inducing, status quo–enforcing belief system but as a source of inspiration and aspiration. Lucille animated and placated the world through a system of signs and gestures, and Grey, with his Trickster, Coyote, defined himself as a gnostic, if not as a Manichaean. And while I wondered at Western people, like Kelly, who embraced Eastern ideas, I supposed that it *was* one world; and although sometimes his fidelity to any set of ideas seemed superficial, Kelly was a person who subscribed to an ethical life. I, like Narcissus, wanted to *do* good, but found myself usually at odds with everything around me.

"They are invisible friends, Aunt Matilda, my saints, like the kind of friends lonely children make for themselves. They keep me company. They give me a sense of continuity with history, with time. And the only time I felt part of the universe was when I gave birth."

"Oh, my dear." Aunt Matilda clutched her chest.

"You are not having a heart attack?" I asked.

"Good heavens, no. I'm healthy as a horse, because, as you know, I eat oats."

"But vitamins, Aunt Matilda, and protein?"

"Oh, what are they, my dear, but sheer illusions? You see, I believe in a world behind this world, too."

"But . . ." I could feel her bones, her wrists against my shoulder, her arms barely able to bear the weight of my head. She was like a little bird.

Light was making its way between the lace of my curtain, the little squares and loops—bits and pieces of light, tentative, less than enthusiastic light.

"Do you believe in prayer, Zoe?"

"Yes, in a way." I believed that once one was deliberate, it helped.

"Our ancestors prayed their hearts out, you know."

This was the Mormon epic, the trek across the country after being **307** kicked out of Missouri and Illinois, the women in the homespun gingham dresses walking in back of the covered wagons, the men on the buckboard and the valuables inside. Of course, in the first wave, there had only been two women. More came later, more and more.

"That first year after they planted the corn, the locusts came and gnawed away, Zoe, gnawed down their crop."

I thought of the sound of the million locusts like car engines and the sun blasting down and winter up ahead like the fringe on death's overcoat.

"They prayed because they would have died just like the Pilgrims would have that first Thanksgiving without the Indians. They prayed their poor hearts out."

To me, that was like the Catholics and their sacred pictures, Christ with a window in his chest and a cuckoo heart ready to pop out.

"They prayed their brains out."

That brought to mind worms popping out of their heads, or maybe they were little slips of paper, the brain a ticker tape bearing fortunes like fortune cookies. You will be saved—in bed. That was my other aunt, the one in Pacific Grove, my mother's sister, whose ballet school had failed. It seemed strange to me that I found solace in the aunts, not my mother.

"They were all there, kneeling in the fields, Zoe, dear, and, lo and behold, out of the west came a great flock of sea gulls."

Aunt Matilda got up and stood on the bed, sweeping her hands back and forth. Her bald head was as flushed as her cheeks.

"And then do you know what happened?"

Of course I knew, but still, this rendition seemed rather exciting.

"Those sea gulls, Zoe, darling, ate up those bad locusts all the way up." Matilda jumped off the bed and, making like Superman, ran from one corner of the room to the other, scooping up pretend locusts, stuffing them in her mouth, mashing them with her good Mormon teeth—gobble, gobble, popcorn sack.

"Matilda!" It was Aunt Martha below us, banging the kitchen ceiling with a broom handle.

"And that, Zoe, sweetheart, is why there is a big statue of a sea gull in Salt Lake today. It's gold or golden or gold-plated or gold-leafed, something gold."

Secretly I pretended that some Mormon along the way, the long trek west, had been good to a sea gull, spared a sea gull, helped a sea gull out, as in a fairy tale, and, thereafter, the whole sea-gull nation rallied to the rescue. I could imagine one sea gull squawking to another: Pass it on, locust trouble in Salt Lake.

I had no such fondness for the bird. In Monterey Bay they coated the rocks with their droppings, thick white splotches, and their squawking always sounded like quarreling.

"So that is why, today, I eat only what Moroni tells me to," Aunt Matilda said. "It is my way of saying thank you."

[**I HAD TO PASS** the golden sea gull every day on my way to work in Woolworth's dime store, in downtown Salt Lake City. I gave the old bird a frown. It was my way of saying drop dead.

My job was that of cashier, standing on my feet all day, except for lunch, which I took at the soda fountain in the store, and two ten-minute breaks, which I took in the storeroom in the back. On the form I lied on the question Have you ever been arrested?

Unfortunately, the cash register was by the turtle tank, the smelliest spot in the store. There were about fifty tiny turtles in that tank with bright pictures painted on their backs, pyramiding the sides of the tank in a mad scramble to get out. Manny, the high school boy helper, a beast and a bore, had the job of cleaning out the tank, but he hardly ever did it. Turtles died in droves, and the bottom layer of the pyramid was stinky little turtle corpses with Bugs Bunny and Mickey Mouse gaily painted on their backs.

Alongside the turtle tank was the churning watch tank. This was the mighty Timex watch on a mechanical plastic holder which plunged into the water every few minutes. In, out, in, out. Perfect timing. Next came the rows of alarm clocks, across the aisle from the hair accoutrements—plastic curlers with rubber bands, Toni home perms, barrettes and bobby pins, combs, brushes, bright plastic headbands, shower caps. Sewing accessories were kept in the adjacent counter. Embroidery hoops and threads, the white cloth blue-stamped with patterns to trace. Cardinals and blue jays, little girls opening gates, flowers, cute animals. Then the yarns and knitting needles, crochet hooks. A little open cabinet of threads on wooden spools arranged by color and shade. Red, magenta, orange-red, orange, dark pink, pink pink, pale pink. Then there were the aging, yellowing cards, all seasons: Thanksgiving, Halloween, Christmas, and Valentine cards and red paper, doilies, big books of punch-out cards for kids. The bolts of cloth and patterns were kept in the back. Clair, a lady who had worked there twenty years, cut the cloth, measuring it along a yardstick nailed to the counter. Once a month a man came and demonstrated an implement which could chop vegetables with a mere flick of his wrist. Mr. Smiths.

So, besides the occasional presence of Mr. Smiths, there were Clair and Manny and the manager, Mr. Stewart, and Edith, who like Clair was ancient and did the back counter, and me. Aunt Martha bought me comfortable shoes to keep my arches from falling, but the floor was the soft, dark wood, narrow planks of all dime stores *in perpetuum*, and my legs were okay. It was my mind that was in trouble. I thought I was going to die of boredom.

I couldn't read on the job, except during the one hour Mr. Stewart went to lunch. Every day from one-thirty to two-thirty he went next door to a cafe for a hot turkey sandwich, which was a heap of turkey on two triangular pieces of white bread, topped with a scoop of mashed potatoes and lots of gravy, something my mother used to make; a Coca Cola; and a deep-dish apple pie.

I always had the blue-plate special at the counter. Fried fish or chicken, or a hamburger patty with lettuce and tomato, and either Campbell's tomato soup or green Jell-O salad.

Our customers were mostly old ladies, regulars. Some came in every day just to buy one thing, a skein of embroidery thread or a set of jacks for a grandchild, and then they stayed for a cup of coffee at the counter. On Saturdays, for I worked six days, our customers were primarily Negroes, and they did not use the lunch counter.

I really didn't notice that until after I received the letter from Margo, which had been forwarded from my father's house.

June 10, 1958
Did I tell you that I am writing for the school paper, The Hilltop?
Our editor is a Jamaican, very smart. I have also submitted some poetry to the
creative writing magazine Dasein.

I want to see your baby.
I have cut my hair. It is still wild, but curlier, more kneegrow.

July 20, 1958
Dear Margo (I didn't write back), I work in a damn Woolworth and live in the driest town (in all ways) in the United States. Every day I go home to my three elderly great-aunts. For entertainment, we play Go Fish and Hearts, sometimes Authors, whoever gets four Hawthornes, Louisa May Alcotts. You know. On Sundays we go to church. On the other hand, Nadja is growing. They dote on her, take excellent care of her. She has dark hair like Grey, is a very smart little miss. I long for Grey terribly. Whoops, didn't mean that. To continue, I carry Nadja about on my back with a little homemade papoose board. I don't know if our dime-store counter is integrated. The Negroes never sit down, the few who come in on Saturday. Love, Zoe.

I noticed one Saturday, though, that while the manager, Mr. Stewart, was over at lunch at the Lunchbox, one of the customers, a Negro woman buying a scrub brush and tin pail, had in her purse bunches of earrings, new ones from the store, still on their cardboard. I caught a glimpse when the woman got her wallet to pay for her scrub brush and pail. Was it a mistake? I didn't say anything.

But the next Saturday the same woman came at the same time, and I could see in an inside pocket of her coat a bulge that looked like a row of fountain pens.

I wanted to tell her to put them back because Mr. Stewart did an inventory every week, matching the cash register receipts with the stock. But I merely cleared my throat. I was embarrassed, for one, and, also, her dress, her purse, the earrings, the pens all reminded me of myself, Nadja's Easter dress, the special pockets Lucille made in my raincoat for "going shopping" at Macy's.

The following Saturday during Mr. Stewart's lunch hour, the

woman brought a friend. They took bundles of yarn, knitting needles, children's socks and underwear, and lipsticks.

"Please," I said when they came to the counter.

"Yes?" The woman looked up. She had very dark skin, a large mole on her nose. Her hair was pressed flat in parallel waves, and I could see that she had sewn the runs in her nylons, no small feat. I wondered where she lived, how she could live in Salt Lake City, for at that time there were no Negro Mormons. Negroes were the children of Ham, cursed for having seen his father, Noah, naked. That's what my father told me.

"Yes?" the woman repeated.

"Ah," and I couldn't say more.

I wondered if Clair or Edith detected anything.

The next Saturday, the two women came with a man. It seemed that they gave me a special look. Was it a signal? A thank you? Or the pity you bestow on the ignorant?

"Listen," I said, thinking, I could get into trouble, lose my job.

"Yes?"

"Nothing."

"You're not from around here, are you?" the woman said.

"No."

"Where are you from?" she asked. She was wearing a pink cotton dress and a brown hat with a veil. The dress didn't fit her that well, but the hat, its perky angle, reminded me of Aunt Mercy.

"California." I began to blink. "I'm from California."

"Is there something in your eye?"

"No, it's a nervous habit. I got over it a little while, but it comes back from time to time."

"Whenever you think you're going to blink, take a deep breath, count to ten."

"That works for blinking? I thought you did that for hiccups."

"Both. You have beautiful eyes. You should keep them open."

"And see everything? Do you think I should see everything?"

"You have soft eyes," she continued.

Soft eyes? It sounded like soft-boiled eggs.

"You do see everything," she went on. "I think you see more than most people. But if you keep your eyes open, people can see you."

"Well," I said, thinking, as Mary Ellen had said, that flattery is skin-deep, "it's not that I want to be invisible. It's just . . ." and I was reminded of the time with Aaron that I stumbled on the truth by saying that it was not a father I was looking for but a mother. "I sometimes don't want to be where I am, and by closing my eyes just for a second, I can sort of not be there."

And by saying that, the words leading me to the truth, I realized that was exactly what the mother I didn't have wanted to do by drinking. She wanted to close her eyes.

"So where do you want to be, Hawaii?"

"Yeah," I said, "someplace like that."

[**IT WAS LATE** July and sweltering. Instead of a high chair, Nadja now sat on a little chair Aunt Mercy had bought at Sears, which was placed on a big grown-up chair. She had already grown out of her first shoes, and Aunt Matilda had them bronzed. They sat on the mantel beside a studio photograph of Nadja and me.

Rubber beach balls, sprinkling buckets, sun hats were being stolen. Mr. Stewart, even as inattentive as he was, was aware that the inventory was not matching up with the receipts. I was worried.

"What would you do?" I asked Aunt Martha over dinner, which was a delicious chicken salad with strawberries for dessert. "What do you do when you see somebody doing something wrong, which could be costly to you, but to tell on them would be to betray something in you?"

"You have to pray," Aunt Martha said without a moment's hesitation, "and do what God tells you to do."

"What if He doesn't say anything?"

"He will."

"I don't think so."

"Spend a good hour with him. We'll keep Nadja downstairs. You go up and kneel down in your room. If the Heavenly Father is for you, who can be against you?"

I went upstairs and knelt in front of the side window, the one facing away from the Temple and downtown. I could see the houses next door and the dry, empty fields beyond. I thought of where the Negroes might live. Mr. Stewart said that the Negroes who came to the dime store lived in the colored section. But I had never seen that part of Salt Lake City. I wondered if it might be near the lake, tin shanties dusted with salt. Or on the way out of town, on State Street, where there were rows of pawnshops and a figure of a giant bowling pin atop Classic Bowl, and auto paint places and Auto Truefit Seatcovers, Hotel Pandone, great places like that.

I imagined the lipsticks lined up like toy soldiers on a windowsill and the jewelry pinned to a wall patched with bunched newspaper. No, they would have sold the lipsticks. Maybe they saved the children's things—the children in their new underwear and bright white socks would be jumping on the bed.

"Dear Sweet Jesus," I began, "love of my life, tell me what is right and I will suck on your bones."

Okay, Zoe, I said, stop being excessive.

"Dear God, You who art in Heaven, grant me this wish today."

Nothing. Not a word.

"Saint Anthony, old man, old fool, listen to me."

Suddenly it started to rain.

"It's raining," I heard Aunt Mercy exclaim downstairs, "in July. Can you believe that?"

I ran past the stairway portrait gallery, ran outside the back door just in my dress, let the screen door slam.

"Zoe, come in," Aunt Martha called to me. "You'll catch your death."

I hopped back on the porch, but it was not cold.

I stood beside the washing machine, which had a wringer on top with big round lips. I wrapped my arms around my sides to keep warm. Everything was wet and the world was exquisitely beautiful.

I heard a rumble and some squeaking. I looked around.

"She should do what she should do. Papa God has spoken," the washing machine lips rolled out. It was like print coming off the press, but in invisible ink on invisible paper and in a deep movie voice. I was not surprised. On the other hand, maybe, like Grey, I was having religious delusions.

"What kind of answer is that, Papa God? I should do what I should do?"

The rain was coming faster now. How very lovely it was, everything was, and I thought of Grey in New York. Was it raining there? I reorganized my memory of the time he tried to run me down on the Gorda hill to include rain. It was raining so hard on the hill that he didn't see me. The car was like a massive fish, a prehistoric whale newly awakened from its watery depths, and, with a blind will of its own, it swam down the hill.

"Remember the categorical imperative," the washing machine heaved out. "Remember what Aaron has taught you."

"Aaron is dead."

"No matter. So is Immanuel Kant. Neither died of the categorical imperative."

"Aaron might have died of the categorical imperative, that is, that do-unto-others thing is only for the very healthiest, not for masochistic people."

"Oh Zoe," Papa God said. "Go with your instincts."

"That's what's been getting me into so much trouble."

The machine wheezed.

"Are you laughing at me, Papa God?"

"No, little one."

"What does *The Book of Mormon* say?" I asked.

"And it came to pass that in the three hundred and sixty-third year the Nephites did go up with their armies to battle against the Lamanites, out of the Land of Desolation.

"But, behold, the judgments of God will overtake the wicked; and it is by the wicked that the wicked are punished; for it is the wicked that stir up the hearts of the children of men unto bloodshed."

"Thanks a lot." The Land of Desolation was right.

"Zoe, come inside this instant," Aunt Martha commanded, holding up the curtain to the side, shaking her head a little, but still smiling at me through the window. I ran into the house and looked out the front window. And then, there in the rain layering the ground in thin sheets and painting the sky a skim of gray, I saw right on West Temple Street a coyote. No, not a dog. A coyote. It looked at me straight in the eyes.

Little Mole, Little Mole, I am coming to get you.

I knew then that Narcissus was right in warning me. My longing was over. Grey would destroy me.

I ran into the kitchen as fast as I could.

"We don't usually get rain this time of year," Aunt Martha said.

"Are you all right, dear?" Aunt Matilda asked.

"Were your prayers, do you think, perhaps . . . What I mean is, do you think they were successful?" Aunt Martha asked.

"I got scared," I said.

"Ah, fear is not always the worst thing, my dear."

"A cup of tea for the weary?" Aunt Matilda offered.

"Where's Nadja?"

Her playpen was in the kitchen, as it had been in Lucille's house. But she was hardly ever in it. We had baby-proofed the house, moving everything she could swallow or hurt herself with out of reach. I found her in the living room watching television with Aunt Mercy. I picked her up. I tried to put Grey out of my mind. Seeing the coyote reminded me. It was a sign, a bad sign. I had to put it out of my mind.

So it was that each day I left with trepidation the yellow brick house with its sagging metal awning and walked down West Temple, passing the Royal Arms apartments. Temple Square with the Tabernacle—a half eggshell where the famous organ was housed and the choir sang. I took a left on South Temple, where the statue of Brigham Young and the Pioneers and two Indians stood, and passed the white Utah Hotel. Inside the hotel were columns and golden pineapples hanging from the white columns. Nearby were Brigham Young's house and the Lion House, really the Beehive House and the Lion House. Industry was the idea behind the beehive symbol on the flag. No coyote was visible.

The Temple was open only to Mormons in Good Standing with Letters from their Bishops. It was made of granite blocks pulled by oxen from a quarry nearby. I hadn't seen the coyote. Grey was far away, part of another life.

[**THEY CAME** every Saturday. There were four. And I watched as they emptied the front of the store before my nose. They seemed to swoop down like the legendary sea gulls eating up all the locusts.

Toys—small rubber balls and balsa-wood airplane models to build, marbles, white baby dolls, wind-up cars, bubble mix with plastic holders, dollhouse furniture, little Golden Books about the three pigs, *Little Red Riding-Hood*, and paper-doll books.

Have mercy, I thought.

Bracelets with charms on them; rings with stones for each day of the week—Monday was pink glass, Tuesday blue, Wednesday emerald green; a music box like mine at home with twirling ballerinas and tinkly music; round, creamy white compacts.

But not tool sets, which were in the back with the fabric, dog-food bowls, bird cages, and tiny gold fish in aquariums. What they took was all to the front. They knew. They knew me, but I dared not look in anybody's eyes, as they bought one coloring book and a small box of Crayolas.

"God helps those who help themselves," Aunt Martha said.

"You sound like my father."

"Well, we are related, although Melba and I could never see eye to eye on how she raised that boy. She did not spare the rod, and, as far as I could tell, that child never once stepped out of line. He grew up frightened. Then she got so fat and all. I don't know, Zoe. Let me say that you can only try and hope it is for the best. If you have a good heart, surely . . . Oh, did I tell you, I have a letter for you."

"A letter?"

"It looks like a book." She handed me a thick envelope with many stamps on it.

I recognized the handwriting. I put the envelope in my pocket. Aunt Mercy was knitting Nadja a sweater. And Aunt Matilda, feeling a bit on the weak side, was snoozing on the couch. Nadja was crawling about, going from one of us to the other. She was in her sleepers.

"Matilda doesn't look well these days; I don't think the oatmeal diet is the best, and apparently the pendulum is not going to change its mind," Aunt Martha said to Aunt Mercy. "Do you think we should take her to the hospital?"

"What are you saying, dear?"

"I am saying she looks like she's dying."

"I don't want to go to the hospital," Aunt Matilda said. "And I am not dying."

"So you are not asleep."

"Well, you have to eat more than oatmeal," Aunt Martha said. "We are not going to sit here and watch you starve to death."

"I think we should go to the hospital right now," Aunt Mercy said.

"Zoe, would you go upstairs and get Matilda's shoes?" Aunt Martha asked.

They were going to take Matilda to the hospital? Just like that? Right now? What was happening? Matilda, yes, was getting thinner every day, but wasn't that expected? Nobody seemed that alarmed before this moment. I ran upstairs, got Matilda's shoes. The letter from Grey, tucked in my pocket, was burning my thigh, but first things first, as my father would say.

Of course, I had been in Matilda's room before, but I was struck by it differently this time as I fetched her shoes. The fact that she was going to leave the room made me see it anew. One wall was stacked high with newspapers, *National Geographics*, and travel brochures. Over her lean spinster bed were taped highway maps of various states put out by the American Automobile Association. Wyoming, North Dakota, the Badlands. Matilda did not know how to drive. Aunt Martha was the driver of the family. And Aunt Mercy got to sit up front. The coat was in with the dresses. Rooting about for it reminded me of the times my mother had taken me into the closet. I had been terrified, confused.

My mother always had that effect on me.

"Zoe."

"Coming."

"Now, Matilda, we don't want you to resist this."

"It's raining," I said lamely.

"Mama," Nadja cooed.

"Just a minute, sweetie." She was holding on to one of their overstuffed chairs with one hand, holding her rattle with the other.

"Maybe Matilda needs her galoshes," Aunt Mercy said.

"I'll get them." I ran back upstairs, rooted among her shoes, got out her old-lady, clear-plastic galoshes, ran back downstairs. Mercy knelt in front of her sister, slipped them on over the grandmother shoes. The sidewalk was wet.

"Shall we come?" I asked.

"No, dear, you stay with Nadja. We'll be back soon."

"Don't forget my pendulum," Aunt Matilda said.

"That stupid pendulum is why you have to go to the hospital," Aunt Martha said. "Sorry, but this is a moment of truth, Matilda."

"She's not in her right mind," Aunt Mercy explained.

"Who is not in their right mind? My brain is not damaged, Mercy. You, Zoe, take care of my pendulum."

"Of course."

I noticed then how feeble her voice sounded, how they had to help her walk, how weak she had become.

Where had I been?

At the dime store.

I heard the grand old Lincoln start up. Aunt Martha started it with great vigor, but drove about five miles an hour.

I picked up Nadja, watched the car from the window.

"Do you want a story?"

I knew she couldn't follow the stories I read, but she sat quietly and looked at the pictures. It was a little Golden Book about Cinderella I had gotten from work. Cinderella swept the ashes, hoping for deliverance. I considered the possibility that this might not be the best story for an impressionable young mind. But what Nadja liked was the Pumpkin.

She liked bright colors and she liked animals. Maybe we could get a cat, a calico cat. I'd have to see what the aunts said. I still felt the letter in my pocket. I nursed Nadja and took her upstairs to her crib. I didn't like to be too far from her, even if she was sleeping, but I went downstairs, washed the dinner dishes.

Was Aunt Matilda seriously malnourished? I remembered when I was in the hospital with an ulcer, and Aaron had leaned over the bed railings. Let me see you, he said. Open your eyes, the Negro woman said, so people can see you. Mr. Stewart, the manager, had scheduled a meeting for Monday. I cleaned the fridge out, sponged the stove, swept the floor, got the toothbrush we used for cleaning behind the tap, did that, and then decided to mop the floor. I wished my father could see me. Matilda's pendulum lay on the table. I picked it up, asked it if I was a fool.

Yes, it swung, yes, yes, yes.

[**S O I S A T D O W N ,** took the letter out of my pocket, began to read it.

August 1, 1958

The telling is New York and I am Coyote crying in the hallway to a tiny kitchen, and keep going and you will find, after a bicycle hung on a wall, two tiny rooms at the back, like testicles on either side of a long narrow penis. Oak and the baby in one room, me in another, and in the afternoon when I sit there, one piece of sunlight that comes between the brick buildings laps in, whole yellow waves of it, like the tide coming in; the sky lingers, like Neptune in the depths, calling in his pretty white sea horses slowly, no hurry about it. And it becomes muzzy, indistinct, and without fuss the warm yellow is sucked back home, taken in, given dinner, and sent to bed, a black bed of kelp and dinner of sea slugs.

People look at Coyote on the street, coming in bunches at me and laughing in bundles. Yes, Coyote, there is a world, but you must bring it all back home and take it out one by one to spread on the floor one by one. You are a little pup, and a priest is coming out of you with his golden bowl hooked on a chain. Holy, holy, holy. Letting out the scent and steam, like an engine. Creation is a catastrophe wrought upon us by a cruel demiurge. There is nothing but darkness and deep.

It is summer and summer sits atop their skin like jellyfish on the beach, translucent bubbles. I am of the People and live in the Turtle Land. Bring it all back home, baby, and let it grow inside you, so that your flesh contains the world.

In the market a basket of figs, rows of cantaloupes, buds of garlic, garlands of onions.

It says: Coyote, taste of me, California.

"What's the matter with you?" Oak says. "Be cool."

"It's a lovely day," Grey giggles.

"What's so funny all the time?"

Coyote sees Mole sometimes, Zoe, walking along the street very orange, a navel orange. She is glowing in the dark. Her aura is magenta. She is the Corn Maiden, the eternal virgin, Isis, the soul of light, the truth behind the veil. She carries a basket and is shopping in the village for flowers.

"Oh Zoe, come to me, California."

"What are you saying, Grey?"

"I see a pachyderm, no, a dromedary, Oak, with a tight, mealy mouth, long eyelashes, humpbacked, listlessly wavering. It is a mirage. Look, Oak."

"Hush, Grey, no silly stuff."

Oak is tall and strong. Oak is mighty and brave.

> My ancestors chant:
> Dance for rain.
> It is always drought in California.
> Do the Deer Dance.
> The deer is Zoe's totem, the power of gentleness.
> The bench in the park says: Sit down.

"Where are we going, what is the hurry, Oak?"

"God, Grey. Get up. Don't poop out on me, now."

We go a-gallerying gallery to gallery.

Oak's pictures are vegetables. Green peppers that look like green asses, butting out juicy with an occasional black spot. Tomato breasts, squash penises —a fecund garden of delights. Often I stay in the apartment with the baby while she makes her rounds. I lie in the shade of the afternoon in the quiet room, the fan poised to my neck, blades slicing the air and singing to me, and the baby boy on my stomach.

Coyote, this is Dragonfly, the fan says. I have a secret message from my secret garden. The real vegetables are rotting on the vine, bursting open in the sun, becoming tangled. Come home, native son, come home.

I bring it all back home. The ancestors have given each thing a power and a meaning, so I know what to eat and what not to eat, and how to thread my way through objects. I must mediate, meditate, machinate, masturbate. Sometimes I can't keep my hands off myself, and must do, do, do it. So that deer is there. I, Coyote, am riding her between my legs, and I feel the vibrations of her muscles. This is the secret, she says. I am the secret.

Oak, Redwood, and me, we are shambling, ambling down the street, all three of us. Oak, tall and blond, a golden daffodil. And me—small, furtive. I am, my dear Mole, of the earth, but seldom do my feet touch earth. Miles and miles of sidewalk, as if spilled out of the sky by a giant cement mixer, a celestial machine. All must wear and rub in time, wind down. But not the sidewalk which carries us along, like it or not. At night I look for the Big Dipper, for I wish to follow the drinking gourd north into Canada and on up through the glacial forest, sparkling like glass, until I get to the castle of the Ice Queen. Oh, crack open my heart, please break it, and set me free. But the city is lit up like a birthday cake, the icing made of soft sugar, and I cannot see the sky for lights.

My ancestors say: Read the ground, and bring it all back home. What does the earth tell you as we pound in dance?

The ground is our Mother Earth.

"This woman we are going to meet goes with the guy that runs that gallery I was telling you about. He's going to be there, and I don't want her nervous about me. That, Grey, is, like, why I had to drag you along. We are going to have coffee or sherry or something, and I am, like, counting on you not to giggle or play with yourself."

When did it start?

Ohio? South Dakota? Montana? What states did we go through? The window must have been open and the dry wind blowing when my mind left me, rolling into a large ball of tumbleweed.

"My dear, I think I've lost my mind. Could you stop the car a minute while I go look for it?"

Maybe camping in Colorado. Just as soon as she can, she's going to put me in a box and ship me back to California.

"You can't even, like, fuck anymore," she said one night in utter disgust astride me. "You are good for nothing."

We are now in the East Village, standing outside a warehouse. We go up the lift, huge, industrial. From below, one can see the cables, like vocal cords to the voice box, Vox, his Master's Voice climbing, climbing.

"Oh, Oak, how nice to see you."

All in black, small, shiny, an ant of a woman, busy, busy, made miniature by the huge walls, high ceilings, everything white, white and black.

I no longer feel like love, but Oak likes to get on top of me and straddle me in my sleep, the rider on the horse, the cocoon around the dragonfly. And flopping up and down, her buttery hind and her long, ponderous breasts. Her snake tongue long and wet, a little sour and acid at the end, like pot. And the cocoon would tighten to make poor dragonfly buzz and buzz, but no buzzing. Coyote must howl.

"This is Grey, Grey Cloud."

You want me to rattle my beads, Oak, and do my dance. Heap Big Brave.

"In the Sioux tradition, it is necessary to purify oneself in the sweat lodge in order to speak of sacred things. Everything connected with the sweat lodge is done carefully. The trees to build the sweat lodge are spoken to, and the bent saplings are covered with buffalo robes. Men must rub themselves with sage held over the fire while prayers are chanted. The water must not be spilled, otherwise Thunder Beings will be angry. Then the chosen young man is sent in search of a vision. For four days and nights, he is watching everything for a sign."

"I warned you, Grey, you mess this up and I will, like, kill you."

Somewhere outside New Jersey is when we knew we hated each other. The Garden State, but full of sooty, dilapidated little buildings of aging brick, and red rusted railroad cars, and barrels of garbage.

If you breathe a word, the priest said.

Even in confession, Father?

Do you want to die?

I thought I was dying so God would not have to kill me outright. Killed in the sacristy, the thing exploding up my ass like a fat stick of dynamite. I was torn apart. And later the blood staining my underpants, so I had to hide them. The twelve-year-olds were put in the west wing. That night the snow fell in thick clumps, fistfuls. The bleeding stopped, but I walked with difficulty, still feeling the thing up me, a fat hot dog.

No, that is not the story. The story is, I got back in the car, in the back of my mother's car, a pack rat, in with everything, and bled silently on the dirty clothes.

"Grey, what are you doing in there? Max is here."

The boyfriend, fiancé, lover, whatever, also in black. I wonder that they like Oak's vegetables in their obscene reds and greens, brilliant yellows.

Greylen, you have sinned.

Father, you have sinned. Even I, an ignorant Indian orphan boy, knew that, but did not say. Twelve, thirteen. Snow, sun.

Fourteen, I ran away in a Greyhound, all my possessions in a paper bag. In San Francisco, you were paid to have your ass split open.

"Sometimes we have poetry readings at our openings."

I understand, Zoe, you are trying to divorce me.

Nothing in the world could persuade me to let you divorce me. I would rather die, I would rather us both be dead. I am coming back.

Mecca is not Mexico City or New York City. It is Salt Lake. I am coming to get you.

Nirvana is not here or there.

Nobody knows.

[**I WENT UPSTAIRS,** crawled into bed, pulled the sheet over my head.

"Matilda," Aunt Martha whispered to me that night through the sheet, "Matilda is very sick. We waited too long this time. Pray for her, my dear. Give God your young heart."

Before I came to Utah, I had only sincerely prayed a few times in my life, and here I was being asked to pray two times in one month.

"Sweet Jesus," I said aloud, this time kneeling in front of Nadja's crib at two o'clock in the morning, not daring to look out the window. "My Aunt Matilda is so harmless, so gentle . . ." Her room was her getaway, wasn't it. The maps, the travel brochures. She wanted to get away, and the only way she could get away, get away with it, plan her getaway, was to starve herself to death . . . Like me blinking, my mother drinking. "Sweet Jesus, spare her life, and . . ." I didn't know what I had to offer. Devotion apparently did not do the trick. I remembered that in the old days people offered up sacrifices. I could understand that inclination. But I was not an eye for an eye sort of person. I was not Abraham. And I needed my hands. I needed my feet. I had no lamb to kill. Then I remembered a story we had to read in school, that stupid Maupassant story. "Dear Jesus, I offer you my hair."

I had read somewhere that the Nazis used Jewish hair for making rope, cloth, carpets, mattress stuffing, all sorts of things. It was shorn off them after they were gassed, and those strong enough to work had it cut before they died. And then collaborators, women in France who went with Nazi soldiers, had their hair shaved by their own French countrymen and were paraded in the streets for loving young soldier boys. Nuns shaved their hair in supreme sacrifice. I knew I had hit on it. Perfecto.

[**S U N D A Y   M O R N I N G**   when I came down to breakfast, Aunt Martha said: "My, but you look stylish. I like that short hair.
It becomes you. Quite the modern lady."

Aunt Mercy concurred. I noticed she had done some snipping,
too.

My short hair did not lie down flat, though. It popped up like
little licks of flame. After my aunts left for church, I went out in the
backyard and buried what I had chopped off. I could swear that it
burned my hands. I arranged two combs in the shape of a cross to mark
the spot.

Sunday night I heard that they were keeping Aunt Matilda at the
hospital to be force-fed and that she was going to live.

Monday morning I had to go to work.

"My God," Mr. Stewart said, when he walked into the stockroom
Monday morning for our big meeting, "run into a threshing machine?"

"Your crowning glory," Mr. Smiths added.

"Penance," Mr. Stewart went on.

There were not enough chairs for our dime store meeting, so the
men graciously sat on boxes, except for Mr. Stewart, who stood up. He
had on his red tie, the short-sleeved white shirt he wore every day, and
his blue slacks. The bathroom door was open and you could see the
sign that said: EMPLOYEES, WASH HANDS BEFORE RETURNING TO WORK.

"There's been a discrepancy," Mr. Stewart said.

Edith looked at her hands. They were her pride and joy. Each nail was tenderly tended to, filed, polished, buffed, shaped, and refiled, cuticles pushed down. Breakage was tantamount to tragedy. They were a shiny pink this week, and she wore a handkerchief fanned up like a peacock tail in her dress pocket. Clair bit her nails, and her bobby socks slipped down and her heels were worn down at the back. I think that in terms of grooming I was between the two. But I had no idea what either of them did when they went home from work, although Clair mentioned a mother sometimes. My mother bought me this dress. Or: We had fried potatoes last night. I was sure they were Mormon, though, as was Mr. Stewart. Manny was something else. Maybe a Lutheran.

All I could think of, though, was Grey's letter. It scared me. He scared me. I remembered, with edgy lucidity, that he tried to run me over. I didn't let my brain contain it, didn't let myself quite put my mind around it. Now I thought of the pink bumps of my brain enfolding a car, a gray Volvo. The image was sinking in.

"I have noticed a distinct decrease in some areas which do not show up on the cash register receipts," Mr. Stewart began.

Here it comes, I thought.

"Now, I have been checking each day, and it seems . . ."

I tuned out. I had been in Salt Lake City almost three months. Soon it would be fall, Thanksgiving, Christmas, then Nadja's first birthday. Except for the public library and the church, I had been nowhere. Where was there to go?

"Manny is an honest boy."

I looked at Manny. His real name was not Manuel, which would make him Mexican, but Manfred. Good German stock. He narrowed his blue eyes at me to bare slits. Once, he had pressed me to the wall in the stockroom, put his hands on my breasts.

"You want to live?" I had asked. "My brother will . . ."

"You ain't got a brother."

"You want to bet?" Actually I was thinking of Sister Martha, master baker, ex–phys ed teacher. She would beat him up. "You want hands, Manny?"

He dropped his hands. "Ugly woman." He spat.

"You," I said. "What you look like I don't mention."

I had picked up a few tips in San Francisco from Lucille, the girls at the club, riding public transportation late at night, living in the Fillmore District. A girl learns.

"And Mr. Smiths, well . . . 'nough said," Mr. Stewart continued.

Mr. Smiths smiled shyly, but with guile. He liked women with big asses, that I had observed, and he, he was all belly, no ass, a fine specimen of American manhood, but every Friday, chop, chop, chop, the magic chopping machine.

"Step right up, ladies. This may look just like a jar and some blades to you, but let me tell you, in the kitchen you will not have a better tool. Cukes, 'matoes, taters, you name it, my handy-dandy chopper machine." And big sweat stains under his shirt sleeves, even on cold days. Edith told me he was going to be getting married soon. We couldn't imagine it, or the poor woman.

"And Clair. Well . . . Also Edith . . . Not from their departments."

Clair looked at me sympathetically. Edith gave Mr. Stewart devil's horns behind his back.

I remembered the football chant in high school.

"Give 'em the ax, the ax, the ax."

"So the only one responsible," Mr. Stewart said.

"I didn't take anything," I said.

"I could have you arrested," he said.

I closed my eyes.

"I could have you thrown in jail."

I opened my eyes, looked straight at him.

"I have been arrested," I said.

"But instead," he said, as if not hearing me, "I am firing you."

Clair looked as if somebody had punched her in the stomach, and she started crying.

"Oh, Mr. Stewart, don't do that," she said. "She didn't take anything. It was the niggers."

I felt as if *my* stomach had been punched.

"What niggers?" Mr. Stewart asked.

"The ones who come in every Saturday during your lunch. They take advantage of her."

"Well, Edith?"

Edith was examining her nails assiduously.

"I don't know nothing about it," Edith said. "Don't ask me."

"Zoe?"

I didn't say anything.

"Are you going to defend yourself?"

Manny was smiling. Mr. Smiths was perspiring. Chop, chop, chop. This *was Dragnet*, except the names were not changed to protect the innocent.

"So why didn't you say anything?" Mr. Stewart asked Clair.

"Me, me, I was scared, sir. Scared they might come in the night to kill me. And Zoe, she was scared, too."

"Zoe, were you scared?"

"No."

"What were you arrested for?"

"Shoplifting."

"Well," Mr. Stewart said. "That settles that. Get your things, Zoe Cloud, and get out of here."

Clair followed me back to my locker in the infamous back room.

"I wish we could give you a going-away party," she said.

"It's all right, Clair."

"Some Tupperware or something. A cake dish with a cover on a pedestal, or a manicure set with extra polish, like Edith has."

"Don't worry, Clair. I have to leave town anyway."

I thought of the Negroes coming next Saturday, a legion of them, maybe talking in the morning about all the stuff they would get and then arriving. Mr. Stewart would be there at the cash register. The store would be eerily quiet.

"Where, where'd she go?" they'd whisper.

"She gone. She gone, gone."

[**BIG DEAL,** I said to myself walking home. So I lost my job. Joseph Smith, the founder of our church, was murdered for polygamy. So I've lost every job I've had. What the hell. So I'm a failure. Who cares? I was dying to hear some music. Connie Francis singing "Who's Sorry Now?" I longed to be near somebody my age. I wanted a drink. I wanted a cigarette. I wanted to get out of there. I wanted to be on the road. I had better be on the road.

"My, you're home early," Aunt Mercy said.

"Where is Nadja?"

"Taking a nap."

"I was fired."

"Oh no."

"Yes."

I opened the fridge.

"And I'm hungry as a horse."

"Speaking of food," Aunt Martha said, coming into the kitchen, "I decided to make some cookies today in honor of Matilda's recovery."

"Cookies on Monday?" It smelled wonderful in the kitchen. I sat down at the table. Aunt Mercy sat across from me.

"Martha, Zoe lost her job."

"I am so glad," Martha said. "I always thought that dime store was not worthy of your talents."

Martha took off her apron and pushed the cookie jar, which was in the shape of a hen, my way.

"I was fired," I repeated, "and I can't stay here anymore."

"Why ever not? You could get another job."

"No, this is not my place." I didn't want to tell them that I was frightened that Grey would find me. Then what? Would he run me over again? I doubted that. Perhaps what I feared was my own weakness. We were almost divorced now. By the end of December. I could recall the lawyer's door rippling behind me, his red face before me, Extreme Cruelty written on a yellow notepad.

"We love you, love Nadja," Aunt Martha said. "We will take care of you. Is it because we are Mormon, too Mormon for you?"

I laughed, thinking of Narcissus. Is it because I'm a Negro?

"Oh no."

"Where will you go?" Aunt Mercy asked. "To your mother's?"

"No. I can't go there."

"To your house in the forest?"

"No, never."

"So where will you go?"

"I don't know."

"*That* is a problem," Aunt Martha said.

We were all quiet for a minute.

"Put on your thinking caps," Aunt Martha said.

I opened the drawer under the silverware drawer. My thinking cap was a yellow bathing cap. I looked like Donald Duck. Aunt Mercy's was black felt. She looked like Felix the Cat, who always said Drats. Aunt Martha wore a handkerchief like a Catholic lady at mass. Matilda's was an old pioneer bonnet. We sat there thinking.

"I know where you could go. You could go to our cousin's. He and his wife live in a big house in Santa Barbara."

"It is sunshine there all the time," Aunt Mercy said. "They have oranges and lemons."

"But what makes you think they would want me?"

"Why not?"

"Why not indeed," Aunt Martha said. "Good thinking, Mercy."

"And I am taking Matilda with me." I had thought about this a little, but only when I said it had I decided.

"What?"

"I am taking Aunt Matilda with me."

"Why?"

"Because she wants to leave, to go somewhere, and wherever I am I will need to work and have a babysitter. Is their house big enough for the three of us, them and us?"

"But Matilda has always lived in Salt Lake City."

"All the more reason. It is killing her. Look at her room, Aunt Martha. She wants to get away, to go somewhere. This would suit both of us."

Aunt Martha looked at me long and hard.

"You know I am right," I said.

"But we have always lived together, except for those few short, misguided months when, when . . ." Aunt Mercy began crying.

"Now, now, Mercy," Aunt Martha said.

"I think Aunt Matilda would love to go on a trip," I said.

"Well, we will see what we will see," Aunt Martha said.

And that is how Aunt Matilda learned how to drive, riding with me and Nadja through the desert in a 1954 maroon Studebaker with a pointy tin nose. It looked like a rocket bent for the moon.

There is a theory that the people who originally went to California were social misfits, that the movement west was composed of those who could not live in the civilized east, that the cowboy who slept out on the range alone and came into town once a week to shoot up the saloon was your basic everyday sociopath. And as soon as little towns would sprout up, the surge was ever westward. Finally these loners hit the Pacific, and later, after it was built, they could jump off the Golden Gate Bridge.

Some don't jump off the bridge, but just wade out, letting the waves carry them to our First Mother, as if cradled in the dream of all dreams: love.

[**WE WENT** the northern route because Aunt Matilda wanted to see San Francisco and stop in Reno. In Reno we stayed in a hotel with an indoor swimming pool, and after a short swim in her first bathing suit, hastily bought on the one street in town, Aunt Matilda put on her best church dress and went to play the slot machines— which with a pull of the arm could yield a lemon–lemon–lemon, a cherry–cherry–cherry, a bell–bell–bell, a clown–clown–clown, or a 7–7–7.

Then she played poker, five-card draw, in the midst of the clinging and the ringing and the tiresome glitz, and when I came down at eight-thirty in the morning to find her, she was winning. She won enough to finance the rest of our trip, so we could stay in the new motels cropping up all along the highway.

I could remember as a kid how there were only a few seedy motels in Seaside near Fort Ord for servicemen's families. But now, outside every city, there was at least one fine sprawling establishment where you could simply drive in, park, and get out near your room, and this was not a dilapidated Dew Drop Inn, with a lopsided sign swinging VACANCY but a spiffy motel with a shimmering turquoise swimming pool and wall-to-wall carpeted bedrooms, outfitted with your own TV.

We crossed the Sierras at Donner Pass, where the pioneers (not Mormon) starved to death. The story was, caught in a snow storm, they had to eat their shoes and belts and then each other, one of the few high points of grade-school California history. Aunt Matilda and I stopped in San Francisco, and she marveled at all the hills, the flowers, the palm trees in the middle of Dolores Street. We went on a cable car to Fisherman's Wharf, actually had dinner at the Cliff House while watching the sea lions on the rocks below, and in Macy's Aunt Matilda bought me a brown silk dress.

I am ashamed to say that I did not drop in on Lucille and the members of the household in the Zone (did I doubt Aunt Matilda?) but that after shopping and sightseeing we drove straight on down to Pacific Grove and stopped to see my mother and father—they were fine, I suppose, but I did not inquire too closely, curiosity killing the cat. My father, understandably distant, having "told me so" about Grey and everything else, mentioned something about my mother belonging to AA, which I knew about and had initially thought meant a car club; and Aunt Pearl, who had been promoted to buyer at JCPenney, could not stop talking about her customers, how she outfitted whole families, and what each woman bought—the girls' school clothes and the mothers' housedresses and the grandmothers' housecoats. The Baron had been replaced by a Vietnamese man who taught at the Army Language School, Monsieur Pierre Van Dong, who liked his Vodka neat, his pork skewered on little sticks, and who French-kissed—in bed.

Matilda, Nadja, and I did not take highway 1 to Santa Barbara, which would have passed through Big Sur, but highway 101, inland. Matilda took her hair down and we let the wind blow through the car. When we arrived in Santa Barbara, even though it was seven at night, the first thing I did was go to the beach.

I walked close to the shoreline, where the sand was damp and firm. My body in clear outline, the warm September wind wrapping around my elbows and knees like obliging scarves, my short hair sprung up from my head like new grass, I felt light-headed, clear-headed; and though I missed the beauty of the San Francisco streets—people spouting poetry and arguing in Italian, the pungent smell of strong espresso and sourdough bread—and the dear, funny company of my Great-aunt Martha and Great-aunt Mercy in Salt Lake, and the great drama of the Big Sur coastline, for the first time in ages I felt young. In fact, walking on the beach next to the sea—my real mother, my mother the sea—I felt almost immortal and certainly beyond harm. The coyotes I had imagined standing sentry along the road from Salt Lake were gone.

And yes, although I was remembering Grey, his smell, his skin from a lifetime of cigarettes, as often as I would remember some little thing about him, I could not bring up the exact image of the face which I had known more than my own. Of course, we had no photographs of each other, yet I certainly looked at him enough to remember him, and in the dark I used to trace his face with my finger—the sharp nose, tight twist of his thin mouth, and his arrow cheekbones.

The problem was, I think, that we had no long nights of love I could dwell on, no special tenderness, no endearing gifts, no funny quirks I could summon to my attention. Our lovemaking had been short and rather harsh, our intimacies generated by peyote and pot.

And as my feeling for him departed, I filled up with myself. No more You Tarzan, therefore me Jane. I was Zoe, simply myself, and in one piece, brain intact. Somehow that was enough; it was all. I don't know how it had happened. Maybe somewhere between Salt Lake City and Santa Barbara, when the windows were open and Aunt Matilda and I were drinking forbidden Coca-Colas, Grey was finally let go, dropped off in some small town where the gas station was the post office and the post office was the grocery store. Do you live here, I might have asked the attendant incredulously. Yes. And if the attendant was a woman, of all things, with long hair and a weathered face and wonderful clear eyes, I would know that all things were possible, and I most of all.

[**DURING THE DAY**, while Aunt Matilda watched Nadja, I worked in a nursery in Carpinteria, a small agricultural town nearby. I would drive over in the early morning light from Santa Barbara. Despite the dusty ride west, the Studebaker was still in mint condition and the velvety maroon upholstery smelled as new as cloth straight from the fabric store. Riding to work, on my right was the ocean, tame and swimmable, fronted by rows of skinny-bean palm trees; on my left, soft green mountains. The landscape, much less dramatic than Big Sur, was lovely, friendly.

In the Ocean Breeze Nursery, we grew azaleas and marigolds for retailers. Azaleas are little bushes with rose, pink, lavender, salmon, or white flowers. And the marigolds, of course, reminding me of Margo, are individual flowers, fuzzy orange and yellow, brown-rimmed. I worked in the shade house, which was just a bare skeleton with wooden slates for a roof, and the potting shed. We had one thousand azalea plants, the cuttings imported from the East, and who knows how many marigolds on the fifty acres. I wore big rubber boots, and my job was to plant and weed and water, to spray, to keep the smudge pots and wind machine going in case it got too cold, and to keep track of the hoes, rakes, hoses, pots, and shovels. It sounds simple, but the azaleas were delicate, and there always seemed to be some kind of crisis in the temperature, or the aphids would be on the attack, or somebody had quit, and the flowers always needed coaxing and special attention.

All around the nursery were orange and avocado groves and rows and rows of lettuce going in a straight line to the beach. I was deft and fast, said to have a green thumb, and the only Anglo besides the boss, the rest of the workers being Mexican. I was the *gringa*, the *gringuita*, and, finally, *guapa*, good-looking. I wore army-issue khaki shorts and a gray short-sleeved shirt and my hair, which was lengthening again, in a Christopher Columbus shower cap (just as Mother had worn *her* shower cap to work in the canneries), to keep the dirt off it. But after I started seeing Carlos, I wore a blue cotton scarf around my head instead of the cap.

In any event, I would emerge from work clothed in mud, my sweat holding a thick film of dirt on all the hairs of my arms and legs, which *were* hairy, for after working as an exotic dancer, standing in a pool of blood after shaving, I had sworn off razors. I suppose I was quite a sight, but I felt strong, as if I were a sabra on a kibbutz with the ghost of Aaron, who was actually against Zionism, hovering over my shoulder. I am making the desert bloom, I could have said.

Meanwhile, Aunt Matilda, in beach sandals, took Nadja on strolls in her new stroller with a fringe on top. They went to the wharf, the art museum, the park, around the courthouse, and down the main street of Santa Barbara. They stopped for coffee and orange juice. In the afternoon, they took naps together.

We started at seven in the morning in a pastel and very gentle sky. For an hour or so it would be cool and pleasant. In early fall, by eleven the nursery buildings with the marigolds heated up like blazes despite the fans. The few times it rained, it steamed afterward for an hour.

For lunch, I ate peanut-butter-and-jelly sandwiches with my fellow workers, crouched outside against the wall of the nursery office if it was not raining. Their lunches were wrapped in large, soft tortillas, and after they gulped down their *jugo*, they would stretch out on the hot earth, nap into a deep slumber for about fifteen minutes before the whistle blew. I read. I was reading an author Margo had recommended, Zora Neale Hurston.

In the greenhouses, the men sang all day. They sang sad Mexican songs about love and loss.

Tu eres lo que deseo—You are my heart's desire / *Mi único amor*—My very own love / *Por favor, no te vayas*—Please don't go from me / *Te amo más que a la vida misma*—I love you more than life / *O mi niña linda*—Oh, my beautiful girl / *Mujer de mis sueños*—Woman of my dreams / Come close, come closer—*Acércate, acércate un poquito más.*

At three, when the whistle blew, we would all rush out like freed schoolchildren under the orange and lemon trees, between the lettuce rows, running to the beach. I still had my black one-piece bathing suit from high school, a Jantzen, like the ones Esther Williams wore in her movies with the synchronized water ballets. It felt like a piece of armor, and I was very conscious of the little pubis part and fearful something might peek below the stiff panel over it. I had to keep pulling my bathing suit down in the front. And sometimes a little flap of ass would slip below the back and I would have to stretch the back down. Then the damned front would creep up again.

People who had known me in San Francisco would have been amazed at my recently acquired modesty. But this was different. *I* was different. I was no longer onstage in a mask. When I went into the water with my multipurpose yellow thinking cap, Carlos would lift me way out of the ocean and throw me back in. Oopa, oopa. Carlos would be careful to hold me by the waist, but still sometimes his hand slipped down to my hips or up to my breasts. Just an accident.

Our cousin Charlie, whom Matilda, Nadja, and I were staying with in Santa Barbara, was really a third or fourth cousin, yet peripheral as he was to the whole Utah clan, he had kindly agreed to let us live with him and his wife. He was a jack Mormon, he explained, that is, he had left the church, not through a grand gesture of excommunication or anything like that. No, he just slid away from the path. He described it as a little venture here, a little venture there, and anyway, he "just couldn't buy the whole Mormon thing," that is, "that Joseph Smith in 1825 or so had found plates in New York state, the Urim and Thummim, which were the records of the people of Nephi and Lamanites and Jared, which became, when translated (and from what language, I ask you), *The Book of Mormon*. And that Christ had come again, resurrected was it in A.D. 34 or A.D. 64, to the Americas? Who were they? Incas, Aztecs, Mayas? What's the deal, you tell me?"

Cousin Charlie, Charles McIntosh, called himself Mr. Sinaman.

"Hey, Mr. Sinaman, where you going Mr. Sinaman?" he would sing, dancing soft-shoe. He prided himself on his house, which was supposed to be a tabernacle of hedonism.

True enough, it was full of mirrors and fake fur, if that constituted hedonistic decor. Like Margo's glass house, there was hardly any privacy; everything was spaciously, modernly open. Most of the furniture was low and upholstered in some kind of sexy synthetic cloth that seemed **347** to sizzle and simper when you sat on it. The towels in the bathroom were like velvet, and the bathtub was deep, not long. You had to stand up in it or sit on the little cement ledges on the sides. Aunt Matilda said she felt pickled when she took a bath, pickled and canned. Cousin Charlie, who had read about Japan, said it was like what they had in Japan, and soon it would catch on all over America. He was very interested in fads, and considered himself in the vanguard.

The other furniture, in the kitchen and bedrooms, was spindly and skittish, on thin legs. I feared the whole breakfast nook might just tiptoe off one day, if not melt in the heat, for all the materials were plastic. Cousin Charlie had a lot of nudes on the wall, nudes with long hair, waiflike expressions, and sad puppy-dog eyes. I had a hard time believing that anybody so well endowed by their creator could be that sad. Anyway, Cousin Charlie had not hired a decorator but had personally done the whole place, with a little help from Lois, his wife, who in her next life, she confided, *wanted* to be an interior decorator.

"Our modular environment expresses us," Charlie explained to Aunt Matilda. On the outside, Cousin Charlie's house was traditionally Spanish, white stucco with the red tile roof. Thick blocks of glass formed the windows that let the light in, but you couldn't see out of them. There were five extra bedrooms in the designated sleeping area, solitary-confinement cubicles with one small, high window per room, which, of course, you could not see out of, so that the outside world was mere speculation. Sometimes I imagined people whispering along our cell block. Pass the word: Life exists on the outside.

Charlie's lapse from Mormonism had occurred when he left Salt Lake City and entered the "real world," which was "tooth and nail," and now he was "in" advertising for the aerospace industry near L.A. Thank God for the Cold War, he often said. "Uncle Sam wants you," he would declare, grabbing *me* in not so cousinly a fashion. "Where there's a will, there's a way," he would continue, sounding like my father. Luckily, they had a maid, and actually there was no woodwork. And besides, everything was automatic. They even had an upright freezer. All the appliances hummed in the dark, aerodynamically. They kept the cocktail glasses in the refrigerator of their full bar, which had black imitation leather stools and a paneled, mirrored wall.

I was impressed.

"Tea and coffee and tobacco we despise," my cousin would sing from Sunday school. "Drink no liquor and we eat but very little meat. Hark, hark, the children sing."

Charlie and Lois, like Lois Lane, were very much in love. That was what Lois told Aunt Matilda and me, confidentially. She had been a stewardess and was, of course, beautiful. During the day she went out to lunch, window-shopped, and had her hair done.

"At fourteen," Cousin Charlie liked to recite nightly, "I was a deacon. At sixteen a teacher, at eighteen a priest, and at nineteen an elder, my mission confirmed, and ready I was in the name of the Father, the Son, and the Holy Ghost to cast out devils. Devils I say unto you."

"I don't think that's very funny," Aunt Matilda would say tartly, although, in all honesty, she had lapsed in many ways, too. It seemed contagious.

One night a week—Sunday—Charlie and Lois ate in. The rest of the time they went out to dinner—Monday, Mexican; Tuesday, Chinese; Wednesday, German; Thursday, French; Friday, fish; and Saturday, a hamburger place. It was a very European habit, Lois explained to me —eating out, having your own special table, being on good terms with the maître d'. Sundays, dubbed Family Home Night, Lois and Charlie raided the refrigerator, which was well stocked with bologna, already packaged in slices, and bright American cheese, also sliced and wrapped in cellophane. They shopped at a huge grocery store called Safeway, dropping packages of food into a little wire cart they pushed up and down the aisles. Their freezer featured steaks and contained any number of already packaged meats and frozen vegetables. They were very happy and very full, and, of course, very much in love.

Aunt Matilda, Nadja, and I always ate in, but we were very happy, too. Why not? The sun, the stars, the sand, meat loaf and tuna salad. Carlos winked at me at work. I was learning Spanish. And when I would return from my walks, I read as I had in high school, hand over fist, avidly, uncritically, fast. I started to smoke cigarettes elegantly like Lauren Bacall, inhaling like the Philip Morris man advised us to do, and parroted a sentence Jim Thompson used in his cold-blooded tale *The Killer Inside Me*.

"Dirty habit," he said, in just a quiet conversation voice. "Got it young, though, and I reckon I'll keep it."

At our Mormon cocktail hour I'd drink a Coke, and Matilda would have a sarsaparilla, which she got God knows where, and sometimes right before I fell asleep, 'round midnight, I listened to late-night jazz on the radio real soft. The Duke. Art Tatum. Miles Davis, George Shearing, and our own cool California jazz: Dave Brubeck, Gerry Mulligan, and Chet Baker. A couple of times Carlos took me to the Spanish movie house. I liked being surrounded by a language I did not understand, while beautiful black-eyed señoritas gesticulated and wept, and men with hair like Valentino flung cigarettes to the floor, stamped their feet click-click-click, and left a room slamming the door nearly off its hinges.

Me traisionas.

You are betraying me.

No, nunca.

No, never.

Yo lo se.

I can tell.

No, nunca.

No, never.

Tu olor es mentiras.

You smell of lies.

No, nunca.

No, never.

Tienes un corazon negro.

Your heart is black.

Aunt Matilda ate everything now, and she told me that in her walks she had met a retired man who took her to lunch at McDonald's, a new kind of place where they had hamburgers with french fries and Cokes, "just like teenagers."

"I even feel like a teenager," Aunt Matilda said. Except that when she *was* a teenager, they didn't have such things to eat. For her lunch dates, she bought a new wardrobe, all California clothes: dresses with tropical patterns and bright colors, Bermuda shorts that showed her knobby knees. She still had to wear her hair in a kind of Victorian bundle over her bald front, but she wore it looser, and every day she took Nadja to the flower shop to buy a single flower. It was a kind of thing with them.

Although they didn't need the money, I gave Charlie and Lois one week's pay every month, and Aunt Matilda another week's. Out of the rest, I bought a red gathered skirt and a big white ruffled blouse, for sometimes on payday all of us from work would go dancing at a little cantina outside town. Carlos was usually my partner. He was beginning to kiss me. His lips were salty and large, and he had a little pointy tongue. He was short and thick, and it was nice for me to take him in *my* arms and have him rest his head on my shoulder. There, there, Carlos. There, there.

There seemed to be more stars in the sky of southern California than in northern California or Utah. The Sioux, according to Grey, called the Big Dipper the Big Bear, the North Star the Fixed Star, and the Milky Way the Great White River in the Sky. The story was that if you tried to count the stars, you were doomed, for death was certain before the counting was finished.

I didn't count the stars. I just looked at them. They were cold and remote, unattainable, almost abstractions. The oil drills along some of the shoreline, however, could be counted, and they looked like sex to me. Boy-dream Erector sets, perpetual penetration. And the ocean at night, black and opaque, resembled a thick layer of oil. I claimed her as my real mother because my other mother was as unreachable as the stars. The air, thick and sticky on my night walks, was also oil, everything oil. In several millennia, I would be oil. But it didn't seem terrible. I could imagine my body floating along in an underground river of black, circling the inside of the globe like blood in the body. When I die, I thought, bury my heart not at Wounded Knee but in California, on the beach, in the sand, and let my body get lapped, coated with black, let me brush against roots and rocks as I course through the veins of the earth.

I was nineteen and living in southern California the fall of '58. My uncle's television was kept on all the time, and so I began to see what was going on in the world. Through the Huntley-Brinkley Report, I learned that Castro had come down from the hills, that de Gaulle was proclaimed President of the Fifth Republic in France, that Khrushchev was the Russian premier, that Vice President Nixon was not well received on his goodwill tour of South America, and that tension was growing between desegregationists and the Old South, and I was hearing and seeing more and more of that minister, Martin Luther King, Jr. I realized

I had missed, in my family and in Big Sur, a decade of "news." During the Stevenson-Eisenhower presidential campaign, when Nixon was accused of accepting money from a special fund, I hadn't heard Nixon's Checkers speech, when he said that his wife had "a perfectly respectable Republican cloth coat" and that regardless of what happened, his family was going to keep their dog, Checkers. I had never watched NBC news with John Chancellor, who was intensely moved when the 101st Airborne arrived in Little Rock to protect the Constitutional rights of the Little Rock Nine to go to school. I did not know about the Russian satellite *Sputnik*, meaning fellow traveler.

When I had been an exotic dancer, my father had said something about "the rest of your life." Is this how you want to spend the rest of your life? Lucille, too, had alluded to my life as if it were something to be planned. At those times, "the rest of my life" seemed a long time and something far away, and my sense of possibilities was blunted and limited. But now, perhaps being able to swim daily in the ocean and not feeling powerless in the midst of nature, and being able to make a living at something not absolutely awful (they had not asked me if I had an arrest record), I was thinking of the rest of my life as if it was something I could control. Grey, my refuge, my solution, had proved unsafe. We were soon to be divorced, and the land, which I had not claimed in any kind of settlement, Grey was welcome to cultivate or sell.

Aunt Matilda said, "When Nadja can go to the child-care center, I can watch her at night and you can go to night school. Harry Truman went to night school, you know."

"Does that mean I have a chance at the Presidency?"

Cousin Charlie said, "If I were you, Zoe, I would go into fashion, or maybe cardboard boxes. Packaging is the wave of the future."

Typing, night school, cardboard? The world stretched out before me.

Cocktail hour.

We were all standing around. Nadja with her bottle filled with orange juice, Matilda with her sarsaparilla, I with my Coca-Cola with a maraschino cherry in it. Charlie's wife, Lois, was on tippy-toe, in very high heels. Charlie, a sharp dresser, too, almost zoot-suity, was on his second martini. About forty-five, he sported a deep tan and a ducktail hairdo, liked to rumba and do the tango. Lois was getting a little thick around the middle, and her girdle bubbled at the top, so she had a little extra roll of fat, but no matter, her bullet bra made her appear ready to launch, aerodynamically. She was actually nice in a hard-boiled Rosalind Russell sort of way, but Charlie, Charlie had taken a shine to me and could be moody and pouty and rather difficult.

Once, when he took me for a ride in their car, a 1958 Chevrolet Corvette, black with a patch of white in an oblong around the front wheels, he put his hand on my knee. I took it off, and he looked at me in such a way that I could tell Nadja and I would have to move despite the convenience of it all.

My friend Carlos drove a 1950 Mercury coupe, canary yellow, with a track of little red pom-poms all around the windows and a tiny soccer ball in a net hanging from his mirror. His car was like a little house, and we made out in the backseat like high school kids. It surprised me that he liked me. I was so tall and pale, my hair now a mass of red curls bobbing on top of my head, my black plastic cat-woman glasses making me look very alert. But when he touched me in his expert way, I was aware that nobody had ever done that, just touched me, my chin, my eyebrows—*cejas*—which he declared his favorite part of me. He was actually courting me. And as he touched my eyes, gently removing my glasses, I stopped blinking, and as he fondled my ears, I could hear beautiful words. *Dulce. Agua. Mango. Verde. Verde.* It reminded me of an account I had read about an autistic child whose first word at seven years old was *dandelion*. Dandelion. Is there no word more beautiful?

[**I WAS IN** the kitchen. Aunt Matilda and I usually cooked the old Utah recipes and things I had learned from Lucille in the Zone. Aunt Matilda was unusually late. I was making a quick chili of browned hamburger, a can of kidney beans, a can of tomatoes, and chili powder. Charlie came up behind me, put his hands on my ass spread-eagle, like two cockleshells.

"Don't," I said.

"You smell good."

I smelled like the ocean.

"I like you, you know."

"I like you, too, Charlie—you and Lois. You are family to us."

And we were living at his house, I reminded myself.

"You know what I mean."

"Charlie, I think we might have to move out."

"Is that so?"

I nodded.

"Well, you can forget Santa Barbara on your salary."

"Aunt Matilda has a little money."

"Matilda is getting married."

"What?"

"She didn't tell you?"

"Who to? To whom?"

"Mr. Smorgasbord."

I blinked very fast.

"The man who took her for a hamburger?"

"A hamburger, breaded shrimp, a steak, spaghetti and meatballs.

The guy is serious."

In fact, where were Aunt Matilda and Nadja right now? It was six and they were out. Out eating? Then I heard the door, the stroller rolling in.

"Nadja," I said, running out of the kitchen area to the hallway area.

"Little late," Aunt Matilda giggled like a teenager.

"Are you getting married?" I didn't believe it for a second. Charlie could be such a card.

"Let's go into my bedroom, Zoe, and discuss this after dinner."

"Charlie said you are getting married."

"We'll talk about it."

"Just tell me."

"Yes, I am."

"Who is going to marry you?" I don't know why I said that.

"A very nice man," she said peevishly, "if you must know this instant."

She took Nadja out of the stroller. Nadja crawled over to me. She could stand up and move about holding on to things. I still nursed her in the morning and evening, sometimes during the night. The other times she took a bottle, and I had started her at three months on solid food.

Charlie scrutinized us with his hands on his hips. I was wearing my red-and-white-polka-dotted pedal pushers, a sleeveless white blouse. I fastened my hair back with white plastic barrettes in the shape of Scotty dogs. As my father would say, What was the world coming to, for here I was wearing pedal pushers and Matilda was getting married. What next?

"But you're . . ." I protested.

"Old?"

"No, I don't mean that." I did mean it.

"Mama," Nadja said.

"Yes, Mama still loves Nadja."

"What are you saying? Nana *still* loves Nadja, too."

"But *you're* getting married."

"And so?"

Nadja was sucking a lollipop, and looking quite dirty but very proud of herself. Was she in on this, too? This defection from the ranks?

"Married, Aunt Matilda, married?" That wasn't part of the plan.

Charlie winked at me. I began to blink like a berserk railroad crossing sign.

"Soon as you let them out of Salt Lake City," Charlie began.

"Don't try to close your eyes to the world, Zoe McLaren. And if I want to get married, I will."

"But you've never been married, Aunt Matilda."

"All the more reason."

"What about Aunt Martha and Aunt Mercy?"

"What about them? They are invited to the wedding. If they want to get married, stopping them I'm not."

Lois strolled in. Her dress was tight as a leopard skin and the same pattern, too. I expected to hear her snarl. *Her* needs were obvious enough. Charlie grabbed her around the waist, spun her around. He was the animal trainer in the crowd. Aunt Matilda was the romantic, and I guessed I was the spoilsport.

"Grrr," Cousin Charlie said to his leopardess.

Nadja held up her hands for patty-cake.

"Not right now, honey," I said.

"Do I hear wedding bells?" Lois asked sweetly.

"You do, indeed." Aunt Matilda folded her arms.

In all fairness, let me say that Aunt Matilda had amazing blue eyes, and her long white hair, although starting back a bit on her forehead, had potential. She let me brush it each night and I would tell her, as she sat before the mirror, that she looked like a queen. Apparently she had taken me seriously, for what was a bride but a Queen for a Day, as Aunt Matilda's favorite new TV program was called? Nadja liked watching *Captain Kangaroo*, and Lois fancied *This Is Your Life*. Charlie enjoyed *What's My Line?* Except for watching the news, the fifteen minutes daily on NBC, I was the only one in the house who wasn't periodically glued to the lighted screen.

"This is the man who takes you out to lunch?" How much spaghetti can you eat, I was thinking.

"Yes."

"Because he takes you to lunch?"

"There are other things."

"Other things?"

Cousin Charlie winked.

There she was, my great-aunt, in pale blue Bermuda shorts and matching checked blouse. Her hair was in a bun, but professionally done, with little tendrils of hair dripping down, and the flower of the day was a bright red hibiscus. The pistil and stamen of that flower were not discreetly shielded as were regular northern California flowers, but the yellow sticky wand with a tight fuzzy ball at the end stuck out shamelessly from the soft loopy petals like the engorged sexual organ it was. This was definitely the southern California mode. My great-aunt Matilda looked like a Caribbean Ophelia who perhaps did get to the nunnery, but some years later jumped over the wall (which, I had to admit, I had loved to read about as a kid) and was *persona grata* in the Santa Barbara bachelor crowd. Furthermore, I noticed that she had changed her staid blue plastic-rimmed glasses for harlequin glasses, new ones with embedded diamonds.

"Are those real diamonds in your glasses?" I asked.

"Of course not, Zoe."

I pictured her fiancé, a slight California widower in khakis and ribboned belt, polo shirt, canvas hat and shoes, a man on the dried-out side, somebody hanging on by a thread, cooking on a hot plate.

"I can still take care of Nadja," she said. "I think you feel jealous of me because you are getting a divorce. But we won't be living far. You can bring her on the way to work. We would love to have her. Benjamin and I have talked about it. I am not deserting you."

"Benjamin." That was his name.

"Benjamin Feldstein."

"You are marrying a Jew?" I knew it. I just knew it.

"The Mormons are also a lost tribe, Zoe; we are both desert peoples. We have a deep and abiding affinity with each other, and a mutual distrust of Gentiles." Actually we Mormons, interestingly, did call other Christians Gentiles. But, then, what were Jews? I wondered if I had paid attention at all in Sunday school. It was really all very confusing. And I could see how Mormons would have an affinity with Jews. *The*

Book of Mormon, except for the presence of the resurrected and earth-visiting Jesus, was, certainly in language and content, much like the Old Testament.

"But you can't be married for time and all eternity in the Temple, **357** Aunt Matilda, or get magic underwear, as my parents did."

"Ah shucks," Cousin Charlie said.

"I can't believe you are saying these things, Zoe. I thought you believed in freedom, in love, in life." Aunt Matilda looked at me, sadly shook her head. "I'll take twenty good years," she said. "To tell you the truth, I've never been that up on the finer points of our faith."

"But the angel Moroni." Suddenly *I* was the fundamentalist.

"Thank the Lord that Moroni is the last chapter in *The Book of Mormon*. Do you remember what he said: Infant baptism is an evil abomination. 'Behold I say unto you, that he that supposeth little children need baptism is the gall of bitterness and in the bonds of iniquity.' Pretty strong language, I must say, not gentle at all."

"Aunt Matilda, I thought the angel Moroni was . . . I mean, remember how you followed his word and ate only oatmeal?"

"I must have been out of my mind. Oatmeal? When you can have onion rings and cheeseburgers?"

"Your Aunt Matilda has a good point," Cousin Charlie said.

Lois shook her head.

I blinked. Clearly, I was jealous.

Nadja, crawling around, was not taking sides.

"I know this is quite sudden, my dear, but the marriage of true minds admitting impediments is of utmost importance to me, as is sex. I believe in mind, not just brain. Besides, we have decided not to have children, but that doesn't mean we don't want you to come swimming in our swimming pool or leave Nadja during the weekdays, and we're going to have a barbecue every Friday."

I put my head in my hands. Nadja extended her arms to be picked up. She had lollipop goo all over her face (a lollipop before dinner?), and her hair, Nadja's straight black hair, was fastened in a barrette so that it stood up straight on the top of her little head like a water fountain. She had Lucille's hairdo, and Aunt Matilda had never met Lucille. But Nadja also had on blue shorts and a blue checkered shirt, and her toenails were polished pink just like Aunt Matilda's.

"I'm not sure nail polish is good for babies," I said, remembering the poor turtles in the turtle tank in the dime store.

They were twinsies, in a mother-daughter outfit—she and Matilda, a zany toothsome twosome out on the town—and who knows what Nadja had witnessed on their daily jaunts?

"Does Nana want her dinner," Aunt Matilda crooned, picking her up off my lap and rubbing her face like a purring cat all over Nadja's dirty face.

"Yaya."

Could Nadja possibly think that Aunt Matilda was her mother?

"Jesus Christ," I groaned, putting my face in my hand.

"I don't see how He enters into this. We are going to have an interdenominational wedding, a rabbi *and* a Unitarian minister. The emphasis is going to be on the spirit as it is embodied in all religions."

"I suppose," Cousin Charlie said, rolling his eyes, "that you are going to wear Hawaiian leis, too."

"That's not a bad idea, Charles."

Nadja gurgled and ran her hands flat over her great-great-aunt's face. What did she care that it was wrinkled. What did she care that her nana was basically bald? Aunt Matilda often pushed the stroller as if it were a ride in a carnival, twirling it and speeding it up, and even making it dance as Margo's mother had danced in the wheelchair. The two of them doted on each other.

"Nana."

"Nana's precious Nadja."

"When *is* the wedding?" In a way, I thought it was a rhetorical question. Wedding? There was going to be a wedding? Not really. Not for real.

"Next week. Small, at Benjamin's house—carrot cake, champagne, nothing fancy, mind you."

"Am I invited?"

"But of course you are."

"Charlie and Lois?"

"Best people, and you can be an honored matron of honor, and, oh yes, you invite Carlos, the more the merrier. Just a few close family friends."

"What does Benjamin do?"

I knew I was sounding like Margo when she asked me what Grey "did," but it popped out. I expected to hear: retired contractor of a cement business, retired general manager of a dogfood supply store.

"He writes music for movies."

"Movies?"

"He does scores."

"Better than cardboard, in terms of the wave of the future," Cousin Charlie conceded.

"He's rich," Lois giggled. "He has that big house, you know, on the hill in back of us." She pointed east.

"He is?"

"You bet," Aunt Matilda said. "Do I know how to pick them or do I know how to pick them?"

"I guess you do."

"See you girls later," Charlie said, sashaying by. It was Mexican night. He had a smirk on his face, like: I told you.

"There is a letter for you upstairs," Aunt Matilda said. "Two letters actually."

"From whom?"

"I don't know, dear, but I'll feed Nadja. We can have a nice salad. I had a rather big lunch today."

"I was making chili."

"Chili and salad, wonderful."

She put Nadja in her high chair.

"Nana needs a little face wash," Aunt Matilda cooed, picking up the dishrag.

Nana? Nadja was Nana? Wasn't Great-Great-Aunt Matilda the nana? Oh well. At least I was still Mama. I had to find the washcloth. I went upstairs. It wasn't up the stairs but, rather up a couple of stairs into the bedroom area of the house. I'll have to move, I said to myself, looking at Nadja's mobile over her crib, a bunch of plastic airplanes, and my bedspread, which resembled my Tibetan peyote visions, big elephants on the march. Now I'll definitely have to move.

The letters were on my desk underneath the little goosenecked lamp, and they seemed to vibrate with their own pernicious energy. Both letters were forwarded. One from Pacific Grove to Salt Lake to Santa Barbara, and the other from Big Sur. I recognized both handwritings and, of course, the green ink.

October 6, 1958

Dear Zoe,

360

> *My life is at a crisis point, supposedly that word in Greek,* krisis, *means opportunity for change.*
>
> *I am very sorry I could not respond to your emergency. In medias ras, you know, or is it res. Did you ever get your husband in a hospital? Or is he better? Those things tend to happen and then iron out. Your baby, how is the baby?*
>
> *Love, Margo*

Things tend to happen? And then iron out? This was from Miss Change-the-World?

The other letter was from Grey. It said:

Coyote returns.

Coyote returns?

I started to blink. My hands began to shake, and I started looking toward the window, but, of course, in the bedrooms the windows were too high. Yet I made believe it was snowing outside and a skim of white, like milk on hot chocolate, coated the sky. But it was not snowing, and the sky was a hot rubber sheet.

[**THE WEDDING** was not small and not modest. It was huge and lavish, with a green-and-white-striped tent, caterers, a string quartet, flowers all over the place, champagne in tiny thin glasses, and a whole bunch of people in tuxedos and cocktail dresses; and it was there, poolside, that I met the director of Thoreau College, David.

The Thoreau "campus," David described, was just a big ramshackle house, in the Santa Barbara hills, in which all the students lived and went to school. They shared all household duties, and there was an elaborate sexual arrangement. He cleared his throat at this.

"Yes?" I asked sweetly, wondering why Thoreau was such a hero in California.

"I'm not so keen on going into the woods," I said, remembering Grey.

"Oh, we aren't either. Our Thoreau is the one who was socially involved."

Of the twenty "students," some chose to be in the heterosexual best-friend unit, others in the homosexual best-friend unit. You could only sleep within your best-friend unit, and you had to share each other equally. Jealousy was the tragedy of the Judeo-Christian West, emanating from the concept of a jealous God.

"Oh really?"

"I kid you not," David said.

"Cool," I answered, looking around to spot Nadja with Lois.

It was the kind of collective that emphasized free choice, he continued. For instance, they could choose what they wanted to study, a kind of Great Books approach.

David was actually Aunt Matilda's new husband's son. It couldn't be simpler. David had recently returned from Harvard, and yet he had a heart, he said. He had not lost his simple California idealism. He was all of twenty-three.

Harvard, so soon out of his mouth, could have been Parnassus as far as I was concerned. It was that remote from my dirty California life in the azalea shed.

"I graduated from Monterey Union High School. And as far as my heart goes, well, it's not that I've lost it. It's tired."

He raised his eyebrows.

I shrugged my shoulders.

"Easy come, easy go," I said, thinking of dear old Dad.

For his father's wedding, this arrogant young man wore a lavender silk shirt, a yellow tie, and the most beautiful suit I have ever seen. It was raw silk, a creamy, nubby cloth which I coveted. Perhaps he had misinterpreted my intentions. I did want to disrobe him, but it was not for his body.

"So you graduated from Monterey High, and I hear you are Matilda's great-niece." The man was smooth as a salamander.

"Yes." I was in one of my two dresses. The green wool, not suitable for the occasion or the locale, was in the closet. I had on the brown silk Matilda had bought me at Macy's in San Francisco. It draped about my body loosely, the silk making me look shapely. No doubt, David's and my attraction was a meeting of clothes.

"Matilda tells us you were a good student in high school."

"That was a long time ago." Really only about two years ago, but I remembered Aaron saying that prodigies grow up. I knew I was beyond recall in some ways.

He smiled, swirling the champagne in his glass.

I wondered if this was flirting.

"You are a very beautiful woman," he said.

"Really?" So he *was* flirting.

"You *are* beautiful."

"Thank you, David." Without my glasses and with a little wine,

I was perceiving everything in a kind of happy blur, although I had to
make sure I did not get too close to the edge of the pool. I looked over
at Nadja and Lois. Soon I would have to take over.

"Would you like to fuck?" he asked.

"I beg your pardon."

Aunt Matilda was flitting about, checking on everybody's good
time. She was in a wonderful straw hat, with real flowers about the
brim and multicolored shiny silk ribbons hanging down her back. Her
dress, expensive I could tell, was a sky-blue gauzy thing. She was wearing
not her granny shoes but high-heeled sandals, mere wisps of shoes. The
Mormon women in our family, despite the long trek west, had great
legs. My mother's were thick, but mine, like Aunt Matilda's, were
shapely. Aunt Mercy and Aunt Martha, of course, *were* in their granny
shoes—looking terribly dowdy next to their sister—and appeared in a
state of shock.

"Would you like to fuck, I said," he repeated.

"No, thank you." I blinked just once, I think. I was getting better.

"You might like to visit our school. It's unique in that we practice
what we preach." He hadn't missed a beat. "We are a real university
—a community of scholars. We live together in peace and harmony."

"Well, a regular university . . ."

"Regular?"

"I mean a real . . ."

"Real?"

"Dormitories, that sort of thing."

"You find that if you shit beside somebody, you can have very
few pretensions," David countered.

"I don't know about that." Did he mean coed bathrooms without
doors? Holes in the ground like the Essenes had dug, according to Grey,
which meant that Christ himself . . .

"We share everything," David persisted. "Our meals. We buy our
food at a co-op, take turns cooking, and we discuss our problems out
in the open, and have a system of sexual pairing which is just and
equitable. We have the heterosexual unit and the homosexual unit, and
within your unit you have free access to each person."

"You told me about that, but what if you like somebody outside
your unit?"

"Then the unit has to agree on the inclusion of that party."

"Hmm."

David was awfully chummy. Meanwhile, my cousin Charlie was giving me the old eye from across the pool, and Carlos, my real partner, who had come as my guest, was being taken for a busboy. Lois was managing Nadja, but I worried about them getting too close to the pool, and Grey, soon to be an ex, was dogging my tracks in true coyote fashion. Great, I thought, just great, everything was great.

"A quickie in the bathroom," David said. "I have a small dick and I come fast. In and out, you will hardly know what happened."

"For your information, that's my boyfriend," I said, nodding over Mexico way.

"The spic?"

"*Si.*"

Carlos waved at me. I smiled back.

"Would you like to meet him hombre to hombre, David?"

"That's all right." He smiled nervously.

"I thought so. When you bullshit next to somebody, you can have very few pretensions."

"Hah, hah."

"But what about the money part of your school?" I asked. I noticed that people in southern California seemed to leave that aspect of existence out. Of course, there it *did* grow on trees.

"Oh, we all have jobs, outside jobs, except of course the teachers-administrators unit, and we pool our money, whatever it might be."

"The teachers-administrators, do they pool their money?"

I was thinking of the swimming pool overflowing with dollars.

"Of course not."

"A true republic," I said.

"What do you mean?"

"As in Plato. Oligarchy."

"*You* read Plato?"

"I'll overlook that, David. Are there any people with children in your utopia?"

"No, not as yet, but we, of course, welcome children in our

midst. Are you familiar with the work of Kahlil Gibran? He says children . . ."

I thought Gibran very lowbrow, very sentimental, but then, again . . . it was southern California.

"And do people get their own room?"

"Yes, they do."

I knew I had to move out of Charlie's and, like, soon. Sometimes we would meet accidentally in the hallway and he would ask for a big hug. It sounded friendly enough, and it seemed silly to make an issue of it, but when he pressed me to him, his penis pressed against me like a big banana. Then if Grey arrived . . . But Thoreau College might be an out, the cheapest out, the easiest out, unless the sexual unit thing got out of hand, then I'd be out of luck and out on the street. O-U-T, out.

Meantime, people at the wedding were clinking their glasses with spoons. The happy couple had to keep kissing. Later on, Aunt Matilda said her mouth was tired at the end of that day. By then, the guests had gone home and I was taking Nadja for a little swim in the pool. I held her up, bounced her up and down. She was giggling. She loved water, but one of my nightmares was that she was drowning in muddy water and I couldn't reach her, couldn't find her. But that seemed so unlikely. Murky water.

"You should go to David's school," Benjamin said, rolling his cigar around in his fingers. "People your age. Have you ever been with people your age?"

"In high school."

"I mean socially. Since?"

"Carlos." Actually Carlos was twenty-three. I thought of Aaron, Aunt Pearl, my mother and father, Grey and Kelly, Lucille, the Mormon great-aunts—they were all older.

"I thought we forfeit youth when we get married, Benjamin."

"Look at Matilda and me." Benjamin gave my great-aunt a tickle.

"Remember," Matilda said, leaning forward, "when I was in that room in the yellow house with the maps on the wall? Now Ben and I are going to Hawaii, can you imagine that, and, after that, Australia. I have always wanted to travel, see the world."

I was thinking of the rent and Cousin Charlie's continued atten-

365

tions. All I would have to pay at Thoreau College was some portion of what I earned, and Nadja and I would have a safe place to live. Not only that, but we would get food and I, night school. David had said he would be my tutor. It was modeled on the English system at Oxford. One big exam at the end.

Jolly good, I thought.

[**AT THOREAU,** breakfast time was when we all told our dreams. People dreamed of boats sinking, people flying, trees growing in steamy forests, their first-grade teachers, Johnny Appleseed, and sex, of course, always sex, and not just within the regulated best-friend unit but with comic-book heroes and animals and strangers on the street and basketball players and the girls at the co-op, and the boys who worked in the bookstore. Luscious guys.

I could never remember my dreams. There didn't seem to be any room for them. The others' dreams filled up all the space; the house was like a hive bulging with dreams, the walls collaged with scenes of cocktail parties and first-birthday parties, and montages of ranting parents and space monsters. There was so much going on dreamwise that I slept with the sheet over my head, hoping not to be called up for jury duty or anything.

Yes, life at Thoreau College was certainly not like working at Clothing Classics, the garment factory, or dancing at the Eagle's Nest, or working with Edith and Clair at Woolworth's, or living with the great-aunts or Lucille. For one, everything took longer. All decisions were democratic, so the slightest move was a massive undertaking. Should we buy carrots? Are pancakes for breakfast too bourgeois? Who gets to use the Thoreau College vehicles when? What about pets? Our ten cats, three dogs, one hamster, and three parakeets were eating up a good part of the food budget and were the only nonvegetarians in the household. But animals had rights, too. Which included sleeping on the dining room table? Ten were in favor, eight opposed. People, that is. Ten cats slept on the dining room table, for it was the sunniest spot in the house. And we spread a menstrual-blood-spotted mattress pad over the velvet couch inherited by David from his mother, so the dogs wouldn't mess it up. We did need a new roof—that was agreed upon the few times it rained.

Another thing: people tended to take their studies not only seriously but audibly. People liked to quote at length and in loud voices.

For instance, those of us who had been deprived of television as kids and accused of being eggheads in high school would be sitting in the living room watching *Father Knows Best* or *The Adventures of Ozzie and Harriet* or *Leave It to Beaver*, and the Nietzsche person would parade before us, tromping mud from the communal garden all over David's real Oriental rug that he bought in Iran when he was an exchange student, and declaiming:

What is great in man is that he is a bridge and not an end: what can be loved in man is that he is an overture and a going under.

I forgive you what you did to me; but that you have done it to yourself—*how can I forgive that?*

Thus spake Freddy-spaghetti, our Nietzsche scholar.

The Plato person was a small, woebegone girl, a mere waif, who, I had heard, had a ferocious sex drive. The metaphor of the cave was her specialty, and she always looked like she had just come *from* a cave, with her rumpled hair and sleepy eyes.

"Shadows, shadows, all is shadow."

The woman who was studying Emma Goldman was in the homosexual unit, but she looked just like a regular woman to me. She had long hair and was pretty and pert: "The greatest shortcoming of the emancipation of the present day lies in its artificial stiffness and its narrow respectabilities, which produce an emptiness in woman's soul that will not let her drink from the fountain of life . . . The demand for equal rights in every vocation of life is just and fair; but, after all, the most vital right is the right to love and be loved."

"David," the Plato person would say, "if all we see are shadows, are we not shadows also? Do you think the most vital right is the right to love? Do the male and female homosexuals in the homo unit fuck each other?"

"Stop, Zarathustra. Wait. It is I, O Zarathustra, I, your shadow." Freddy was always underfoot. People kidded that he had a venereal disease and would soon, very soon—"Stop, wait—"—be as mad as his hero and have to be confined to his room.

Actually, we had other candidates for that distinction.

Then there was Christa, who would wander through the living room, her head thrown back. She was reading Ibsen's A Doll's House, and there was not a man she would not slander or a door she would not slam behind her. Her stamping and fuming reminded me of the Spanish movies Carlos and I saw together after we gorged on tacos, tostadas, enchiladas, and my favorite, chili rellenos.

Marshall was our dipso unemployed poet, who told us about Dylan Thomas's last words.

" 'Thirteen shots, not a bad record.' And the man immediately went into a coma. They say he was a horrible houseguest, that he messed in his bed and also ate a great deal of chocolate, so you could never tell what was what."

Amy wanted to be a confectionary chef in order to make madeleines—or was it marzipan—and had applied to a culinary school in Switzerland. Meantime, she was reading Proust.

Thomas was Melville's Bartleby. He preferred not to come out of his room if at all possible, but did appear for meals on a regular basis, although he neglected his turn at kitchen duty.

Then there was the Hemingway bunch. They were brusque and alert.

"Pass the salt."

"I hate your guts."

"Don't give me that shit."

"The first thing I'm going to do when I get to New York is go to the White Horse Tavern." Thus spake the Dylan Thomas person.

"And shit your pants."

"Shut up Freddy-spaghetti."

The beats were going to congregate at Vesuvio's, and eat dinner at the New Pisa.

"Fall off your stool?"

"Hah, hah."

"Hey, I've eaten there," I said, not elaborating on the occasion, or mentioning that I had actually worked in North Beach.

"If you die by the sword, you die by the sword."

"Pass the goddamn fish, goddamn it."

"Going fishing tomorrow, Sally?"

"You bet, damn it."

"The whiteness of the whale. Have any of you considered that it is one of the very few times in Western literature that white, not black, is a symbol of evil?" Sometimes the Melville person preferred to say something.

"I say it's about time," I said, thinking of friends and neighbors and assorted folk about the earth who would be happy to get this info pony express pronto Tonto.

Sometimes Carlos came for dinner. An outsider, he did not understand much, nor did he like the salads we ate of dandelion greens and raisins and grains, but he smiled warmly at everybody, and under the table put his hand on my thigh. His silence was a relief. We would go up to my bedroom, and he would kiss me, saying, *"Chica, chica, querida, querida."* Which must have been out of some Mexican novel for was anybody capable of original dialogue anymore?

And shortly we began to make love, something I would have to confess in group, during group-meet night, I knew, having sex outside our best-friend unit, but I did not want to share Carlos with Amy and Freddy and Christa and David and Mitchell and Sally and the Melville person and the Plato person. Thank God the Goldman woman was a lesbian, for she was by far the most attractive.

[**WHAT DID I** choose for my Great Books project?

Othello, of course. I had all of Aaron's notes. Furthermore, I considered myself an expert on the tragedy of the Judeo-Christian West emanating from the concept of a jealous God.

Frankly, I was planning to rehash Aaron's notes, for I had been the only one to go back to his office, empty his desk, and gather his belongings. He had drawers of notes. It seemed that Aaron had been like Mr. Casaubon in George Eliot's *Middlemarch*—the man was always writing the book but never quite finishing it.

"The Greenness of Othello" was the title I chose, he chose.

"By that I mean, of course, jealousy, but also naïveté," I explained to David. "I got the idea from the whiteness of the whale."

"Please just read it, Zoe," David said wearily.

We were in his study with several house pets. The house was getting a distinctly doggy odor, and the equal allocation of resources and chores was not working out Utopia fashion. Some people were complaining that they were doing all the work. For instance, Freddy-spaghetti. Naturally, the Melville person preferred not to. Amy, the Proust girl, was too dreamy for dishes, and too aristocratic for bathroom duties. Emma Goldman was always rolling up her sleeves, taking up the slack. The Hemingway people did their chores if they were manly enough. Taking out the garbage, yes. Vacuuming, no.

"So," David said. "Update me on *Othello*. Give me your own personal point of view."

"Okay." It was also Aaron's point of view. But one thing, I never

wore my red pedal pushers to tutorial or shorts or anything that didn't look like a sack around David. I liked Carlos. What he lacked in the English language he made up for in eye and hand language. I didn't have to constantly justify my existence around him. He didn't tell me what to do. He loved Nadja, and sometimes I knew that when we were out with her, he let people think she was ours.

"So you are interested in jealousy?" David put his hand on his chin. "The green-eyed monster?"

I had not talked about my own gullibility or jealousy in any serious way, but I intended to use my paper on *Othello* as a means of exploring myself. If literature, as Aaron believed, taught us something and was not a mere Platonic mimicry of reality, we should be able to learn from it.

"I have a different point of view, David," I warned. "To me jealousy is not just destructive and awful"—I took a breath—"but also life-giving and wonderful, a gem, yes, an emerald at the heart of our existence, ourselves. I see it as a sign of life. We must have, we must be, we are. What we wish to possess in our possessiveness is ourselves. Man as magnet. World as filings." The last bit was not Aaron. It was pure, sophomoric Zoe.

David said: "Do you really believe that crap?"

"Yes."

"Yes and no?" He moved closer to me.

"Plain yes. Yes."

"Go on." His study had a couch, a chaise, the kind of one-sided thing you see in cartoons of psychiatrists. You are getting very sleepy, my dear. Your eyelids are getting heavy.

"In the play *Othello*, everybody literally and figuratively pales beside Othello, David. He is the only truly majestic character, and in his passion he is redeemed beyond redemption. The black man who marries the white girl who plays out his destiny on such scanty-hanky evidence is naïveté incarnate, green as they come."

Coyote Incarnate, I remembered. You think you are a big woman, Grey had said to me. Yes, I could now answer, I do, I am.

I had known about but never seen the Orson Welles movie of

Othello. Welles was a giant man who played giants. Hearst. Othello. I wanted to make my paper tie in with Grey and my life in Big Sur and what had happened at Nepenthe, the former hideaway of Orson Welles and Rita Hayworth. I wanted to get my mind around all of it, as I had once tried to understand why Grey wanted to run me over. I thought if I could assimilate my experiences without pain and then correlate my life with another reference point, with literature and Shakespeare's knowledge of human nature, that I would not only process understanding but, in doing so, free myself from many bad feelings.

David looked depressed. He looked bored. How many great books can you take, I wondered. How many kids have you misled?

"*Othello* is a map misread," I continued.

He had sidled over, was diddling with my leg, my hairy, nonexotic dancer's leg. If my father's head was the Red Sea, complete with Hebrew part, then my legs could be called the Red Forest. Necessary and sufficient.

"I wish you wouldn't do that, David."

"Do what?"

"You know."

"Are we talking private property, here?"

"Yes. You are not in my unit."

"I thought you were a free agent."

"That makes you King of the Mountain?"

"Mentors-administrators . . ."

"You know those connect-the-dot pictures, David? Each thing, each dot in the line leads to the next? In *Othello*, we are irrevocably led to our hero/villain's demise and death." I took a breath, went on. "Nothing has innate meaning in itself. The eye of the beholder is all. Each dot read is on a domino. One falls, the others go. Chain reactions. Time to go." I jumped up. "Nadja. It's her feeding time."

"She is going to grow up, Zoe, and then what will you do?"

Suddenly I was stricken with sadness.

"What do you mean? I am going to write a book about *Othello*."

I ran upstairs. Amy, who was baby-sitting, was singing "Joe Hill" to her, and Nadja was playing with her toes, gurgling.

"Amy," I asked. "Does David ever, you know, like, bother you?"

"He likes redheads. His senior thesis was on the Pre-Raphaelites and . . ." She drifted away.

"I see."

"Yeah. Well, he won't kick you out of the school or anything, but he can make it difficult." In some ways, Amy reminded me of Oak. She was dreamy.

"Thanks for nothing."

"You're very welcome. You want tomorrow, same time, same station?"

"Sure."

"I love the little monkey," she said, nudging Nadja's nose. "Be cool, Zoe."

"I've never been cool in my life, Amy. Maybe Nadja and I should move out of California? You think? A place where people are more intense?"

"To New York?"

"Yeah."

"They'll eat you alive there."

"The crocodiles?"

"What crocodiles?"

"When I was a kid my father said that crocodiles grew in the New York City sewers."

"San Francisco is where it's at," Amy said.

"I don't know."

"Don't tell anybody, but I've applied to Berkeley."

"I thought you wanted to go to culinary school in France."

"Switzerland. Nope, not anymore."

"Why?"

"Emma Goldman."

"I thought Proust was your thing."

"Nope, not anymore." She smiled mysteriously.

Nadja crawled over to me, grabbed my hair, gave a grand pull. Our room was large and looked out over the hills. I was lucky, I knew. We had drawn lots and I had gotten the corner room with two sets of windows. The house itself was that rare thing in southern California, a Victorian, with outdoor carvings and indoor nooks and built-in drawers and a real attic.

"Why don't you just sleep with him, get it over with. You get to be teacher's pet for a week, and then he forgets you."

"I fall in love with people I sleep with, Amy. I take it literally, you know, when I make love, I *make* love."

"Oh, too bad."

"Anyway, what would Othello or Plato or Melville say about it, you know, not being sincere?"

"Oh sin-sear, Zoe? We are at the dawn of a new age. Melville, Othello, and Plato are dead." She seemed to swoon a little.

"Not to me."

"Well . . . what can I say, then." She waved her hand as if she were doing the Charleston.

I took my shoe box from under my bed. These were my personal notes, written on small cards. Keeping books and notes under my bed was a habit left over from childhood, even though, at Thoreau College, all rooms, men's and women's, were provided with desks and bookcases, and supposedly we respected each other's differing beliefs. I was still furtive. Hide it. Deny it. I have never nor am I now. Go out to the bomb shelter. Fold, duck, cover. I couldn't help it, I had been schooled in deception and concealment.

I picked a card from my shoe box.

Pick a card, any card. It was like Lucille's fatal tarot card illustrating my misfortune.

"The Greenness of Zoe":

When Grey betrayed me, truly betrayed me (one difference among many between Othello and me, Grey and Desdemona)—how did I feel? I think at first maybe I ignored signs—the map of fate was not misread, just unread. Unlike Othello, who was so assiduous in his jealousy, I was lackadaisical, unwilling at first to be drawn in. I think my body took over and said: Don't look now. Don't see that.

Another card:

When I was jealous, I was brilliantly alert, lividly alive, righteously sure of myself. And at no other time did I love Grey so much as when I was jealous.

On the other hand, my jealousy, as if it were a seed, took root and grew into a tree of self-doubt, sprouted branches of I-hate-myself. Once I was sure of Grey's infidelity, to know was to doubt love.

Another card:

Maybe I was just waiting to be knocked about, run down, left, and abandoned. It was the accumulated force of guilt, perhaps? Because of Aaron, because of no Aaron, hide-and-seek, here today, gone tomorrow? To be the other woman was to be no woman at all? And then he had to up and die, just like that, so that I, the other woman, was the black widow, the real femme fatale. Watch out, the kiss of death is the lipstick of my desire, not Ruby Red, but Zoe Zip. Or maybe, it was one of those children's games played out at home. Teach me how to kneel and scrub, for when you are poor, sewing what you rip comes out of the woodwork. And when your mother loves a liquid more than you, what are you but nothing deserving nothing, if not the worst. My daily bread and most humble pie, give me a clue.

Another card:

The Sun Dance Grey had told me about—when the bravest of the brave would have pegs with long thongs attached to their chests, the ends tied to a sacred tree—is like a maypole dance. They would make their way around the tree, letting the thongs tighten until the pegs tore the body. This offering of flesh was made to Wakantanka as a sacrifice for the People. The maypole was the manhole.

Those were my notes to myself kept for myself in a shoe box under my bed in a packet of 3″ x 5″ cards held together by a rubber band. November 1958.

[**THE SLOW** working out of the inevitable seemed like a movie you go to, sit through feeling sick all the while, and while watching it you scrunch down in your seat, close your eyes, peek occasionally, but stay. You stay.

One day, coming down the hill after visiting Matilda, Nadja in my arms, hitting a late cocktail hour at Charlie's, I was struck by how much their house resembled the White Palace, not a winter wonderland, skating on very thin ice in the midst of the tropics, but a hamburger joint. Or rather, it was not what it seemed and, in fact, was your typical one-dimensional movie set in lovely Burbank, California.

In this scene, my cousin Charlie and his wife, Lois, are made up like movie stars, and in their midst stands a lost soldier from a forgotten war, an anachronism, a creature from the black lagoon, an alien from another planet. Grey Cloud.

"Your friend Carlos," Charlie said.

Actually, Carlos's sperm was seeping out of me. I had not taken my diaphragm out from the night before. Cousin Charlie was drunk and apparently took dark Grey for dark Carlos. All the same to him, I supposed, spic, Injun. Meanwhile, I felt a Hemingway bout of succinct short answers coming on like a premenstrual cramp.

"Not Carlos." I winced, blinking very fast.

Grey turned to me. His head, his eyes, his body met me full force. He had become old, older. Gray streaks in his long hair, and his face a map of wrinkles. His eyes shone like obsidian, though, polished coal, hot oil, the pupils hugely black, so that there was only a tiny rim of dark brown. Where are your irises? I wanted to ask. He was on

something.

"Zoe," he said, opening his arms. "The baby."

I recognized his voice from a dream. I didn't move.

"Nadja, her name is Nadja."

"Carlos has come to pay us a visit."

"Not Carlos."

"Who's Carlos?" Grey asked.

"Would you like a drink, Zoe?" This was Lois, trying to be perky and bright, save the situation.

"Yes," I said dully, for where was my heart in all this? I could see it pickled in the bottle of Jim Beam behind the black vinyl bar.

Or my heart. Strung up on the Utah clothesline to dry, clothespins pinching it, the sun drying it out, after being through the roller-wringer.

Or my heart. Caught like an old sock in the dryer of the laundromat in the Zone. Resting on a pile of clothes. Riches to rags.

Or my heart. Hanging by a thread from the big stand-up fan in the garment factory, Mary Ellen's wedding dress blowing up and down like a dreadful kite.

Or my heart. Put in a drawer, the underclothes drawer beneath the underpants in my Pacific Grove girl's room. I was reminded of the line in a stupid song we sang in chorus, "and the clock stopped, never to run again."

Grey was wearing blue jeans, of course, and a large canvaslike coat. He looked like a refugee from a cattle drive.

"Carlos, would *you* like a drink?" Charlie asked. "Is there something in your eye, Zoe?"

"He is not Carlos."

"Nadja is getting big," Grey said, as if he had ever seen her. "She is beautiful. You have taken good care of her."

I walked closer to him. Your child, I wanted to say. See, see what I have done without you, and where is your Oak? I want to kill her, kill you.

"Here's a drink, Carlos." Charlie shoved a cocktail glass in his hand. Grey had probably never had a martini in his life.

"Don't drink firewater," he said.

I looked at him. Still the Indian, I thought. When was he ever going to let up.

Lois gave me vodka. Two shots, woman to woman. A wise choice. Actually, I had nothing against her. She had told me once that she was from Texarkana and was raised dirt-poor. She had met Charlie on a flight, of course, and he had promised she would never have to serve a tray again.

Luckily I was born with long legs, she had said, as if she had been a colt.

Was Grey looking at her?

Oh no, I thought, I'm jealous. I hate him and I'm jealous.

"I was in New York," he said.

"Yes, I know."

"And in Boston for a while."

"Oh."

"All over, really."

"Where's Oak?"

"I don't know. Still in New York, I guess. She's a famous artist now."

"Oh." He smelled different. Not Oak's patchouli but something acrid and odd. "And how did you get here?"

"On the bus. I went back to Big Sur and then to your aunt's house. I understand we're getting divorced." He said the last word with great disgust. "They couldn't find me to serve the papers, but they caught up."

"Right."

"I will never accept a divorce. It is impossible for us to be divorced."

"No it isn't." He had said that before.

"And then I went to Salt Lake City," he picked up again.

"Salt Lake?" I thought of that desolate landscape. Lake? Hardly.

"Your aunts."

"Yes, in that house. The Henhouse."

Grey and I were standing face-to-face. Charlie was pacing. Lois was perched on a bar stool as if ready to take flight. I was wondering if he and Lois were going out to dinner soon, and if they were, then what? Grey and I? Well, so what are you doing these days? How's life treating you? Have you heard the latest knock, knock? Knock, knock? Who's there? Nobody is home. Nobody is home, Grey.

"I love Zoe," Grey announced.

"I love Zoe, too," Charlie said, lurching toward me drunkenly.

"No, you don't understand, I love her like a lover."

"Me, too," my cousin said.

"I'm going to put Nadja down," I said tartly. It was our old room, when Nadja and I still lived there and not at Thoreau, but I didn't tell Grey that. Let him think we lived there. Actually it was eight o'clock. Nadja and I had stopped for dinner at Aunt Matilda's and Benjamin's. It was barbecue night.

"See, the secret of a good barbecue," Benjamin told me, "is letting it burn down so it's just warm coals."

I didn't tell him that I had cooked over campfires and on a woodstove. Benjamin was kind of the expert on everything. A big, strapping man of sixty-five, he called Matilda the little woman, which she *was* compared to him.

"I'll be right back," I told Grey, Charlie, and Lois.

I went up the two stairs and into the bedroom, put Nadja in the crib I still kept there, changed her diapers. My hands were trembling, my knees shaking, and I almost stuck her with her safety pin. Nadja looked up at me.

"Mama?" she queried.

"Don't be worried," I said to her, catching a sob. "I'm here."

She lifted her arms.

"Hungry?" I asked.

I had eaten at Aunt Matilda's, but Nadja had not been interested. Now, it seemed, she was hungry.

"Mama."

She wanted to nurse. I knew she was too big, going on one year, but I still had not weaned her. I knew that when I did, she would be on her way to growing up, being on her own.

"Yes, little papoose, little rabbit, in a minute, in a minute, everything."

I sat down on the bed, remembering the night of my high school graduation, how I had run from my home to Grey's little room along Cannery Row. Let's get married, I had said. And the first time, we made love in the room of skins. Flayed alive. There had been months when I would have given my life to see him again, despite the divorce proceedings, and now he was here and I wanted to get rid of him once and for all and as fast as possible.

I brought Nadja back into the living room, put her in the playpen. She had three, one in Aunt Matilda's and Uncle Ben's, one here, and one at Thoreau.

"How can you keep her in a cage?" Grey asked.

"It's not a cage. It's for her own safety. Otherwise she'll be picking things off the floor, putting them in her mouth, swallowing them, choking. Unless I can watch her every second, it's the safest place."

"Oh."

"Does Oak still have her car?"

"Zoe, that, that was . . ."

"A mistake?"

"I wasn't in my right mind."

"Are you now in your right mind?"

"Am I missing something here?" Charlie asked.

"Just life," Lois replied.

"I have to nurse Nadja," I said, going behind the bar. Lois had poured me another vodka. I accepted it, despite the fact I was nursing.

"Shall we get rid of him?" Lois said, coming behind me and whispering to my shoulder. "He's your ex, the ex-con, isn't he?"

We could see the men over the bar. My cousin had his arm on Grey's shoulder.

"I love her, too," he kept saying.

"Can you?" I said.

"You're not going with him, are you, back with him?"

"No, no, not on your life."

"I really do love her," Grey said.

"Don't go to dinner," I whispered to Lois. "Stay here."

"You're scared of him?"

"Yes."

"I don't think Charlie can make it out for dinner tonight," Lois announced loudly. "Let's all have some sandwiches."

"I'm going to give Nadja some food and then nurse her," I said brightly.

"I can make dinner out," Charlie said, wobbling a little. "What do you mean we can't make it out?"

"You're drunk, Charlie. You'd embarrass yourself, embarrass me."

I walked across the room, got out a jar of Gerber puréed meat and vegetables, and put it in a saucepan with a little water. Then I turned on the burner. Then I turned off the burner. Grey and Charlie were busy saying how much they loved me. I wiped off the stove top. When in distress, I become a compulsive housecleaner. The stove was electric. My aunts in the Henhouse had an old stove from the thirties. It was green and on tall legs. It said Detroit on it. This stove was state-of-the-art. Everything in the house was up-to-the-minute modern. Soon it would be the sixties. The end of the century was growing closer. Then we would all be riding around in spaceships. I could hardly wait.

Charlie came into the kitchen, lunged at me.

"No," I said. "No."

"Charlie, behave yourself," Lois threatened.

"Hey," Grey said. "She's my wife."

"No, Grey, not anymore."

I got Nadja out of the playpen, put her on the floor, and sat down opposite her.

"Nana."

"Not tonight, sweetheart, let Mama help you." I fed Nadja while everybody watched in silence, then I took her into the bedroom, put her in her pajamas. I sat down in the plastic chair, nursed her. She sucked a few minutes. I felt the warm flow come from deep inside my chest. My milk. My baby. My poor baby. She was tired. It had been a long day. Her eyes would close and then she would open them again in an effort to stay awake.

"I'm here, darling," I said. "Right here." I had quieted my shaking hands, but my heart was going wild. I tried to breathe normally, slowly calm myself down.

She fell asleep shortly, a little puddle of milk in her mouth. I put her over my shoulder, burped her, and put her down on her stomach in the crib.

When I returned to the living room, my cousin had passed out on the floor. It reminded me of my mother.

Lois and Grey lifted Charlie onto the couch.

"Thanks," Lois said.

"No bother," Grey said.

"Want to play cards?" Lois said, taking Charlie's shoes off. "A little poker? How about checkers? Grey, do you play checkers?"

"Maybe Grey has to go," I said.

"Take a walk, Zoe?"

"No. I have to keep an eye on Nadja," I said, my voice shaking. "Excuse me a minute, just want to check on her."

Grey followed me into the bedroom.

She was awake again, had rolled over, and was looking up at her mobile.

"I want to try again," Grey whispered. "I haven't forgotten you for a day."

"No more tries," I said.

"Oh, Zoe, look at me."

I turned. He looked like the tobacco leaf I had once envisioned, the one sandwiched under the cornflake boxes of a grocery store waiting for the manager to lock up. He was a criminal, but a folded and faded one, an old dollar bill that had been crumpled and smoothed, crumpled and smoothed.

Nadja giggled.

"She likes me," he said. "Dada," he said, leaning down. "Say Dada."

She began to cry.

"No, Grey, no."

"I *am* her father, Zoe."

I shuddered.

"Grey, please go. It's over."

"How did you manage?" he asked.

"I managed."

"It's summer, Zoe."

It *was* early December.

"The easiest time."

"The hardest time. Sell it," I said. "Sell the house, the land. Marry somebody else. Do anything, but not me, not us, Grey."

"Give it a try, Zoe. Give me a month, give me one month and I will prove to you that we can begin again." He put his face down to Nadja in the crib. She patted his face with her palms as if she had known him all her life.

"See?" he said, as if something was settled.

I didn't even want her touching him, him touching her.

"Just let's do it, do what I say, and all will be fine."

He smiled at his baby.

"We are family, you know, Zoe. You can't deny that. You can't deny that we belong together. That we are kin."

Then he smiled at me for the first time, and lifted his eyebrows in his way, in the way I knew more than my own face.

"You can relax," he said. "I will take care of you, Nadja."

"I can take care of myself and Nadja."

"I am her father. You can't deny that."

"You abandoned us, Grey. You tried to run me over. Before that you beat me so that I almost lost her. You did not want me. You did not want her. The child is mine. We are over. It's over. Please leave us alone. I can't say it more simply. You know, you could be arrested for what you did, and I could sue you for the land."

"You were going to put me in a mental asylum."

"A hospital, Grey. You needed help."

"It's not over, Zoe, until I say it's over, and it will never, never be over. You thought you could get rid of me by putting me in a prison, but it didn't work. I'm free. I'm here. I'm going to take you back. I know you still love me."

"Sit down, Grey." He sat on the bed.

"Let me tell you something. Listen to what I say. Remember what I say." I stood above him, took a big breath. "I do not love you. That's number two. I know you live in your own realm, but listen, get this straight, you tried to kill me. That's number one. You ran off with Oak. You neglected your child. You beat me up. How can I impress on you that I mean, really, really and truly, I have had enough. I am good-natured and soft-hearted, but, my God, enough is enough. You impressed on *me*, I finally got it: YOU DON'T WANT ME, I mean, so much so that you would knock me down, kill me. When I was a kid, I used to worry about the bomb, the A-bomb, something coming from overseas to Get Me, flatten me to the asphalt of my school playground. Well, I didn't have to worry about some big airplane coming from overseas. I was wrong. My husband, right here in the good old U.S. of A., home sweet home, tried to flatten me. I had to worry about my own family doing me in, not some 'foreigners,' not strangers. You, my own husband.

The enemy, my friend, my husband, is you. And even had you been 'not in your right mind,' I would have been just as dead. Don't you see, can't you see, that it was a mistake from the beginning? I wanted to get away from my dead-end life and guilt over Aaron and did not have the courage or intelligence to do it myself, and you needed some innocent creature to go along with your plans. It seemed perfect, but it was all wrong. It was all wrong from the very beginning."

"You are in love with somebody else," he said.

"My love life is not your business, Grey."

"It is my business. I love you."

"Sure. Tell that to the judge."

He came over, slapped my face.

Tears started in my eyes. I put my hand up to my face. "I am going to call the police, Grey, and if you come near me again, you will be put in jail."

"They won't take me alive."

"God, Grey, get out of here."

"Everything all right?" Lois said, popping her head in.

"Grey is just leaving," I said.

"Is that what you want?"

"Yes, Grey, that is what I want."

"Is that really what you want?"

"Yes. Yes." I let myself flop down on the bed. I had said it, done it, it was over. "Yes, I mean it, go." And I did mean it.

"The divorce is not final," Grey said.

"It will be," I said, "in about a month."

"You think so?"

"I know so."

[**B U T I S H O O K** for days. At first I could not understand how somebody I had loved so much had become nothing to me, worse than nothing. The pet had become a pest. In our house group meeting at Thoreau, I tried to see it from different perspectives. We were both older. I had grown up. He was the rebound from Aaron and all that Aaron stood for, a jump from the intellectual man of ideas to the elemental man of the earth. But Grey had ideas, too.

I had to begin again. Nobody in the group was buying it.

Going from the idealistic materialist (Marxist) to the materialistic idealist (Pragmatist). Or perhaps it was the thesis, the antithesis; yet, I saw no synthesis.

Amy said that kind of analysis did make some kind of sense, but perhaps, she suggested, I had simply married Grey because I had nothing better to do.

She was right. I really didn't.

The Platonist in the household thought that maybe I was emerging from the cave is all, that from the very beginning I saw shadows and that now I hungered for a real world of Pure Idea.

The Goldman woman knew I was declaring my independence as a person. The Nietzsche man knew I liked to be whipped. The Melvillean said I preferred not to, just call me Ishmael, and the Hemingway team went fishing.

It was the beat group who made the most sense of the scenario.

If I was a rebel with a cause, as I had once told Margo, the cause was not freedom, walking freely in the street, as I had expressed to her, but excitement. Grey was exciting to me.

Yes, I said. At one time.

Now I couldn't understand what I had found so exciting. The most exciting thing, it seemed, was the former power and energy of my love for him. The dynamics of our relationship were complex, I realized, and perhaps, as the Platonist might agree, Grey was *my* projection, that is, rather than his giving me life, perhaps my attention had imbued him, suffused him, given him the life energy which was my life and made *his* life possible. Once that evaporated, drained out, once I withdrew, there was nothing left. No wonder that my impression of him was that of a dry leaf. He was a shell, a residue. And maybe he would find, as he had hoped to find in Oak, somebody else who would blow wind into his empty frame so he could set sail. He was not a lone wolf, the coyote he imagined himself. He needed a sidekick, a double, a prop, a person who would hold him up. He was a kind of fraud, a make-believe Indian. No wonder he did not want me to look in the mirror. No wonder he forged checks for work he had never done, taken land he had never worked. He wanted a family without earning it. Well, the house, the house was his monument, a stone house. That was his.

David thought I had worked through the problem like a pro, and would I like a nightcap in the study.

No, thank you. Nobody seemed to understand how frightened I was, but a week went by and I settled down. Another week and we started getting ready for Christmas at Thoreau College with a big party featuring red. Red wine. Borscht. Tomatoes. Radishes. Valentine cookies with red sparkles on them. We had to wear red, too. Carlos came as a hot pepper. And afterward, when we were upstairs in my bedroom, I told him, halting, as simply as I could, about Grey's sudden appearance. He said: *Cuidado*, Zoe, *cuidado*.

Prophetic words. Old, familiar words.

For one morning after the new year I was at Thoreau College alone with Nadja when Grey turned up again. Everybody else had gone to the co-op. They were only going to be gone an hour. I was reading or straightening up, listening to records—a Miles Davis LP, *Kinda Blue*, I think. I listened to jazz because I began to understand it and because I had first heard it at Aaron's, and it corresponded to a time in my life when I was open and alive to all sorts of new things, and I could feel that accessibility and potential in myself again.

The song was "Blue in Green," and Nadja was in her playpen very intently examining some colorful blocks. I remember thinking: She's bright. She's going to be bright. And I could see us, in a sense, growing up together, she in school, I in school. I had decided that I was going to study psychology. Now she was almost one year old, then she would be two. When she was three, I would have enough money for her to go to nursery school, and we would move to Berkeley. Amy said I could stay with them until I found a place. We would be poor, but we would be poor anyway, no matter what. And so I would start college when I was twenty-two. Big deal. Maybe I would graduate when I was twenty-seven or twenty-eight. That was not one hundred years old, as I had complained to Lucille, and she was right, the time would go by anyway. I might as well be in school.

The sun. I remember the sun coming in our windows that day. People say California does not have seasons, but they are wrong. And it is not just the winter rains but something more subtle, a feeling, the air. It changes from day to day. That day it was a wintry, feeble sun. We had to keep the smudge pots on the windmill going in the azalea shed for seven days. I only worked there three days a week since starting school.

Amy, who had been baby-sitting the day before while I went to the library to get a book on Shakespeare's fools, made beaded necklaces and earrings, and she had left some of her equipment on my bureau. I was sitting on the bed. I had taken out my library book to look at the chapter headings and index, and thumbed through it to see what I wanted to come back to later. I was interested in the relationships between Lear and his fool and Iago and Othello, that is, who was whose fool. The room was in a kind of disarray. My note cards were out, as well as clothes to be washed. Maybe I should return Amy's beads to her, I remember thinking. We all kept our doors unlocked. I picked up the string of beads, some fell off. I bent down to pick them up. I got up, turned to the door, sensing something, and there was Grey.

"Grey? What are you doing here?"

"What do you think?"

"I'm going to call the police, Grey, if you don't go. Please."

And it seemed almost simultaneous with those words that Nadja began choking.

"Nadja." I picked her up, thumped her back. I reached into her mouth, down her throat, felt nothing. I hit her across the back again. I held her by her feet and jerked her up and down. She continued to gasp for breath.

"Grey." He was still standing in the doorway.

"What is it?"

"She's swallowed something. Call the ambulance. The phone is right at the base of the stairs. Do you have a car?"

"Maybe she was bit by a spider."

"Bit by a spider? No."

"Here, let me see her."

"She needs a doctor, Grey, fast."

Grey took her from me.

"See, she's in trouble." Her little face was suffused with red. Her chest was heaving in and out.

"She'll be all right," Grey said.

"Give her back. I'll call. She's swallowed something."

"Nadja," he said. "How could you be so stupid as to swallow something?"

"Grey, if you don't call, I will."

I was beyond panic. I pulled Nadja away from him. Frantically, I ran to the doorway with her choking in my arms.

Grey blocked the doorway.

"You are not going anywhere," he said.

"What?"

Nadja was changing color. Oh God, have mercy, I breathed.

"You are not moving."

"She needs a doctor, Grey. Oh, Grey, please. Please, please."

"Do you think a Harvard doctor knows more about your child than you do?"

"Yes, yes, Grey. Yes, yes, I do, I need a doctor, a real doctor to operate on her. They can get air down her throat. Let me pass."

"Over my dead body," he said, barring the door with his hands.

I looked beyond him and thought I saw a figure, the figure from my dreams, the upright coyote, only hoofed, not a coyote, but a leering goat. I saw Death.

"Oh God, Grey," I screamed. "She is going to die if we don't get help. Let me by. Please, I beg you."

I hung her upside down again by her feet, shook and shook. "If she dies, Grey, if she dies." I put her on the floor on her stomach, pushed her back in artificial respiration, the kind I had been taught in first aid, my lifesaver badge on P.G. Beach, in, out, in, out.

"If she dies," Grey said, "we will bury her out in the back. That's what they did in the old days, that's what country people did. We'll have other children."

"Grey. You're crazy. Please, I beg you, let me by."

I got up, leaving her on the floor, flung myself forward against him.

He held fast.

Quickly, I looked through the room for something I could use. The broom, an umbrella. I picked up the umbrella, charged toward him. He grabbed the end, pushed back on it, pushed me down.

"Grey, I will kill you if you don't let me through."

He began to laugh in his old crazy way.

I picked up Nadja, who was hiccuping and coughing, hugged her to me and rushed for the door. He threw us back. We fell on the floor. I got up, and rushed for the door again. Nadja was throbbing against my breasts.

"Please God. Please help me." I bit Grey's hand hard, kneed his groin, got through.

I ran down the stairs and through the hallway. The child was turning blue. I ran, stumbled, fell, got up, holding one hand around her head, and started running again. Behind me. He was behind me. I heard him, heard him behind me. I heard him, felt him behind me, and then his hand went out, and he grabbed my hair, turned me around, tore the child away from me.

"Grey, she's going to die," I screamed.

He walked back up the stairs. I took the chair by the phone, lifted it high above my head, and knocked it down around his head. His head started to bleed, but he kept walking. I ran in front of him, pulled the baby from him, and then, then I saw his fist coming. I thought he missed me, but I felt something very hard hit my face, and then, as darkness closed in around me, I prayed.

"Baby Jesus, take her now," I muttered. "Let her die now and suffer no more. Saint Anthony, have mercy." This was a human being, my child.

I was in a long tunnel. She was in a long tunnel. She was getting born, born again in darkness and silence. I heard echoes, the flap of wings. Black bats and white feathers.

Then I awakened. Nadja was lying across my chest.

She was still. Her face was relaxed. Her arms and feet warm. For a moment, I thought I might have dreamed everything. She was alive. She was all right. Except that her eyes were wide open and her little chest felt hollow, motionless. Everything in her, all her tiny organs were curled up, contained, stilled, without life.

"Heavenly Father," I prayed. Then I saw that Grey was dancing, dancing and whispering, dancing around the stairs, and his whispers were getting louder.

"The Ghost Dance," he said. "The Ghost Dance will raise the dead."

I sat up, holding the dead child to my chest, cradling her head as I had when she was a newborn. I stood up with Nadja. She was dead. I was going to vomit. I swallowed it, but it couldn't stop. It came up. I vomited all over the floor, holding Nadja to my side, not letting go of her. It kept coming and coming. I had to sit down on the stairs, I was so weak. Nadja lay so still. She was so patient. Oh, Saint Anthony, I thought, resisting temptations has taught you nothing. Jesus, you are truly dead. And Grey kept dancing, just kept dancing.

"She is dead," I said to Grey. "Dead. She is dead." It was a dirge. Dead.

"We will bury her," Grey whispered between his chanting and stepping, "behind the house, and she will rise up."

I got up with difficulty, holding my dead child to my beating heart and nearly stumbling down the hallway, then I gained my footing. This time Grey did not stop me. He kept dancing, kept dancing. She was dead.

I walked out of the house. The sun practically blinded me. I walked down the hill to a neighbor's house. I knocked on the door, and when she opened it I started screaming.

[**THE END** should have been before the beginning. When your baby dies, you want to die, too; you want to die instead of the baby; you want never to have been alive. You want nothing ever to have been in the world before, during, or ever after. You want the seasons to stop. When your baby dies, *you* are an orphan in the universe.

I would not let her go out of my arms. The nurse wanted to take her from me when the doctor examined her dead body, but I clutched her to me, and held her as she grew stiffer and stiffer and colder and colder.

The End should have been before my mother *held* me, not that she did much. That time in the Turkish room of my aunt's house, my father's missionary zeal getting the better of him, the dark angel, the bird of ill omen should have raised his claws, shown him the golden Moroni tablets: Thou shalt not.

The End should have been the realization of the motorcycle dream, actually getting on the wheels with no brakes, no handlebars, and knowing then and there, Get off, get off while you can. You will do anything, Margo marveled. The devil does dare, and all *my* temptations were followed.

The End should have been joining Aaron, lying down beside him, one sand angel to another flying to our sand castle in the sky, because it was my fault.

The End should have been: No, thank you. I do not cut hair, camp, live in a trailer, roll Sisyphean stones to make a House of Despair on a haunted hill in a Land of Desolation.

The End should have been the recognition of the Grand Trickster prancing outside the house, coming closer and closer, that east wind of braves gone to dust while Father Peyote-Coyote laughed in his hat.

I was a crazy woman in the hands of a crazy man.

The End was owl boy eyeing me while the trees turned red with writhing snakes as Grey kicked me.

The End was the second I laid eyes on Grey. Poetry is a living thing, he had said, trickster of death.

The End was our talk in the coffeehouse in San Francisco. We will live on the land, be as gods.

The End was the big bug lights of the car coming at me during the consummation ceremony long ago, Kelly saying, Go home, Narcissus saying, Do some good.

Mary Ellen, the wooden-legged seamstress, said the secret is four words, her fingers raised, one, two, three, four. Be Good to Yourself.

The End was when Grey said: Do you think a Harvard doctor knows more than you about your baby?

The End was the string of beads, Amy's beads on the bureau, one fallen in the playpen, it took only one.

The End was when I gave Nadja over to the mortuary to be prepared for burial. After sitting a little while, I simply handed her over.

"Now where?" David asked, as if we were on a shopping expedition. We were standing outside a mortuary in Santa Barbara, not unlike the one I went to with Margo for Aaron. First Aaron, now my child. I had the golden touch.

"To the sheriff's office."

"Are you sure, Zoe?"

"Yes, I am sure."

We drove down the street to the police station, a few blocks over from the courthouse to still one more red-tiled-roof building with the American flag and the California state flag, that old grizzly bear, in front of it.

Sitting across from a large man in front of the desk, I told my story and swore out a warrant for Grey's arrest. The charge was second-degree manslaughter.

"You mean," the cop said in a Southern accent, "he prevented you from getting the child medical attention."

"Yes."

"Mercy, mercy." The policeman shook his head back and forth. It looked like he was going to cry, too.

"The child would have died anyway," David put in. "The doctor said that in a few minutes brain damage occurs. Without oxygen, the cells . . ."

"Hush." The policeman looked at David with some distaste. "We don't deal in would have/could have here. The facts is what counts. And we don't want to cause more grief to the little lady, now, do we. California protects its women. Seems to me we have sufficient cause here. Seems to me that we don't know everything, even doctors. Seems to me we have sufficient cause to call this man in. You say his name is Grey Cloud? What kind of name is that?"

My child is dead. Nadja is dead, I said to myself. I closed my eyes, let myself swoon.

"Does she have relatives?" I heard the cop say softly.

"I'm taking her home right now," David said.

My child is dead. Nadja is dead.

Sitting in the front seat of David's car, I felt weightless. No child to hold. An empty lap. Milk was dripping out of my breasts, wetting my blouse. I was bleeding milk. The engine hummed. I was vaguely aware of the ocean on one side, mountains on the other, but nothing held its meaning. The meaning slipped off like slippery veneer. Nothing meant anything. Mountains, ocean, what did they mean? I saw people standing around on the street. People. I couldn't think about anything, and I couldn't not think.

As we neared Thoreau College, I said: "Take me to my Aunt Matilda's."

The moment she opened the door, I fell into her arms and slipped down to the floor.

"Where is Nadja?"

"She's dead."

"Oh my baby," she cried. "My poor baby."

"*I* am not the poor baby."

"Oh Zoe, Zoe, my poor Zoe. Ben, come here, please come right now."

They got me upstairs, and apparently called a doctor because in a little while a man was sitting on the bed.

"This will calm you down," he said, taking out a needle from a brown leather bag.

And so I slept. It seemed days, but it was only one day. And when I woke up Benjamin was there, sitting on the edge of his and Aunt Matilda's bed, and my Aunt Pearl was there, Cousin Charlie and Lois, and my mother and father and Carlos. My breasts were still leaking. My gown was caked in old, sour, dried-up milk.

"My baby is dead," I moaned.

"Oh," Aunt Pearl keened. "Oh."

"Everybody is dead," I said.

"You are not," my Aunt Pearl ventured.

"I wish to be."

"Oh honey," Aunt Pearl crooned.

"Nadja is to be buried on Wednesday," my father said.

"Did you have to tell her like that?" my mother said.

"It's true."

"Nadja is with the angels," Aunt Matilda said, taking my hand.

"I killed her," I said. "It was my fault."

"It was not your fault, Zoe. You were a wonderful mother."

"But . . ."

Carlos was crying. He stood in the corner, shook his head, and cried.

"It was an accident," Benjamin insisted, "a tragic, tragic accident."

I remembered the sign in the garment factory: ACCIDENTS DON'T JUST HAPPEN. I remembered Mary Ellen. I remembered her ghostly wedding gown on the fan breezing in and out. Lucille, everybody had warned me.

"Grey . . ."

"They haven't found him," Benjamin said.

"When they do," Lois put in, "you can be assured they'll string him up."

"He thinks he's a shaman, a coyote."

"*Es un perro.* He is . . ." Carlos began, "*un perro. Peor que un perro.*" He is a dog. He is worse than a dog.

"What?"

"A dog," Carlos said, "the very worst of all dogs."

They looked at me.

"My baby is dead," I said.

"We know," Aunt Matilda said. "We know."

"Es hijo de puta, y su hermana también es puta. Toda la familia son gusanos." He is the son of a whore, and his sister is also a whore. All of his family are worms.

"Where is Margo?"

"We have wired her," my aunt said. "She is on her way."

"You wired her? You know about *her?"*

"Yes, Zoe, I wired her," my aunt replied. "I knew about her."

I looked at my mother, wondering why I survived and Nadja died. Wasn't I at least as good a mother as my mother? Didn't I try harder? Didn't I at least try?

"Zoe," my mother said, "you must forgive yourself."

I had never heard my mother speak this way.

"Why?"

"Because," and she gave a darting look at my father. "Because God forgives, and if He forgives, so can you. You have done nothing wrong, nothing bad. You were a good child and a wonderful mother. What happened, happened. You will never forget, but you can forgive. Forgive yourself. Yield to your Higher Power."

I looked at her, my eyes wide open. She nodded.

"It was my fault for marrying Grey and staying with him so long. He has the excuse of being crazy."

"It is not your fault for being young, for loving," Benjamin consoled. "It was an accident, a bead from a necklace. Somehow it got in the playpen. It could happen any time, any place."

Amy was not there. Had she flown to Berkeley, as Nadja had flown to God, if she had flown to God? Amy's fault for making a necklace in my room, my fault for going to the library to get a book on fools, Grey's fault for being crazy and stupid. I couldn't blame Amy.

"Nadja is with the angels," Aunt Matilda said again.

"Do you believe that?" I asked. But I could hate Amy.

"Yes, Zoe, I believe it with all my heart."

"We'll let the experts determine what is what," Cousin Charlie said. "Anyway, they'll find Grey. He's obviously a danger to himself and society. They'll find him, bring him in."

"What is today?" I asked. I hated everybody.

"Tuesday."

Monday, Tuesday. Words, words didn't work. I couldn't understand how the week worked either. Monday, and this was Tuesday, and
therefore when had Nadja died?

"Wednesday, tomorrow," my father said, sensing my confusion.
"She's to be buried tomorrow."

I have a day, I mused. I have one day.

"What, dear?"

"She's tired, let her sleep," my Aunt Matilda said.

"I still don't know why you had to be so blunt," my mother said,
sniping at my father, something I had never seen her do before.

You reap what you sow. You weep what you sew. I closed my
eyes, tried to concentrate, for I had to be clear, very, very clear.

[**I GOT UP** early the next morning in that California room with the sliding doors opening out onto a terrace which overlooked the ocean. It was a gray day at the beginning of January, 1959. I was nineteen years old, soon to be twenty. My baby was dead. Her first birthday was three weeks away. I took Benjamin's car keys from the front table, the keys to his BMW. I felt so sick of everything, it was all I could do to hold on to the wheel, keep my foot on the gas. Keep going, I willed myself, it is only a little longer. In fact, I could hardly believe I was still alive. How could I be alive? I felt completely insubstantial.

I remembered things, though, which held me to the earth, and that was why I had to get away. Heavy memories. Aaron on the beach, the pharaoh with his retinue of feathers and shells ready for imminent departure. Margo in a land where east was east and west was west and white was white and black was black and she was everything rolled into one big blanket. Smallpox wrapped around Grey. Grey had been my husband. Husband, I said over and over again. Your husband your husband your husband. My baby is dead.

Margo had gone to college, I had been an exotic dancer, stripped my clothes off, traitor to myself. I had loved an Indian, she loved Howard University. In the early days all continents were one and lava flowed from every mountaintop. Rivers of black oil circulated underground after the ferns molted and drooped, and orchids came out and yams were born. Then the lizards moved up into the sleeve of your coat and held on to your skin in the throes of death. Horny snakes and fiery salamanders and Gila monsters and iguanas and toxic toads. A long way from baby applesauce and high chairs and stolen little dresses. A long way even from spells to spills to kill your enemy. Orishas, voodoo queens, and snow sacrifices of human hair, washing machines personifying God. I was going to go with her. Be there with Nadja. Wherever it was, even if it was nowhere. My dear daughter had died in my arms and I wanted to go to her place, her country.

When I got to the Carpinteria beach it was about seven, I figured, and of course it was deserted. It was a cold winter day. The water would be freezing. Good, I thought, I not only needed to die, I needed to suffer as she did. I parked the car on the road. They would think a strange winter picnic, and then lovers making out, and then lovers making out some more. My only wish was that before my body got completely awful they would find me. Or, better yet, I would never be recovered. It surprised me how vanity held up to the end, or I wasn't surprised. In movies the undersea was silent and blue-green, very solitary. Being cradled by the original mother in the first amniotic fluid would not be all that cozy. There are deaths and there are deaths, Kelly had said once, some worse than others. Narcissus, Narcissus, have you found the Good?

It should have been Jade Beach in Big Sur, where green cliffs cascaded to the ocean. Every rock at Jade Beach was green, the very pebbles thrown ashore green, green, I love you green. The story was that the Japanese had come across the ocean to mine the jade, and all the expensive pieces were gone, but it was still magnificently green. Once, a woman scorned in love had cut her wrists and ankles and tried to die on Jade Beach. Some tourists had found her, saved her.

I had to dispense with the romance of Jade Beach, the beautiful beaches of the world. Instead, it was the regular Carpinteria beach, the one everybody went to on sunny summer Sundays to get tans, to be seen. Behind me was the Ocean Breeze Nursery full of azaleas and marigolds, and the rows of lemon and orange trees, the lettuce, just planted, stretched out all the way to the sea.

I spread the blanket on the sand. It is amazing how things that you think are inconsequential become extremely important. Even in concentration camps, I had read, there was modesty and a sense of aesthetics. I had my black Esther Williams bathing suit on, my bathing-thinking cap, and I waded in looking like I was going to star in some water ballet. But then I thought, No, I will be more honest, and go back to the sea unclothed, as I came. I pulled off my bathing suit, put

it on the blanket, neatly folded it, and took off my thinking cap.

Did I hear mermaids calling me?

No.

Had Neptune seduced me?

No.

Did I feel the great pull of the mother sea to her daughter?

No.

It was cold. I was raw with grief.

I picked up a small shell, fit it to my ear.

Don't do this, came the deep voice. This is Papa God.

Popsicle, I wish you would just shut up. It is all over.

I will not shut up. It is not over.

I am not now one of your true believers.

Despair is the greatest sin, Zoe.

I put my fingers in my ears, but, of course, his voice was inside me, there at the base of my belly. Popsicle, you let me down. I let myself down. Worst of all, I failed my child.

In the shallows there were little stones and bits of seaweed, but as I waded out, the sand got smoother and the water was not as chilling. It was a gray day, an early morning, nobody about but me and sea gulls, the sea gulls who had saved the Mormons.

"Goodbye, sea gulls."

You fool, they squawked back. Generations, white girl, they said, have gone into you. You think you have the right to destroy that, destroy all that pioneer blood. People died on the Mormon Trail west, going to the new Zion, people who didn't want to die.

Popsicle, Papa God, do not be a bird of ill omen. Do not send me these mixed messages.

I saw a lone old fisherman on the dock with a squashed hat, but he didn't see me.

It was getting deeper, the water up to my crotch, my sex, which had caused me so much trouble I hated it, and my waist, here I was thinking of my waist, my breasts, which I had shaken for money, and then my neck. My self-loathing was beyond description. I decided to swim a little first, get far enough out, I thought, so my body would not float in immediately. I had never seen a drowned person, only a seal without eyes dead on the beach and the clean shells. Far better than being in the earth, although the fish would nibble me, I was sure, and I had heard of sea worms, too. I had seen people in movies drown. Gangsters with their feet in tubs of cement. They went straight down, and pirates who had to walk the plank, the dark waves lapping over them.

They say that after you give up breathing, trying to breathe, it happens fast. I took a test run, or rather test dunk, but quickly bobbed up. I decided to swim out a little more. The sun was coming up. I had seen sunsets, but it had been a long time, or maybe never, that I had actually seen the sun rise over the mountains.

Maybe choking on water would be similar to Nadja choking to death, and if she could do it, I could go as she had. I kept going. The breast stroke. There were a few boats around the pier, and I could see that lone fisherman on the dock. It seemed that he might have seen me after all. Maybe he thought I was a seal.

I thought of Ginsberg's "Kaddish," his poem to his poor, demented mother:

> And how Death is that remedy all singers dream of, singer remember, prophesy as in the Hebrew Anthem, or the Buddhist Book of Answers.

At the end of the poem, he kept saying: O mother. O mother. I swam. Nearing the spot I had chosen, I repeated to myself: O mother. O mother.

I was where the waves overlap themselves, swell up like big breasts, and pull down, down, down. I was tired, very tired, and I let myself float a little. The fisherman on the wharf started waving.

"Hey, hey, what you doing, girl?" There was somebody else with him, a woman.

I let myself go down a little. I closed my eyes, let my shoulders go. O mother, I hummed inside, O mother. I went down, down, my breath going, my air, no air. O mother. No air. O mother. No air. I let myself go down, down. No air, no air.

Suddenly, I was drowning. I couldn't breathe. I opened my mouth and water rushed into it. I began to choke. I choked . . . I was going to die. I couldn't get my breath. I couldn't breathe. I was choking. I pushed, pushed myself up to the light, to the small funnel of light, the surface coming closer. I popped up, my head came up above the surface. I took a deep breath.

"Help!" I screamed. "Help me!"

And I was sucked down again. I struggled to get to the surface. I flailed.

"Help!" I screamed.

"Hold on," the fisherman on the wharf said.

"Zoe, Zoe," another voice called out.

I went down again. I closed my eyes. I was going to die. I was going down. I pushed up again.

"Help!"

"Hang on."

"Zoe, hang on."

I went down again. This was it, I realized. This was the Real End. But then, way up on the surface, there was a splash. And where there had been water was an orange circle of rope.

I pushed up. I kept pushing up. I reached the surface again.

"Grab hold," the fisherman shouted. "It's a life preserver, child. Just grab hold."

It *was* a life preserver. I did grab hold with both hands.

"Pull yourself up on it. Use your arms, girl, use all your strength."

I was able to pull myself up a little so my chest lay across it. By then more people had gathered, and several strong men began pulling on the rope. Then I saw, I think I saw, was it?

"Hold on," the fisherman kept saying as I approached the dock. Then they began to draw me up, hand over hand.

I caught my breath. I could breathe. I was getting there.

"Quite a trickeroo," Margo shouted out. "Thought we almost lost you, and just when we need you the most."

I started to cry. "Oh, Margo . . ."

"Yes, I know. I know."

"Hang on, girl," the old man said. "Just hang on while we pull you up level to the dock."

And that is what I did.